Winter's Song

THEN, NOW, &

Always

A Three Kings Novel

A.E. VALDEZ

To my found family-
Maria, Adolfo, Giselle, Verdi, Kassie, & Tuti.
Thank you for loving me. I never thought a cup of coffee would
change my life.

Author's Note

To My Amazing Readers:

There's heartbreak, grief, healing, and a whole lotta love in these pages.

This book also contains discussions of death, mentions of suicide, addiction, violence, explicit language, mentions of abuse, and vivid descriptions of sex.

Please take care of yourself!

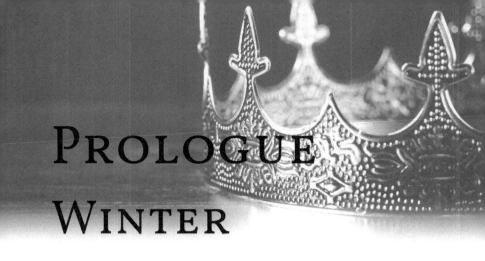

Prologue
Winter

MOST NIGHTS I GET drunk to numb the ache of the hole in my chest and bring someone home to silence the loneliness. Neither vice is bringing me comfort tonight.

The woman on top of me is beautiful. But even with her wrapped tightly around me, I don't feel shit. Her mouth is moving, but her moans sound faint with the ringing in my ears drowning her out. It's been a while since I disassociated during sex, putting my body on auto pilot, getting lost in my thoughts. Not focusing on any particular thought or memory... just mentally taking myself anywhere but the present.

I'm pulled back into my body when she digs her nails into my chest, breathing heavily as she chants my name and tells me she's coming. At first, I think she's faking it. I've done nothing for her to come other than provide hard dick, but her pussy grips me so hard I feel myself teetering on the edge of my own release. Before I can join her, she succumbs to her own pleasure. She rides me until her hips slow and she collapses onto my chest.

"I needed that," she sighs.

I wait a few seconds before moving to get out from underneath her. She climbs off me, and lies on the bed. Getting up, I pull the condom off and disappear into the bathroom to throw it away. This isn't how

I imagined my night ending. My distraction's eyes remain on me as I reenter the bedroom.

"Feel free to stay. I'm not tired." I pull on boxers and a robe before sliding my feet into some Prada slippers. I really am tired, but I don't want to sleep beside her. And while I'm an asshole, I don't want to kick her out. So, I'll stay up until she leaves or fall asleep watching TV in the living room.

"I know the drill, Winter. Don't pretend to spare my feelings. You call, I come–literally–and then we part ways." She gets up with a sigh, picking up her discarded clothing from the floor.

"That's all I have to give." Honesty spills from my lips.

She pulls on her shirt, fixing her hair. Approaching me, she smiles as she reaches out and gently touches my face. "You have everything to give. Just not to me."

Without another word, she pulls on her jeans, fastens them, and grants me my unspoken wish of solitude. The sound of her heels clicking across the marble floors fades as she makes her way to the front door.

Feeling relief, I collapse onto the bed and stare up at the ceiling. I know nothing will bring me comfort tonight. Not in the way I felt in the presence of Eve Valentine.

1

EVE

PICKING UP THE CHAMPAGNE flute, filled to the brim with a pomegranate mimosa, I take a gulp after breaking surprising news to my two best friends. If the café we're in wasn't bustling with people, the silence following my confession would be deafening. It takes them a few seconds to process my words.

"A boyfriend?" Noelle sputters on her drink, wiping her mouth with a napkin.

"Yes." I smile brightly. "Is that so hard to believe?"

"We've known you nine–" Aspen starts.

"Ten. Almost eleven years," Noelle fills in.

"Right." Aspen nods. "And you've never been remotely interested in dating. In fact, you act like it's the bubonic plague."

I down the rest of my drink. It's not even nine a.m. and I'm already feeling a little tipsy. "Things can change." I shrug nonchalantly. The waitress walks past our table, I hold up my hand to stop her. "Can I get two more of these, please?" I point to the empty glass. "Don't be afraid to add a little extra champagne either."

"Sure." The waitress smiles, taking my glass and disappearing with it.

Noelle and Aspen are looking at me curiously. "What?"

"Who is it?" Aspen asks, cocking her head to the side, pinning her arms across her chest.

"You remember Noah, right? Noah Kincaid."

Noelle's brows knit together. "The guy who annoys you?"

"Didn't she say he was clingy?" Aspen points at me while asking Noelle.

The waitress reappears with the drinks. My temporary saving grace as I take another sip that's mostly champagne, causing me to slow down.

"Did I say that?" I wipe my mouth with a napkin, knowing damn well I said it.

Noelle opens her phone, scrolling furiously, until she finds what she's looking for in our group chat. "And I quote, 'He's annoying and a little clingy. Doesn't understand the friends with benefits concept.' Another one says, 'He sends me flowers with hopes of more, knowing they'll sit and die on my counter.' You also graciously attached a photo of the dying flowers to the chat." She holds up her phone, displaying the wilted vase of long-stemmed roses.

"Apparently the flowers worked," Aspen quips.

"At least you're regularly watering your most important flower now." Noelle grins.

Aspen chokes on her drink before falling into a fit of laughter. "She could do that without forcing herself to date him!"

"I'm not! I do like him. He's handsome, good in bed, cooks, is successful..." I tick each one off on a finger. "Noah checks every single box of the ideal boyfriend." I dare another sip of my mimosa, immediately regretting it and setting it aside.

"You're gauging how much you like him by a list of... imaginary boxes?" Aspen scrunches up her face.

I avoid eye contact, noticing a diamond on Noelle's left hand that could be seen from miles away. "What is that?" I point at the ring on her finger.

"What is— Oh." She looks down at her hand, grinning before holding it up. "Snow proposed while we were at his mom's place."

"Why didn't you tell me?!" I grab her hand, inspecting the brilliant diamond ring in the shape of a snowflake. "Elle, this is gorgeous." I'm hit with an unexpected wave of emotions and a lump forms in my throat. "I'm so happy for you..."

"I wanted to tell you in person." She says, squeezing my hand.

I pull her into a hug, ignoring the twinge of pain in my chest and the breath that's caught in my throat. "You're right because I wouldn't have been able to hug you. How do you feel?" I ask, pulling away, dabbing at the inner corners of my eyes.

I've never seen her smile so bright as she says, "Happy."

"Tell me every single detail of how he proposed."

Noelle's eyes twinkle with excitement as she launches into the tale of how Snow gave her a movie worthy proposal. The happiness radiates from her, making me smile. As she talks, I push the green eyed monster of jealousy back in its cage, attempting to keep it at bay. She's my best friend. No. She's my *sister*. The only person I truly let my guard down for after my heart was ripped from my chest. I'm happy for her.

Are you? A little voice whispers.

Can I be happy for her and... jealous at the same time? Is it jealousy or sadness for what could've been? Or maybe I'm just a selfish, cold-hearted bitch for only thinking of myself when my soulmate is experiencing the happiest time of her life.

I remember being in the chapter of my life she's in now. Freshly engaged to the man I saw eternity with. The dream she's living was once mine too. I believed nothing could ever come between me and my fiancé–*until it did*.

A meteorite in the form of grief and pain split us in two and created a bottomless chasm, and we lost sight of each other in its wake. The sadness turned to anger that festered into resentment. A bitterness, borderline hatred, for the person and life I wanted being wrenched from my grasp.

I flinch when I feel a tear rolling down my cheek, realizing the memories elicit the same response they have for the past decade.

"How gorgeous would a Christmas wedding be?" Noelle asks as I tune back into her words. "So elegant and charming! Oh, and will you be my maid of honor? You'll be sharing the title with Aspen of course."

"You don't even have to ask!" I say, blinking rapidly as another tear rolls down my cheek.

Noelle swipes it away. "Stop. You're going to make me cry. I'm so happy you're going to share this moment with me." She gives me another hug while I feel guilty because the stray tears weren't induced by happiness.

"Always here for you, Elle."

Aspen picks up her glass, raising it in the air. "To exceptional, top tier dick and happily ever afters!" she announces loudly.

"A word!" I clink my glass against hers.

"Aspen!" Noelle hisses, falling into a fit of laughter as the people around us stare at our table.

"Toast your glass with mine, Elle, before I have to repeat myself louder."

"You know she will," I warn, laughing.

We toast our glasses together, downing our mimosas. This one goes straight to my head. I'm grateful I planned a chill day because I'm going to be useless after this. After our toast, we order our food and discuss possible bridesmaids dresses while we wait. My phone vibrates, pulling me from our conversation.

Noah: Hey babe. Will you be busy later? I wanted to see you.

Babe? We've only been officially dating a few days. Fucking for years, but he's never used any terms of endearment... unless I'm underneath him. I ignore the feeling of annoyance and respond.

Eve: Hi ba-

I feel the threat of vomit before I can even finish the word. *Delete. Delete. Delete.*

Eve: Hey. I plan to spend the day at my place. I need to decompress.

As the clinical director of Hope's Village, the only pediatric clinic in our city, it's been busy since the grand opening just a few weeks ago.

"Noah?" Aspen asks, wagging her brows.

"This isn't about Winter is it?" Noelle asks, taking a bite of her pancakes.

My phone slips from my hand, clattering to the floor. "What does he have to do with this?" I pick my phone up, relieved the screen isn't shattered.

"Everything," Noelle says. "You're not wrong, Noah is an exceptional candidate for a boyfriend with top tier dick, I'm sure. But," she sighs, "you two have been friends with benefits for years, and now, after seeing Winter, you start dating him? Do you really like Noah?"

My skin heats and my palms become clammy. "Winter has nothing to do with Noah and me."

Winter King. The *only* man I've ever seen eternity with. And now Noelle is engaged to his brother. For ten, almost eleven years, Winter and I have managed to not cross paths… until we crashed into each other again.

Noelle studies me before deciding to drop it and resumes eating her pancakes.

"Noah is delectable." Aspen licks her fork. "If you're happy, we're happy, Eve."

"I wasn't asking because I'm not happy for you, I asked because— "

"You care," I finish for Noelle, giving her a small smile. "I know."

Noelle is all love and always means well. She's the quietest of our trio, but that doesn't mean she won't go toe to toe when necessary. Aspen and I are more impulsive while Noelle is thoughtful.

I steer the conversation away from Noah and me. "Are you seeing anyone, Aspen?"

"I'm a free agent." She smiles.

"I thought you and North hit it off."

She scrunches up her face. "Yeah… as friends. Don't get me wrong, I'd let him smack it, flip it, and reverse it, but he wants forever while I want right now. So instead of falling into bed with him, I've been helping him find dates. He's a little shy." Aspen smiles brilliantly as she holds her fingers a pinch apart. "But it's ridiculous he's single."

North is shy, but he's comfortable talking to her. Aspen is what I like to call *confidently* single. She's single because she *wants* to be. Not because she can't find a man or some traumatic past love–she genuinely is vibing to the beat of her own drum. I wish I had her confidence.

"I'm sure he loves that." I laugh.

"There's been a bit of reluctance, but he's been on three dates so far."
She smiles proudly.

Noelle looks at her phone. "I've got an assignment due in a few hours
that I need to get home and do." She gathers her things. "I didn't have
time to get it done yesterday and then I have a meeting with Winter."

"What were you busy with?" I side eye her with a smirk on my lips.

"Oh... you know." She waves her hand airily. "Snow. I should really
make his ass do my assignment."

"You know he would. Has he ever told you no?" Aspen asks, applying
some lip gloss.

Noelle's eyes flit up to the ceiling. "Mmm... yes. He has."

"And how long did that last?" I pop a piece of gum in my mouth and
offer them some. They both take a piece.

"Not long." Noelle grins, positioning her designer bag, courtesy of
Snow, across her body. I can't help but envy her a little bit. Snow would
hold all the galaxies in the palm of his hand for her if he could. I miss that
feeling.

"Spoiled. As you should be," Aspen says, rising from her seat.

Leaving our tips on the table, we head for the front of the café. "Let
me grab a coffee before we head out." Looking up at the menu, I act as
though I'm going to change the order I've been getting since high school.
"Breve caramel macchiato, please."

"You should've told me you guys were coming here!" Noelle exclaims.
Turning to face her, I'm met by the sight of the King brothers. She
presses onto her tiptoes to give Snow a kiss.

"I wasn't planning on coming out, but these two were complaining
like children." Snow points toward North and Winter.

To my misfortune, Winter is the epitome of getting better with age.
I doubt his smooth sepia skin will ever see a wrinkle. Tattoos cover the

length of his arms, and his lean build is enhanced by the muscle he's gained. His velvety brown eyes have always been warm and inviting, although now, there's a hint of distance in them. He smiles when he looks at Noelle, and it's still charming. I remember the first time he smiled at me. It felt like he had knocked me off my feet.

"Miss Mistletoe Mountain." Winter gives her a bear hug.

Noelle laughs. "You're dramatic. We see each other every day."

Winter and Noelle work together at North Star Toys, the King brothers' company. They're managing the marketing department together. Noelle seems to like it. I made the mistake of letting my jealousy get the best of me when she first announced she'd be working with Winter. She forgave me, but I can tell she's hesitant to share details. I can't blame her when I know I didn't handle myself well.

"Leave my future wife alone." Snow playfully nudges Winter's arm.

Winter lets her go. "She's *my* future sister-in-law."

North cocks a brow, shaking his head. "You're really going to fight Snow over who has a higher status with Noelle?"

"If it comes down to it." Winter shrugs his broad shoulders, making his muscles strain against his white t-shirt.

Noelle and Aspen laugh. I even crack a smile, trying to hide it by biting my bottom lip. North lets out an exasperated sigh, turning his attention to me.

"Hey, Eve."

"Hi." I smile.

"Eve." Snow gives me a nod, wrapping his arm around Noelle's neck, kissing her temple.

Winter doesn't say 'hi' or even glance in my direction. It's as if his brain has edited me out of his reality. Instead, he turns his attention to Aspen and gives her a hug.

"Are you coming over tonight?"

I try to keep my expression stoic as my mind reels. Aspen... hangs out with him? Alone?

"Yeah." Aspen smiles. "What am I bringing?"

How much do Aspen and Noelle not share with me about Winter for the sake of my feelings? I wonder if they're... doing more than just hanging out. Not that I could blame them. Aspen is drop dead gorgeous, and Winter is— I'm not going to allow my mind to go there. I don't even care.

I miss the rest of their conversation when Noelle nudges my arm. "Your order's up, babe."

"Oh... right." I blink, forgetting I had ordered a coffee. When I turn back around, Noelle is saying her goodbyes to the boys. Each of them genuinely loves her.

The jealousy claws at the surface again. I remember being a part of the King family once upon a time. They're close knit, and I've always admired that. When Winter and I were together, his family welcomed me with open arms, and I viewed them as my own. When I lost Winter... I lost them too. I stifle the feelings and put the smile back on I let slip for a fraction of a second.

"See you at home." Snow plants a kiss on Noelle's lips. "Bye, Aspen. I'm sure I'll see you later."

"Of course you will." She smiles sweetly. "I'm glad you've accepted Elle and I are a package deal."

"Expected nothing less." Snow chuckles. "Later, Eve." He nods in my direction before turning to his brothers.

North simply waves with a smile before talking to Aspen, and Winter turns his back on me, heading toward a table. When we first reconnected,

Winter tried to talk to me. I was the one who met him with my claws out.

I should be happy he's no longer trying... right?

Pulling out my phone, I send a text to Noah.

Eve: Would you still want to spend the day with me? I just got done with the girls.

Noah: Of course. Meet you at your place.

I'll decompress with him as my stress reliever.

2

WINTER

NOSTALGIC MEMORIES OF ME and my brothers coming to Flapjack's Brew with Dad for a steaming stack of pancakes flood my mind. The smell of freshly brewed coffee and warm pastries permeate the air. This café has been in Hope Valley for as long as I can remember. We don't come as often as we used to, still much hasn't changed. The sun shines through the large windows giving the earthen brown colors of the café a warm glow. Fresh flowers sit at the center of every table, adding a touch of vibrant color.

I head toward a table near the back of the café, waiting for Snow and North to say their goodbyes to Noelle, Aspen, and Eve. I've learned it's best to not even try with Eve. No matter what I do, apologizing or otherwise, she has a problem sharing air with me.

"Well... that went well," Snow says, taking a seat at the table with a smile on his face.

"What do you mean?" I ask, sliding my arms out of my coat's sleeves, hanging it over the back of the chair.

"Eve," North says simply. "You two decide not talking is the best option?"

"Nonverbally? Yes. We did."

They both chuckle. "I guess if it works..." Snow shrugs.

"I've been cordial. She's the one who wants to rip my nuts out of their sack."

"True..." Snow nods. "You have been."

I lean back in my chair, cocking my head to the side. "You're not going to side with her and say I deserve it?"

Snow's brow furrows. "Why would I?"

"Because... I thought you'd side with her since you also agree that I'm a fuck up."

"Can we please not start this conversation over breakfast?" North sighs exasperatedly.

Snow leans forward, resting his forearms on the table. "Do you honestly think I'd condone someone talking shit about *or* to you?"

My eyes remain locked with his as I say, "No."

"Good, because if you would've said otherwise we would've been kicked out of here for fighting." I can't help but laugh. "What's happened in the past doesn't pertain to what's happening right now. I always have both of your backs."

Despite all Snow's shit talking, I know he'd never leave me in the dark. Even when I was at my lowest, he was there, holding out his hand. Unfortunately, I can't say I've done the same for him.

"That went over more smoothly then what I thought. Progress, boys."

"You have such a dad spirit, North," I jest.

"What kind of dad are we talking about here?" North smiles.

"That's how you feel?" Snow laughs. "Go on a few little dates and now you think you're a daddy?"

"Know," North corrects.

I lean back in my seat, getting a better look at him. "Let me find out Aspen is bringing out the King arrogance in you."

North's first girlfriend was his worst and he's been weary of dating ever since. I'm happy Aspen has been getting him to come out of his shell a little more.

"All the King men in my café?" Sunday, the owner of Flapjack's Brew, beams as she approaches our table. "To what do I owe this pleasure?" She gives each of us hugs.

"Thought we'd stop by for the best pancakes in the city." Snow smiles, releasing her from the hug.

"You flatter me." She splays her hand over her heart. "How's your mama?"

"Good." North smiles. "She'll be visiting us in a few weeks. I'm sure she'll stop by."

"Always does. I miss that woman." She smiles wistfully. Sunday and our mom grew up together. Even though they live twelve hours apart, they're as close as if they still lived on the same street.

"I'm sure she'd love it if you visited her in Sapphire Shores," I suggest.

"She's been saying the same thing. Maybe you three showing up together is my sign to go."

Indigo, her daughter appears at her side. "I thought I saw the three of you walk in."

"Isn't it nice to see them, Indigo? Congratulations on the engagement, Snow." He smiles at her. "Now, are either of you two single?" Sunday asks brazenly, pointing at North and me. "Because Indigo—"

"Mama!" Indigo protests, covering her face with the tablet in her hands.

"You miss every shot you don't take, darling. Isn't that what you kids say now a days?"

We try to spare Indigo the embarrassment, but we can't help our laughter.

"I don't need you taking shots on my behalf," Indigo says sternly, looking everywhere but at us.

"It's a simple question. They're handsome and come from a good family. It wouldn't be—"

"What can I get started for you guys?" Indigo's voice overpowers her mother's.

Sunday nudges her shoulder with a smirk. "I'll leave you to it. Good to see you boys." We wave her off as she leaves our table.

"A pitcher of fresh squeezed orange juice and Flapjack's leaning stack of pancakes." Snow orders.

"Got it. The order hasn't changed, I see." She smiles. "Coming right up." Turning on her heel, she disappears into the kitchen.

"You should take her on a date, North."

"Me?" He adjusts his thick black framed glasses. "Nah. There would be too much meddling on Sunday's part. Besides, didn't you two have something?"

"Hope Valley's very own man whore," Snow says with a smirk, shaking his head while side eyeing me.

"I've never touched Indigo. Her friend on the other hand..." I smile. "C'mon, we're three, excuse me, Mr. Mistletoe Mountain, two of the most eligible bachelors in the city, and if they're offering, I'm gonna eat it."

"So... you're just giving up on Eve?" North asks.

Indigo reappears, setting down a carafe of orange juice along with three glasses. "Pancakes will be out in just a moment."

"Thanks, Indigo," we say in unison.

"Like I said earlier..." I pour orange juice into each of our glasses. "She doesn't want me anymore, and I'm not going smash myself against a brick wall."

"It really is sad..." North picks up his glass, taking a sip.

"What?"

"That she's already snatched your nuts from your sack and you don't even realize it."

Snow snorts into his glass of orange juice while North grins at me.

"Fuck you both."

Moments later, Indigo sets a steaming stack of pancakes down in front of us, followed by plates. We waste no time digging in. Sunday has truly perfected the art of a melt in your mouth pancake.

"It's different with Eve. We have history." A sordid one at that.

"Yeah, but that doesn't mean she has the right to use you as a punching bag," Snow says in between bites of pancake. "All North is saying is, you may have fucked up, but that doesn't mean you can't have a backbone."

I shovel a bite of pancake in my mouth, choosing to end the conversation. Eve has only let her guard down one time since we reconnected. It was the night at Fireside when Snow introduced us to Noelle. Once the initial shock of seeing each other again wore off, and no one was around, Eve talked to me.

Stepping out onto the balcony to clear my head, I see the silhouette of a woman. I don't need to see her face to know it's Eve. I've recognized her energy since the first time I met her. For a moment, I consider heading back inside to avoid her wrath. I can't help myself though and continue walking toward her like we're two magnets. Masochist? Maybe. Initially, I don't say anything, just stand beside her near the railing, staring out at glittering city lights.

"What are the odds?" She lets out a huff of laughter. "That they'd meet on the side of a fucking mountain."

My shoulders shake with silent laughter. "Before today, I would've said slim to fucking none."

"And then for them to not even meet here, but some far away, straight out of a fairytale place."

"I believe that is what people call... kismet."

"Yeah..." She crosses her arms, hugging herself. I shrug out of my jacket, wrapping it around her shoulders. For the first time all night, she looks at me with a familiar softness in her eyes. "Thank you."

I nod, turning my attention back to the city lights. We stand in silence, side by side, when I feel her hand brush against mine. I don't dare steal a glance, thinking it was an accident, until her slender fingers intertwine with mine. The jolt of electric recognition reminds me she still commands my heart.

"There's so many things I've wanted to say to you over the years... some beautiful and some vile." A smile tugs at my lips. "But all of it would convey the same message that was confirmed when I saw you tonight."

"What's that?"

She turns to face me. "That I still love you as much as the first time I told you."

My heart stops in my chest. After what I did, and the way I left, these are the last words I expected to hear. "Eve, I'm sorry for leaving you... and not being strong enough for us."

She silences me with a kiss. I place my hands on her hips, reacquainting myself with the shape of her as I pull her against my body. She fists my shirt, moaning into my mouth. Ten long fucking years without her touch. Pulling away much too soon, she rests her head on my shoulder.

"I know you're sorry, but forgiveness is hard for me to find."

Cupping her chin, I bring her gaze to mine. "I'll wait as long as you need."

I watch her eyes become glossy. "You'll be waiting for eternity... when you left, I made a promise to myself. To never fall back into you... no matter

*how much I still love you." She takes a step back, pulling my jacket from
her shoulders. "And I intend to keep it."*

*We hold each other's gaze as she hands me my jacket. I watch Eve walk
away from me like I did her all those years ago.*

She allowed me those few moments of grace and has been giving me
the ninth circle of hell attitude ever since.

"What are you doing the rest of today?" Snow pulls me from my trip
down memory lane.

"Uh..." I look at my plate, realizing I cleared it and theirs are empty
too. "Elle and I are going to work on some social media content and go
through influencer applications."

"Was there enough money allocated or do we need to go over the
budget again?" North asks, putting his accountant hat on.

"The current budget is perfect. We decided to keep the first group
small to see if working with influencers makes a noticeable difference for
us."

"It's crazy how marketing has changed." Snow says, shaking his head.

"It definitely has. Imagine being eight years old with a decent following and being offered ten plus grand for a fifteen second video. It's the
new wave and allows for authenticity. That eight year old can connect
with others in a way that I never could."

Once I got my shit together, Snow wanted me to work at North Star
Toys alongside him and North. The original plan was for me, the oldest,
to take over once Dad retired, except he never got the chance. He died
unexpectedly, creating a fracture, not only in our family, but each of us
as well. We handled the grief differently. Losing Dad was my green light
to speed down the path of self-destruction, trying like hell to rid myself
of the pain. The man who I aspired to be, who I thought was invincible,
was gone.

I was treading in the bottomless abyss of grief while Snow held it together for Mom and North. He took over the dream I could no longer carry. I was lost for a long time, and in many ways I still am. I've been stable for three years now. Initially, Snow wanted to share the CEO title with me. After considering it, I decided I wanted to try something different. That's how I became the president of our marketing department.

Before I took over, the team was stuck in their ways. Initially, they were resistant due to my murky past and didn't believe my ideas would work. One thing about me is, I love proving people wrong. Three years later, I've done what they believed I couldn't.

"That's an insane amount of money for an eight year old." Snow says.

"It is. That's why Elle suggested setting up a financial literacy program for our influencers to take part in. Paychecks are nice, but so is building sustainable wealth."

"I love what you two are doing." Snow smiles proudly. "The influencer program is an amazing idea, Winter."

"Thank you." I clear my throat, unsure of how to take his compliment. I know Snow and North are proud of me, but I still struggle to accept it. Or maybe I struggle to be proud of myself? My phone chimes, reminding me I have somewhere to be. Finishing off my orange juice, I rise from my seat.

"Where are you off to?" North asks.

I pull on my jacket. "I have something I need to do."

Snow leans back in his seat, giving me a skeptical look. "Someone throw up the batman whore signal?"

"Not all superheroes wear capes." I grin, throwing a hundred dollar bill down on the table. "Leave the rest for Indigo."

"I got it." Snow says, pulling out his wallet.

"Thank you for breakfast. Leave it all for Indigo then. Sunday didn't have to do her dirty like that."

"She really didn't." North agrees. "Will you be in the office today?"

"Yeah. What about you, Snow?"

"I have a riveting afternoon full of meetings. I hope your..." His voice trails off as he meets my gaze. "Rendezvous goes well." The look in his eyes lets me know he knows I'm hiding something. Instead of questioning me further, he gives me a wave.

My Saint Laurent boots sink into the lush emerald grass as I amble across it. The morning's dew is still clinging to the freshly cut blades. Looking around, I'm grateful to see that no one else is here. Not that this is a place where anyone would willingly want to hang out. Unless you're me, then it happens to be the only place you find peace. My steps slow as I get closer to the gray stone that's been my point of focus since stepping out of the car.

I shove my hands in my jacket pockets when I'm a few feet away from it, reading the inscription.

Christopher Dane King

1956 - 2012

"Living on in the hearts of loved ones."

I remember stressing out over that simple sentence. All of us were drowning in grief, yet I found myself with the responsibility of taking care of Dad's headstone.

Closing the door, I rest my head against it and take a deep, shuddering breath, listening to Mom cry. She told me she's fine, but none of us are fucking fine. There's not a fray of a thread to hold onto when the anchor of our family is lying six feet under. I slide down the door, sitting on the floor and listen to her cries become more hysterical. There's no consoling her. She buried her other half today. There are no words or comfort to soothe this kind of ache.

Bringing my knees to my chest, I rest my elbows on them and cradle my head in my hands. Tears that I've given up on trying to control fall onto my jeans. Emotional pain cuts much deeper than physical pain ever could. It imbeds itself in your soul, taking root. I don't even startle when I feel a warm body sit next to mine.

Eve drapes her arm over my shoulders, resting her head against me. "Have you eaten?" Her voice is soft and soothing.

It's such a random question given the events of today, but it puts me in the moment. "No. I'm not hungry." I don't look at her even though she's watched me relentlessly cry since the day Dad died.

She gently places her hand on my cheek, bringing my gaze to hers. "You need to eat something, Winter."

Her soft brown eyes bring a spark of warmth to the chill that's settled over me. "I... don't want to leave her."

"What if I bring you something? We can sit right here. That way she's not alone and you're not alone either."

I can't remember the last time I gave food a thought. The realization makes me aware of the pain in my stomach. "Okay." I nod my head.

She presses a kiss to my temple. "I'll be right back."

Eve is on her feet and halfway down the hallway before I can formulate a response. Mom's cries subside, meaning she's probably falling asleep. North locked himself in his room hours ago, and Snow left, going for a drive. I don't blame him. The air in our house is stale with a suffocating grief.

The silence becomes deafening as Mom falls asleep on the other side of the door. I'm not sure how long I sit before I hear Eve's approaching steps. She's carrying a tray with two plates that each have bowls of steaming soup and a slice of bread on the side with butter melting on top. When she sits beside me, my mouth waters as the smell of broccoli cheddar soup wafts toward me.

"You made this?" I ask, sitting up.

"No. Mom did. She dropped it off a little bit ago."

"Tell her I said thank you." I grab a plate from the tray.

Eve smiles, displaying the dimple I've kissed infinite times on her left cheek. Grabbing her own plate, she settles beside me. My body welcomes the warmth of her and the soup. We sit eating in silence. Each bite makes me feel a little better as I fill my stomach.

"I can't remember when I last ate. Everything's been a blur..." Setting my empty bowl and plate on the tray, I lean against the door again.

"You haven't been eating. That's why I asked." She keeps her eyes on the bowl of soup in her hands.

"Thank you for being here with me."

"Winter... you don't have to thank me."

"I know, but—"

She shakes her head. "No buts. I'm here and wouldn't want to be any-where else."

We're three months away from our wedding. The joy and excitement I'd been feeling has been snuffed out. I know she'd rather be in those moments where we're planning for the happiest time of our lives, but instead she's here, sitting on the floor with me, making sure I've eaten.

Resting my head against the door, I let the exhaustion take over me. "Every time I think something will be the hardest part... another thing comes up." I shift my gaze to her. "Mom wants me to come up with Dad's epitaph. How the fuck am I supposed to sum up fifty-six years of life in a single sentence?"

She sets her empty bowl aside. "Did you talk to Snow and North?"

I rub my tired, burning eyes. "Everyone is... drained. Mom was hysterical because she didn't realize the headstone would take four to six weeks to be made. She started screaming 'How will we find him?' and that—" My voice cracks, and Eve scoots closer to me, wrapping her arms around my middle. "—that moment chipped away another piece of me. I never imagined having to see Mom like this. Or myself. It's all just..." My voice trails off as fresh tears fall from my eyes.

Eve holds onto me. "You don't have to explain your pain to me when I can feel it too."

I kiss the top of her head and lean into her as she rests her head on my shoulder. Of course she understands without me having to say a word. After four years together, we know one another better than we know ourselves.

"Dad is gone..." she says. "But the essence of who he was lives on in each of our hearts. A sentence won't change that. Your existence is honoring his life."

"Living on in the hearts of loved ones..." The smile that tugs at my lips feels foreign. A stark contrast to grief. "That's perfect." Wrapping my arms around her, I pull her into me. "I'm not sure I've said this lately," I say as I bury my face in her curls, inhaling deeply. "But you're my soul."

"Forever." She hugs me tightly.

Squatting down, I brush stray leaves from around the headstone. I run my fingertips over the inscription before laying down on the grass beside Dad. For a moment, I gaze up at the clouds lazily passing in the sky.

"Not a day goes by that I don't wish you were here or see the reflection of you when I look in the mirror." I sink my fingers into the earth as if I can reach him. "You've missed so much... we've missed you so much. Snow is engaged. North is dating. Mom is happy in her house by the sea. All that's missing is you."

Sometimes I can't help but wonder if I was always meant to veer off the path or if I'm exactly where I need to be. Would my life be different if Dad were still here? Would Eve and I be married with kids?

"I hope that despite my fuck ups–mistakes–that you're still proud of me..."

Closing my eyes, I wish I could hear his voice. Mom, Snow, and North reassure me Dad would be proud regardless of what I've done. I know they're right, but I still long to hear it from him... to talk to him again. Lying beside his grave is the closest I'll get now. So, I lie here, feeling the peace that's only present when I'm in the cemetery. There's been countless times where I've dozed off and the groundskeeper has had to wake me up. If he didn't take such good care of the grass, I'm sure there'd be a permanent indentation from how many times I've laid here.

I'm on the verge of falling asleep when my phone vibrates in my pocket. I ignore it, not wanting to move. It eventually falls silent again. I close my eyes, letting myself enjoy the peace a little longer. A few minutes later, my phone vibrates again.

"Dad... I've gotta go. Know that I love you and I'm fucking trying. Shit. Damn. I mean— I'm trying. If you haven't noticed, I still curse like a sailor as you used to say." I smile, rising to my feet. "Until next time..."

I press a kiss to my fingertips and touch his headstone. "Watch out for us, okay? Especially Mom. Love you."

Turning away, I head toward my car and pull my phone from my pocket. "Shit." I look at the time. "Better late than never I guess."

"Winter," my "rendezvous" glances at the clock. "I didn't think you'd make it."

"I'm here, aren't I?" Hanging my jacket, I slide into the plush chair.

"In the flesh. Even if it seems reluctantly."

"There are other things I'd rather be doing right now, Dr. Maddox." I let out an exasperated sigh, getting comfortable in the tufted velvet seat.

"Yet here you are. Why?"

"We have an appointment."

"That's the obvious answer." He waves his hand airily. "Why did you decide to show up today after missing," he flips through his notepad, "the last month's worth of sessions?"

I'm running from myself. "Because we have an appointment, don't we? Why am I still on your schedule, anyway?"

"You pay me," he says plainly, making me want to smile, but I keep my expression neutral. Dr. Maddox shifts in his seat, setting his notepad aside. He seems to be about the same age as my dad. Or the same age Dad would be if he were still here. He has richly colored brown skin, hair with signs of gray, and deep brown eyes framed by glasses he slides off, pinching the bridge of his nose.

"Winter..." His tone sounds worn. "May I speak honestly?"

"Isn't that what I pay you for? Honesty."

"Why the hell are you in my office today?"

This time I allow myself to smile. "There you are."

"What?" he asks, confused.

I sit up, resting my forearms on my thighs. "I wondered when you were going to drop the clinical bullshit and speak to me like a human with a beating heart instead of a patient you're attempting to dissect."

I don't expect to be best friends with Dr. Maddox. Although, I must admit to myself his style is impeccable. When I saw his picture on his website, his style and warm demeanor were what caused me to reach out to him. I'm sure befriending your psychologist is against the rules anyway. I do need to feel human though. Feel like I could be catching up with an old friend and not like I'm a puzzle to be solved.

He freezes, holding eye contact. Leaning back, he tilts his head slightly as if he's getting a better look at me. "I-I'm sorry you've felt that way." Clearing his throat, he says, "It wasn't my intention."

I study him a moment before speaking. "It's alright." I shrug, leaning back in the seat. "We're all performing in some way."

He hesitates, his demeanor more relaxed than it was when I walked in. "Do you feel like you're performing?"

"Depends on the situation." Silence fills the room, letting me know he's waiting for me to expound on that thought. However, that's not what's on my mind today. "I'm here because my brother claims this works and I can't seem to sort through my thoughts. Or forgive myself for putting my family through hell."

I look out the window, trying to decide how much I want to share.

"For seven years, my coping mechanisms were drugs, gambling, and women. The latter is still my vice of choice" I meet his gaze. "But... unfortunately, that no longer seems to be working."

"Do you still use drugs and gamble?"

"Marijuana? Yes, occasionally. Gambling and coke? Fuck no."

He chuckles, resting his ankle on his knee. "Did you attend rehab?"

"Yeah..." I look away from him as memories of Snow dropping me off at rehab, twice, replay in my head. "And before you give me shit about the marijuana, it helps with my anxiety and insomnia."

"Everyone's path looks different." Dr. Maddox puts his glasses back on. "I'm not here to judge your choices or what works for you. Unless it's harmful. Then it'll become something we have to address together."

His response makes me pause. "I've seen my fair share of therapists, and I'm not sure if it's sad or refreshing that you're the first one I believe isn't judging me."

Finding a therapist hasn't been easy. Too many of them felt like I was in a doctor's office when they asked you the standard questions. There was a sterility to their aura. I need to know someone sees *me* and not just another patient in their chair.

I've been seeing Dr. Maddox sporadically for a few months. Due to my inconsistency, I was expecting him to drop me as a client. Instead, he met my inconsistency with what I now understand was genuine caring. When you've made mistakes such as mine, people think that tough love is the only way to love you. I guess I needed to know that Dr. Maddox didn't share that sentiment before I told him the things I'm afraid to say out loud to myself in the mirror.

"I'm here for you, Winter."

Another silence settles between us before I speak again. "Have you ever lost someone you love?"

"Yes."

"So you know the feeling of emptiness even when you're still surrounded by loved ones?"

"Unfortunately, I do."

"Does that feeling ever go away?"

Dr. Maddox clasps his hands together, resting them in his lap. "Honestly, no." His answer startles me. I expected him to give me a bullshit inspirational line. "The feeling never goes away. However, we learn to cope... adjust to life without them. As painful as that may be." He pauses before asking, "Who did you lose?"

"My dad." I swallow the lump in my throat. "I know a lot of kids say their parent is the best, but he really was."

"How long has it been since his passing?"

"A decade. We were close. As a kid, I was his shadow." Dr. Maddox smiles. "As an adult, I knew I could go to him with anything. I never felt alone between him, my mom, and brothers. We're close-knit, but then a pillar to our foundation crumbled... and I toppled right along with it." Sitting up, I run my hand along the back of my neck. "And now, even though I have my mom and brothers... there's a void. To be honest... I don't know who I am without the chaos and grief."

Dr. Maddox offers a beat of silence before speaking. "Are you afraid to know who you are now?"

"Yeah. I am." My eyes meet his. "That's why I try not to be alone even though I perpetually feel I am. I saw my..." *Eve.* My voice trails off before I utter her name. "Never mind. I feel like I know who people think I am, you know? Winter King, the charismatic, recovering mess with a face and last name that opens legs and doors. That shit is all a performance. To keep people at bay. The only people who truly know me are my family and..."

My voice trails off as images of Eve flit through my mind. I'm not sure I can even say Eve knows me anymore. Does a soul ever forget its other half? Her name sits on the tip of my tongue before I swallow it back down.

"I don't know who I am without the chaos, addiction, and grief. I change out one vice for another because I'm scared of who I'll be without them."

With sobriety came new coping mechanisms. Some are healthy like working out and talking about things while others are unhealthy – drinking just enough to blur the edges of reality and the dopamine I get from being between a woman's legs. It makes me wonder if I'll always be an addict. Or maybe Dr. Maddox is right, everyone's path to recovery looks different.

"I can tell you one thing." Dr. Maddox smiles.

Resting my elbow on the armrest, I rest my chin on my fist. "What's that?"

"You don't have to face yourself alone. Getting to know who you are underneath the... performance, the façade, doesn't have to be a solo discovery. Others, especially those we love, tend to be our mirrors. Revealing the best and worst in us."

"Yeah... I think I got the worst part down pat."

He chuckles. "May I give you an assignment?"

"Didn't realize therapy required homework..." I say ruefully.

"Nothing arduous. You can do it anywhere, anytime. You have an imagination, correct?"

In spite of myself, I chuckle. "Homework and a smartass therapist?"

He ignores my remark, continuing on. "Before our next meeting, take time, even if it's just a moment, to imagine what it looks like to forgive yourself."

Forgive myself for abandoning those I love? "You said it was nothing arduous..."

"Has your family forgiven you?"

I take a steady, long inhale. "They say they have, but..." My voice trails off as realization washes over me. "Fuck... I guess you're right." Thinking back to breakfast this morning, *I* accused Snow of calling me a fuck up despite him telling me a thousand times over he has my back.

Dr. Maddox smiles. "It's harder to accept forgiveness if we haven't forgiven ourselves." I nod, acknowledging I hear his words. "Do you think you could try the homework?"

I meet his gaze, briefly glancing at the clock, realizing I've been here for almost an hour already. He's easy to talk to. "I'll try. No promises."

He glances at his watch, noticing the time too. "I am here for *you*, Winter. Not myself." Hesitating for only a moment, he asks, "Shall I keep you on the schedule for next week?"

"Yes." I stand, grabbing my coat. "I'll stop being a prick and be on time."

He lets out a hearty chuckle. "Very well."

Buttoning my coat, a curiosity crosses my mind. "May I ask who you lost?"

Dr. Maddox slips his hands into his pocket, looking at the floor before meeting my gaze again. "My son."

Despite his put together composure, I recognize the pain laced in his voice. "I'm sorry." I hang my head with my hand resting on the door handle. "I don't wish navigating the waters of grief upon anyone."

He smiles, but his eyes are distant. I know my question brought up memories. "Nor do I." His eyes come into focus on me. "Thank you for being here with me today, Winter."

"Thanks, Dr. Maddox." I nod, slipping out the door.

3
EVE

LYING WRAPPED UP IN a fluffy white down comforter, I watch Noah pull on his hunter green scrubs. I bite my bottom lip, appreciating the way his muscles flex beneath his smooth mahogany skin as he moves. He catches my eye, giving me a brilliant smile as he pauses getting dressed and climbs back onto the bed.

Hovering over me, he presses his lips to mine. They're soft and full. "You're beautiful to wake up to."

It's been nearly a month since we've gotten together, spending intentional time with one another. Noah is attentive, caring, and... familiar. He's the only man who I've consistently allowed in my life since— I stifle that thought.

"It has its perks." I bring my hands to his hair, rearranging some of his brown coils that are still damp from his shower. "Are you coming to my place tonight?"

"Of course." He rubs his thumb along my cheek. I relax into his touch. "Did you still want to meet for lunch?"

"Yes, unless something comes up. The clinic is still so new and—"

"I'm proud of you. I know how much Hope's Village means to you and the community."

A warm sensation that isn't related to how handsome Noah is heats my skin. I smile up at him. "Thank you."

He presses a kiss to my forehead before getting up to continue getting ready. "What time do you have to be in?"

"Not until ten today. All the work that went into opening up the clinic feels like it's finally catching up to me. And I'm realizing there is still so much to do."

"Eve, there's always something to do, but don't forget there will always be tomorrow too."

"I know, but if this clinic fails it—"

"It's not even eight in the morning and you're already spiraling." He chuckles, pressing a kiss to my temple. "Not everything can be accomplished in a day. Rest so that you can accomplish the things you want too."

I want to argue with him, but I know he's right. "Fine..."

"Your drive is admirable, but don't let it drive you into the ground. I know all too well what that's like."

Noah is a surgeon. We've known each other since high school, but fell out of touch once I started dating Winter. He came back to the Valley to complete his residency and be near his family. We crossed paths and went from being friends, to hooking up, and now we're together. Back then, I would've never looked at Noah the way I do now. Time has a way of adjusting our lens.

"I guess I'll take your advice, Dr. Kincaid," I say smugly.

He trains his brown eyes on me. "My name sounds like temptation on your lips."

Letting the blanket slip from my curves, I climb off the bed and stand in front of him. "You'll be late." I press a soft kiss to his lips. "I'll see you this afternoon."

He rests his hand on my bare hip. "Are you lunch?"

"I can be."

"You will be." He punctuates his sentence with his palm smacking my ass.

Laughter bubbles up in my throat as he kisses my neck. "See you later, Noah."

Jude: Are you at work or home?
Eve: Work. Why?

I stare at my screen, waiting for a response that doesn't come. Locking the phone, I set it aside, rolling my eyes. Jude, my little brother, recently moved back to the Valley from New York City when the company he works for offered him a remote position as a data scientist. Living on the other side of the country was hard for him.

He's twenty-eight now, but when he got the job in New York City, he was twenty-four and it was the first time he'd been away from home. Unlike Fox, who loves to travel, Jude was homesick and there were multiple times I had to talk him out of quitting his job. Now, four years later, he's making six-figures working from home in his pajamas most days. I'm proud of him. Even if he does annoy me sometimes. *A lot of the time.*

Settling at my desk, I curse myself for not stopping to get a coffee before coming in. We have a coffee maker here. It works well enough. It isn't a match for the coffee from Flapjack's Brew though. I decide to settle on a London Fog tea instead, knowing we have all the ingredients in the break room.

Grabbing a mug, I pour in a bit of French vanilla syrup, a dash of lavender, and then drop in an earl grey tea bag before filling it with scolding hot water. I aimlessly scroll through my phone while it steeps.

Peering into the cup, the water is now a golden brown color, letting me know it's ready. After I throw the tea bag away, I grab the can of cold foam from the fridge and put some on top before returning back to my office. I lick some of the sweet cold foam off the top. If I don't have coffee, this will always be the perfect substitute for me.

Rounding the corner into my office, I stop in my tracks when I see my brother sitting in front of my desk. His feet are propped up on it, casually sipping a coffee and eating a croissant.

"Excuse you. Get your filthy feet off my desk."

Jude turns around, grinning at me. "Always so sweet in the morning." He waits a few seconds too long for my liking to put his boots on the ground. "I come bearing gifts."

There's a clear to go cup filled with coffee from Flapjack's Brew and one of their melt in your mouth croissants on my desk. I look at my tea, deciding it can wait as I set it aside. "Thank you." I smile.

"Anything for my favorite sister."

I suck my teeth, taking a seat at my desk. "I'm your only sister."

"Lucky for you, you have no competition then." He winks.

"No work today or what?"

"I have a meeting I have to get ready for in a few hours. Until then, I thought I'd drop by and pester you before I run a few errands for mom."

I smile, shaking my head as I take a sip of my coffee. It's nice having him home, although I'd never tell him that. He'd gloat about it endlessly. Jude left four years ago as a boy and came back a man. His physical appearance is just one indication, like how he has a perpetual five o' clock shadow outlining his jaw these days. Or how his once lanky frame is now filled out with muscles to prove he spends time in the gym. He'll always be my little brother, but now he does adult-like, manly things like bringing me coffee, checking in to make sure I'm good, and going out of his way to spend time with me.

"I'll endure your presence since you brought me stuff." I take a bite of my chocolate croissant. "How are you liking being back at home?"

A smile slowly spreads across his face. "I missed it. It's good to be around family again. I know this is where I'll settle down... one day."

"Are you ready to settle down?"

"Depends on the day." He smirks. "I've hung out with Aspen a few times. Nobody could ever tell her she's ugly. Ever. And she knows it."

I let out a peal of laughter. "Never. I didn't realize you two were hanging out."

"It's casual. We're just friends."

"Uh huh..." I jest, knowing it's more casual for Aspen then him.

"It is! Aye, and don't tell her nothin' either." He points his finger at me, narrowing his eyes.

I give him a scandalized look. "I'd never! That's not my business to tell."

"Right... remember when you told our – " I wheeze with laughter because I already know what he's going to say " – next door neighbor with your big ass mouth that I thought she was cute and then she asked me if it was true and when I said no, out of fucking fear, she punched me in the fucking eye? Do you remember that, Little Miss I'd Never?"

I hold onto the arm rests of my chair, trying not to slide out of it as I laugh. "Why did you lie to her?"

"I was twelve and scared as hell! The first girl I ever liked punched me in the fucking eye!"

"She wouldn't have been good for you anyway!"

"I do have to agree with you on that." He smiles. "But I still would've preferred if you had kept your trap shut."

"Mom made me do your chores for a month. I learned not to say shit about other people's business after that."

"At least something got through that big head of yours."

Sucking my teeth, I glare at him. "Fuck you."

"Do you want to go look at places with me if you have time? I'd take Mama, but she's pushy, talking about I need to consider my non-existent future wife and kids."

I snort with laughter. "Yeah, let me know when you want to go."

"Cool. I need my own space as soon as possible. It's nice being home. I just want my *own* home." He glances at his phone. "I better get going. Dad asked me to pick up his medicine at the pharmacy."

I stand, walking him to the door. "Thank you for the coffee and croissant."

"Don't mention." He gives me a tight hug as he kisses my cheek. "I'll text you later. Love you.

"Love you, too."

After enjoying my coffee, and answering a few e-mails, I decide to start my day. Before I can get too deep into my work, there's a knock at the door. Looking up, I'm met by Ilaria and Silas, the two pediatricians who are the heart of Hope's Village.

"Good morning." I smile. "Should I be worried that both of you are in my office?"

"Some of us know how to take breaks." Silas smirks, taking a seat with a cup of coffee in hand.

I give him a bemused expression as Ilaria rolls her eyes. "We have a few minutes before our next appointments."

"Is everything okay?" I ask.

"Yeah, everything's fine, but..." Her voice trails off. I raise a brow, waiting for her to continue. "Silas and I were talking—"

Silas sits up, letting out an exasperated sigh, setting his cup on my desk. "We need more funding for services." He looks at Ilaria. "You don't need to sugar coat with Eve. She gets it."

"I know, but I didn't want to stress her out."

"I'm not stressed." I smooth my hands over the front of my blouse, attempting to ignore the knots of stress in my stomach.

"Families are still having to travel forty-five minutes to an hour away for services. Not only that, but wait lists are long in other areas, leaving children without crucial services. Especially children with special needs," Silas says.

"I can contact the grant writer and see if—"

Ilaria begins shaking her head before I can finish my sentence. "That takes too long. The sooner we have these services, the better."

My brow furrows as the knots tighten. Where am I supposed to get more money? It's not like we opened this with our own bank accounts. It took years of planning, grants, loans, and not to mention countless hours of stress that apparently are never ending.

"What other services are needed?"

"Early intervention services." Silas speaks first. "A speech therapist who has experience with AAC devices would be beneficial."

"Experience with what?"

"Augmentative and alternative communication," Ilaria fills in. "They are devices, such as an iPad, that can help children who are unable to use verbal speech to communicate."

"Think of it as their voice," Silas adds. "If a speech therapist were here, it would mean that families could get services in a timely manner instead of having to wait six months."

"Six months?" I raise my brows. I may not be a doctor, but I do know how imperative it is for children to have access to early intervention services when needed.

"We also need a pediatric occupational therapist. OT is beneficial for children who have motor delays, sensory processing disorders, and coordination issues. It can help them regulate their nervous system."

"I can see the benefits of these services, but where are we going to find a speech and occupational therapists?"

Silas looks at Ilaria, smiling. "We can take care of that if you can take care of funding."

The anxious knots loosen themselves a little. "Okay, but where would we offer occupational services?"

"Do we really need two conference rooms?" Ilaria raises a brow.

"Did you two already have this figured out?"

"Ilaria was worried if we sprung this on you without a plan, we'd be throwing you into the deep end... again."

I can't help but laugh. "You two have never thrown me into the deep end."

"No. But without you, Hope's Village wouldn't be here," Ilaria says.

Being a clinical director wasn't my life's dream. At one point, I thought I'd be wearing a white coat with Dr.Valentine embroidered on the front. A year into medical school, where I met Ilaria and Silas, life happened, and it changed the trajectory of my plans. Looking back now, I realize, while it may have been the darkest time of my life, it also set me on the path I feel was made for me.

In spite of the change in plans, I knew I still wanted to be in the medical field but switched my focus to managing. I applied to be a clinical director at the facility I worked at, got the job, and fell in love with it. When Ilaria approached me about the possibility of being a clinical director for a pediatric practice, I gave her a wholehearted yes.

"Thank you." I give them a warm smile. "I know grants take time, but that's our best bet for funding."

"Lucky for you," Silas says as he claps his hands together with excitement, "The Mayor's Charity Gala is in just a few weeks."

"They do an auction for fundraising to benefit local businesses," Ilaria adds.

"Is there anything you two didn't think of?"

"No, because our window of opportunity is closing for us to not have to worry ourselves with grants and loans," Silas says.

Hope Valley is one of the richest cities on the West Coast. If there is anywhere to get funding, it would certainly be at the Mayor's Charity Gala.

"The only problem is – " Ilaria begins.

"Problem?" I ask. My voice a little too high.

"Calm down." Silas sighs, waving his hand airily. "We need tickets, and they're no longer available on the website."

I lean back in my seat, letting out an exasperated sigh, rubbing my temples. "Do you know how much easier this meeting would've been if you two would've simply asked for tickets to the Mayor's Charity Gala for funding? The stress the past few minutes has caused me is ridiculous."

Silas lets out a hearty laugh and Ilaria gives me an apologetic smile. "We wanted you to realize how important these services are," Ilaria reassures me.

"If either of you say we need something, I trust that it's true."

"I told you we should've led with the Gala," Silas says to Ilaria.

Haven, the receptionist, pokes her head into my office with a smile. "Sorry to interrupt, but your one o' clock appointments are here," she says to Ilaria and Silas.

"Thank you, Haven." I smile before she heads back to the receptionist desk. "I'll get us to the mayor's charity Gala."

"We knew you could." Silas smiles, rising from his feet. "Thank you for all you do, Eve."

"Anytime, Dr. Bradford." I nod.

"Silas," he corrects. "Just Silas."

I snort with laughter, knowing he hates formalities. "Why did you work so hard to get the white coat only to tell people to call you Silas?"

He shrugs. "Sometimes I'm a mystery even to myself."

Ilaria smiles at him, shaking her head as he disappears out the door. Her eyes meet mine again. "What?" She adjusts the stethoscope around her neck.

"Nothing." I shrug nonchalantly. "It's just... you never look at me like that."

She sucks her teeth, narrowing her eyes. "I have appointments."

I can't help the laugh that escapes me. "Have a good day, Dr. Solis." She gives me a dismissive wave of her hand as she walks out the door.

Rising from my seat, I stretch my hands to the ceiling, feeling the tension leave my body. I hope that we're able to get enough funding from the mayor's charity Gala. I'd hate to disappoint Ilaria and Silas... even myself. Pushing the negative thoughts from my mind, I reach for my phone on my desk to find Mayor Price's number. She answers on the third ring.

"Hi, Mayor Price. It's Eve Valentine." I lean against my desk.

"Eve! How are things?"

"Amazing." I smile. "I'm reaching out to see if you'd have time to meet today?"

"If you could make it to my office in the next hour, I'd be more than happy to meet with you."

"I can be there."

"Perfect!" she says happily. "I'll see you in just a bit."

Hanging up the phone, I shoot a text to Noah.

Eve: I can't do lunch today. I've gotta meet with the mayor. See you tonight.

Grabbing my bag, I head out the door. "I'll be back, Haven. Let me know what you guys would like for lunch and I'll pick it up."

"Okay, I'll text you once they're done." She smiles.

Sitting on a stiff leather sofa, I wait for Mayor Price in the lobby of the city council's office. My phone vibrates with a text in my bag.

Noah: The mayor?
Eve: Yeah. I'll tell you about it when I see you later.
Noah: Are we cooking tonight or do you want me to pick something up?
Eve: Cooking together sounds fun.
Noah: I'll pick up some stuff.

"Eve," the receptionist calls my name.

Standing, I smile and follow her into the office.

"Eve Valentine." Mayor Price exclaims, foregoing a handshake, pulling me into a hug.

I've known Eliza for years. She's the youngest Mayor in Hope Valley history at only three years older than me, making her thirty-six.

"Mayor Price." I pat her back. "Thank you for meeting with me on such short notice."

"You've helped bring a much needed service to our city. You'll always have my time. Please sit down." She gestures toward a seat in front of her desk.

"Thank you." I sit in the much softer, more luxurious leather seat.

"How's your brother doing?"

I rub my lips together, trying to hide a smile. "Which one?" I ask, knowing full well which one she's most curious about.

"Both," she says casually.

I give her what she wants because she's giving me her time. "Fox is great. Still traveling."

"He sure loves his travel doesn't he?"

"Yeah." I nod my head. "He's currently in South Africa."

She looks out the window with a glimmer of longing in her eye. "Tell him I said hi when you talk to him next."

"I will."

My oldest brother, Fox, was home from college when he and Eliza started spending more time together. It didn't last long because he wanted to travel the world while she wanted to stay here. He may have left, but Eliza never misses an opportunity to ask how he's doing.

"What can I help you with today?" she asks, forgetting about my middle brother, Jude.

I swallow a laugh, giving her a smile. "The charity gala. Is it possible Hope's Village can participate in the auction?"

"We'd love to have you. However—" My heart sinks with her hesitation. "We do ask that guests pay the table fee."

"Oh." I blink. "Okay, how much is that?"

"Twenty thousand per table."

"Twenty grand? For a table?" I can't keep the surprise or annoyance out of my tone.

"It's steep, but every penny goes toward charities in the valley. The hospital, the schools, shelters, scholarships, and we're even starting a community therapy fund for those who can't afford it. It's going back to the people. Not to me or the council."

This wasn't an anticipated expense. I can't ask Ilaria or Silas to dig into their own bank accounts after already putting so much on the line already.

"I understand."

"Of course, there are always other businesses who are not participating in the gala or auction who may be willing to sponsor your table. The only catch is— " She grabs a paper from her desk, handing it to me. "—they cannot sponsor more than one table. Since the gala is only weeks away, most businesses are already providing sponsorship."

Taking the paper, I glance over it. "Are the ones with asterisks beside them already sponsoring a table?"

"Yes." She nods. "If you do get a sponsor, we ask that you be open to sponsoring another business at next year's gala."

"You're doing amazing work, Eliza. I mean, Mayor Price."

"No need to correct yourself." She chuckles. "I never wanted to leave because the community is amazing."

Hope Valley is a progressive city with the heart of a small town. People move and stay here for that very reason.

"I have to agree since I'm still here too."

"Reach out to the businesses. I know investing twenty grand in something you weren't expecting to as a new business can put a strain on the budget. That's why we have a sponsorship program. Once you've secured a table, contact Mason Hawthorne." She hands me a card. "He is the one coordinating the auction."

"What do you suggest we put up for auction?"

"Anything." She gives a wave of her hand. "From baked goods to vacations. It's really up to you at Hope's Village. I would suggest making it something unique and enticing. Most businesses will give away services, but you can't really do that with the pediatric clinic. Think about collaborating with one of the spas or wineries."

"Unique and enticing. I'm sure the three of us can come up with something."

"I'm looking forward to seeing you all at the gala." She glances at the clock on the wall. "Oh, I have to get to another meeting."

Standing, I wait for her to gather her things and follow her out of the office. "Thank you for your time."

"Of course. Let me know if you need anything or have trouble with sponsorship. I'm sure we can work something out, but I do like to encourage participants to give back to the community they are asking to invest in them."

"I understand, and we will most certainly give back."

She smiles. "Take care, Eve."

Walking back to my car in the warm spring sun, my phone vibrates in my bag. Pulling it out, I'm met by a picture of me with Dad as he kisses my cheek.

"Hey Daddy!" I smile as I answer the video call.

"How's my girl?"

"I'm good. Just got done talking to Mayor Price about attending the charity gala in hopes of getting more funding."

"How did that go?" he asks, tinkering around the garage.

"Good," I reply even though I'm now stressed about finding the funding to pay for the table.

"Is Eliza still hung up on Fox?" he asks with a chuckle.

"Always." I press the button to unlock my car before pulling on the handle. "Asked about the boys and only cared to hear about Fox."

"I run into her around town on occasion, and she always asks about him. She's a nice woman."

Closing the door and starting the car, I set my phone on the dash mount. "She is sweet which is why Fox didn't allow the relationship to go any further because he knew he wasn't going to be around."

"Speakin' of Fox, have you talked to him lately?"

"We email more than talk. His reception is always questionable depending on where he is."

"Good, good." He grumbles distractedly as he rummages through his toolbox before turning his attention back to me. "It's been a few days since I've seen you and wanted to check in."

The stress and tension that had crept into my body, eases up with his words. "I know, Dad. I've just been busy with work and—"

He holds up a hand with a warm smile on his face. "You don't have to explain to me, Bug. I'm proud of you. I'll never not want to know what you're up to and how you are. I just wanted to let you know you're missed."

I give him my brightest smile. I'm close to both my parents, but Dad and I have always been a little closer. He knows exactly what to say at the moment I need to hear it. "I miss you and Mom, too. I'll stop by tomorrow evening, okay?"

"Can't wait to see you. Tell Noah he's welcome to join us." He winks.

"I'll bring him, too." I smirk.

"Good. I won't keep you any longer. Love you, Bug."

"Love you too, Dad."

Ending the call, I let out a contented sigh, feeling rejuvenated after talking to Dad.

Noelle gives me a hug and kiss on the cheek as I step into her apartment. "Did you want to eat with us tonight?"

"No, thank you." I set my bag down on the countertop, side stepping a box. "Noah and I have plans to cook dinner together."

"That sounds better than having dinner with Snow and me." She moves the boxes off the kitchen island. "I was just packing some more stuff up."

"Are you excited to move into the new house?"

Noelle and Snow purchased their first home together in Citrine Grove. It's about a fifteen minute drive east from the heart of the Valley. It's a beautiful, gated community with homes that are Architectural Digest worthy with coveted views.

The smile on her face tells me how she feels before her words do. "Eve... I really can't believe this is my life. Engaged to the love of my life, buying a house together, and planning a dream wedding."

"And you're deserving of it all." I pull her into a hug, holding her tight.

"Thank you... for always being by my side." Releasing me, she dabs the inner corners of her eyes with her fingertips. "So, how was your day?" she asks, grabbing a bottle of wine and some glasses.

Between sips of white wine, I fill her in on the quest to secure more funding and the Mayor's Charity Gala. "Sometimes I feel as though I bit off more than I can chew. When I think we can coast a little bit, there's another hurdle. What if..." I lick my lips, not wanting to verbalize my worst fear. "What if it all falls apart?"

She grabs my hand. "Take a deep breath with me." I roll my eyes but follow her lead. "While failure is a very real possibility, it's *always* a possibility with everything we do. Hope's Village is new. Not even three months old. There will be bumps, curves, and scary moments, but you have an amazing team and support system. *Breathe*, before you die holding your breath, wanting it to be perfect."

I let out a puff of air, trying to ease the anxiousness. "I'll try to remember to breathe."

Noelle smiles. "I'll be here to remind you when you forget. Now," she downs the last sip of her wine, "is there any way I can help?"

I watch her get up, putting her glass in the sink. I'm not sure how Noelle became my best friend. One day it was just me and then it was us. I only hope I can be half the friend to her that she is to me. Because times like these, where she's willing to help without hesitation, I wonder if I deserve her.

"I have to find a sponsor for the insanely priced table."

"How much is it?"

"Twenty grand..."

"For a fucking table?!" Noelle's eyes widen as her eyebrows shoot up. A chuckle tickles my throat. "Your reaction is the same as mine."

"That's robbery!" she exclaims.

"I have to agree... but, it all goes back to the community. I know Eliza isn't lining her pockets with it. Not as though she'd need it anyway."

The Price family is well off. Her parents own a luxury car dealership that sells to customers from all over the world.

"I guess the people who attend have bank accounts that won't notice the cash is missing. But I didn't think you'd have to pay for a table given you're a business who's participating in the auction."

"I don't make the rules, babe. Besides, she did say we can have another business sponsor us." Grabbing for my purse, I pull the paper with the list of businesses out of my bag. "The ones with the asterisks beside them are already sponsoring someone."

Taking it, Noelle looks it over. "Um... well more than half are taken."

"All." I let out a long, low sigh. "I called the few that were left. Most are sponsoring others or participating themselves this year."

Her brow furrows. "Why isn't North Star Toys on here?"

Before I can respond, the door opens and Snow appears. Noelle lights up, setting the paper aside, and makes her way over to him. Wrapping her arms around his middle, she presses up onto her toes, giving him a kiss.

"Snowflake." He smiles, wrapping his arm around her waist, kissing her again.

They're hopelessly lost in each other. Not in a sappy, lovesick way. It's the rare occurrence of witnessing two souls who've found each other. A thought invades my mind... *is it possible to ever feel that way about Noah?* We go together as well as any two people can, but the spark I see between Snow and Noelle, the one that I've felt before... we don't have that.

Can two people kindle a spark? Or are we already carrying a spark that blazes when we find the soul whose light matches yours?

Tearing his eyes away from his world, Snow smiles at me. "Hi, Eve! Where's the third member of TLC this evening?"

Noelle and I laugh. "Stop it!" Elle playfully shoves his arm. "She's getting off soon and then she'll stop by."

"I won't interrupt your time together." He grins, starting toward the bedroom.

"Hold on." Elle grabs his arm. "Why isn't North Star Toys sponsoring anyone for the Mayor's Charity Gala?" She holds up the paper in his face.

He takes it from her hand, looking at it. "Because we make donations to the city throughout the year. We felt that would help more. Why do you ask?"

"The clinic needs more funding." I speak up. "We thought the auction at the charity gala would be a good place to raise money without having to worry about trying to get a grant. To participate in that, we have to purchase a table and the price of that is steep for us at the moment. Mayor Price suggested a sponsor, but since we're down to the wire, everyone on the list is already providing sponsorship."

"Couldn't North Star Toys sponsor them?" Elle looks at Snow expectantly.

As if the man could deny her anything. "We can..."

Noelle squeals, clapping her hands, and I gape at him, relief washing over me. I was ready to be stressed about this for the next few days.

"But—" He begins, making my elation ebb. "You'll have to talk to Winter."

Noelle's eyes dart to mine as I deflate with his words. "Why?" I ask, trying not to sound like a whining, petulant child.

"He's the president of marketing," Snow says plainly. "This is marketing."

"Elle works in the marketing department. Can't she just approve—"

"I just work there... I don't make decisions," she answers before I can finish my sentence.

"What about North?" I ask. "Isn't he in charge of finances?"

"Yes, he is." Snow nods. "But Winter also handles public relations within his department."

A silence falls between the three of us. *Ask Winter for help*? I feel ridiculous for wanting to pull the money from my own account just to avoid talking to him. Aspen walks through the door as if this is her place seconds later.

"Why do the three of you look like you're in a standoff?"

"Eve's being... difficult." Noelle crosses her arms, letting out an exasperated sigh.

"When is she not?" She hangs her bag on the hooks near the door.

"I am not!" I defend, feeling ganged up on.

Snow glances at me before turning his attention back to Noelle. "I'm going to change." He kisses her temple without saying another word.

Once the bedroom door closes, Noelle turns to me. "You're being unreasonable."

"I am not!" I repeat myself, knowing full well I am.

"Want to fill me in on what's going on?" Aspen grabs the bottle of wine, filling her glass.

Before I can get a word out, Noelle fills her in on my dilemma. "And now, she's being a brat about asking Winter to sponsor them."

Aspen snorts into her wine glass, eyeing me over the rim. "Eve, I love you. And because I love you, I say this respectfully. You are your own fucking problem. Winter isn't the devil. Get over yourself."

"Damn." Noelle looks into her wine glass she's holding in her hand.

I gape at both of them. "Get over myself? Do you know what he—"

"No." Aspen cuts me off. "Elle and I don't have a clue what Winter did because you *refuse* to talk about it. You're still holding onto that pain over a decade later, expecting us to pat your back and justify why you've been a certified grade A bitch to him."

"Aspen," Elle hisses, giving her a warning look.

"Don't Aspen me." She imitates Elle's tone. "Eve doesn't need to be coddled." Aspen crosses her arms, holding her wine glass, looking me up and down. "She needs to face her shit."

Aspen's words feel like a smack to the face. Every single one is true, even if they are hard to swallow. I stare at her, feeling the tears. Looking away, I blink, not giving them a chance to fall.

"This really isn't about you or Winter, is it?" Elle places her hand on my shoulder. "It's about getting what you want so you can make a dream come true. Winter aside, is throwing away the possibility of securing funding worth it?"

"No." I blink, looking down at my hands. Letting out a sigh, feeling the threat of tears again, I say, "I'll talk to him."

"Yes you will," Aspen says, making my eyes snap to hers. "And do you know why?" I shake my head. "Because you've come too fucking far to let this stand in your way of getting what you want."

Noelle wraps her arm around my shoulder. "Although Aspen's delivery could be better, she's right."

"Yeah..." It seems simple enough, but neither of them know I'm still in love with Winter.

4
WINTER

KNOCKING ON THE DOORFRAME, I peek into Snow's office. It's pointless to do this since the walls are glass and he can see me, but I'll never miss an opportunity to be obnoxious. He holds up a finger, signaling me to wait, and then points to the ear bud. I lean against the doorframe, waiting for him to finish. Once done, he gives me his full attention.

"What's up, man?" He pulls the earbud out, setting it on his desk.

Noelle tries to enter Snow's office, but I wrap my arm around her neck. She lets out a laugh as she stands beside me. "Nothing. I came to inform you I'm taking *your* fiancée to lunch. Since you're too busy to do it."

Snow lets out an annoyed sigh. "Thank you for reminding me... again."

"You sure you can't come with us?" Noelle pushes my arm off her shoulders, making her way to Snow.

She leans down to kiss him, and I clear my throat loudly. "You're on company time, Miss Frost. I'd hate to have to call HR." This elicits a laugh from Snow.

Noelle side eyes me as she leans forward, pressing her lips to his. I gape at her, faking offense. After kissing him, she straightens up, squaring her shoulders. "Fire me if you want, but you'd be lost without me. I'd hate to have to tell them you're having a fling with the receptionist on the first floor."

"*Winter*," Snow says irritably, giving me a look of indignation.

"Throw me under the fucking bus, Noelle!"

She cackles in response.

"Please tell me you're not having a... fuckship with someone here in the office. If you are, HR really will be involved and—"

Holding up my hands, I take a seat in one of the chairs in front of his desk. "Listen, it's not like that." He looks at me with disbelief. "Okay... it was initially."

"Are you having sex with her or not?"

"No. I'm not. Although, I will admit it was my intent."

Snow raises a brow. "Did she reject you?"

I let out a hearty laugh. "Please. Look at me." Noelle snorts with laughter and Snow rolls his eyes as I flash them both a smile. "To be honest, she was boring and talked a lot about nothing. I need both brains stimulated. Not just one."

"Since when?" Snow asks incredulously.

"Damn, bruh. I can't change and want more?"

His face softens. "Of course you can."

I'd rather claim I want to change when the truth is, I don't really have a choice. My usual vices failing me as of late have caused me to be aware of things I normally overlook. Historically, if a woman was annoying, or seemed to not be the brightest color in the box, that was fine because I only wanted one thing. But lately... that hasn't been enough. I find myself attempting to dig below the surface talk. Not only is it exhausting, but it's disappointing to discover that they're all hollow beneath the alluring appearance.

North appears, bringing a lighter mood to the office. "Staff meeting without me?"

"No, I'm taking Noelle out to lunch since Snow will be neglecting her for a meeting."

"Do you want to go to the meeting and I'll go out to lunch with her?" Snow asks.

"Fuck no. That's your job. Want to come with, North?"

"Yeah, that's why I came up here in the first place."

"Are you guys at least going to bring me back food or is it just fuck me?" Snow asks.

"Are you... pouting?" Noelle tilts her head to the side, surveying her future husband.

The crease between his brow deepens, giving him away. "I don't pout."

"He's definitely pouting," I say with a sigh, rising to my feet.

Noelle reassures Snow we'll bring him back food. It's refreshing to see him genuinely happy with her. I can't help the thought that creeps in.

I wonder if I'll ever feel that happiness again?

After a delicious plate of chicken fettuccine alfredo at Urbane Bites, North, Noelle, and I let our food settle while we talk. I've enjoyed getting to know Noelle over the past few months. She's become more of a confidant than just a future sister-in-law to me. Noelle is the only one from the family who knows I'm disappearing to therapy and not to fuck someone. I haven't told the rest of the family because I don't want the pressure of having expectations placed on me to do better or change.

I'm doing what I can. For right now, that has to be enough.

Noelle grumbles at her phone before tossing it in her bag. "Trouble in paradise?"

Shaking her glass, making the ice clink against it, she slurps down the rest of her lemonade. "No. Snow and I don't argue much."

"Not that it's any of our business," North interjects, giving me a look.

"Unless he's being an idiot," I add.

"Oh yeah, then let us know." North stretches out in his seat, adjusting his glasses. "We'll set him straight."

She chuckles, making her shoulders shake with laughter. "Thanks for having my back guys, but that's not..." Her voice trails off as she turns toward me. "Eve wants to talk to you."

I don't move or allow any emotion to cross my face. North leans forward, resting his forearms on the table. They both look at me expectantly. Before I respond, I take a long sip of water. Not to be dramatic, but my throat suddenly feels too dry. Setting it back on the table, I keep my hand around the cool glass because her name makes my body respond in a way I wish it didn't.

"Does she really? Or are you just saying that?"

"You know me, Winter. This isn't something I'd lie about. Besides," she pokes at the ice in her glass with her straw, meeting my gaze again. "She doesn't really have a choice."

I try to keep the devilish grin off my face but fail miserably. North snorts with laughter. "She's fucked."

I'm reveling in this news. She *has* to talk to me? After months of arctic shoulders and venomous glares, Eve Valentine *has* to talk to me? The smile on my face doesn't waver.

"Tell me more," I urge.

Shaking her head, the corners of her mouth tip up. "I knew this would delight you."

"More than you could ever fathom. After Fireside, I've been waiting for the day."

"Fireside?" North cocks a brow.

Noelle tilts her head to the side. "What happened there?"

"Nothing." I lean back in my seat, letting out a sigh. Of course Eve didn't tell her.

"What was it?"

I decide against sharing the moment between Eve and I, wanting to keep it to myself. "She just seemed to warm up to me a little before going subzero."

"Oh, we've all noticed that," North says, stating the obvious.

I ignore him. "What does she want?"

"That's for you two to sort out. I'm simply giving you a heads up. She wanted me to ask about meeting times."

"Did she?" I splay my hand across my chest. "Are you my assistant now, Noelle?"

"Oh, God," Noelle groans, cradling her head in her hand.

North chuckles. "You should've known good and damn well he was going to eat this up."

"At North Star Toys, we are professionals." I square my shoulders. "Please direct her to make an appointment to speak with me through the appropriate channels. I'm a busy man. Not at anyone's leisure."

"Can you see that?" North asks.

Noelle peeks through the slits of her fingers. "What?"

"His head has grown three times since you've told him this news."

We burst into laughter. "I'm simply following protocol."

"Yeah, since when have you given a fuck about that?" North grins.

"Since Eve discovered she *has* to speak with me."

Pulling up my calendar, I check the time of my therapy appointment this afternoon, making sure I can stop by Dad's grave beforehand. As I'm looking over my appointments, an email comes in from my assistant. It's an approval request for a meeting with Eve. I read her name multiple times in the subject line before opening it. A part of me wants to decline and make her choose another time, but I'm too interested in what she could possibly want to talk to me about.

To be an asshole or not to be an asshole? That's always my fucking question. When we first met, I wasn't jaded. My edges were smooth and touchable. I became enamored with her quickly, wanting to know her, *needing* to know her. Now, my edges are sharp with ridges, cliffs, and canyons. Some of them I dug myself while the deepest ones were out of my control. I know I hurt Eve, but she hurt me too. I'm not sure she'll ever see it that way because I'm the one who left.

Attempting to smooth out my perilous edges, I accept the meeting time for Friday at three o' clock. Leaning back in my seat, I let out a satisfied sigh. Soon, Eve will be in my office, forced to let her guard down enough to talk to me. All I need is a hairline fracture in that fortress of hers.

"What do I do if... someone doesn't forgive me?"

I can endlessly imagine forgiving myself, and even if I do, that doesn't mean the other person will.

Dr. Maddox offers me a smile before setting his notepad aside. "Forgiveness isn't for the other person. Quite frankly, fuck them." His words jolt me. "You're aware you made a mistake, correct?"

"Yes." I know it to the depths of my soul.

He nods. "We hold ourselves prisoners to the past by not forgiving ourselves. When you truly forgive yourself, you're cutting the tie to the anchor that is holding you prisoner to your own self-judgement and resentment. No one else can cut that rope but you."

Taking in his words, I consider how I'm holding onto mistakes of the past, wishing I could correct them, but knowing I can't. Can I let them go and forgive myself? Could finding peace within myself be so simple?

I don't realize I'm lost in thought until Dr. Maddox speaks again. "It's easy to let other's narratives of us become our beliefs. Getting to know yourself means writing your own narrative. I also believe as you discover who you are, forgiveness will follow."

I've only thought about forgiveness. It's hard to visualize something I never imagined for myself. Ten years ago I didn't imagine this is what my life would look like. It's not just about forgiveness, it's also making peace with the dreams that never came to fruition.

Knowing what I have to do, I say, "I'll make a real effort... for myself."

"You're already doing the work, Winter."

The corners of my mouth tip up. "Thank you, Dr. Maddox."

Glancing at the clock, he asks, "Same time next week?"

"I'll be here." I let out a sigh, rising to my feet.

"Actually, before you go," Dr. Maddox stands, heading to his desk. "I wanted to ask if you'd be interested in something. Are you familiar with True's House?"

"Yes." I nod. "We donate to them regularly." True's House is a non-profit organization that has multiple youth and young adult programs such as behavioral health services, housing, and support for at-risk youth.

"They have a mentorship program called True's Circle that is for children who have lost a loved one."

"You want me," I point at myself, "to be a mentor?"

"No. I don't *want* you to be a mentor. I'm wondering if you'd be interested in being one?"

"Why..." I can't imagine a parent, given what I've been through, wanting me mentoring their grieving child. "I can barely mentor myself and you're wondering if I can guide the youth of tomorrow?"

Dr. Maddox gives me a patient smile. "I think any child would be lucky to have you by their side."

Not only does he call me on my shit, but he also *believes* in me. "What would it entail?"

"You'll be paired with a child they feel you'll be a good fit with. Once you're paired, you can attend the activities at True's House or you can take them on outings you've planned."

"That sounds relatively painless."

He rifles through some papers on his desk. "Is it something you'd be interested in?"

"A mentor..." I mutter more for me then Dr. Maddox while I mull over his question. "Uh... yeah. I guess I'll give it a go. But," I point my finger at him, "if anything goes left, I'm blaming you."

"I doubt it, but will accept the blame." He chuckles, handing me a card. "The application is online. Fill it out, and I'll let Hudson, the director, know to look out for it."

I stare at the card, wondering if this could be exactly what I need or another mistake?

Later in the afternoon, Noelle and I are going through influencer applications. The response to the open call was overwhelming. We've finally made it to the last few applicants, and we couldn't be happier to be nearly done.

"Three more left and then we can narrow it down." Noelle sighs. "I think once we have our chosen applicants, we should get input from the rest of the team as well as North and Snow."

"I agree. We need fresh eyes." I say, stretching out on the couch. "I'm fucking tired of watching videos. Next time, it would be wise to assemble a team to sift through the applications before us."

"That definitely would've been helpful."

After my appointment with Dr. Maddox, becoming a mentor has been on my mind. It's not something I can pick up and drop if I don't like it. I have to be committed. Once I arrived at the office, I pulled up the application and read through the information. It's not a short term commitment. I'd be paired with a child until they turn eighteen or graduate from high school.

"Do you think I'd be a good mentor?"

Noelle blinks at me, clearly taken aback by my question. "I mean... yeah. You've taught me—"

"No. I mean for a kid."

"Oh, yeah. For sure." She smiles.

"Seriously?" I cock a brow.

"Yes. Why do you ask?"

I reiterate my conversation with Dr. Maddox to her. "I'm not sure it's a good idea, though. Me? A mentor?"

Grabbing her bottle of water off the table, she side eyes me as she takes a longer than necessary sip. It makes me worried.

"Winter..." She screws the cap back on. "You're the only one who thinks you're not capable."

"I..." My voice trails off as her words slap me with a reality check.

"Am right." She smiles, finishing my sentence for me. "I'm surprised there's any room for doubt with that big ego of yours."

I match her smile. "It may come as a shock to you, given my godly physique—" she gives me the whites of her eyes as she rolls them "—but I'm a mere mortal."

"Listen, drama *King*. You're human. If you want to be a mentor, commit to that shit and be a mentor. None of us are fucking qualified half the damn time, but you know what?"

"What?"

"They're not looking for qualified—" she makes air quotes with her hands "—they're looking for someone who's willing to show up. Qualifications don't matter when you *need* someone, Winter. If you want to do it, do it." She holds my gaze for a few seconds before turning her attention back to the list of applicants.

My routine is pretty mundane. Work, hang out with family, go home, get tired of the silence, and then I go out to fill the void with something. The problem is, filling the void means that I'm not making the best decisions. I'm surrounded by people who are also trying to ignore their issues. I'm realizing the importance of the company I keep which is why my circle has dwindled down to my brothers, Elle, and Aspen.

Becoming a mentor would give me something refreshing and positive outside of myself. At least I hope it will.

"Thanks, Elle," I say, making up my mind to fill out the application tonight.

"Tom Ford suit today?" North brushes off my shoulders with a smirk.

I swat his hand away as he lets out a bark of laughter. "Don't you have somewhere to be instead of bothering me?"

"Actually, no. I don't." He takes off his suit jacket, laying it over the chair.

Glancing at the clock, I say, "Don't get to fucking comfortable. This is a meeting for two."

"Chill." He flops down onto the couch, pulling some candy out of his pocket. "Not like Eve will give you any play once she gets here anyway." Unwrapping it, he puts it in his mouth, giving me a smug smile.

"I'd hate for you to choke..." I glare at him as he takes up unnecessary space in my office. Eve should be here in fifteen minutes. But if I still know her, she'll be here ten minutes early which means North has five minutes to get the fuck out of my office. He meticulously chose today to play the role of the obnoxious little brother. I was hoping to have a few minutes alone to compose myself.

"So..." He stretches out, placing his hands behind his head. "Are you trying to get back with her or what?"

His blatant question makes me pause. *What the fuck am I doing?* Eve made it clear she's going to do everything she can to keep the bullshit promise she made to herself. I'd be more inclined to make an effort to respect it if she hadn't said she's still in love with me. For me, and my ego, that was an open invitation to put that shaky ass promise to the test. It's been easy for her to keep it because she's been avoiding me like the plague, but today she's going to be in my space. All I know is, I want her to come to me because she knows where her heart feels at home like mine does. Not because I wore her down.

"The only thing I'm trying to do is see what she could possibly need me for."

My assistant's voice disrupts our conversation. "Your three o' clock is here, Mr. King."

"Thank you, Willa. Give me a few minutes to get rid of North."

He smiles at her from the couch. She returns it, shaking her head. "Will do."

Once she closes the door again, I turn my attention to North. "Get the fuck out."

He slowly sits up, taking his sweet time gathering his jacket. "You avoided my question." Standing, he pulls it on. I remember when he was shorter than me. Now, we're eye to eye. "I may be the youngest, but I also see everything." He adjusts his suit jacket, intentionally moving at a snail's pace. His eyes meet mine. "Have you ever thought maybe it's not about her forgiving you... but about you showing up for her?"

"Showing up for her..." I repeat his words, more for myself.

"Don't let your abnormally large ego get in the way of your heart. You can't change the past nor can you control the present, but you can show her that you're not going anywhere now... even if you did leave all those years ago."

Show up for her... us? Something I didn't – *couldn't* – do all those years ago?

"I don't want to be the only one trying, North." I admit.

He claps my shoulder, giving it a squeeze. "Shit. Maybe she's just waiting for you to make the first move."

North doesn't give me an opportunity to respond, exiting my office. I hear him greet Eve as I take a calming breath. We may view him as the baby, but he just hit me with some old soul advice that forced things into a new perspective. I don't have much time to ponder them when Eve enters my office.

I attempt to look casual, leaning against my desk with my legs crossed at the ankles as she invades my senses, sending them into overdrive. Eve's velvety sable skin looks like it's glowing against her white blouse that dips low in the front, giving me a tempting peek of the swell of her breasts. I used to know the shape of her as if it were my favorite sonnet. She's always been willowy. But now, with a decade passed, her curves are slightly more defined and supple. Soft in all the right places. Her deep brown hair is freshly pressed, cascading over her shoulders like the finest strands of silk. Nothing I couldn't sweat out to make her hair revert to its natural curly state.

Her eyes look everywhere but at me. It makes my lips twitch with amusement. She really doesn't want to be here. I motion for her to have a seat at one of the chairs before rounding the desk and taking my own.

Her sleek strands momentarily obstruct my view of her heart shaped face as she gets as comfortable as one can in a place they don't want to be. As she sweeps her hair out of her face with her fingertip, our gazes collide for the first time in months. Her brown eyes have always reminded me of an autumn sunset.

She offers me an "I come in peace" smile, displaying her dimple and all her teeth. Even the one on the bottom row that is slightly crooked.

It's not even noticeable, but somehow she got it in her head that she needed to get it fixed before the wedding. I told her that I loved her and that damned snaggletooth and she looked like she wanted to throat chop me. Instead, she fell into a fit of laughter and then we ended up fucking on the bathroom counter. There was no way I'd ever allow her to feel less than in my presence. Not then and not even now.

I match her smile and she inhales deeply, causing her breasts to look like they just might bless me and spill out of her top. *They don't.*

"Good morning, Win— Mr. King."

She's laying on the sweetness extra thick. Luckily, I've never had a sweet tooth. Unless I'm eating my way through a honey pot.

"Miss Valentine." Her smile wavers slightly with my formality. I'm just matching energy. "Can I get you anything? Water, tea, coffee?"

"No." She sweeps her hair over her shoulder. "I'm fine. Thank you."

I nod, leaning back in my seat, steepling my hands as I study her. A silence ensues that is clearly uncomfortable for her, but enjoyable for me as I freely drink her in.

"To what do I owe the pleasure, Eve?"

5

EVE

THE WORD *PLEASURE* SPILLS from his full lips like a promise of sin. I'm no longer used to being the center of his attention. But in this moment, he gives me *all* of it. His basalt eyes, unwavering as they roam over every inch of my body he can see. My skin heats under his gaze. Maybe coming here wasn't a good idea. Winter raises his eyebrows, waiting for me to speak. *Shit.* I've been staring at him for far too long.

"Um..." My voice trails off. I struggle to remember his question.

He chuckles low and smooth. The sound resonates in my heart as if it's calling me home. "I asked to what do I owe the pleasure of you being here with me today?"

"Right." I clear my throat. "I need your help..."

"Do you?" he asks, a hint of indifference in his voice.

I refrain from rolling my eyes and smile instead. "Yes."

"Care to elaborate? Or are you going to continue to stare at me?"

My lips part as my brows pinch together. "I wasn't staring – I..." Stumbling over my words is proving I was. "I don't personally need your help. The clinic needs a sponsor for the Mayor's Charity Gala. Most of the businesses are already sponsoring someone. And Elle had the idea to have North Star Toys sponsor us, but Snow said—"

"Done."

"What?" I blink at him.

"North Star Toys will sponsor Hope's Village."

I shift in my seat, crossing my legs. He holds my gaze, with a smile on his face that I'm not sure I should trust. "Just like that?"

"Just like," he snaps his fingers as he says, "that."

I arch a brow. "Really?"

"Yes. Really." He nods. "Is that all?"

This is far too easy. I cross my arms, cocking my head to the side. "No fight? No nothing? You're just going to give me what I want?"

"What is there to fight about, Miss Valentine? You asked for help, and I'm willing to give it. What's the problem?" He shrugs, lifting his hands into the air.

"I just... haven't been the nicest to you as of late and—"

"Mmm..." He rumbles lowly, making my stomach feel like I've dropped off a cliff. "So you're aware you've been unreasonable?"

"I wouldn't say unreasonable. I'm simply keeping the promise I made to myself."

"At my expense?" The look on his face is no longer light. His gaze is pensive.

I tug at my earrings. "You make it seem like I'm hurting your feelings, Winter. We both know you don't have those."

Anger flashes in his eyes, before he closes them. Shit. I've always sucked at holding my tongue. When he looks at me again, the playful twinkle that was in them seconds ago is gone.

"What you're not gonna do, Miss Valentine, is treat me like dog shit on the bottom of your Giuseppe heel. Is that understood?" I blink at him, unsure how to respond. He's never been... stern with me before. Heat crawls up my neck as it spreads in other places, making me squeeze my thighs together a little tighter.

You have a boyfriend, Eve. A good boyfriend.

"I know you're used to getting what you want, Miss Valentine." I hate that I'm annoyed he won't say my name. "And I'm letting you know that shit stops now." He rests his large forearms on the desk, leaning toward me. "Do you understand? Or you can walk right back out that door and find another sponsor."

Instead of rolling my eyes, I let out a huff of laughter and glide my tongue across my teeth. "Would you like me to say 'yes, sir'?"

He chuckles, making my skin prick with sweat. "That's up to you. Call me what you want. But I need to know you understand that you will no longer be treating me the way you have."

As badly as I want to tell him to go fuck himself, I remember Elle's words. Getting funding for the clinic isn't about me or him. It's about children who need accessible services.

"Yes." I nod curtly. "I understand."

"You're not going to call me sir?" He leans back in his seat with a raised eyebrow, looking unnecessarily handsome. The playful twinkle is back in his eye.

I can't help but roll my eyes. "Not today."

"So, it's a someday option?" A sexy, slow smile spreads across his full, entirely to kissable, lips.

"Winter." I say his name in an attempt to clear my thoughts of calling him sir from my head. "I'm here for Hope's Village." The statement is more of a reminder to me than him.

He nods. "I understand that, and lucky for you, I'm here to help."

"And..." He raises his brows, waiting for me to finish my sentence. "I have a boyfriend."

I expect him to falter. Show some hint of annoyance. Except, he doesn't miss a beat.

"That sounds like a personal problem." He gives me an unbothered shrug of his shoulders, sitting back in his chair.

"You don't care?" I bite my bottom lip, annoyed with myself. There goes my mouth again, speaking before my brain forms a coherent thought.

"I don't give a damn." He stands, rounding his desk, and holds his hand out to me. "We have to go talk to North. He can get you the money today."

"Right." I ignore his hand, standing on my own, and grab my purse from the other chair. When I straighten up, we're chest to chest. My breasts brush against him, and I swallow the moan that threatens to slip from my lips. The right thing to do would be to take a step back, but I don't for reasons I'm not even willing to admit to myself. Instead, I tip my head back, looking up at him.

He leans closer, keeping his hands to himself, leveling his mouth with my ear. "I need you to remember *who* your heart beats for. Longs for." His voice is deep and gravelly, pulling me closer to him. "He may have the title of being your boyfriend. And that's cute. I'm happy for you. Shit, I'll even tell the motherfucker congratulations. But titles don't mean shit when you're in love with somebody else."

He pulls away, breaking what little physical contact we had, and his eyes flit to my lips. I close my own, anticipating him closing the small distance between us.

"Miss Valentine..." My eyes snap open. All I see is him, taking up every frame of my vision and his lips hovering over mine. "We must think of your *boyfriend*." Abruptly, he pulls away, taking his warmth with him.

Adjusting the strap of my purse on my shoulder, I attempt to regain my composure. "Don't flatter yourself," I snap, and he gives me a bright smile.

He pulled away. I didn't. Truth is, *I wanted him to kiss me.*

Noah grazes his teeth against my neck, making me inhale sharply. He goes deeper, taking me on the ascent to a much needed climax. His hand grips my thigh, pulling it higher up his waist as I bring my other leg up over his shoulder. I fist the sheets as he repeatedly hits the spot that promises ecstasy. I close my eyes, submerging myself in the pleasure.

I open them just as quickly when Winter's face flashes in my mind's eye. "Fuck..." I hiss.

"You gonna cum for me, baby?" He wraps his strong hand around my throat, not applying any pressure. Noah has a good stroke and a decent tongue. My need to be handled and choked is lost on him. He tries *sometimes.* Smacks my ass from behind, pulls my hair (not hard enough), and is getting better at talking nasty shit. Choking is something he still hasn't been able to do.

If he knew I was seeing Winter instead of him, his grip would certainly tighten. I'm not imagining Winter on purpose, but he's been on my mind since I left his office hours ago. I focus on Noah and his look of determination to give me every ounce of pleasure my body deserves. His furrowed brows, smooth, rich mahogany skin, cheeks that have dimples when he smiles for me, strong jaw, and full lips that I bring to my own. I moan into his mouth as his tongue dips into mine.

I match his thrusts, feeling the edge of my release. Bringing my hands to his forearms, I hold on as I tip over the edge, calling out his name. My body floods with pleasure, and my mind silences as every thought melts away. Noah follows me seconds later. His hips stutter as his thrusts slow. I dissolve into the mattress, letting out a satisfied sigh as he gives me all his body weight. I groan with delight and laugh when he buries his face in my neck, nipping at it and soothing it with a kiss.

"Are you spending the night?" I ask, wrapping my arms and legs around him.

He pulls away just enough to look at my face. "Do you want me to?"

"Yes."

"Then I'll stay." He kisses me. "Shall we order in?"

"Ohh yes! I've been craving the chicken alfredo from Urbane Bites."

He chuckles, reaching down between us, and pulls out of me, holding the base of the condom. "I think you're single handedly keeping that place in business."

"Excuse you!" I laugh as he heads to the bathroom to throw the condom away. "You're right alongside me."

"I'm not complaining." He reappears, grabbing a fresh pair of boxers from his designated drawer. "Simply making an observation." Lying beside me, he pulls me into his arms. "Shit, I didn't have a chance to ask, how was your meeting with Winter?"

"Good." I nod, tucking my hair behind my ear. "He agreed to sponsor the clinic."

"That's amazing!" He squeezes me tighter, pressing a kiss to the top of my head. "You were stressing over nothing."

While I was stressed about finding additional funding, he doesn't know I was also stressing about being in close proximity to Winter again.

"Yeah... well you know me, and we haven't talked in quite a while."

"True." He shrugs. "But sponsoring Hope's Village is for a good cause. Were you worried he'd say no?"

"To spite me? Hell yeah." We laugh. I leave out the part where he told me to get my attitude in check or find another sponsor.

Winter was right. I'm used to either getting what I want or making my way. I say strong-willed, but Winter basically called me a spoiled brat. There was a time he saw the sun rise and set in my eyes. I wanted for nothing with him. Not that I want for anything now, aside from funding, but I didn't have to worry about anything with him because he took care of it all. Before I asked, it was given.

I spent more time than I cared to admit this afternoon, trying to recall a memory with Winter where he talked to me like he did today. It's never happened. He used to be... softer. The years have made him more calloused and rugged. And to my dismay, he wears it so fucking well. I wish he still had the softness about him. He probably does, just not for me. In fact... I know he does. I replay the memory of him resting his hand on the small of Aspen's back at Flapjack's Brew as they talked.

"I doubt that. If Winter is anything like how I remember him, he's a man of honor and wouldn't do anything out of spite."

He doesn't know the Winter I do. Honorable? Yes. Petty? Absolutely. "Yeah... you have a point there."

Before I left his office, I had a check in my hand. Once North handed it off to me, Winter left without a word. I thought he would've at least tried to talk to me some more. Actually, I expected him too. I've been annoyed with myself for how disappointed I am due to his fleeting attention.

"I'm happy things went well for you today." He smiles.

Noah believes I've moved on. That I've healed and Winter still isn't invading my thoughts. I fooled myself too, thinking the feelings I had for him disappeared when really they were dormant, waiting to be awakened again.

The next day, Elle and I stroll through the park while I tell her about my meeting with Winter.

"See." Elle nudges my shoulder. "You survived a little thirty minute meeting."

"Barely," I say, the heat of invisible blush warming my cheeks at the memory of me *wanting* to kiss him.

Elle snorts with laughter. "You could win an academy award for dramatics."

"Can I ask you something?" I take a seat on one of the vacant park benches. Elle sits beside me, looking out at the lake that sits in the center of the park. "And I need you to be honest with me. Even if you think it'll hurt my feelings."

"Okay..." she says with an air of caution.

"Do you think I've been too unforgiving of Winter?"

She inhales deeply, exhaling as she slips her hands into the pocket of her hoodie. "Honestly, yeah." Her brown eyes meet my own. "It's one thing to be hurt, but it's another thing entirely to be deliberately mean to someone." I nibble on my bottom lip. "I say this with love, but sometimes you're a nasty bitch. And not the good kind." I snort with laughter and she gives me a bright smile. "Look, you two don't have to be best friends, but what good is holding onto the past doing you?"

"It's keeping me safe..." I say softly, looking down at my hands. My vision blurs as tears prick my eyes.

"From what?" She gently places her hand over my own.

I look up at the sky, blinking back the tears. Looking at her, I know that if anyone will understand me it's Noelle. "I'm still in love with him."

I let out a noise that's a mix of a strangled sob and an exhale. A small bit of relief washes over me, admitting it out loud to someone instead of keeping it bottled inside.

She wraps her arm around my shoulder, pulling me closer. Grabbing my chin, she pulls my gaze to hers. She wipes my tears with the sleeve of her hoodie. "Babe, you can't admit what I already know."

For some reason this makes me cry harder. I rarely cry, but my soul feels like it needs to be cleansed. "And I told him."

She gapes at me, eyes wide. "Like recently?"

I nod vigorously. "The first night we saw each other at Fireside."

"Is that why you left early?"

"Yeah, I freaked out. We were talking on the balcony, he apologized, and then... I kissed him." Covering my face with my hands, I lean forward resting my elbows on my thighs. "I shouldn't have fucking kissed him or admitted to *still* loving him."

Noelle rubs my back in soothing circles. "Eve... why are you fighting your feelings for him tooth and nail?"

Sitting up, I run a hand through my hair. "Because," I face her. "After he left... I made a promise to myself to never fall back into him. I know it's stupid, but I was so broken after he left. That pain was unbearable... "

Rolling onto my side, I reach my hand out for Winter, except his side is cold. Opening my eyes, I can tell it's still dark outside. Ever since his dad passed, sleep evades him. Climbing out of bed, I pull on my robe and slide into my slippers. I head toward the living room, usually that's where he hangs out if he can't sleep. The glow of the TV illuminates the hallway as I approach it.

"Winter..." I say, rounding the corner. "Come to—" My sentence falls short when I realize he isn't here. I grab the remote, turning off the TV, making the house eerily quiet.

Tossing the remote back onto the couch, I head to the garage to see if he's even home. He's been going out more lately, but he usually tells me. Opening the garage door, the car he usually drives is no longer parked beside mine. I try to ignore the sinking feeling in my stomach as I head back to our room to find my phone.

Grabbing it, there's no missed calls or notifications. I call Winter and it rings for what feels like an eternity before going to voicemail.

"Hey... I'm just calling to check on you." I rub my eyes. "I'm sorry about our fight earlier. Can you please just call me back to let me know you're okay?" I hesitate. "I love you, Winter... and if you want to—" I close my eyes, taking a deep breath. "Just please call me back, okay? I love you so much, and I know we can get through this together."

Flopping back onto the bed, I let out an exasperated sigh, replaying our fight earlier at our wedding venue. Fighting wasn't an issue for us, but now it seems like an everyday occurrence. I can feel him slipping away from me, and I feel like there's nothing I can do to stop it. Tears sting my eyes at the thought of losing him. I can tell he's trying, but his grief is too strong.

Getting up, I head to the closet to put on some sweats, deciding I'll wait up for him. Something feels off, but nothing has felt right lately. I'm not sure what "normal" is for us anymore. Or if we'll have any semblance of it anymore.

Looking around the closet, I still. It feels too large. My heart jackhammers in my chest and sweat makes my palms slick. Almost everything is gone from his side. I tear open the drawers of his dresser and they're empty too. Heading to the back of the closet, I look for his luggage. It's gone. He's... gone?

"No... he can't just leave. Can he?" I mutter to myself, collapsing to the floor. The panic sets in. I try to take deep breaths that turn into hyperventilating. "This cannot be happening." I squeeze my eyes shut. "You're still

sleeping. He's in the living room watching TV like he always does when he can't sleep." I repeat this multiple times, knowing it isn't true because my heart hurts in my chest.

Warm tears stream down my face. Maybe he just needed space? Scrambling to my feet, I grab my phone again. I call Snow first.

"Please don't go to voicemail. Please don't go to voicemail." I chant.

On the sixth ring, he answers.

"Hey, Eve." He sounds wide awake for it being two in the morning.

I cut to the chase. "Is Winter with you by chance? Or staying with you?" I try to keep my voice even and nonchalant.

"Nah. He was here earlier, but he left to go to North and Mom's place."

My hopes rise. It'd make sense for him to stay with his mom right now. Carol needs all the support she can get after losing Chris.

"Thank you."

"Everything okay?" I can hear the confusion in his tone.

"I hope so... I'm going to call North."

"Alright... call me if you need anything."

"Thanks, Snow."

Hanging up, I immediately try Winter's cell again. It rings and rings before his voice fills the line. My heart leaps in my chest for a fraction of a second before I realize it's his voicemail message. I don't bother leaving one. Instead, I call North.

He sounds half asleep when he answers.

"Hello..."

"Hey, North. Is Winter with you?"

"Nah. He left a couple of hours ago. Said he was heading home. Is he not there?"

My lip quivers, and I bite on it as fresh tears blur my vision. "No, he's not. And... and his clothes are gone too."

"*What?*" *He sounds fully awake now.* "*I'm gonna have to call you back, Eve.*"

"*Wait –* "

He hangs up before I can respond. I stare at the screen. Unsure of what to do. It's the middle of the night, there are only so many places he could've gone at this hour. I pace our room, wracking my brain for where he could be. Why would he just leave? It was just a fight. I didn't think it would've led to this. I should've just held my tongue and changed the plans like he asked. But—

My phone cuts through my spiraling thoughts. I'm disappointed to see Snow's name instead of Winter's.

"*I got ahold of Winter...*"

"*And? Where is he? Is he okay?*" *I hop off the bed, heading toward the closet to put on my shoes and jacket.*

Snow lets out a weary sigh. "*Yeah... he's okay.*"

"*Where is he?*" *I slip my foot into a sneaker.*

"*I don't know...*"

I stop in my tracks. "*What do you mean you don't know? He's my fiancé. Where the fuck is he, Snow?*" *My fear quickly morphs into anger.* "*You don't fucking know or you're refusing to tell me?*"

"*No. I really don't know. He answered and said he needed some time and he was going to get out of Hope Valley for a bit. But he wouldn't tell me where he was or where he was going.*"

"*A bit?*"

"*Yeah...*"

"*Days? Weeks? Months—*"

"*I don't know, Eve,*" *he says sympathetically.* "*I'm in the dark like you are on this.*"

"No you're not." My voice cracks. "At least he'll talk to you." He remains silent because he knows it's true. "So what? I just wait for him? I mean w–what am I supposed to do, Snow? We have a whole fucking life? Had..."

"Honestly... I don't know what any of us are supposed to do right now." The sadness in his voice makes me feel selfish.

"I'm sorry to add to—"

"You don't need to apologize, Eve. I just wanted to—"

"Did he ask about me? At all? Say anything to tell me?" I'm sure I sound like a desperate dog looking for a scrap, but I never thought it'd come to this. The thought pushes a sob from my throat.

I'm not sure how long Snow listens to me cry before he speaks. "He... didn't ask about you."

"Earth to Eve." Noelle gently squeezes my hand. "Are you okay? If you don't want to talk about it, I understand."

"Yeah." I wipe my nose on my sleeve. "I'm fine." She gives me a severe look. "I'm not fine... but I feel better talking to you." She wraps her arms around my shoulders again.

"Do you want to talk about it anymore?"

I take a shaky, deep breath, weighing whether I want to give her a play by play of the memory I just got lost in. I've never talked about it in detail. No one dared to ask. Those that did, felt more sympathetic for Winter losing his dad then for me losing *him*.

"Give him time." They said. No one predicted it'd be a decade. And even with time, he still wasn't back. We're just in each other's orbit because his brother and my best friend found forever in each other.

I met Noelle after losing Winter. It was by chance. We were both taking a communications course at Hope Valley University and got paired for a project. At that point, anything that was a stark contrast to my grief annoyed me.

Noelle is the antonym of grief. Except her presence wasn't annoying, it was comforting. We became fast friends. As I got more comfortable with her, she asked if I was seeing anyone. I told her I was fresh off a breakup. She wrapped me in a hug, let me know she was here for me, and has been ever since. I know if I don't want to tell her, she won't press me.

Since Winter, I let people get close enough to give them the illusion that they know me. It's not a character trait I'm proud of, but it's one that makes me feel safe. Despite my efforts to keep Noelle and Aspen close at a distance, they still know me better than I know myself most days. I'm the only one dead set on being an enigma.

"I've never told someone *all* the details before..." My voice is barely audible against the wind rippling over the lake and the chattering birds.

Noelle doesn't speak. She waits, arm looped through mine, holding space for me like she always does even if I don't deserve it. I fill that space with the memory of Winter leaving and the pitch-black darkness I plummeted into. By the time I've recounted every detail, we're both crying.

"Even now," I hike my shoulder. "I *still* don't know why he left. I can't let that happen again, Elle, even though I love him and probably always will. And... maybe if I knew why, we could... never mind." If I knew why, we could what? Fix it? Be together again?

Maybe, a little voice whispers.

She wraps me in her arms. "It's okay to love Winter still, Eve. It's also okay to feel a kaleidoscope of emotions toward him. Give yourself some grace for not having killed him just yet."

The laugh I let out startles me and the birds around us. For feeling like lead seconds ago, I feel lighter as a sense of relief settles into my being. "Thank you, Elle." I pull away, looking at her.

She smiles. "It's been a decade, but have you given yourself time to process?"

I didn't allow it. *Couldn't* allow it if I wanted to keep my sanity intact. It was a domino effect after he left. I lost him... and just kept losing.

"No..." I answer honestly.

"What if you just let yourself feel what you want without trying to fix it?"

I screw up my face, rearing my head back. "You realize who you're talking to, right?"

It's her turn to laugh. "Yes. Which is why I said *try*." She draws out the word for longer than necessary.

"You realize I'm a fixer. I don't just wait to see what happens. I fix. Correct. I—"

"You fall apart while holding everything and everybody else together. I get it." She nudges against my arm. "You're the real life Olivia Pope, managing it well and doing a good fucking job. But ignoring the past and how you feel isn't doing you any favors."

"Neither is being faced with my past either..." My voice trails off as I look out at the lake. "When I was at Winter's office," I turn my attention back to her, "I wanted him to kiss me. The only reason a kiss didn't happen is because *he* pulled away to remind *me* of my boyfriend. I didn't even flinch."

Noelle clamps her mouth shut in an attempt to hide a smile. "It's not funny!" I playfully shove her arm. "I lose all sense around that man. It's like time doesn't exist with us, it's just me and him."

She lets me marinate in that thought before speaking again. "What about Noah?"

"I really like him." I can't help the smile that spreads across my face.

"That makes me happy for you..."

"But?" I coax her.

Noelle tousles her curls, letting out a sigh before she tugs at the neck of her hoodie. Well, Snow's hoodie because it's much too large for her. "Eve... it's not fair to Noah. Even if you really like him."

"But—"

"You would've kissed Winter if he didn't pull away. How would you feel if Noah did that to you?"

I clamp my mouth shut, pulling my bottom lip between my teeth as I nibble at it. "Terrible. Probably volatile."

"If you really like Noah, you need to be all in with him."

"*I am.*" I stress the word. "It won't happen again."

Tilting her head to the side, her brows pinch together, looking as though she's about to question me further. Instead, her lips turn up into a smile as she stands, grabbing my hands, and pulling me with her. She changes the subject to outfits for the charity gala as we continue our walk.

One thought tickles at the back of my mind as we walk: am I trying to trick myself into believing I'll never hurt Noah just like I tricked myself into believing I've fallen out of love with Winter?

6
WINTER

SHE HAS A BOYFRIEND. It's the thought that's been on my mind since my meeting with Eve. There's been no one since her. Not for lack of trying on the other parties' part, but I decided if I couldn't commit to Eve Valentine, I wouldn't commit to anyone. I guess in a way I made my own promise to myself.

I've only been tempted to break that unspoken promise once, and she's currently smiling at me.

"All I'm saying, Brielle, is if it were you and me, you'd never have to work behind the bar."

Her husband, Ezra, scowls at me from the register a few feet away. I grin at him, raising my bottle of beer, tipping it appreciatively in his direction.

"Have you ever thought, Winter, that maybe I *like* working behind the bar? And that Ezra supports what makes me happy?"

Leaning forward, I hold her gaze. "Then why doesn't he support me?"

Blinking, her full lips, painted in a deep red, part before she tosses her head back with laughter. "You're so full of yourself.

"Tell me something I don't know."

"Why are you here bothering me at my job?" Her tone is laced with annoyance.

"Stop with the theatrics, Brielle. We both know I'm the highlight of your shift."

The smile on her face confirms my statement. Instead of acknowledging it, she switches gears. "How's the love of your life?"

I pause, mulling over the question, wanting to be a smart ass and say *"I'm looking at her"* even if we both know it's not true. I love Brielle, just not in the way she deserves to be loved. That's why she's married to Ezra because he loves her deep. Anyone who sees them together knows that they're each other's *one*. Instead of answering, I watch her gracefully flit around the bar, her waist length locs trailing behind her as she organizes bottles and glasses.

Brielle is the only woman I allowed into my space after Eve. We never put a label on what we had. All we knew was that we enjoyed each other beyond the release sex brought us. It went from casual to spending all our free time together. I was physically with her, but Brielle felt my distance. I was performing even if I was happy. I found myself trying to say the right things because that's what she deserved even if my heart wasn't punctuating them. Six months into our unlabeled relationship, we stopped physical contact and remained friends. Eventually she met Ezra, and the rest is history.

When she notices I haven't responded, she stops, raising a sharply arched brow. "Are you staring at my ass, or are things that bad?"

A smile spreads across my face. "No. Not bad. She came by my office the other day."

This information causes her to press her palms into the bar, leaning forward with interest. "And?"

"It's not as exciting as you're imagining" I down the rest of my beer. "She needed a sponsor for the mayor's charity gala."

"Of all the businesses, she chose yours?"

"No." I set the beer bottle aside and she grabs it, tossing it in a bin. "More like she didn't have a choice."

"Oh, babe." She pushes away from the bar, crossing her arms as she flashes me a smile. "We *always* have a choice."

There are other businesses in the valley. Hundreds of them actually. Letting out a sigh, I cut the string of thoughts before they spiral. I'm not going to allow myself to get my hopes up about Eve. She looked ready to claw her way out of my office if necessary. But then... she also was *waiting* for me to kiss her. I would've given her what she wanted if she wasn't being such a spoiled brat. Oh... and her other personal problem.

"She has a boyfriend. There's nothing to romanticize about her asking North Star Toys to sponsor her clinic."

"That's right." Brielle nods. "I've seen her in here a few times with a tall guy." She leans against the counter behind her, resting her hands on it near her hips. "They may fuck and have a title, but she doesn't look at him the way she looks at you."

"Of course she doesn't, Brielle." I scoff. "If she could laser my head off with her eyes, she would."

She snorts with laughter. "No. She wouldn't. Even if she could, those eyes were made only for you."

I narrow my own at her, raising a brow. "Why are you so invested in 'the love of my life'?"

"Because..." Her face lights with a smile. "You deserve to be happy, Winter King."

After a particularly draining therapy session, instead of returning to the office, I decide to head home. Emptying my mind with Dr. Maddox only seems to fill it with more thoughts. But instead of them being anxious and chaotic, they're more organized and subdued.

He pushed me today, asking the right questions to dig deeper. I pushed back, trying to keep a handle on dredging up unwanted feelings, until something broke in the middle and the hemmed up wound split open.

Dr. Maddox picked up on me skirting around the issue of how I felt about his death. Of course I was traumatized and depressed. I'm the one who was with him when he went down. I'm the one who started chest compressions, trying like fucking hell to save him even though I had no clue what was wrong. So when he died, I felt like I failed even though I knew his death wasn't my fault.

Underneath the grief of losing Dad is... anger. I was mad at him, myself, my family... and shit. In the end, I was even mad at Eve. I had the weight of the world on my fucking shoulders. My father was gone, instantly making me the head of our household and his million dollar company on top of navigating emotions that were foreign. Mom was fragile, Snow and North were looking to me to figure shit out, and Eve still expected me to carry on with life. How the fuck do you carry on with life and meet demands when, internally, you're broken?

After Dad died, Mom wasn't fit to make decisions, and as the oldest it was ingrained in us since childhood that I'd take over. Everyone looked to me. Everything fell on me. From having to cease life support because there was no brain activity, to picking out a casket, to arranging a funeral, to the goddamn headstone. The expectations were mounting and the weight quickly became unbearable.

It seemed no matter what I did or fixed – it was never enough. There was always more to be given. I felt like I was suffocating because the demands were relentless. Dad gave me an unrealistic expectation for what it'd be like to fill his shoes. I wasn't given an opportunity to say no to becoming his protégé... it just was. While my brothers had the freedom to choose what their lives would be, my fate was sealed to responsibilities I quickly realized I didn't want. This made me fucking angry and bitter. I tamped it down because what use is it to be angry at a dead man?

And in spite of it all, Dad loved us fiercely. Unconditionally. Dr. Maddox assured me two conflicting emotions can co-exist. I can feel the grief and the anger. Today, I feel they're warring against one another. When I went off the deep end... everyone thought it was because Dad died. That was the catalyst, but the anger and continuous expectations were overbearing. I needed to get away. I got so far away I was lost. And I still fucking am.

My phone rings as I step into the foyer of my home. Pulling it out of my pocket, Snow's name lights up my screen. I consider ignoring it, but I know he'll call me incessantly or come over if I do. I was hoping the text that I'd be out of the office for the rest of the day would suffice.

"What's up, man?" I try to sound upbeat but the weariness wins.

"You good?"

"Fine."

The line is quiet for a bit. I can tell he's wondering if he should dig further. "Come over for dinner tonight."

"Snow – "

"Come over for dinner or we're coming over there."

I let out an exasperated sigh. "Why the fuck are you and North tag teaming the annoying little brother role so well lately? Can't I just be?"

"You can... after you come over for dinner. Then you can go be whatever the hell you want." I hear the smile in his voice.

"What time?" I grumble.

"Six."

"Alright. See you then."

He pauses again before saying, "You sound like shit by the way."

For whatever reason this makes me laugh. "Fuck you."

"See you at six, dipshit."

He hangs up before I can respond. We're in our thirties and will always fight like we're children.

Arriving at Snow and Noelle's apartment, I let myself in. Elle doesn't spare me a glance.

"Hey, Winter." She pulls the top off a skillet on the stove, stirring the contents.

"How'd you know it was me?"

"Because," She puts the top back on. "Everyone else knocks besides you and Aspen and she's already here." Rounding the counter, she gives me a hug. "Missed you at work today."

"Honestly, Elle, you don't have to tell me what I already know." She pinches the shit out of my arm. "Ow! Snow!" I cower away. "Your wife is abusing me!"

"I'm sure you deserved it," he says from the living room.

Elle smiles at me triumphantly. "He loves me more."

I laugh. "Damn, would've never guessed you had a mean streak."

"I tried to be nice, and you gave me your deflective sarcasm."

"It's not you..." I let out a sigh, running a hand down my face. "It was just a long fucking day." Glancing at the living room, Snow is busy talking to North and Aspen. "I saw Dr. Maddox and dug up shit I was trying to keep buried."

Elle glances over her shoulder at Snow and North. When her gaze meets mine again, her brow is furrowed with worry. "You can tell them you're in therapy, you know?"

"I know... but I'm not ready." She nods, pursing her lips, clearly not satisfied with my answer, but letting it go. "I just don't want to fuck up another thing or... have another expectation."

She gives me an understanding smile. "You know I'm proud of you, right? It's not easy what you're doing."

This takes me by surprise. "Thanks, Elle." She didn't see me at my darkest, but she sees me now and is proud. I can't help but feel my family says it out of obligation. Even if it's not. It feels good to hear these words from her. "I also finished the mentorship application, did the interview, got a tour, and submitted the background check information."

"And?" She asks excitedly. "How do you feel?"

"Good." I smile. "Something to look forward to."

"I can't wait for you to– "

"What are you two whispering about?" Snow gives me a hug before standing beside Elle, draping his arm over her shoulders.

"I was giving Winter shit for abandoning me today."

"Why did you take the rest of the day off?" Snow inquires.

"My insomnia is creeping up on me again which led to a migraine today." I hate using that as an excuse because now he'll worry about what I'll get into all night long. "I needed some rest is all."

"Are you feeling better?" I see the concern in his eyes.

"Yeah. Thanks for inviting me."

"Always welcome." Snow smiles and North enters the kitchen followed by Aspen.

"Is the food done yet?" North tries to pick in the bowl on the counter and Aspen slaps his hand. "Shit!" He snatches it away, covering it protectively with his other.

"Did you wash your hands?" Aspen crosses her arms, glaring at him. "No telling where they've been lately."

"For fuck's sake." Snow sighs while Elle and I try to hold in our laughs.

"You're the one setting me up on all these damn dates!" North defends. "I'm fine sitting at home, playing video games, smoking the occasional blunt, but here your happy ass comes."

"You shouldn't have grandpa behavior at your age. It isn't healthy," Aspen says, stepping in front of the sink to wash her hands. "I mean honestly, North, you were going to bed at nine. You should be *grateful* for my happy ass."

"I have to be well rested," he says as if it's the most logical thing ever. "Sleep is crucial for proper brain function."

Aspen gives him a bemused expression as she dries her hands. "You're lucky you're a hot nerd."

North straightens up, adjusting his glasses. "You think I'm hot?" Aspen scoffs, rolling her eyes as she throws the towel in his face and saunters toward the dinner table.

"You're smart, but you miss the signs, bruh." I pat his shoulder.

Sitting around the table with them helps alleviate the stress of today. I'm glad I came instead of staying home, thinking of everything that's gone wrong.

As we're finishing up dinner, a knock echoes through the apartment.

"Oh, that's Eve," Elle says, jumping up from her seat to answer the door.

I let out a much louder sigh then I intended, feeling the stress creep back in. Chuckles ripple around the table. "I'm gonna go chill in front of the TV for a bit." Snow and North give me a knowing nod, feeling the tension radiating off me. I can tamp it down for them, but I can't go toe to toe with Eve right now.

Before we talked the other day, one of us used to leave when the other would arrive. It ended up being me taking off most of the time because I didn't want to invade a space she made for herself with Elle and Aspen. Snow and North gave me shit about it because Eve takes up space and they encouraged me to do the same.

Ten years ago, I would've allowed her to chastise me. I would've been crawling on my hands and knees, begging for forgiveness. That was before I snuffed being a people pleaser out of my life. The life I immersed myself into let me be selfish. Sure, I was lost, but it let me be whoever the fuck I wanted to be without having to worry about somebody else's needs. I was free of expectations. While I have no desire to ever be a part of that lifestyle again, it gave me a different perspective.

I own up to leaving. If I could go back, I'd do things differently. Still, Eve can't act like everything was all on me. As prim, proper, and perfect as she may want to pretend to be – she's far from it. She's guilty too, and I refuse to shoulder the blame.

Turning up the TV to drown out the cadence of her voice, I close my eyes, attempting to let the anger from earlier settle. Instead of letting it settle, I fall asleep.

I wake a while later, keeping my eyes closed when I feel the couch dip as someone sits beside me. I can feel it's Eve. Taking a deep breath, stretching out my legs, her familiar lingering scent of vanilla and sandalwood fills my lungs. Opening my eyes, I don't look at her, instead I focus on the TV, wondering why she's sitting next to me.

"Hi..."

Turning my head, I take in her side profile. High cheek bones, plush lips, and tendrils of hair framing her face. "Hey..." I look over my shoulder and the rest of them are playing a board game. Elle steals a glance at us, but doesn't say anything. "Where's your boyfriend you were so eager to tell me about?" I turn my attention back to her.

Her eyes narrow as she meets my gaze. "Surgery. He's a surgeon."

I nod my head. "I bet he's good for you. Reliable... predictable," she scowls, making me smile, "in the best way."

"He *is* good for me." She focuses on the TV. I can't help but wonder if he's right for her. "You okay?"

"Do you even care?" It doesn't matter if she does. At least I tell myself it doesn't matter.

When her bright brown eyes meet mine, I see the sadness. "I never stopped."

The weight of her words don't blanket me with comfort like I thought they would. They annoy me. "You say these things, Eve, that are contradictory to you having a boyfriend."

"I can't care about someone?"

"See, that's your fucking problem." I chuckle.

"What?" She gives me an annoyed look.

"Stop saying shit in secret with me if you're not ready to stand by it."

"So I can't ask if you're okay, or what?" She crosses her arms.

I lean closer so only she can hear my next words. She inhales sharply, responding to my proximity. The chatter in the dining room ceases behind us, but I don't care. They can't hear over the TV anyway.

"Your boyfriend knows you wanted me to kiss you then?" She opens her mouth to respond, but no words come out. "Does he know he'll only ever have the ghost of you because you're in love with me?"

I'm surprised she leans closer to me. "Do you love me, Winter?" Her eyes search my face for an answer.

"Does it matter?" She pulls back slightly with my question. I could tell her the past ten years apart have been hell. Instead, I say, "You can't have me and him at the same time. I never learned to share."

Getting up from the couch, I put distance between us. Disappointment shadows her face. I know what I want. She knows what she wants but refuses to allow herself to have it. I won't settle for anything less than *all* of her.

It's Saturday. The one day of the week I can sit at home and do nothing. Still, my brothers have found some way to drag me out of the comfort of my home as if we don't see each other every day. I have sweat dripping down my back and my boxers are sticking to my nutsack because Snow thought it'd be fun to come hiking.

"Fix your face," Snow says as we trek up the incline.

"I'm here. Don't ask for more."

North snorts to my left. "You're in the gym the most. This should be slight work for you."

"What's slight about hiking up the side of a mountain at eight a.m. on a Saturday?" The gravel of the trail crunches beneath our feet.

"It's good to get the heart pumping," Snow says.

"I can think of more pleasurable ways to do that."

"Quit crying. If we wouldn't have invited you, you would've talked shit for weeks about us leaving you out," North says over his shoulder as he pulls ahead of us.

I crack a smile because he's right. While this isn't the ideal activity, I'd rather be here with them then home by myself. Doesn't mean I'm not going to talk my shit. We continue the hike in a companionable silence. Once we're at the top, we take in the grander snowcapped mountains that surround the Valley. Snow settles on the ledge of the lookout, letting his legs and feet dangle over. North joins him, sitting on his right, and I settle on his left. It reminds me of when we came up here together and sat in silence after Dad died.

"Are you ever carrying on and suddenly you miss him?" I welcome the soft breeze as it cools my skin.

"Every damn day," Snow says first.

"Multiple times a day," North adds.

"I didn't think we'd be experiencing life without him."

We sit in silence, appreciating the breathtaking view before us.

"He didn't either." Pressing his palms into the dirt, Snow leans back.

"But we are." North brings his leg up, hooking his arm around his knee while the other one dangles over the ledge. "And I'd say we're doing a pretty damn good job."

I open my mouth to say something, but Snow speaks first. "Yeah, even your crazy ass, Winter." We share a laugh. "You always have to be the dramatic one and count yourself out."

"You win the fuck up award. We get it," North says exasperatedly. "I'm about to start fucking up just so you'll shut the hell up."

"I'd love to see you try," Snow says, warningly.

"Damn. Tell me how you feel, North."

"We." Snow scratches his neatly groomed beard.

I splay my hand across my chest, looking aghast. "You're tired of me pulling the fuck up card, too?"

"Exhausted." North unzips his sweater, pulling it off.

"Beat down." Snow picks up a small rock, throwing it over the ledge.

"Ragged." North takes a sip of water.

"Bone fucking ti–"

"Alright!" I interrupt Snow. "Damn! Didn't realize you motherfuckers were so weary!"

They lean against each other, laughing.

"Listen, we know you're sorry," Snow says through laughter. "But forgive yourself and get the fuck over it."

"Wow..." I nod my head slowly. "You two were just holding this shit in huh?"

"Not holding it in. We'd talk shit behind your back but—"

I lunge for North, sandwiching Snow in the middle. North hollers, trying to get away as he laughs, but I grab his shirt, keeping him in place. Snow smacks me on the back of my head. I reciprocate and smack his head.

Snow jabs my side with his elbow. "Grow the fuck up."

North catches me off guard by smacking the side of my face.

"You little shit! I need to grow up? You two are ganging up on me." I try to hit North, but hit Snow.

"I swear I'm gonna knock your ass out," Snow warns, shoving me. Instead of letting go of North's shirt, I keep a firm hold on it, making us all fall into the dirt as we topple backward.

I clamber over Snow to get to North who's still laughing hysterically. Cocking my arm back to punch him, Snow tackles me to the ground before my hand can connect.

"North, you bitch!" I shout, rolling on the ground with Snow. "Always hiding behind Snow."

"Never that," North says, punching my arm so hard I know it's going to be sore.

He tries to get away, but I grab his ankle, making him eat dirt. Snow wraps his arm around my neck, putting me in a headlock. North sees it as a window of opportunity when I let go of his ankle, and he comes for me. I let him get close enough to think he'll be successful before kicking his feet out from under him. We continue fighting, rolling around in the dirt, and shouting expletives.

Never mind that we're grown ass men who look like fools. We're having fun even if it comes in the form of trying to knock the dog shit out of each other. I know I wouldn't be here without them. I hear my phone ringing from somewhere on the ground.

"Get off me!" I push at them to get to my phone. Snow won't let up, so I jab him in the side until he finally lets go to catch his breath.

"You're the one who started this." Snow kicks the back of my knees, making them buckle. "Bitch."

North is a dick and kicks my phone away from me as I reach for it. "If the screen is cracked, you're buying me a new one."

"You broke my glasses!" They're askew on his face, making me double over with laughter. Snow tries to be the better brother, but laughs too.

"Can't be talking shit then!" I say, finally reaching my phone. Picking it up, it's a number I don't recognize.

"Winter King," I answer, trying to not sound winded as I brush dirt and twigs out of my curls. "Bastards," I mouth at Snow and North. They both reply by giving me their middle fingers.

"Hi. This is Hudson from True's Circle." I take a few steps from the guys, turning my back to them. "We've found you a match."

Scuffing my sneaker in the dirt, I rub the back of my neck. "Okay..."

"The child is older and..." When his voice trails off, I pull my phone away from my ear to make sure we're still connected. "Well, he's a been a little more difficult to match."

"Is that a good or bad thing?"

"All about perspective, Mr. King," he says a little too brightly as if he's trying to convince me it'll be okay.

"Right..." I say warily, wondering what I'm getting myself into.

"He's a good kid. Just needs some stability and guidance. If you'd like me to search for another ma – "

"No! I'll take him." I smack my hand against my forehead. "I mean, I'll be his mentor..."

"Perfect. I think he'll be excited to meet you. He'll be here today if you wanted to drop by and meet him?"

"What time?"

"In an hour." I glance down at my clothes covered in dirt and the sweat seeping through my t-shirt. "But take your time. He'll be here most the afternoon."

"Okay, I'll be there as soon as I can."

"Great! I look forward to meeting you, Mr. King."

Hanging up the phone, I let out a low sigh, tapping the phone against my forehead. "Fuck it..." I mutter to myself. When I turn to face Snow and North, they're right behind me and I nearly run into them. "Eavesdropping, assholes?"

"You're going to be a mentor?"

"Can't see for shit, but you sure can hear." I narrow my eyes at North.

"Fuck you," he grumbles, attempting to fix his ruined glasses once again.

Snow is looking at me with his head cocked to the side.

"What?"

"Nothing..." He shrugs with a smile. "I just think this will be good for you."

"Yeah..." I nod, taken aback by his response. "Me too."

7

WINTER

NORTH AND SNOW DIDN'T get an opportunity to question me about the mentorship any further. We were too busy racing to see who could make it to the car first. Then we started playing dirty and fighting again. I got back first, then Snow, and since North was last we locked the doors and made him jog alongside the car for good measure before letting him in. Needless to say, he's pissed and not talking to either of us. Little brother woes.

After a shower to wash all the muck and grime from my body, I walk through True's House doors just under two hours later. Hudson is waiting for me by the front desk. He's a little shorter than me with tan skin and brown hair that's tapered on the sides, long on top, and pulled up into the proverbial man bun. The receptionist who was eager to talk to me when I was here last ignores Hudson, turning her attention to me.

"Mr. King," she says brightly.

"Please, call me Winter."

Hudson straightens up, giving me a warm smile and firm handshake. "Winter. Glad you could make it."

"I would've been here sooner, but I was on a hike with my brothers."

"Not a problem. How are they?"

Hudson has met us in passing at community events since we're donors, but we've never held a conversation. "They're great."

"Happy to hear. This way." He holds open the door that leads into the center. "We typically have activities planned every other weekend. Today, kids are welcome to come and hang out in the recreational room. We stay open until nine and provide transportation if needed."

The recreational room is flooded with natural light and painted in bright colors. It has a little of everything. Books, foosball table, two arcade machines, lounge area, computers, a television equipped with the latest gaming system, and an area that looks like it'd be perfect for studying. I'm an adult and I'd love to hang out here.

"This is amazing." I continue to take in the little details of the room. There's a girl watering a few plants near the window and a boy sitting in what looks like a cocoon hanging from the ceiling, reading a book.

"We've tried to create a welcoming and safe space."

"You've accomplished it."

"Thank you." I see pride in Hudson's demeanor as he smiles. "His name is Reign DeLeon and he is..." Hudson's green eyes scan the room. "Sitting right over there near the window."

I follow his line of sight until my eyes land on a mass of black curls. He's splayed out in an overstuffed chair, staring intently at what looks like a comic in his lap.

"Do I just go up to him or... ?" The only time I've been this nervous to approach someone was when I first met Eve. I'm acutely aware of my heart hammering in my chest and the clamminess of my hands.

"I'll introduce you." Hudson smiles, walking toward where Reign is sitting. I stay rooted in place. He turns back when he notices I'm not beside him. "Everything okay?"

I glance between him and the kid a few times before settling on Hudson. "What if I fuck this up?"

He gives my arm a reassuring pat. "Whoever said we expected you to be perfect?" Some tension leaves my body with his words. "You can be a friend, right?" I nod. "Then take a deep breath. That's all he needs."

I inhale deeply, attempting to calm my nerves. When I'm certain I'm not going to throw up, I fall in step with Hudson.

"Hey, Reign. How are you man?"

He doesn't move. At first it seems he didn't hear his greeting until he shifts his gaze to my sneakers. He keeps his eyes there for a second before tipping his head back to meet my eyes. At least I think he can see me behind the curtain of curls covering his face. "Nice sneakers."

"Thanks." I look down at my red, black, and white Griffey's.

"Reign, this is Winter. He came to spend some time with you."

"If you want...," I add, not wanting him to feel obligated.

Reign looks between Hudson and I, considering our words. "Okay." He shrugs, turning his attention back to his comic.

I guess we're doing this then. Thank the universe because I wasn't prepared to get my feelings hurt by a teenager not wanting to spend time with me.

Hudson lets out a small, surprising sigh of relief. "Awesome. I'll leave you two to get to know each other."

I smile, letting him know we'll be alright. Grabbing a chair from nearby, I slide it closer to Reign and take a seat. He hasn't moved much since we came over here, but I notice he slightly turns his head to see if Hudson left. Turning his attention back to his comic, he runs a hand through his loose curls, revealing his face.

He has hazel eyes, with his right eye being a little greener and the left a little browner. They stand out against his deep tawny skin. A cross is dangling from one ear and the other has a black diamond stud with a helix piercing. For barely looking at me seconds ago, he stares intently at me now.

"Did he tell you I'm difficult?"

I wonder how many matches he's had before me. "Honestly, yeah. He did."

He nods his head, averting his gaze to the comic in his lap. "I'm not difficult." He mumbles. "I'm just trying to make sense of who I am."

His words resonate with me because I know what it's like to be labeled before people know you. To an outsider, it looks like you're trying to make your life hell when really, you're trying to navigate the storm inside to find yourself. "How old are you?"

"Seventeen."

"Are you graduating soon?"

"No." He shakes his head. "Just turned Seventeen. I graduate next year... if I keep my grades up."

My brows knit together. "If?"

"Yeah." He keeps his eyes on the comic book in his lap. "My mind has been preoccupied with other things."

A million thoughts race through my head. I didn't get much background on Reign because we're expected to get to know each other. All I know is he's a part of True's Circle which means he lost someone close to him. Who that someone is, I don't know. After Dad died, when someone would ask about him it felt like they were twisting the knife that was already lodged in my chest. Asking him is the only way I'm going to get an answer. I could ask Hudson, but I'd rather get to know Reign on my own. If he knows he's been labeled as difficult, he knows we've talked about him. That's never a good feeling, even if good things were said. That's why I was honest with him when he asked. I want him to trust me.

His stomach growls loud enough for me to hear. I watch him place his hand on his stomach and rub it, but it growls even louder. "Do they feed you here?"

"Yeah... but there are other kids who come through here worse off than me, so I only eat enough to take the edge off."

"The edge off?" I can't see his eyes, but I can tell by the angle of his head he's looking at me. "What do you like?" He smooths his hair out of his eyes, giving me a skeptical look. "It can be anything."

"Pizza," he says without hesitation.

"With?"

"Pepperoni... extra pepperonis."

"Alright, I'll be right back." He doesn't respond, just watches me get up from my seat. Leaving him to his comic, I try to find Hudson. I see his man bun in an office that's near the receptionist desk.

"Hey Hudson, can you order some pizza for the kids? I'm not sure how many are here or I'd do it myself." He blinks at me with his mouth open. "I'll cover the cost."

"Uh... yeah. Sure. Wait, are *you* sure?"

"Positive. Order enough for everyone and I'll take care of it when they arrive."

"Okay." He blinks again.

"Who makes the food here?"

"Volunteers."

"You don't have a chef... cook? Someone who runs the kitchen?" If this is the only place some of the kids get a meal, then there needs to be someone here who knows what the fuck they're doing.

"No... that's not really in the budget. Almost a hundred percent of what we get here is donated or volunteers pitch in."

"What if North Star Toys funded a cook or cooks to come in for meals?"

"I couldn't ask—"

"Maybe you can't, but I can offer. Is that something we could do?"

"Yes." He nods. "I— thank you."

"Pizza," I remind him, and he immediately grabs his phone. "Make sure there's one with extra pepperoni." He nods, staring at me as I exit his office.

Reign is sitting where I left him a few minutes ago. "Where'd you go?" He asks.

"To talk to Hudson." His shoulders tense. "Not about you," I add. "Do you not get along with him or something?"

"It's not that..." His voice trails off as he closes the comic in his lap. I take a peek at the cover, seeing Stranger Comics printed across the top. He obscures the name when he puts his arm across it. "He tries too hard..."

"Wait." My eyes slide from the comic to him. "Is that a bad thing?"

"Nah. Not at all. He... Hudson tries to be cool, ya know? Whereas you," he waves a hand down the length of my body, "are cool. You know what I mean?"

"How do you know I'm not a square like Hudson?"

This elicits a smile from him. "I never said he was a square. And you're cool without even trying. Hudson's a try hard. That's the only way I know how to say it. He's not bad, but I doubt he can relate to me."

Leaning forward I rest my forearms on my thighs. "And I can?"

"Yeah... at least I hope you can." He shrugs, propping his ankle on his knee, fidgeting with the laces of his worn Chuck Taylors.

"For the record..." I lean back in the chair. "I don't think you're difficult." Pushing the hair out of his face, he gives me a genuine smile. "So... what do you like to do?"

"Depends on the day..."

It's silent for a few beats, and then he starts rattling off things he likes to do – skateboarding, playing video games, drawing, reading, and he really wants to see the world. He talks about a lot of things that bring him joy, but he's most animated when he talks about art. We have an art museum that has some cool exhibits. I'll have to figure out what kind of art he's into. I'm simply happy he's talking to me for as quiet as I thought he was going to be. He's asking me questions about where I've been in the world when Hudson appears with the pizza delivery person.

"Okay, guys. Winter was kind enough to order pizza for everyone today." He's balancing a stack of pizzas in his arms. "Please make sure you thank him." Hudson slides them onto the table in the center of the room.

Reign gapes at me. Even behind his curtain of hair, I can tell his eyes are widened. "You got me pizza?"

"Yeah... I hope you weren't just saying pizza when you really—"

"No!" He holds his hands up. "It's my favorite food, but I didn't expect you to actually get it for me."

"You said you like pizza..."

"Yeah, but..." He scrubs his hands down his face. "I'm not used to people doing things for me not since – well not in a while..."

To me it's a simple pizza. For Reign, it's more than that. "It's cool. I got you."

Standing, I head toward Hudson to pay for the pizzas. I'm surprised Reign follows behind me.

"It's one hundred and fifty dollars," the delivery guy says.

Pulling a wad of cash from my pocket, I count out a hundred and eighty. "Thank you." I hand him the money. "Keep the change."

"You're rich?" Reign asks, eyeing the money in my hand.

"Comfortable." I smile. "Are you going to eat?"

"Yes." He licks his lips, grabbing a plate.

"Thank you for this, Winter." Hudson nods with a smile.

"Anytime."

I wait for everyone else to get a slice before grabbing my own. Reign is sitting with the girl who was watering the plants. I don't want to impose, but he waves me over just as quickly as the thought enters my head. Sitting at the table, Reign smiles. His hair is pulled back with what I'm assuming is the girl's scrunchie.

"Calliope, this is Winter." He introduces us. She holds her hand out.

Shaking it, I smile. "Nice to meet you."

"Thanks for the pizza. Better than the crap they serve here." Clearly she's more extroverted then Reign.

I snort with laughter. "That bad?"

"Have you played Russian Roulette?" she asks.

"Hopefully we can change that."

"The food isn't terrible," Reign adds. "It really just depends on who's cooking and what supplies are available."

"Exactly," Calliope says. "Russian Roulette."

A phone vibrates on the table. She reaches for it, unlocking it, and then lets out a sigh. "My dad's a block away. Did you want to ride with us?"

"Uh... " Reign sets his half eaten slice of pizza down. "Nah. I'm going to chill with Winter for a little while. Thanks though."

Calliope beams at him before turning her attention to me. "He must really like you."

"Shut up, Calliope." He looks down at his plate with a smile.

I take a bite of my pizza to hide my own.

Her phone buzzes again, and she looks toward the entrance. A tall man with deep brown skin and jet black curly hair that matches Calliope's is standing outside it with a smile. Hudson intercepts him, striking up a conversation.

"Text me when you get home, kay?" Calliope snatches her phone off the table and plants a kiss on the top of his head.

Reign looks like he wants to melt with embarrassment as he stares, eyes wide, at a spot just over my shoulder. I really have to shove the laugh threatening to come up back down my throat. Calliope gets about five steps away before she turns back around.

"Okay?" She repeats herself, waiting for a response.

"'Kay...," he says, eyes still fixed over my shoulder.

She gives him a satisfied smile even though he isn't looking at her. "See you around, Winter."

"Nice to meet you, Calliope." Reign still hasn't moved. "What were you reading earlier?" I ask, changing the subject entirely.

"Oh, a comic Calliope gave me." He blinks, finally looking at me after Calliope's kiss. "Niobe by Stranger Comics."

"Is it good?"

"Amazing. It's one of my favorites."

I make a mental note to look it up when I get home. "How's the pizza?"

"Delicious. I haven't had it since..." His voice trails off and he sets the pizza down again. "How much did Hudson tell you?"

"Nothing." I shrug my shoulders. "All I know is that your name is Reign, you're seventeen, and love art."

He smiles, but it fades as he looks down at his pizza. "Hudson didn't tell you why I'm here."

"No... but," his eyes snap to mine, "I do know that True's Circle is for kids who have lost a loved one." I'm trying to tread lightly even though you can't really tread lightly around death.

His eyes well with emotions before he closes them, taking a deep breath and swallowing hard. "Yeah..." He nods, pulling the scrunchie from his hair, making it cover his face again. "My dad..." His voice is barely audible.

I understand the pain in his voice so deeply I feel the sting of tears and feel the ache in my chest. The wound never fucking heals. I was twenty-five when I lost my dad. Reign is seventeen, trying to navigate emotions that I'm grappling with as a grown man. Instead of filling the silence that's fallen between us, I wait for him.

"It was me, my dad, and grandma. But... Dad was a firefighter, and the fires last summer were really bad. He left to help and didn't come home."

I remember seeing on the news that a local firefighter had passed. They shut the city down for his funeral.

"At first, we were heavily supported..." He wrings his hands in his lap. "Almost suffocated. He died in the line of duty, and they wanted to memorialize him. I'm proud of him, who he was and what he did. As the months went on, it kind of felt like he was remembered and we were forgotten. The support died... just like he did. His friends still check up on me, out of duty I think, but they have families of their own." Bringing his hands up he swipes at his face, keeping his eyes on the floor.

"People get to a point where they want you to move on – expect you to – and I'm not there yet. Not sure if I ever will be." He lets out a sigh, his body relaxing as if saying those words out loud alleviated some of the pressure. Smoothing his hair back, he steals a glance at me before looking away again.

Setting my pizza down, I clear my throat. "I think that's one of the hardest things." My words catch his attention. "That life goes on as if nothing happened. It adds to the feeling of loneliness... at least for me it did."

"You lost someone?" His eyes meet mine.

"Yeah. I lost my dad too."

He tilts his head to the side, making his curls move to get a better view of me. "You look so... happy... put together."

"In many ways I am happy and put together." I chuckle. "For all the ways that I am, I'm also not." He leans forward, waiting for me to say more. "I can't promise that you won't feel the pain, but it does become more bearable... eventually. No one can make you get there any faster. Take your time."

His leg bounces as he sits back in his seat, shoving his hands into the pocket of his hoodie. "So... it does get better?"

"Yes, Reign." I smile. "It does get better."

After swimming countless laps, I lay floating on my back in the pool, eyes shut, as my heart rate slows. Dad taught me and my brothers how to swim when we were babies, but it wasn't something I fell in love with until a few years ago.

The feeling of being weightless in the water when it feels like the world is crushing you is liberating. Initially, it was just exercise. Now it's therapy. I listen to the comforting sounds of my breathing and heart rate. Lately, I've been feeling lighter without the help of the pool. When I started therapy, I had zero expectations. I didn't want to get my hopes up that there'd be some kind of relief even if I do like Dr. Maddox. Some sessions are harder than others, depending on what my mind's trying to process. Judging by how I feel lately, it's helping. Therapy, along with hanging out with Reign and focusing on myself, has helped me feel less chaotic. I'm learning new ways of coping that don't leave me feeling empty afterward.

Not only new ways of coping. New ways of living. My days were filled with activities that made me look happy, successful, and busy. Everything was meaningless aside from what I did with my family. I've felt happier than I can remember feeling in long time.

Opening my eyes, I look up at the clouds through the glass ceiling. I'd considered taking the day off. Then I remembered if I did, I'd have the little brother brigade knocking at my door later this evening. I settled for a late start because Elle and I need to contact the influencers we've selected. She's also someone who I don't mind spending time with. It's going to be hell when she graduates with her master's.

Reluctantly swimming to the edge of the pool and climbing out, I grab my towel and dry off while I check my phone. I press the missed call notification to return the call to Mom.

"Hey, Mom."

"How's my boy?"

I chuckle, shaking my head as I swipe the towel over my face. Never mind that I'm six-four and thirty-five, I'll always be 'her boy'. "I'm good. Just got done with a swim and now I have to get ready to go into the office. What are you up to this morning?"

"Surfing," she says nonchalantly.

"Surfing? When did you take that up?"

"Oh…" She clicks her tongue a few times. "A few weeks ago. Needed a little something to do."

I let out a rumble of laughter. "Cycling, yoga, and salsa dancing weren't enough?"

"No." I hear the smile in her voice. "Being active is good for me." She's the most active fifty-four year old I know.

"Yeah it is. I miss you, Mom. When are you coming to visit?"

"Miss you too. I'll be there in a few weeks. Sunday insisted I stay with her this time."

"You know she's still trying to marry off that daughter of hers?" I chuckle.

"Yes." She sucks her teeth. "I told her if she keeps asking every young man if he's single on her daughter's behalf, she's not going to find one."

"She means well." I toss the towel into a hamper as I pad toward the bathroom.

"Always. I don't want to keep you. Only wanted to hear your voice and check in."

"I'm good, Mom. Just been focusing on myself."

"I know you don't believe me, but I'm so damn proud of you, Winter. Not only because you're still here, but you're an amazing man."

Pinching the bridge of my nose to stop the tears, I take a breath before responding. "I'm working on accepting those words from you."

"That's alright. For now, let them lay over you like a blanket until they can soak in."

"I love you, Mom," is all I can manage.

"Love you too, Winter."

Hanging up the phone, I set it atop the marble sink before stepping into the shower. I wasn't around much after my dad died, and if I was, I'd avoid her. Snow wouldn't have let me see her anyway. At that time, I thought he was being a controlling prick. I now know he was protecting her. We lost Dad. She didn't need to see her son lost too. As far as I know, Snow told her I needed time. Anything besides the fact that I was so far gone she wouldn't have recognized me. Snow was really the only one who saw me at rock bottom. My mom didn't realize how bad it was until I went to rehab.

It's becoming more apparent that the forgiveness of others isn't as crucial as the forgiveness of myself.

8

WINTER

AFTER SENDING OUT THE invites to our chosen influencers, Elle and I join Snow in his office.

"Hey, North." Elle smiles.

"Is this a family meeting?" North returns her smile.

"Got new glasses?" I ask smugly, side eyeing him.

"Fuck off," he sneers before returning back to texting on his phone.

"Who're you talking to?" I knock it out his hands as I sit next to him. He sucks his teeth. "You're annoying as fuck."

"Tell me something I don't know. Talking to a new honey or what?"

"No." He gives me a look of indignation as if it's a wild idea. "I'm talking to Aspen. She wants to meet for lunch. Which sounds a little more appealing now that you're here."

"Why didn't you want to go in the first place?" Elle grabs a small bottle of water from the mini fridge before sitting beside Snow.

North lets out a heavy sigh as he sinks further into the leather chair. "She wants to set me up with one of her friends. I appreciate her efforts in demolishing my 'tragically single life' as she calls it, but I'm tired. If I find someone, great. If not, trust me when I say I'd rather be single for the rest of my days before I settle for the women she's been putting on the roster."

Noelle tosses her head back with laughter. "I think that's the most I've ever heard you speak!"

"Man..." North smiles. "I'm fucking tired. I can only sling so much dick." Snow and I succumb to laughter. "I'm not afraid to admit that I'd rather be with one person or no one. I don't know how you do it, Winter."

"You do know Aspen would hang out with you even if she's not setting you up on dates, right?" Elle quirks a brow. North blinks at her as if the thought truly never occurred to him. "Just text her and say you'd rather go to lunch with just *her*."

He looks at her, then at his phone for a minute before typing out a text.

"What are you two doing for lunch?" I ask Snow.

"I don't know, but you're not invited," Snow says with his eyes on Noelle.

"Snow!" She gapes at him before turning her attention to me. "Winter, you're always welcome to come to lunch with us."

"Thank you, Elle. It's why you're my favorite." Both Snow and North scowl at me. "Now I know what people mean when they say, 'it be your own family'."

"Are you ready for the charity gala next week?" Snow asks.

I shrug, trying to ignore the fact Eve has occupied my brain more then I care to admit. "Yeah, I guess."

"Have you even been to Hope's Village?"

I knit my brows. "Am I a child? It's a pediatric clinic."

North removes his glasses, pinching the bridge of his nose while letting out an annoyed sigh. "You spent twenty grand on a table and you've never been to the clinic in person?"

"Well, shit. Eve is as inviting as a thorn on a rose. How would I—"

"It's not about her," North interrupts. "It's about knowing what North Star Toys is attaching its name to."

"It's a pediatric clinic!"

"Yeah..." Snow chimes in. "You definitely sponsored Hope's Village for Eve. Not the damn children."

Elle snorts with laughter and swallows it when I cut my eyes at her. "Winter, you do know they interview the sponsors and the businesses, right? Did you not read the email?" My blank expression is an answer. "They do a news special to get the buzz going the evening before. You should probably know what you're talking about."

"Thank you, Elle." North stands, turning his attention to me. "This isn't a situation you can throw money at and keep going. It's a commitment. Hence the reason we usually don't sponsor."

"Why the hell did you let me sponsor then?"

"Would you have told Eve no?" Snow asks, already knowing the answer.

While her attitude is a problem, I clearly still struggle to not give her everything she wants.

"Exactly our point," North says, walking toward the door. "I'll see you guys later."

Snow gets up from the couch, pulling Noelle with him. "Are you third wheeling?" He turns his attention to me. I shake my head, following them to the door. "Thank fuck. Let's go home, Snowflake."

I chuckle. "If you two wanted to get it in, you could've just said that."

"I'm a lady!" Elle says over her shoulder as Snow pulls her in the opposite direction.

"No need to tell lies, Elle," I say. She narrows her eyes at me as they turn the corner.

These two make me acutely aware of how lonely I am. Letting out a sigh, I head toward the parking garage. Once I slide into my matte gray Audi RS7, I pull out my phone and type 'Hope's Village' into the search engine. Less than a second later, I'm staring at the picture and address. Would it be a bad idea to stop by unannounced? It's not like I have Eve's number to ask her. For all I know, she may not even be there today. It would be nice to meet the doctors if I'm expected to speak to the media. Weighing my options, I start the car and put it in drive.

The clinic is in a nice area about a twenty-minute drive from North Star Toys. It's surrounded by trees and quite literally looks like a treehouse with a wooden exterior and a bridge to cross to get to the entrance. Looking around the parking lot, there are six other cars and one of them looks like Eve's. Taking a deep breath, I climb out of my car and head toward the entrance. My footsteps make a hollowed sound as I cross the bridge.

A child comes barreling out of the entrance with a wide smile and bright eyes. He nearly collides with me before his mom appears, racing after him. She gives me an apologetic smile while holding onto his arm, pulling him around me.

Opening the door, the receptionist speaks without looking up.

"Good morning. I'll be with you in just a moment." She stares intently at her computer.

I wait, turning on the spot, taking the space in. The walls are painted with intricate murals that give the illusion you're deep in the woods. Tall, leafy trees sprout from the ground in a few places, making it feel more like a treehouse. A smile tugs at my lips while I look around. This is amazing. I'd be happy as hell to come here as a child. Shit, even now as an adult it makes me want to build a treehouse.

"Sorry about that wait. What's your child's name?" She looks up from her computer, awaiting my response.

"No kids. I'm here to see Eve."

She presses her palm to her forehead. "I didn't mean to assume."

"It's fine." I chuckle. "Why else would an adult be here except to wish they were a kid again?"

"Right? Isn't this place amazing? I love working here." She grabs the phone on her desk. "Let me see if she's busy."

Before she can press a button, Eve appears from the hallway with a mouth full of food.

"Haven, I—" She stops in her tracks when our gazes collide. Her eyes widen... and then she starts fucking choking on whatever was in her mouth. I take a step toward her, she takes one back, turning away from me.

"Oh my gosh!" The receptionist shoots up from her seat. "Eve, are you okay?"

She's bent over, hands on knees, attempting to cough up a lung all because she saw me. I try to keep the amusement off my face while I take a step back and let her friend attend to her. To keep from embarrassing her further, I pretend to be more interested in my phone instead of the fact she's fighting for her life. She disappears into the back, making me wonder if I should've called instead of surprising her.

Appearing less than a minute later, my eyes track her hands as she smooths them over her blouse and skirt. She's wearing heels that accentuate her already long, toned legs. Trailing my eyes back up her body, I meet her gaze.

"Hi," she squeaks, clearing her throat. "Um... were we supposed to meet today?"

"No." I slide my phone back into my pocket. "But I wasn't aware we'd be doing a news interview prior to the gala and—"

She looks as surprised as I was about the interview. "We will?"

The corner of my mouth tips up. "Yeah... you know North, always reading the fine print."

"I do." She offers me a small smile. "Is that why you're here? To tell me that?"

"Nah. I'm here because I wanted to see what you've built since North Star Toys is your sponsor."

"The clinic's sponsor," she corrects. "Not mine."

"Mmm..." I slip my hands into my pockets, turning on the spot. "No, Miss Valentine." Meeting her gaze again, I smile. "This is all you. I can feel it."

Even if she didn't want to smile, her lips contort into one, making everything in her gravity a little brighter. "Would you like a tour?"

"If you have time."

"I do. This way." She turns around, and I keep my eyes on her sleek ponytail that trails down her back brushing her— "I wish I could take all the credit for this dream come true, but it wouldn't have been possible without the two doctors I work with." She presses the button to call the elevator.

"I'm sure they say the same about you. Just two doctors for now then?"

She smiles, nodding. "Yes. Dr. Solis and Dr. Bradford. I was in..." Her voice trails off and her smile slips. She closes her eyes, seemingly gathering her thoughts before opening them again. "I met them when I was in medical school, and we kept in touch."

The elevator door opens, and I follow her inside. It reminds me of a mine shaft with glass walls and rock on the other side that has pieces of glittering gems imbedded in it. "Did you stop medical school because—"

"You left?" Her eyes meet mine, but there's no malice or even fight in them. It feels as though the air gets sucked out of the cabin as the door slides shut. There's a few beats of silence while she smooths her hand over her ponytail before she responds. "I'm not sure medical school was ever my path. It took me awhile to accept that, but I know that this," she waves her hand around the elevator, "is exactly where I should be."

"In an elevator with me?" I quirk a brow, attempting to lighten the mood.

She smiles, as the door glides open after a short ride. "We don't really use this level yet," Ignoring my question, she continues. "Besides a storage room. We're hopeful that we secure funding at the gala to turn this lower level into therapy spaces."

"What kinds of therapy?" I follow her down the hall. The walls down here are also painted with whimsical forest murals on one side and a row of windows, giving a view of the trees outside, on the other wall.

"Occupational and speech therapy. We are in desperate need of it here."

"What's occupational therapy?"

She stops in front of a room opening the door. "Occupational therapy focuses on motor skills. For example, if a child has trouble running, jumping, or even writing their name – occupational therapy can help."

"Amazing." I peek into the room. "Is this where it'd be?"

"Yes."

"I'll have to come back when it's done."

"That's *if* we get the funding."

"You will," I assure her.

She gives me a sidelong glance as she shuts the door, continuing down the hall. "What makes you so sure?"

I knit my brows together, tilting my head to the side. "You're doubtful?"

"I don't want to get my hopes up. While this has been a rewarding process, none of it has been easy. So yeah... I'm a little skeptical that we'll show up at a gala and magically get funding."

I gently bump into her shoulder as we walk, causing her to look up at me. "There's going to be an open bar and rich people who love to spend money. Trust me, you'll get it."

Laughter tumbles from her lips, echoing through the hallway. The sound resonates in my chest. "Thank you." She places her hand on my arm. "I needed that laugh."

I look down at her dainty hand. Eve hasn't touched me since the night on the balcony. She must have the same thought because she hastily pulls away, looking straight ahead.

"Just be yourself at the gala, Eve. That's all you've ever needed to do."

Eve comes to a stop in front of another door. Instead of opening it, she faces me, tipping her head back to meet my gaze. For a few breaths her brown eyes flit between mine and my lips. The elevator door dings, and she looks away from me, clearing her throat.

I chuckle at her look of confliction when it dawns on me, "You still have the boyfriend problem?

She crosses her arms. "He's *not* a problem."

"You're right. He's not... for me at least." I give her a devilish grin.

Before she can respond, a woman with hair so black it has a hue of blue when the light catches it steps off the elevator. She doesn't notice us at first because her eyes are on her phone. When she looks up, she jumps, stopping in her tracks and places her hand over her heart.

"Shit! You scared me, Eve!"

"Sorry." She smiles. "I was just... showing our sponsor around. Is Silas busy?"

"Yes, he has back to back appointments. One of mine canceled." The woman's brown eyes land on me, and she gives me a brilliant smile. "Oh! Forgive me, I'm Ilaria Solis." She holds her hand out. "One of the pediatricians." There's a smooth, rich accent to her voice.

"Winter King." I take her hand in mine. "Pleasure to meet you, Ilaria."

"It's all mine." Her eyes convey the truth in her words.

"Or should I say, Dr. Solis?" I can't deny this woman's beauty. She's a little shorter than Eve. With deep sepia skin and bright brown eyes.

"Ilaria is – "

Eve clears her throat loudly, interrupting our exchange. "Ilaria, did you need something?"

"No." She slowly slides her hand out of mine, turning her attention to Eve. "I came to get some printer paper for Haven since I had time."

"Okay," Eve deadpans, clearly waiting for Ilaria to leave. I find this behavior amusing, considering she claims to want nothing to do with me.

"It's okay to call you Ilaria then?" I ask, ignoring Eve's silent protests of our conversation.

"Yes." Her eyes meet mine again as she smiles. "Maybe we'll get to know each other another time?"

I love a bold woman. The tension radiating from Eve is palpable despite her stoic expression. I doubt she's told Ilaria I'm her ex-fiancé. After I left, I rarely talked about her unless it was to family or people that knew both of us. Most people didn't bring her up out of fear of leading to an awkward conversation.

"That'd be nice." I smile at Ilaria.

If Eve is moving on, maybe I should too. It's not something I truly considered until this moment. What if Eve really does like her boyfriend? Maybe even loves him? I've been running on the energy that somehow we'd be together again. I wonder if that's even a possibility anymore?

"I'll let you two get back to your tour. See you around, Winter." She smiles before continuing down the hall.

"You're friendly." Eve walks away from the door she was about to open, heading toward the elevator instead.

I guess the tour is over. Letting out a sigh, I follow behind her. Once we step into the elevator, I lean against the glass wall, staring at her. She tries to keep her focus on the elevator doors and fails.

"What?" she snaps.

I chuckle as I press the stop button, suspending us in the elevator shaft. She backs toward the wall, crossing her arms and giving me a defiant expression. Cute. "Eve, you have two options." She narrows her eyes until they're almost slits. "Let me go or stop running."

Her jaw goes slack, making her lips part. She doesn't speak. Only stares at me with wide eyes.

"You've made me the villain. I've accepted that. Accept that I will move how I see fit. If I want to talk to someone else, to move on like you supposedly have, then I will. You can run game on your boyfriend. With me, however," I press the button for the elevator to continue, "I see all the cards in your hand, even if you're pretending to be blind to them." The elevator slows and the doors slide open. Taking a step toward the door, I pause in the frame without looking over my shoulder. "When I move on, Eve, I'll never look back."

I shouldn't have seen her right before therapy. She triggered memories I don't want to dissect today. Or ever. My knee bounces on its own accord as if my body is shaking me to spill my thoughts. I've talked in circles for the past ten minutes in an attempt to not talk about Eve. We've talked about some of my most painful memories, yet I've avoided her.

"Winter, are you okay?"

I press my sweaty palm into my kneecap to soothe the bouncing. "Yes..."

He gives me a skeptical look over the rim of his glasses before sliding them off. Dr. Maddox does this when he knows I'm intentionally being difficult. Apparently I'm an adult with the tendencies of a child. Except this time, he doesn't speak. He simply stares at me. I'm not one to back down from a staring contest until now. I avert my gaze. I'm sure he can see through every ounce of bullshit and what troubles I keep locked away.

After a moment of me pretending not to notice his eyes are on me, he speaks. "Therapy works best when you're honest."

Leaning forward, I press my elbows into my thighs and run my hand over my coils. "I saw someone today." I keep my eyes on my black Christian Louboutin loafers. "My ex-fiancée."

"By chance?"

"No." I meet his gaze. "Intentionally. We hadn't spoken to each other in over a decade. Then Snow fell in love with her best friend. They're getting married. We can no longer avoid each other." More like I can no longer avoid her. When I came back, I decided to stay out of Eve's lane because I knew I fucked up and felt she deserved better. I still feel she deserves better even if it's not me providing it.

"How's the relationship between you two now?"

I snort with laughter, sinking back into the plush leather chair. "Relationship is a stretch."

"May I ask what happened?"

The question I've avoided. I recollect the memory that was the beginning of our end.

"Winter, what do you think?" Eve asks, bringing me back to the present moment.

"It's good," I answer with a tight smile, setting the fork with the untouched piece of cake down on the plate.

The event planner's voice sounds like an incessant fly buzzing in my ear. "And your father will—"

"His father is—"

"Dead," I say hollowly, keeping my eyes on the elaborately decorated cake in the center of the table. It's been six weeks since his funeral and it's felt like hell every day since.

"Oh, I'm—"

"Sorry?" I meet his gaze. Tugging on his collar, he looks between Eve and I as if she'll save him.

"This is my fault." Eve places her hand on my arm. "I didn't tell him. Kylar, may we have a moment?" He bolts up from his seat, happy to give us space. "Winter—"

"I told you I didn't want to be here."

"I know, but we needed to do this today for the wedding and—"

"Eve," I stand, needing room to breathe. "I need time. This," I wave my hand at table covered in cake samples. "Is all too much for me to deal with right now." Grabbing at my collar, I loosen the top few buttons and pull off my suit jacket. "Tasting cakes, seeing venues, taking pictures – having to pretend to be okay when I feel like I'm fucking dying. This is supposed to be the best time of our lives. For me, it's not."

Standing, she meets me in the middle of the room. "What are you saying?"

"I'm saying that I need time." I press the heels of my hands into my eyes, rubbing them. *"I'm not myself."*

"You want me to call off the wedding?" Her voice is small and unsteady.

"Postpone. Not call off." I hold her chin between my forefinger and thumb. *"You're my soul, and I want to marry you. I'm asking for time."*

She moves her chin out of my hold, looking away from me. *"You're asking me to call off the wedding in a roundabout way."*

"I want to enjoy these moments with you, Eve." A tear slides down her cheek, I swipe it away. *"Do you honestly want to marry me in my current state?"*

"Yes!" she says without hesitation, looking up at me. *"We can get through this together, Winter. You're not alone. I'm right here."* I let my hand drop to my side as I search her brown eyes feeling alone even though she's looking at me. *"I can handle the planning and you can focus on yourself so that when the wedding comes, we can walk down the aisle."*

"Eve... it's not about the planning or preparation." Tears sting my eyes, not from grief, but from the fact she's refusing to see me right now. *"Do you know what I see when I look in the mirror?"*

"No," she answers cautiously.

"Neither do I." My vision blurs. *"I've walked through my whole life confident I know who I am. Then Dad died and I realized I don't have a fucking clue who I am. My identity was the one he designed for me. Eve,"* I take a step closer to her, pleading with my eyes that she understands. *"I look in the mirror and am scared of my own reflection because I don't recognize the person looking back at me. You're expecting me to walk down the aisle in three months' time as a ghost of the man you knew. Who I once was no longer exists... and I'm trying to wrap my mind around that."*

She places her hands on either side of my face, wiping my tears and brings my gaze to hers. *"Winter, I had no idea you felt this way. I'm sorry.*

You're not in this alone, you know that right? You have me, your mom, and brothers."

My mom can barely leave her room, North has uttered maybe two words in the past six weeks, and Snow is just as broken as I am, despite acting like everything is okay. It's not just me, it's the whole family. We're all struggling.

She fills the silence between us. "We can get you some help."

"It's not—" I take a deep breath, closing my eyes in an attempt to calm myself. "It's not about help..."

"Can you at least try... for me?"

That's all I've been doing since the day Dad died. Trying. I nod my head, agreeing even though I know she's asking me for more than I can give.

"After that, it seemed we couldn't agree on anything. She wanted to fix me, and I was trying to process losing my dad. I still am." I take a drink of water, swallowing the lump that's lodged in my throat. "Was I being selfish, asking her to postpone our wedding we'd been dreaming up for a year?"

Dr. Maddox puts his glasses back on. "No, Winter. It's never selfish to ask for what you need. Sometimes it's hard for those we love to hear our needs because they may not align with their own."

I stare up at the ceiling, letting the sound of the fountain on his shelf fill the silence. "One day, we had a particularly bad fight. We never yelled at each other. That day we were screaming." Fragments of the memory replay in my head.

"You're the reason we'll never get married because you refuse to try!" Tears stream down her face as she paces the room.

"All I've fucking done is try and all you've done is ask me for thing after fucking thing!"

"Excuse me for wanting what's best for you!"

I let out a cynical laugh. "For me, Eve? The wedding is for the betterment of me?"

"No! It's for us. You and me."

"Us?" I knit my brows together, raising one as I stare at her. "Do it for me, Winter. Try for me, Winter. We – " I motion between us " – are nowhere between those words."

"Stop it!" she cries. "That's not true."

"Every. Fucking. Thing. I do is for you!" I say through gritted teeth. "I ask you for one thing. One fucking thing. And you can't meet me there, can you?"

Her silence is an answer.

"I left later that night. In hindsight, I could've handled that differently... not been a coward."

"You think you're a coward?"

"I dashed outta there like a thief in the night. A coward."

"Winter, can you look at me?" My eyes remain on the ceiling out of fear the flood gate of emotions will open and pull me under. A silence ensues that becomes loud. Slowly, I tip my head forward to look at Dr. Maddox. "You did the best you could at the time." I open my mouth to disagree, but nothing comes out. "You did the best you could at the time. Full stop. Of course you want to say, I'd do things differently now. You're older and wiser. However, we're not talking about now. We are talking about the Winter who was in those moments you just recounted."

"Remember how you told her you couldn't recognize your reflection?" I nod. "If that version of you saw the Winter I'm looking at now, would you recognize yourself?"

"No," I say without having to think. "I'd be surprised I made it this far. At that time, I couldn't fathom being where I am now."

He gives me a patient smile. "Offer yourself some grace. You did the best you could at the time."

"I did the best I could at the time." Every moment I was with her, I gave her my best. "She doesn't see it that way."

He pulls a piece of paper from the table sitting beside him, adjusting his glasses. "Winter King, date of birth June seventeenth nineteen eighty seven, that's you?" His gaze meets mine again.

"Yes..."

"These therapy sessions are for you."

"Smart ass." I chuckle.

Dr. Maddox grins. "We all have different perceptions of our reality even when we're having the same experience. Eve's feelings are valid, but so are yours. Understand that despite the pain you may have caused, you are still deserving of forgiveness."

"It seems everything circles back around to forgiveness and grace."

Slightly tilting his head to the side, he asks, "Have you given yourself either?"

"No."

"*Your* healing, Winter, is not dependent upon those around you. Offer yourself what you seek in others."

9

EVE

SITTING IN MY OFFICE with Ilaria and Silas, I listen to them throw idea after idea out as to what should be auctioned. We need to let the coordinator know what we're offering by this afternoon. My eyes keep focusing on Ilaria. I've caught myself doing this since Winter stopped by the other day. He seemed genuinely interested in her. I can't blame him. Ilaria is intelligent, kind, and gorgeous. Even her laugh is pretty. It fills the room as Silas jokes with her.

I've considered telling her Winter is my ex-fiancé since their exchange. After mulling it over, I realized it's not my place and it doesn't matter. It *shouldn't* matter. He deserves to move on and not look back at what we had. Even if my heart constricts at the thought.

Taking a sip of my coffee, I wince when cold liquid hits my tongue. "It has to be something worth bidding on." I toss the coffee cup in the trash. "We have to think outside the box if we want money."

We've been going back and forth for nearly two hours. You'd think with all the brilliance sitting in the room, we'd be able to come up with something. This has been a humbling experience.

"That's why I suggested the trip." Silas sighs exasperatedly.

"Who's going to bet on a trip when some of them vacation in the South of France on the weekends?" Ilaria clips.

Haven peeks into my office. "Hi." She smiles. "Letting you know there's an hour before the first patients arrive."

"We've been here that long?" Silas sits up straight, looking for his phone.

On a long sigh, Ilaria slumps into her seat.

"Haven, what would you auction?" I ask, desperate for an inkling of an idea.

"Um..." She takes a step into my office, looking at Ilaria and Silas. "You're both single right?"

"Yes," they answer in unison.

"Okay..." She bites her lip before smiling. "My mom does quite a bit of charity work and the most popular charity events are the date auctions."

"Date auctions?" Ilaria asks the question that was on the tip of my tongue.

"Hear me out!" Excitement lights Haven's face, making me smile. "You two are eligible and intelligent. What if you auctioned a date with a doctor for the event? I may or may not have overheard you guys struggling, making me come up with a few of my own ideas." She clears her throat, smiling as they give her skeptical stares. "Twisted Vines would be a good – "

"Their wait list is years long, Haven." Ilaria cuts in.

"Yeah we're in a time crunch." I add. "And I really don't feel like schmoozing for – "

Haven holds up her hand. "If you didn't have a connect, like me," she smiles brightly, "it would be impossible. I've already texted my mom and she'd be more than happy to work something out with the owner."

We gape at her. "Seriously?"

"Honestly, I'll put myself up for auction just to go to Twisted Vines." Ilaria says.

"Sell out." Silas teases.

"What?" Ilaria shrugs. "I like the finer things in life and I've heard amazing things about that place. A ranch with horseback riding, spa, restaurant, and being able to taste the coveted Twisted Vines wine collection. Yes, put me up for auction."

"That took absolutely no convincing." I smirk. "Silas, what about you?"

"For the kids, right?"

"And the experience of Twisted Vines." Ilaria grins.

"I guess, but if my date is some old lady who's handsy, I'm quitting." We burst into laughter. "I'm serious!"

Haven claps her hands together. "Let me text my mom. I'll let you know when everything is settled. What about you, Eve?"

"What about me?" I ask confused.

"You're not offering yourself up as sacrifice?" Silas inquires.

"No. I just coordinate."

"You're willing to miss out on Twisted Vines?" Ilaria gapes at me.

"I am." I lean against my desk, sitting on the edge.

"I'm sure my mom can work something out for you and Noah." Haven smiles.

"No pressure, Haven. I'm just grateful we have something that no one else will have. Exclusivity puts us one step closer to getting the funding we need."

"I'll still ask." She shrugs, pulling her phone out of her pocket as she leaves my office.

"Are you talking about us sacrificing ourselves or Twisted Vines?"

"You're a rare gem, Silas. Of course I'm talking about you." I smirk, pushing away from my desk.

"Glad you recognize my value."

"Are you both sure about this? I don't want to pimp you out against your will."

"If it means we'll get the money we need without having to beg for it, I'm all in," Ilaria says, scrolling through her phone.

"Agreed. We can't wait for another grant. The writing process alone is tedious. I'll whore myself out for the benefit of Hope's Village."

Ilaria and I fall into a fit of laughter. "No one said anything about whoring!"

"Close enough." He shrugs, glancing at his watch. "I take it this meeting is adjourned?"

"One more thing. Our twenty-thousand-dollar table seats ten people. If you want to bring a plus one, feel free to do so."

"Is Winter going to be there?" Ilaria asks.

"Who's Winter?" Silas raises a brow.

"He—" I hadn't considered him being at the gala. "He's our sponsor. Winter King." My heart thrums as I say his name. "He's the marketing director at North Star Toys."

"He was here the other day," Ilaria fills in. "You were busy with patients."

"Hopefully he comes to the gala so I can meet him."

"Yeah." I smile brightly, while internally groaning. "Hopefully."

I pull my car into my parent's horseshoe driveway. With all the stress and emotions I've been swimming in lately, there truly is no place like home. Climbing out of my car, I don't bother knocking. Using my key to open the front door. I'm immediately hit with the savory scent of Mom's cooking. Following the smell into the kitchen, I find her flitting around, humming along to music that's playing.

"Let me guess, lasagna?"

She faces me with a wide smile and open arms. "How's my girl?" I gladly step into her embrace and melt into the hug.

"I'm good, Mom."

Releasing me, she takes a step back, resting her hands on my shoulders as she looks me up and down. "I don't believe that for a second."

"Okay." I huff, setting my bag on the kitchen counter. "There's a lot going on. Nothing I'd like to talk about right now, though."

"I can respect that." She opens the oven, peering inside before closing it again. "You need a break, darling."

My mom thinks I work too hard. Wait, no–she *knows* I work too hard. Loving what I do doesn't mean it isn't stressful. It doesn't help that I'm an anxious being with a heavy case of perfectionism; the two traits clash daily.

"I will. When we can coast—" Before I can finish my sentence, I yelp as two fingers jab into my sides, causing me to jolt forward. "Jude! You little shit! What did I tell you about that? Grow the hell up!"

"Eve!" Mom waves the tongs she's wielding in my direction. "Language! And Jude," she fixes him with her gaze as he straightens up. "Grow the hell up!"

I toss my head back, cackling. "Tell him, Mom."

"I am grown." Jude smiles, grabbing a handful of grapes and popping some into his mouth. "I have a job, pay my own bills—"

"And live at home with mommy and daddy." I finish for him, batting my lashes with a sickly sweet smile on my face. He launches a grape in my direction. I dodge it. "See, this is why you still live at home."

"It's a temporary situation." He shrugs. "Besides, Mom loves having me here, don't you?"

"Oh, yes, son." She pulls the pan of lasagna out of the oven. "I had always imagined that when your father finally retired, I'd be sharing these moments with you."

I snort and pull my bottom lip between my teeth to keep from laughing.

"Damn—" Mom glares at him. "Dang, Mom. I didn't know I was such a burden."

Mom waves him off.

"You know, Jude," I interject. "You just don't care. I'd choose to be rent free too."

"Don't even think about it," Mom warns.

"I love my independence." I smile as Jude flicks me off.

"If you love your independence so much, why are you here?"

"Because unlike you, Mom and Daddy have a chance to miss me." I look him up and down, crossing my arms.

Mom snorts with laughter before stifling it as she cuts the lasagna.

"Mom!" Jude exclaims, gaping at her.

"What?" she asks innocently. "She has a point."

"If it isn't my little sister."

I turn to the sound of a familiar, comforting voice. "Fox!" I launch myself at him. "Why didn't anyone tell me you were back?" My question is muffled against his chest.

"I believe it's called a surprise."

"Smartass." I pinch his arm, pulling away from him. "How long are you here for?"

Fox looks vibrant and happy. He and Jude both resemble Dad with their rich umber skin, tall frames, lean builds, sharp, defined facial features, and thick dark brown coils. While I favor Mom with my heart shaped face, large almond shaped brown eyes, and rich sable skin. The only thing I got from Dad is my brown hair. Mom's hair is jet black.

"I'm back... for good." He beams. "Believe it or not, I'm tired of traveling."

I raise my brows. "Fox Valentine, tired of traveling? What brought on this change?"

He dramatically turns on the spot. "You're looking at the new director of Hope Valley Museum."

"What?" I exclaim, looking between him and Mom, who's smiling brightly. "That's amazing news, Fox!" I hug him again. "I'm proud of you."

"Thanks, Eve."

"Why does Fox receive such a warm welcome?" Jude protests.

I roll my eyes, shaking my head. "You got a whole welcome home party. Are you staying here with Mom and Daddy?" I turn my attention back to Fox.

"No." He chuckles. "Unlike Jude, I got a place before I came back."

"My excitement to spend time with my so called family is dwindling with each second I spend with you all."

We laugh as I pull Jude into a hug and Fox joins us.

"At last." Dad's deep voice fills the kitchen. "All my kids in one place." He wraps his arms around the three of us at once. "I was hoping you'd stop by today, Bug."

"Were you all just not going to tell me my favorite brother is back?"

Jude smacks the back of my head, making me cackle. "How dare you!"

"If it makes you feel any better, I just touched down this morning," Fox fills in. "It's not like I've been hiding out for days."

"It does." I break away from the hug with a smile.

I take a deep breath, looking around the kitchen at my family. For the first time in a while, my heart feels full.

"Dinner's ready," Mom announces.

"Do you need any help, Mom?"

"Set the table, honey. The boys can clean up."

"Hey!" they protest as I laugh my way to set the table.

There's not much chatter between us now that we're eating. This is the first time in over a year that we've been home at the same time. Mom and Dad look undeniably happy.

After Mom takes a sip of wine, she sets the cup aside. "Who's Hope's Village sponsor? I don't think you ever told us, honey."

I've avoided telling them. I take a particularly large bite of lasagna, prolonging my response. "Um... I–no, I haven't told you."

"Who is it?" Dad inquires.

"North Star Toys is our sponsor."

"That's nice of Snow to do that for you, honey." Mom smiles, picking up her fork again.

I could let them believe it's Snow. It'd be easier to let it go. For a moment, I consider it. "Actually, Winter is the one who decided to sponsor the clinic."

Mom pauses with her fork suspended in the air, halfway to her mouth. Time seems to slow down as all eyes are now on me.

"Winter?" Dad asks.

"Mhm..." I become more interested in my plate.

"You two talking again?" Fox grabs his glass of water, leaning back in his seat as he stares at me.

"Occasionally. It's kind of hard not to now that Snow is engaged to Noelle." It's hard not to talk to Winter in general.

"Seriously?" Fox raises his brows.

"Yes." Mom smiles brightly. "They are a beautiful couple."

"That's crazy that your best friend is marrying the brother of your..." Fox's voice trails off before the words tumble from his lips. "Good for them."

"I personally hope you're giving him hell after what he did," Jude says with a smirk.

"Jude!" Mom scolds him before turning his attention to me. "You better not be, Eve. Winter has been through enough without adding your attitude into the mix."

"He deserves her attitude. Who just leaves without a word?" Jude shovels a bite of lasagna into his mouth.

Mom dabs her lips with a napkin. "I think you've been too unforgiving all these years."

I set my fork aside, suddenly losing my appetite. Here we go. If she had it her way, I would've kneeled in front of Winter, asking him to take me back despite him being the one who left. When I introduced them to Noah, she asked if he knew Winter, knowing that they went to school together. It's hard to move on when your Mom believes no one can compare to Winter King.

"How am I being unforgiving?"

"Eve, you can't honestly think he's the only one to blame?"

"He left. Vanished. Disappeared." Digging into past traumas is not what I wanted to do this evening.

Mom nods her head. "He did, but—"

"Vivienne." Dad briefly glances between Mom and I, settling his eyes on her. "It's not our place to tell Eve how to feel."

Mom takes a deep breath. "You're right. Eve, I'm sorry."

"It's fine." I pull my phone from my back pocket, checking the time. "I've gotta get going."

"Honey..." Mom has a pained expression on her face as she watches me get up from the table. "Don't go because of what I said."

"I'm not, Mom. Noah will be off soon, and I told Noelle I'd stop by her place."

"She's definitely leaving because of you," Jude interjects, causing Mom to scowl at him as I simultaneously smack the back of his head. "Only joking." He chuckles.

"Let me make a plate for you to take to Noah," Mom says, getting up from the table.

I stare after her as she heads into the kitchen for a container. She's sending food for Noah as a peace offering. I'll take it.

"When can I stop by to see the clinic?" Fox asks.

"Whenever you want," I beam. "Just text me."

"I will." He stands, giving me a hug. "Good to see you."

"You too." I hug him back.

"Here you go." Mom reappears. "Bring Noah with you next time, okay?"

I release Fox to wrap her in a hug.

She chuckles, patting my back. "I love you, sweet girl."

"Love you too, Mama." I kiss her cheek. I could be seething, and I'd still give Mom a kiss goodbye. I know she means well and only wants what's best for me.

I round the table to say bye to Jude. He tries to wave me off. Ignoring his protests, I place a sloppy kiss on his cheek. "Disgusting!" He nearly topples out of his seat, wiping it away. "I have no clue where your mouth has been!"

I cackle. "Ask Noah."

Every one of them protests, saying my name. "Eve!"

"Yeah, I love you guys, too."

Dad stands, shaking his head with a smile on his face as he grabs the food from my hands. "I'll walk you out."

Once we're outside, I turn to Dad. "Don't tell me you think I'm too unforgiving also."

"No, I say give him hell while also giving him grace." I let out a huff of laughter. "Your Mom means well, Eve."

"I know, Dad." I let out an exasperated sigh, leaning against my car. "It's just... I'm finally trying to move on and she says stuff like this."

He looks down at the food in his hands before meeting his gaze. "She's speaking from experience."

"What do you mean?" I search his face.

"Did Mom ever tell you about me breaking up with her?"

"*You...*" I point at him, "broke up with *Mama*?" My eyes widen with disbelief. "Seriously?" Vivienne and Cole Valentine are the epitome of love. My parent's relationship is what I hope to have for myself one day.

Dad sighs wistfully. "I was young and very, *very* dumb." I can't help the laughter that bubbles up my throat. "I thought the grass was greener on the other side and clearly it wasn't."

"There was another woman?" I curl my lip.

"No. Another opportunity. I was the first in my family to go to college. The only reason I went was because I got a full ride scholarship. It was the opportunity of a lifetime. My parents and friends convinced me I needed to take full advantage of the opportunity and not be tied to anything at home. Including Viv. We dated our Junior and Senior year. She was the only woman I'd ever been with up until that point.

"At first I was reluctant to listen to my family and friends, but then..." He shrugs. "I wondered 'what if there is more out there for me?'. And like a damn fool I broke it off with Viv. As soon as the words were out of my mouth, I regretted it. There was no taking them back. The damage was already done and we went our separate ways. What was supposed to be one of the most exciting times of my life was lackluster without Viv by my side.

"But as you know," he meets my gaze and there's a hint of sadness in them. "You learn to cope. We didn't see each other for four years. I was convinced I got over her until I saw her."

My breath catches in my throat because I know that exact feeling. It's a mix of a sense of relief and pain at the same time. It's easy to convince yourself of things when you can completely avoid what you're so sure you're not missing.

"However, there was a problem. I met someone else and we were engaged."

"Engaged?!" I gasp.

He nods, running a hand over his face, letting out a deep sigh. "I made a damn mess." I chuckle. "I met her at college and I did love her... just not the way I love your mom. When I realized I was still in love with Viv, I had to break it off with my fiancé. It wasn't fair to be stringing her along when I knew she wasn't who I wanted."

I playfully nudge his shoulder. "I didn't realize you were such a heart-breaker."

He lets out a rumble of laughter. "These are not moments I'm proud of. I broke two hearts because I was being stubborn and stupid. Eventually," he continues, "Viv and I found our way back to each other. And believe you me, that woman didn't make anything easy."

I cover my mouth with my hand as I let out a cackle of laughter. "She had every right not to! You left her."

"I did." He nods. "I own up to that mistake, but I tell you this because had it not been for her forgiveness, the life that we have now... this family wouldn't exist."

My face softens as I let his words sink in.

"Your mother told me she tried to move on, like me, and it never felt quite right. You see, Bug, it's one thing to move on because you're ready and want to. It's another thing entirely when you move on out of spite because you refuse to offer someone forgiveness."

I still, holding my breath. "I'm not refusing," I say as I exhale. "I'm... just not there yet."

He gives me an understanding smile, kissing my forehead. "I know. I just don't want you to be stuck in the hurt for longer than you have to."

I want to move on even if I don't know how. The hurt of losing Winter faded as the years passed. I thought I got over him, until he was sitting in front of me. It was as if no time had passed at all. Every emotion – good, bad, and ugly – came rushing back when we laid eyes on each other again. Lying to myself was easier when we ceased to exist in each other's worlds.

"I love you, Bug." He releases me from the hug.

"Love you too, Dad." I meet his gaze.

"Take your time, okay?"

I nod, fearing if I speak I'll cry. Crying in front of him would prove that I care just as much as he suspects I do. He nods, handing me the container with the lasagna and opens my car door for me. Once inside, he closes the door and waves. I return the gesture and blow him a kiss. Turning on the car, he watches me leave. Once I'm in the clear, I let myself feel. It starts as a few tears, quickly turning into warm streams running down my face.

I've been holding in so much lately, feeling like a dam under pressure. Eventually something will break to alleviate the pressure, even if that something is me. I consider heading to my place and then remember Noah will be there. He'll ask questions I don't feel like answering. The answers are truths I don't even want to admit to myself. I decide to stop by Elle and Snow's place. It takes me fifteen minutes to get to their apartment. Before long, I'll be driving to their home in Citrine Grove.

Pulling up beside Elle's car, I take a few minutes to gather myself. I wipe the smudged mascara from under my eyes and blow my nose. Resting my head against the seat, I take a few deep breaths and apply some lip gloss. Once I look as presentable as I can after sobbing, I climb out of the car. I reach back in to grab my bag and when I close my door, I'm met by Winter.

Thank you, Universe. I truly appreciate your fucking sarcasm tonight.

"Hi..." I pull my bag over my shoulder.

Winter knits his brows together, making him even more unnecessarily handsome as he surveys me. "Have you been crying?"

"Allergies." Sniffing, I look away from him.

"Does anyone ever believe that excuse?" He tilts his head to the side, catching my gaze with the hint of a smirk on his lips.

I can't help but smile at him. "Sometimes."

The playfulness that lit his face seconds ago is replaced with concern. "Want to talk about it?"

"No." I shake my head. He nods, rubbing the back of his neck. "Thank you for asking, though."

"Yeah..." He blows out a puff of air. "Well, I'm gonna get going. I just dropped by to help Snow and Elle move some things."

"Oh, yeah. Have a good night, Winter." I hate that everything between us is so formal and rigid. We used to talk with ease and familiarity. Even when we first met.

He gives me a mix of a wave and a salute. Before he gets too far, I holler after him. "Hey..." He stops in his tracks, slowly turning around. "Do you still like lasagna?"

His face lights up in a way I haven't seen in a long time, and it warms my entire being. "Yeah." He makes his way toward me. "Why?"

"I may or may not have some with me." I give him a smug smile.

Looking down at me, he slides his hands into the pockets of his sweats as his eyes roam over my face. "Are you being a tease or you got the goods?"

My smile grows wider as I laugh. "You're making this sound illegal."

"Shit... may as well be." He grins. "Now quit playing with my emotions, Eve. You got lasagna on you or not?"

"I do." Opening my car again, I pull out the perfectly packed lasagna. "Courtesy of Mom – I mean my mom."

We got into the habit of calling each other's parents Mom or Dad when talking about them. Old habits die hard... if they ever do.

I watch him lick his lips, hesitating as he reaches for it. "And you're giving me Mom's lasagna?" Biting my lip, I try to contain my grin. "Is it poisoned?"

I cackle. "No, you dick! Keep talking shit and I'll eat it myself."

He snatches it from my hands. "I'll take my chances." Looking down at the container, he says, "Thank you. Will you eat it with me?"

"What?" I scrunch up my face.

"Eat the lasagna with me." It's more of a statement than request.

"Uh..." I look around. "Okay, are we just going to stand here or...?"

"Nah, Miss Bougie." I suck my teeth as he chuckles, jerking his head at something behind him. "C'mon. I brought my truck. We can sit on the back."

I hesitate before following behind him. He leads us toward a red truck that's a short distance from my car. "Hold this." He hands me the precious lasagna. Turning, he lowers the tailgate.

Setting the container on the gate, I press my palms into it as I hoist myself up. He makes himself comfortable beside me. I wrap my arms around myself as the cool breeze moves over my skin.

"Cold?"

"A little, but—"

He slides off the tailgate and disappears into his truck for a few seconds before reappearing with a hoodie. "Here."

I take it from him and immediately regret it when his scent wraps around me as I pull it over my head. "Thank you."

"Can't have you freezing after you blessed me with Mom's lasagna."

I shake my head, smiling. "You better eat it while it's still warm." Recognizing the familiar look in his eye, I say, "The lasagna, Winter." I shove his arm as he laughs.

"I didn't say anything." He pulls the top off the container.

"You didn't have to..." I mutter.

"Good to know."

I keep my mouth shut before I say something that leads us into a situation I'm not ready for. He unwraps the fork from the napkin and cuts a piece away, holding it out to me.

My eyes cross, staring down at the fork. "I'm capable of feeding myself." He continues to hold it in front of my mouth as he raises a brow, waiting for me. "Winter, I—"

"Eve, eat the damn lasagna. You're already here."

I take a deep breath, matching his glare, and open my mouth. Closing my lips around the bite, he gives me a satisfied smile as he pulls the fork from my mouth. Holding my gaze, he licks it clean. A chill I can't attribute to the breeze ripples through me.

"How's your family, anyway?" He switches gears completely.

I swallow the bite, licking my lips. "Good. Everyone's home again." I tell him about Jude, Fox, and my parents. In between my words, he feeds me bites of lasagna.

"Good to see that smile light up your face again." He takes a bite.

"What smile?"

"The one you wear for those you love." Setting the fork down in the container, he brushes a loose curl behind my ear. My skin tingles, missing his touch as soon as he pulls away. "Thank you for the lasagna."

"Yeah..." I lightly clear my throat. "Any time."

We sit in companionable silence, finishing off the slice of lasagna meant for Noah. He holds the last bite up to my mouth. Wrapping my hand around his, I guide the fork to his lips. Smiling, he lets me take the fork to feed him the last bite. I pull it from his mouth, matching his movements from earlier and lick it clean before setting it back in the container.

"That was good. This," he motions between us, "was good too."

I swing my feet back and forth, watching him put the top back on the container. The last time we talked with such ease was a couple of months before he left. He turns to face me after setting the container aside.

"I–I've... missed you." The words tumble from my mouth before I can stop myself, and the tears from earlier accompany them. I look away, which is pointless. Winter knows me better than I know myself.

He gently places his forefinger under my chin, bringing my gaze to his. "It's okay to miss people, Eve." Wiping a tear from my cheek, he wraps his hand around the back of my neck, pulling me toward him as he plants a kiss over my third eye. "I miss your stubborn ass too sometimes."

I pull away from him, cackling, both annoyed and grateful he broke the heaviness of the moment. "You're the worst!"

"The worst who got you to laugh." He points his finger at me with a raised brow and smug smile.

My phone vibrates in my back pocket, pulling it out, it's a text from Elle.

Elle: Did you leave?

Letting out a sigh, I hop off the tailgate of his truck. "I better get inside before Elle thinks I got kidnapped."

"Shit, we can still make it happen if you wanna spice up your night a little."

The corners of my mouth tip up. "That is a very tempting offer. Raincheck?"

"For you? Yeah."

Butterflies that I attempt to quell flutter through me. "I'll see you around, Winter." I begin walking away when I realize I meant to ask him one more thing. "Wait... can I have your number?"

His jaw drops, splaying his hand over his chest. "My number?"

"Yeah... for the gala and stuff, you know?" I shrug, clearing my throat trying to sound casual even though my palms are sweating.

"For the gala?" The corner of his mouth tips up. "You know, if you wanted my number, you could just—"

"You know what?" I turn around, but he catches my wrist, stopping me.

"I'm fuckin' with you. It'd probably be wise, considering you choked the last time you saw me unexpectedly."

I snort with laughter, covering my face with my hands. "I was mortified by the way."

"I'm not gonna lie, I got a small bit of satisfaction from that."

"Out of me choking?"

"Yes." He gives me a smile. "I enjoy knowing I have that effect on you even if my hand isn't wrapped around your neck."

His words trigger memories I don't need to be having. Swallowing, I trail my fingertips over my throat, remembering what it was like to be underneath him.

"Um... so your number?" I squeak.

He licks his lips, smiling and tells me his number.

"It's..." I read his number again. "It's the same as always?"

"Yeah." He leans against the truck. "Snow kept it active for me while..." His voice trails off.

"You... You got all those voicemails and texts then?" I think of every word I wrote or said, ranging from irate to me begging him to come back. It took me two years to stop trying.

"Some of them. Eventually I got a new phone and different number."

I taught myself not to care what he did. Now, I want to know every detail. "What happened to you?" The words hang heavily between us.

For a few seconds, he doesn't look at me. "Snow didn't tell you?"

"Bits and pieces." I shrug. "I stopped trying eventually."

"Understandable," he nods. "If you really want to know, I can fill in the gaps between the bits and pieces. Not right now, though. I'd rather stay in the moment we're in a little longer."

"I respect that." I give him a smile before typing out a text to him.

His phone chimes seconds later. "Your number hasn't changed either?"

I cock my head to the side. "The better question is, why is *my* number still in *your* phone?"

"Just in case."

"Just in case... what?"

"Just in case I ever figured out what to say to you."

I blink, surprised by his response. "Have you?"

"Hell no!" he exclaims, and I laugh. "But we're here talking, aren't we?"

"We are." My cheeks hurt, making me feel like I haven't smiled in a decade.

"I'll take whatever we got going right here, for now." He matches my smile.

My phone vibrates again. I already know it's Noelle. "I better get going." The words come from my mouth, but my body doesn't listen.

He takes a step into my space, resting a hand on my shoulder. I tip my head back to look up at him as he leans forward and presses a kiss to my cheek. "See you around, Eve."

Without another word, he turns and climbs into his truck, leaving me wrapped up in the scent and feel of him.

10
WINTER

I SWIM TO THE surface after sitting on the bottom of the pool for as long as my lungs would allow. I take a deep breath once the cool air hits my face. Swimming to the ledge, I hoist myself onto it and reach for my phone to check the time.

"Three minutes. Not bad," I mutter. When I first started this exercise, I'd rush to the surface after thirty seconds.

Scrolling through my phone, a text comes through. I'm surprised to see Eve's name.

Eve: Hi.

The other night with her has been stuck in my head. It's been a long time since we had a moment without an undercurrent of animosity. I've thought about texting her since then. As much shit as I talk about her "boyfriend", I respect the fact she's in a relationship. He should be fucking grateful.

Winter: Hey.

I watch the ellipsis bob on the screen as she types.

Eve: Thank you for cheering me up the other night.

Winter: You don't have to thank me. I will say if anyone ever believes your weak ass allergy excuse, they don't really fuck with you.

Eve: LOL Noted.

Eve: Are you bringing anyone to the gala? Our table seats ten. We have room for you to bring a plus one if you wanted.

Grabbing a towel off the chair, I drape it over my head. There's no one, companion wise, I'd want to hang out with a for a few hours.

Winter: It's at the art Museum?

Eve: Yeah, they have a Basquiat exhibit right now.

I wonder if Reign would want to be my guest.

Winter: Yeah, I'll bring a plus one.

Eve: K.

A chuckle resonates in my chest.

Winter: You better fix that salty ass "K" you just sent to my phone.

Eve: It's not salty. I'm just saying okay.

Winter: Fix it.

Eve: I can't wait to meet your plus one, Winter! I'm so excited!

I laugh out loud to myself. She listens so well.

Winter: Better. Will I get to meet your boyfriend?

Eve: Yes. He's my plus one.

Winter: K.

Eve: LMAO Fuck you!

I grin as I send a smiley face in response. Eve brings her boyfriend around when I'm not there. I know Elle and Snow have gone out with them on multiple occasions. Aspen says he's "good looking" and "kinda boring". All I know is he's a surgeon and his name is Nathaniel or some shit like that. I forgot it as soon as I heard it. If she's happy, that's all that matters. Even if I think it's a sham.

Getting up, I head inside to get ready to hang out with Reign for a few hours.

Walking into True's House, I'm met by Hudson. "How's it going, Winter?"

"Good. I wanted to ask you; can I take Reign out?"

"As long as he agrees, you can. Please make sure to sign out when you leave."

"Will do." I open the door to the rec room, but stop and face him again. "Can I buy him stuff?"

Hudson looks taken aback. I'm under the impression he's not used to people wanting to help past a tax write off. "We don't encourage it, but it's your money."

"How's the chef working out?" After my initial visit, a chef was working here within the week. I have more money than I'll ever know what to do with and want to know it's doing some good in the world.

"Great! She's been invaluable to True's House. I sleep a little easier at night knowing the kids aren't going home hungry."

"Glad to hear. Let me know if you ever need anything else."

"Will do." He nods with a smile.

Heading into the rec room, I spot Reign sitting in the corner with Calliope. She's always doing something to Reign's hair. Today, she's braiding it.

"Winter!" Her face lights up when she sees me. "I made you something."

As soon as her hands are out of Reign's hair, he tugs at the braids, taking them out. I chuckle as she sucks her teeth, handing me a small, neatly wrapped package.

"Thank you, Calliope. Did you want me to open it now?"

"Yes." She beams.

Reign's eyes meet mine and he shrugs before shaking his hair back into place so only his lips and nose are visible.

Tearing through the paper with Calliope's bright eyes on me, I pull a bracelet loose from the packaging. Looking closer, I can tell it's made out of hemp with an intricate red and black herringbone design and my initials, W K, in bold, black letters in the center. I stare at it until my vision blurs. I've received a million gifts. None have been as thoughtful as this.

"Do you not like it?" I hear the concern in her voice. "You wear red the most, and I thought the black went nice and—"

I blink, getting rid of the tears, but my voice is thick with emotion. "I love it. Thank you, Calliope."

"You're welcome! Reign has a matching one with his initials and the color blue." Grabbing his wrist, she holds it up, showing a bracelet identical to mine.

He has a few more on his wrist that I'm sure Calliope made for him. "You make nice bracelets."

"I want to open up a shop online." I hear the uncertainty in her voice.

"Why haven't you?" I ask, putting the bracelet on, pulling the sliding knot to tighten it.

"What if no one buys them?"

"You'll never know if you don't try."

"That's what I told her," Reign chimes in.

Calliope narrows her eyes in his direction. "You're one to talk, you won't even share your art with anyone."

"I share it with you," he says defensively.

She rolls her eyes, shaking her head. "I guess that's enough for now."

I chuckle at their exchange. Reign ignores her, giving me his attention. "I didn't think you'd be here till later."

"That was the plan, but I needed to ask you something."

He brushes his hair out of his eyes, giving me a curious look. Calliope lets out a long sigh as she grabs his hair, pulling it into a bun and ties her scrunchie around it. "Cut your hair! No one can see your eyes! I'm surprised you don't run into walls."

Reign scowls, side eyeing her. "What did you want to ask?"

"Would you be interested in going to the Mayor's Charity Gala at the art museum on Friday?"

His eyes widen. "You want to take me?"

"Ooooh, a gala?" Calliope squeals. "Reign, you better go!"

"Yeah." I chuckle.

His brow furrows and his shoulders slump a little. "I don't have anything to wear to that."

"It's fine. I'll take care of everything if you want to go."

"I do." He gives me a rare smile. "I heard they have the Basquiat exhibit there right now."

"Alright, let's get you a tux." I gesture for him to get up and follow me. "Now?"

"Yeah." I look around the rec room. "Unless you're busy."

"He's not," Calliope answers for him, nudging his arm.

"I can speak." Reign looks at her before turning his attention back to me. "I'll go. I'm not busy."

"Okay, let's go."

As soon as Reign stands, Calliope wraps him in a tight hug. "Reign, I'm so excited for you. Have fun for me, okay?"

He holds his arms out to the side as if he's not sure what to do with them, looking down at her. Finally, he hugs her back, saying, "Okay, Calliope."

She releases him and smiles at me. "If anyone deserves good things, it's Reign."

"Thanks, Cal," Reign says with his eyes on the ground.

"Now, go." She gently nudges him, pulling her scrunchie from his hair.

After signing out, he follows me to my car. I open the driver's door and notice Reign is standing there with his hands in his pockets.

"You good?" I open the door.

Looking down at his shoes, he looks back at the car. "I can't get in there. My shoes are dirty and—"

"You belong in every space, Reign. Get in."

I didn't consider taking a less flashy car. The keys to the Bentley Bentayga were the first I grabbed. If I didn't have the customization of the matte white exterior and the red leather interior it'd probably look less luxe. That's not my style though.

Reign looks at it for a few seconds longer, letting out a sigh as he pulls the handle to get in. "This is a really, *really* nice car."

"Thank you." I press the start button, back out, and pull onto the road. "Do you have your license?"

"No." He shakes his head, looking out the window. "My dad was teaching me, though."

"If you want... I could teach you. You can pick any of my cars to learn." His eyes snap toward me. "Within reason," I add.

"How many do you have?"

"Enough." I smile. "Did you still want to learn?"

"Yeah. I'd like that."

"Cool. We can set up some times. Oh, you may want to text your grandma and tell her you'll be a little later this evening."

"I don't have a phone," he mumbles so quietly I almost don't hear him.

Coming to a stop at a red light, I ask, "How do you text Calliope?"

He shrugs. "My grandma's phone."

I couldn't imagine texting the girl I like from my mom's phone let alone my grandma's. "Have you ever had a phone?"

"Yeah, but I shattered the screen after..." His voice trails off. "I got angry and threw it. My grandma said kids my age don't need phones, anyway."

I scowl as I focus on the road. Reign is seventeen. I've seen Kindergarteners with phones. "Would she care if you had one?"

"She doesn't care what I do as long as I don't cause her any trouble."

"Do you get along with her?"

"Yeah..." He shrugs his shoulder. "She's always been there. My mom left shortly after I was born. My grandma has always been my mother figure. She's loving in her own way. If tough love counts."

Being someone who's done their fair share of fucking up, tough love was rarely the answer. I just needed to know someone cared about me beyond my flaws.

"Does she think you're difficult?" The belief that he's difficult had to come from someone. I bet it was his grandma. I'm not one to pass judgement without knowing someone, but I already don't like this woman.

"Yep." He blows out a puff of air, resting his head against the seat.

"You need to stomp that narrative out." I pull to a stop at a red light, looking at him. "You hear me?"

He nods, and I see the uncertainty in his eyes.

"Reign, I'm serious. Stomp that shit out. Create your own narrative. You told me you're not difficult, right?"

"I'm not."

"Believe it when you say it." I focus on the road when the light turns green.

"Did you feel lost without your dad?"

Pulling into the parking lot of the tux shop, I park and turn off the car. "I was terribly lost for a long time."

"And now?"

"Now... I'm learning who I am."

"Will I be lost?" He smooths his hair out of his face, and his eyes are glossy.

"Nah. You'll never be lost. You got me."

I've never seen Reign smile as brightly as he is looking at himself in the mirror dressed in a perfect tailored tux. He even pulled his hair out of his face.

"What do you think?"

"I look like John Wick, but handsomer."

I toss my head back with laughter, enjoying this carefree side of him. "Chill. It's not bullet proof. You look smooth as hell, though."

"Exquisite taste, Mr. DeLeon," Ramsey, the tailor, says as he tilts his head from side to side, admiring his work. "And for you Mr. King?"

"The dark green one we talked about."

"Certainly." Ramsey nods. "Did you want to try it on?"

"I want to see it." Reign looks at me in the mirror.

"I guess I will."

Ramsey leaves briefly to grab the tux and takes it to one of the dressing rooms for me. Disappearing behind the curtain, I try on the tux that perfectly fits thanks to Ramsey. Now that Reign is going, I'm looking forward to the gala. I was dreading it because I usually go to the events for the open bar and beautiful women. While both will be readily available, I have no desire to indulge in either.

Reign is still admiring himself when I step back into the fitting room. Standing beside him, he smiles at me.

"Your tux is nice! I like the dark green." Reign's tux is classic black. I wanted something different and chose dark green, almost black, with some detailing on the satin lapels. "Will we take pictures while we're there? I have to show Calliope."

"Yeah, there will be professional photographers. I'll make sure I'll get some for you and Calliope." I look at myself in the mirror, deciding I want some new shoes to go with it. "Ramsey, do you have brown shoes in stock?"

"Style?"

"Mmm…" I tilt my head to the side. "Oxfords. And then black boots for Reign. I saw the new Gucci ones on the way in. Add a pair for me too. Reign, tell him your size?"

"Isn't Gucci expensive?" Reign wrinkles his brow.

"Yes." I meet his gaze in the mirror.

"I don't know that—"

"Nah," I turn to face him. "Replace that 'I don't know' with 'I deserve'."

He quickly glances at Ramsey and then down to the floor.

Pulling on his shoulder, I coax him to face the mirror. "Look yourself dead in the eye and say, 'I deserve this'. Gotta change that narrative, my boy."

"I… deserve this." His voice rises at the end.

"Is it a question or a statement?" The corner of my mouth tips up.

"I deserve this."

"Good." I clap his shoulder, giving him a smile. "Say it again and mean it."

"I deserve this." Reign grins.

"Damn right you do."

One thing Dad taught me and my brothers is to always lift ourselves up in a world that will try to tear us down. It's the only reason my confidence remains high even when I doubt myself.

"I'll be back with those shoes."

After trying on the shoes and changing back into our clothes, Ramsey lets us know Reign's tux will be ready Thursday.

"If you're comfortable, do you want to come to my place to get ready before the gala on Friday?"

"Yeah."

"Okay, I'll talk to Hudson and see about picking you up after school on Friday."

He groans. "I have to go to school?"

"Go to school or kiss the gala goodbye."

Straightening up, he brushes his hair out of his face, letting me catch the eye roll. I feel a mix of amusement and annoyance. "Fine," he huffs. "I'll go."

"Every single day this week, Reign. Not just Friday."

"I got it." He crosses his arms.

I stop the smile from forming on my lips. Reign is an old soul. It feels good to see him behave like a teenager. He shouldn't have to worry about anything expect going to school. That seems to be an issue for him, even if he is attending more classes since we met.

"Is that all today, Mr. King?" I nod. "Are you wanting to settle your balance now?"

"Yeah, I'll take care of it now."

"Just five thousand two hundred dollars today, Mr. King."

Reign's elbow slips off the counter. Chuckling, I hand my card to Ramsey. "Class, Reign. Every day."

"I promise, Winter." Regaining his composure, he straightens up.

Ramsey hands the card to me. "The items will be delivered to your house Thursday afternoon. Always a pleasure doing business with you, Mr. King."

"See you soon, Ramsey." I nod. "Let's go, Reign. Did you want to look at anything else?"

"No." He shakes his head. "You've done enough for me already. Thank you."

"Are you hungry?"

"I'll never say no to food." He rubs his stomach.

I take him to Urbane Bites and introduce him to their chicken fettuccine alfredo. Watching him eat makes me wonder how my parents kept me and my brothers fed. He's like a loose lawn mower, taking down everything in his path. I'm not sure where it goes either, given his tall and lanky frame.

Slurping down the last of his soda, he leans back against the seat with a satisfied sigh. "That was good."

"Really?" I let my jaw drop dramatically. "I couldn't tell."

He smiles. "Thank you for the food."

"Thanks for agreeing to be my plus one to this gala."

"You didn't want to go?"

"Yes and no. I'm doing it more as a favor for... a friend." That's the easiest explanation.

"That's nice of you. I bet they appreciate it."

I remember Eve reluctantly sitting in my office, asking for help. "I'm sure she does. Did you want dessert?"

"No, thank you." He holds up his hand. "I'm good."

"Alright, let's get out of here. I have one more stop to make before getting you back to True's House."

Twenty minutes later, I pull into a parking space in front of a small shopping mall. "Did you want to get out?" Reign looks like he's two seconds from falling asleep with his head lulling to the side. "You're welcome to wait here, too."

Yawning, he looks around. "I'll go with you."

He falls in step beside me as I make my way to the electronics store. Reign is instantly distracted by the TVs and gaming systems.

"I've just gotta pick something up. I'll be at the counter."

He nods without sparing a glance as he eyes the PS5. I've never asked about his grandma's financial situation. I did a bit of research and know they're receiving survivor benefits since his dad was a firefighter. However, that money goes to his grandma since she's his legal guardian. Reign hasn't said a bad word about her, even if it's clear there's some tension between them.

Reaching the counter, I pay for the item I ordered and head toward where Reign is playing a demo on the PS5. Once he's done, I hold the box in my hands out to him. It takes a second for him to register what I'm holding.

"I can't accept this." He quickly glances at me and then at the box, sliding his hands in his pockets.

"Why not?" I tilt my head to the side.

"Because you've spent a lot of money on me today." He shakes his head, taking a step back.

"Do you want a phone?" I raise my brows.

He rubs his hand along the back of his neck. "Yeah, but that's not the point."

"So... what's the point?"

"I–it's–I'm... why are you so nice to me?" He tilts his head to the side, causing his hair to fall out of his eyes as he looks at me. "Most people haven't given me a second thought, my grandma included, and here you are doing everything you can for me after only meeting a few weeks ago."

It makes sense why he does everything he can to not take up space. "Because you deserve good things, Reign."

"Yeah, but—"

"Nah." I hold up my hand, causing him to close his mouth. "You deserve good things. That's a full sentence. Maybe if you went to English

class you'd know that." He sucks his teeth, laughing. "Take the phone."
I hold it out to him again.

He finally takes the box. "I'll start going to class."

I raise a speculative brow.

"All of them," he adds. "Every day."

"You've gotta show up for yourself, Reign. Even if no one else does." I
offer him a smile. "It's all connected, you only need to turn it on. There
should be a case in there, too. And—"

Reign wraps his arms around me. For a few seconds, I'm unsure of
what to do with myself. After the initial shock, I return the hug.

"Thanks, Winter." He pulls away just as quickly as he hugged me,
sniffing and wiping his nose.

"You're welcome." My voice is heavy with emotion. "Uh... I should
probably get you back so you can catch a ride with Calliope."

He nods, focusing on the box in his hands as he opens it and follows
me out the store. Back in the car, he powers it on, and I see the smile
on his face which makes me smile. I wasn't sure about this mentorship
initially. Now I realize I needed a friend just as much as he does.

"Can I ask you something?" I feel his eyes on me as we speed down the
road.

"Shoot."

"Do you think... if you have time... that you could take me to get a
haircut?"

I glance between him and the road.

"It's just that I want to look nice for the gala and Calliope is always
talking shit – I mean stuff – about my hair being too long."

At a red light, I meet what I can see of his eyes through the curtain of
his hair. "Do you *want* to get a haircut or are you cutting it because of
Calliope?"

He focuses on the red light. "My dad used to cut my hair. He worked at a barbershop before becoming a firefighter. When he died, I let it grow out because I didn't want anyone else touching my hair."

My eyes water. The road becomes blurry, blinking hard, I feel tears clinging to my lashes when I reopen them. "Are you sure you want to get it cut now?"

"I do." He traces the outline of his phone with his finger. "I was just worried no one could cut it how he did. And I mean... I know no one will, but... I want to look nice for this event."

"I can take you to my barber. When did you want to go?"

"Whenever you have time."

Since the gala is on Friday, I have more than usual to do this week than I normally would. "I can take you today or on Thursday. Your choice."

"We can go today since we're already out."

"Are you comfortable with me dropping you off at your house later? I'm not sure how busy he'll be on a Saturday afternoon."

He shrugs as I pull onto the freeway. "That's fine."

"Text Calliope and tell her so she doesn't wait for you."

"I don't have a – never mind." He grabs his phone as I laugh. "It's been a while. She's gonna be so happy she can now bother me whenever she wants."

Something tells me he's also happy about it. I keep the thought to myself. "Have you and Calliope been friends long?"

"Since last summer. Her mom passed away from breast cancer a few weeks before my dad."

"I'm sorry to hear that."

"Yeah. We met in a messed-up way, but I'm happy—" His phone rings before he can finish his sentence.

"Hello," Reign answers and I hear Calliope's energetic voice at the other end.

"Yeah, it's me." He sucks his teeth. "No, Cal, I didn't steal the phone."

I hear her laugh, and I try to keep a straight face.

"Yeah, I'm sure about the ride. I'll be at school tomorrow."

I see him glance my way out of the corner of my eye.

"I promise. Yes, yes I'll call. Bye, Cal." He hangs up the phone.

"If I find out you're skipping school this week—"

"I know. I know. No event. No phone. I got it."

"You better." I pull into a space in front of the barbershop. Unsurprisingly, it's busy. "You're too smart to count yourself out."

He lets out an exasperated sigh. "I know." Even though he's annoyed, there's a faint smile on his lips.

I playfully rub my knuckles against his head, making him laugh as he ducks away from me. "Ready to be able to see where you're going?"

His only response is a smile as we enter the shop.

Cru, the owner, throws up his hands giving me a head nod. "What up, Winter?"

I slap my hand against his, giving him a dap, pulling him into a quick hug. I've known Cru since high school. "My friend here wants a cut. Do you have time?"

"If you don't mind waiting." He glances back at the person in the chair. "I have one person after him. Then I can get to..."

"Cru, this is Reign."

Reign shakes Cru's hand. "Nice to meet you."

"Do you know what you want done? I don't do braiding or—"

"I want the top long, not this long," He runs a hand through his curls. "With faded sides. Like this." He shows him a picture on his phone.

Cru nods. "I got you. How long do you want the top?

"About the same length as the picture."

This is the first time I've heard Reign be assertive. I'm glad to see he'll speak up for himself.

"Bet. Give me about forty-five minutes."

"Thanks, man." I nod to Cru.

We find empty seats, and Reign holds his phone out to me. My eyes focus on a picture from his Instagram. "That's me and my dad."

They look like twins with the same curly black hair, full, defined eyebrows, hazel eyes, deep tawny skin, full lips, and chiseled facial features. "Damn, he made you himself?"

He laughs. "Looks like it, huh?"

"Yeah. You two look like brothers more than father and son." In the picture, his dad is looking at the camera, laughing and Reign is looking at his dad with the biggest smile on his face.

"He was confused for my brother a lot and definitely didn't look his age. Not that he was old. He was only thirty-five."

My eyes widen. "He was the same age as me? That means he had you... in high school?"

"Yeah." He nods his head. "My mom got pregnant their senior year. According to my dad, that was why they split. She wanted to be a teenager with no responsibility even after I was born. Eventually, she left. As I got older, my curiosity grew too, and I looked her up. She's married with two kids. From what she posted online; they have a good life."

My heart sinks for him. "It doesn't bother you?"

"At first it did." He sprawls out in the chair, sliding down so far his head rests on the back of it. "Then I wondered, why would I want someone in my life who so clearly doesn't want me in theirs? That's when I let it go."

"How old were you?"

"This was two years ago... so fifteen."

"Fifteen," I gape at him. "And you came to such a profound realization?"

A smile tugs at his lips. "Just because I'm not in school regularly doesn't mean I'm an idiot."

"No, but you are an idiot if you stifle your brilliance."

"Touché." He makes a finger gun, pointing it at me. "Don't worry, Warden. I'll be in school."

I let out a rumble of laughter. "And I thought you were quiet."

"I am. Until I'm comfortable."

His words make me smile. We continue talking until it's Reign's turn to sit in the chair. He interacts with Cru as if he's known him for years. Cru has that effect on people. He makes you feel comfortable and, above all, welcomed. When I returned to the Valley, he picked up like I never left. I needed that. Someone who didn't give a fuck about the past. Who only saw the version of me that I was in that moment and accepted me.

I watch Reign's curls float to the ground as Cru moves around him. When he told me he wanted to cut his hair, I needed to be sure it was his idea. I know he cares about Calliope, but I don't want him to do things for the sake of her. He needs to consider himself too. That was a hard lesson for me to learn.

Before I went into a tailspin, my life consisted of doing what was expected of me and being a people pleaser. Dad never forced taking over the company on me, but it was an expectation. One that I knew if I didn't fulfill, disappointment would follow. His love for me has never been a question. That doesn't mean it was free of expectations. As the oldest, I was *expected* to be an example and take care of our family's legacy.

Not only did I not know who I was without Dad's guidance, I also struggled with the fact an entire, multi-million dollar company was expecting me to be exactly like Dad, if not better. Those thoughts suffocated me until the only way I felt I could breathe was by leaving it all behind. The issues with Eve only exacerbated the feeling.

I see parts of myself in Reign as if I'm looking in the mirror at a younger version of myself. The version of me who was trying to figure out life without their dad. He has a better head on his shoulders then I did at his age. If I was a disaster losing Dad at twenty-five, I couldn't imagine going through that at seventeen and then having no one. Well, he has his grandma, but I don't entirely trust that relationship yet.

Reign's hair litters the floor around him. I snap a few pictures just in case he wants to remember this moment. A text comes in as I'm putting my phone back in my pocket. Pulling it out, I see it's a text from Snow.

Snow: Are we getting together today?

Looking outside, I didn't realize how late it was. The sun is setting behind the mountains.

Winter: I'll see you guys tomorrow.
North: Where have you been?
Winter: With Reign.
Snow: He's been good for you.
North: Are we not good enough?
Winter: And I'm the dramatic one?
North: Are we allowed to meet him since he seems to be our fourth long lost brother?

I snort with laughter. I've never known North to be jealous. Before I can respond, my attention is pulled back to Reign when Cru pulls the cape from his neck with a snap. For a second, I don't recognize Reign. A man is standing in front of me. Not the shy boy I met weeks ago. His hair looks exactly like it was in the picture with his dad. A wave of emotion ripples through me, and my heart squeezes in my chest. I wish his dad was here to see his boy and not me.

I'm grateful, and honored, Reign trusted me to be a part of this moment with him. Looking in my direction, he gives me a blinding, confident smile, walking toward me. I stand to meet him, ruffling his hair.

"You look sharp, man. Do you like it?"

"I love it." He turns toward the mirror, running his hand through it. "I think it's long enough on top that Calliope can mess around with it if she wants too."

Him and that girl. A chuckle resonates in my chest. "If she recognizes you."

"I was going to send her a picture. I think I'll wait to see if she can find me at school tomorrow."

Cru wraps his arm around Reign's shoulder. "Remember to stop by any time you need a cut."

"I will." His shyness slides back into place.

"And if you need a job, we always need help around here cleaning up, setting appointments, and shit, I just like company. You're a badass kid. I'll see you around."

Taking my wallet out, Cru shoves it back toward me. "Nah, man. Your money is no good here. Get our friend home. I'll see you next time." He gives me a dap.

I've tried arguing with Cru about not paying. He won't allow it since I invested in his shop when the bank told him no. Cru's Cuts has been thriving since he opened, making the money back within the first year.

"See you around." I smile at him.

Once we're in the car, I tell Reign to type his address into the GPS. His house is about ten minutes from the barbershop and twenty minutes from my own. With the windows down, and a smile that hasn't left Reign's face, we talk in between music. I enjoyed getting to know him on a different level today. Since meeting him, I've looked forward to the time we spend together. I'm excited for him to meet Snow and North. Maybe North was right, he is our long lost brother.

I slow down in front of a nice house in a quiet neighborhood. "Is this right?"

"Yeah, that's me."

I take note that there's no car in the driveway and the lights are off. "Is your grandma home?"

He shakes his head. "No. I'm sure she's at the casino."

Pursing my lips, I keep my judgmental thoughts to myself. "Are you going to be okay by yourself?"

"Yeah," he says, unbuckling his seatbelt. "I'm here most the time by myself anyway. I prefer it that way."

I try to keep the surprise off my face and fail. He gives me a sheepish smile.

"She just... things aren't the same without Dad."

"I understand." I say, letting him know he doesn't need to explain himself. Tensions were high between Snow and I for a while after Dad passed.

"Um... this is probably stupid," he looks down at his phone, "but can we take a picture together? We don't have to if—"

"Nah, let's take a picture."

He smiles and I lean toward him to get in the frame as he holds up the phone, snapping a few.

"Thanks... for everything today." His eyes meet mine. "It's the happiest I've been in a long time."

"You're welcome. Text or call if you need me. Did you want me to pick you up after school on Friday?"

His face lights up. "In this?"

"Look at you!" I toss my head back with laughter. "You didn't even want to get in a few hours ago."

"I deserve it." He grins.

"Damn right."

"Yeah, you can pick me up."

"Alright. See you later, Reign."

"Bye, Winter."

Getting out of the car, he waves before crossing the lawn. I wait for him to get inside, and a light illuminates a window on the other side of the house seconds later. I pull away from the curb with a smile on my face.

Truth is, Reign may need me, but I need him too.

11
EVE

NOAH SURPRISED ME WITH a trip to his parent's house in White Pine over the weekend. It's a beautiful, small lake town two hours from Hope Valley. He's been working crazy hours lately. I jumped at the opportunity to spend time with him even if it's alongside his parents. I've met them before when we were in high school and have seen them periodically over the years. Now that we're dating, his mom insists I join him on his visits. I can't complain. They have a beautiful lakehouse, and I don't mind being around his parents... most of the time.

After a nice dinner, Noah's mom, Gwen, and I sit on the veranda, enjoying wine and conversation while Noah plays pool with his dad, Henry. Since Noah is their only child, Gwen is elated that we're together. Like me, Noah hasn't dated a lot. He was too focused on medical school to even entertain the idea. Noah not wanting anything serious and me not being ready to commit to anyone created the perfect situation for us to fulfill each other's base desires. It was perfect until Noah graduated, got his dream job, and wanted more... *with me.*

"How are things at the clinic?" Gwen sets her glass down on the small table sitting between us.

"Great." I smile. "It was worth all the work."

"I'm happy to hear that. Both you and Noah are so goal driven. I can see why you're together."

Pouring myself another glass of red wine, I settle into the seat and cross my legs. "He gets me."

"Now that both of you are secure in your jobs, maybe you can focus on each other a little more."

I watch the sunset glimmer across the lake. Did Noah say something about me not giving him enough attention? The majority of my free time is spent with him. "What do you mean?"

I feel her eyes on me and decide to meet her gaze. "There's more to life then working."

"I know that." I laugh lightly. "Neither Noah nor my friends would ever allow me to bury myself in my work."

Gwen gives me a pointed look that I return with a little more fire while taking a long sip of my wine. "Don't you want kids?"

Catching me off guard, I spill on my white cashmere Chanel jacket. "Um..." I wipe the wine dribbling down my chin. She looks at me unphased, taking a sip from her glass as if to say *'checkmate'*. "One day. Eventually." I add to let her know that 'one day' isn't going to be any day soon.

"I dream of being a grandma. Preferably soon," she sighs. "I'm not getting any younger, and if I'm not, you're definitely not either, are you?" She laughs at her own terrible joke.

If Noah Kincaid has one flaw, it's his mother. "I didn't realize my age was a concern."

"Oh dear, it isn't, but–" she tips her half empty glass in my direction " –if we're talking fertility, yours is declining."

This *bitch*. I set my wine aside to keep from throwing it in her eyes. "I've known plenty of women who have babies in their forties."

"Forties?" Her voice rises. "You plan to wait until your forty to have a baby?!" She literally clutches her string of shimmery pearls around her neck. "Don't you want to get married?"

"Noah and I have only been dating a couple of months." We haven't even gotten to 'I love you' yet, let alone discussing marriage.

"Henry and I were engaged in three months."

No longer caring to keep my attitude locked away, I scoff and I stand. "Unless you're going to be the one who puts a baby in me—" she audibly gasps "—what me and my declining fertility are doing is none of your business. Now if you'll excuse me," I say, my tone brash, "I need to attempt to get this stain out of my sweater before it sets."

I don't bother waiting for a response, heading into the house. The urge to pack my shit and take Noah's car is strong. Instead, I head to the guest room where we're staying. I let out a deep sigh once the door is closed. Calming myself, I take off my jacket, cursing when I see the size of the stain. I mutter angrily as I enter the bathroom and turn on the cold water. Setting my jacket aside, I search the cabinets for a clean washcloth. When I find one, I turn and run into Noah, making me jump.

"Jesus!" I put my hand over my heart as it races. "I didn't hear you."

Placing his hand at the nape of my neck, he pulls me toward him and presses a kiss to my forehead. "Didn't mean to scare you."

I melt into him. "You're fine. I just—"

Pulling back, he searches my face. "What happened?"

"Your mother." I reach around him for the jacket.

He groans, wrapping his arms around my waist and kisses my neck. "What did she say?"

"Oh, you know..." I shrug, dabbing at the stain with the cold water, feeling relief when I see it's coming out. "That we need to focus on each other because I'm not getting any younger. Also, did you know my fertility is declining with each second we stand here talking about it?"

The mortified look on his face makes me laugh.

"And," I point my finger at him, "we're falling behind because your parents were engaged three months after meeting?"

"Did she tell you why they got engaged?" He holds my gaze in the mirror's reflection.

I shake my head, turning off the faucet.

"I am the product of a one-night stand."

My mouth falls open as I gasp. "Perfect little Gwen Kincaid had a one night stand?!"

He chuckles, nodding. "Yep. My dad didn't even want kids, until they had me. He married her because he felt it was the 'right thing to do'."

My eyes widen.

"They love each other now," he continues. "But I'll never let her pressure you or make you feel like shit over something that wasn't a fairytale for her."

"I'm... shocked." No wonder Gwen doesn't seem to care about the emotional aspect of our relationship. "And really grateful I didn't throw my wine in her face like I was itching to do."

He tosses his head back, letting out a rumble of laughter. "You wouldn't have been wrong, however, I'm grateful you didn't."

"I must admit." Turning around in his arms, I wrap mine around his neck. "I got a small bit of satisfaction out of telling her my declining fertility is none of her business unless she's the one putting a baby in me."

He laughs, gaping at me with raised brows. "I am going to hear about that shit for the rest of her life and probably beyond the grave."

"It was that or wine."

"She'll be alright. You're good though, right?" He kisses the top of my head, placing his hands on either side of my face, he brings my gaze to his. "Right?"

"Yeah." I smile, trying to keep her words from repeating in my head. She's not the first or last person who will bring up the fact I'm unmarried and childless. Whenever the topic comes up, I instinctively think of Winter. I dreamed of that with him. For the longest, I was convinced our first child would be a girl because I dreamt of her. When I told Winter about the dream, he wasted no time looking up baby names and insisted we pick one out. He chose the first name, and I picked the middle. There are so many things that will always cause me to think of him, even if someone who is deserving of all of my love is standing in front of me.

"Okay." He presses a kiss to my lips. Pulling away slightly to look into my eyes, he leans in for another kiss.

This time, I deepen it, wrapping my arms tightly around his neck and slipping my tongue into his mouth. He groans, and it has me wanting to climb up his body. As if he's reading my mind, he smooths his hands over the curve of my ass, squeezing it, before gripping my thighs to pick me up. Wrapping my legs around his waist, he takes me to the bedroom.

We crash onto the bed. He breaks the kiss to sit up, grabbing my hips, pulling me to the edge. I can't help but smile as he unbuttons my pants, sliding them off my legs.

"Noah, please tell me that door has a lock." I wouldn't put it past Gwen to interrupt us mid-orgasm.

He gives me a sultry smile as he sinks to his knees. "It's been locked. I came up here with the intention of tasting you."

"Is that right?" I bite my lip as he grips my hips, pulling me closer to the edge of the bed.

Noah places my legs over his shoulders, tugging my panties to the side. "Yes." He slowly drags his tongue over my clit, causing me to fall back onto the bed with a moan.

♔

We arrived home late last night. Thankfully, Gwen didn't bring up marriage or babies the rest of the weekend. She acted as though nothing happened. I don't know if that's better or worse. Regardless, I had fun taking the boat out on the lake with Noah and Henry. What matters most is that Noah enjoyed himself. Sometimes you just need your parents no matter how old you are.

Before heading to the clinic, I stop by Flapjack's Brew for a much needed cup of coffee. I type out a text to the group chat I have with Elle and Aspen.

Eve: Are we still going dress shopping today?

Since I was in White Pine over the weekend, we had to postpone our trip to get gowns for the gala. I have a few on hold. Hopefully one of them fits me like a glove without needing too many alterations. The gala is only days away.

Elle: Yes! I don't have shit to wear.
Aspen: Say the word and I'm there.

I text them the time to meet and the address to the shop. Sliding my phone back into my bag, I smile at the barista when the customer in front of me moves off to the side.

"What can I get you?"

Before I can answer, a voice with a timbre I would recognize anywhere speaks for me. "Iced white chocolate caramel breve with whip for her and I'll have a hazelnut macchiato, please."

The barista nods with a smile. "Name?"

"Winter." Brushing past me, he taps his card to pay.

Our eyes catch. "I can order myself, thank you."

"You're welcome." He gently grabs my arm, pulling me aside to let the next person order.

"What if that's not what I wanted?"

"I can change it." He gives me a nonchalant shrug of his shoulders. "Something tells me if it isn't what you wanted, you wouldn't have hesitated to correct me." Looking down his shoulder at me, he waits for a protest he knows isn't coming.

"I'm surprised you remember."

Winter stares straight ahead as we stand shoulder to shoulder, well more like my shoulder to his upper arm, waiting for our drinks. After a few beats of silence, he speaks.

"I remember everything. Your favorite color is green. You're afraid of the dark and terrified of thunder and lightning, but love dancing in the rain. I remember that you can eat your weight in pasta if given the opportunity. Summer is your favorite season because you hate being cold and you love fourth of July because of the fireworks."

Winter reads me as though he wrote the book. All I can do is listen as he recalls the little things that make up who I am.

"I remember you religiously make wishes on 11:11 and refuse to tell anyone what you wished for because then it won't come true. And surprisingly enough," he says, smiling at me, "you believe in aliens and thought you could work in the X-Files with Scully and Mulder as a kid. I—"

"Winter!" the barista calls, interrupting him.

He leaves my side to grab the coffee and returns seconds later, holding it out to me. I take the cup, grazing my fingertips against his. The smallest touch causes my heart to thrum.

"Thank you, but you forgot one thing." Raising a brow, he brings his cup of coffee to his lips, watching me as he takes a sip. "I'd still like to work in the X-Files."

Winter lets out a deep rumble of laughter. "Do you still binge watch it?"

He bought me the box set for my birthday one year. "Yeah. It's my comfort show." I smile, remembering how my brothers and I used to watch it with Mom on Friday nights when it was on TV.

"I thought you were bullshitting when you told me you believe in aliens that one night. Took everything in me not to talk shit while listening to you state your case as to why we're 'not alone'." He wiggles his fingers as if giving off creepy vibes.

I giggle, remembering stargazing on the trampoline in the backyard with him. "You still don't—"

"Eve and Winter! It's lovely to see you two together again." Sunday comes toward us with open arms and a smile and wraps her arms around us, pushing Winter and I chest to chest. He loops his arm around my waist to keep me steady when Sunday lets go.

"Hi, Sunday." I smile brightly.

"I just knew you two would find your way back to each other." She clasps her hands underneath her chin with stars in her eyes as she looks at us.

"We're not together..." I shift my weight, glancing up at Winter.

"Oh..." Sunday's eyes flit to Winter's arm still wrapped around my waist.

I try to step to the side, but he slides his hand up the column of my spine, bringing it to my shoulder, gently squeezes it. Moving suddenly feels impossible as a subtle shudder ripples through me. Or at least I thought it was subtle. Winter picks up on it, flashing me a smile.

"Only *friends*, Sunday."

The word 'friends' referring to *us* sounds foreign. Could we ever be friends?

"She was in line with me, and I thought I'd buy her coffee."

"Always the gentleman. Well..." She smiles and sighs, looking at Winter's hand still resting on my shoulder, then between the two of us. "I'm happy you two are... friends. It's a start." She winks before moving onto another table of people who are waving her down.

"Thank you for the coffee, friend." I give him a sidelong glance, taking a sip.

He chuckles smoothly. "What else am I to call us? I'd like to think we're friends. You did offer me a piece of Mom's lasagna after all. If that wasn't a peace offering, I don't know what is."

"Yeah." The corners of my mouth tip up. "I guess it was. Friend is good."

"For now." He presses a kiss to my cheek. "Enjoy your coffee. I've gotta get to the office."

His touch and the kiss linger on my skin as I watch him walk out the door.

♛

Later that afternoon, a knock at my office door startles me. Looking up from my computer, I smile when my eyes land on Noah. He looks like he came straight from the hospital dressed in his hunter green scrubs with a black North Face wind breaker.

"Hey." I get up to greet him, planting a kiss on his lips. "You didn't want to go home and get some rest?"

"I will after I spend some time with you." With him on night shift, we weren't getting much time together. "I'm not interrupting, am I?"

"No. And even if you were I'd make time for you."

"Good. You'll have lunch with me then?" He holds up a bag of food that smells so good my mouth waters.

"Of course I will. What did you bring me?"

"Yellow rice with chicken and a side of plantains from that one Puerto Rican restaurant you like."

I give him another kiss. "Thank you."

Handing me the bag, he takes a seat on one of the plush chairs in front of my desk while I pull out the contents of the bag.

"What did you get?" I ask.

"Mofongo with the steak."

"Can I try it?" I give him an impish smile along with my question.

He uncovers his food. "Do I have a choice?"

"Yes, but only one of them is correct." I say, pointing a plastic fork at him.

Noah has a glint of humor in his eyes. "I'll share with you."

"That is correct." I kiss his cheek before taking a seat beside him. Before I can dig into my own food, he holds up his plate, waiting for me to taste it. "You're giving me the first bite?"

"Hurry before I change my mind and don't offer you any."

I gasp, laughing as I listen, dipping my fork into the food, and take a bite. "That's so good," I say, covering my mouth with my hand. "I'll get that next time."

"Good. Then I won't have to share."

I narrow my eyes in his direction. Sharing food is an annoyance Noah tolerates. The first time he told me no, I thought he was joking until we had our first disagreement over it. His point was if I wanted his food then I should've ordered what he got. To be the brat that I am, I took a bite anyway. Now he accepts the fact that I will inevitably ask for a bite and shares with me.

"How's your day been?" he asks.

"Good. I'm going shopping with the girls. I still need a dress for the gala. Do you have a tux?"

He swallows his bite. "Yeah. I just need to pick it up."

"Do you want me to do it?" I take a bite of a tostone.

"If you don't mind? I'm on call until Thursday, and I'd rather not have to worry about it."

"I'll pick it up on my way to get my dress."

Since Noah is an ER doctor, he's often on call. I try to help where I can so he's not stressed. He's a lot like me, trying to do everything on his own. We've had to learn to accept help from one another.

We don't talk much in between bites as we finish our food. Noah takes his last bite before me, closing the lid of the container. Getting up to toss it in the trash, he grabs the now empty coffee cup off my desk. He pauses, looking down at the cup that has Winter's name scrawled across it.

"Winter brought you coffee?" He tears his eyes away from the cup, focusing on me.

I shake my head, swallowing my bite of food. "No. We ran into each other at Flapjack's and he bought me coffee."

Noah nods slowly, looking at Winter's name again. "Oh. That's nice of him."

"Yeah..." My voice trails off, wondering if he's jealous of Winter.

Only weeks ago, he was encouraging me to talk to him about sponsorship. And now he seems... I don't know what he seems like because Noah is usually agreeable. However, with the way he's looking at the cup, like it'll tell him some secret, maybe he's second guessing his past encouragement.

"Come spend the night at my place," he says after a moments silence with his eyes still on the cup.

Setting my fork in the container, I set it aside. "Does it bother you that he bought me coffee?"

"What?" He tears his eyes away from the cup, crushing it in his hand, and he tosses it in the trash along with the food container. "No. You two were just in the same place at the same time, and he was kind enough to pay for your coffee. You got free coffee; how can I be bothered by that?"

Getting up, I wrap my arms around his middle and rest my chin on his chest, looking up at him. "You can be bothered, Noah. It's okay... if the roles were reversed, I'd have your head for even blinking in your exes direction."

He laughs, covering his face with his hands before scrubbing them over his eyes. "I'm not bothered."

I raise my brows, trying to keep the smile off my face.

"Alright, I'm a little bothered. You two have deep history, and I don't feel like him buying you a cup of coffee is just him buying you a cup of coffee."

Knowing Winter, it wasn't solely out of the goodness of his heart even if he was being kind. "Why did you encourage me to talk to him about sponsorship?"

"If I offered, you weren't going to accept it."

"Definitely would've shut that shit down."

He chuckles. "Exactly. So if Winter was your only available option, at least you'd get what you need."

"And what do *you* need?"

"You," he says, leaning closer.

I press up onto my toes for him to kiss me.

"You've got me," I mutter against his lips. "Not just now, but tonight too."

Pulling back slightly, I look at him through my lashes.

Desire flashes in his eyes. "I may quit my job if I get called into work tonight."

My shoulders shake with laughter. "I won't be long dress shopping, then you have me all to yourself."

"Love the sound of that." His words are cut off by a yawn. "Let me get home and sleep before I'm all talk no action."

Noah tightly wraps his arms around me before giving me a kiss that's a preview of what's to come.

After saying goodbye, I finish up my food and return to work. Before Noah stopped by, I was working on the budget for the additional services we want to offer here at Hope's Village. Hopefully we can secure most of the funding at the gala. Which leads me to my next task, finding resources in case the gala isn't as successful as I'm hoping for it to be.

My phone chimes with a text, pulling my attention away from my computer screen.

Winter: How was your coffee?

I lean back in my seat, typing a response with the faintest smile on my lips.

Eve: Good. Although my boyfriend saw your name on my cup.
Winter: My name being on that cup is the least of his worries.
Does he know who I am?
Eve: Yes.

I want to add '*you know him too*' but think better of it. It's hard not to tell him everything. I have to remind myself we're not best friends anymore.

Winter: His eyes are wide shut then. Again, this sounds like a personal issue. You should get that checked out by a doctor.
Eve: You're fucking irritating.
Winter: I'm concerned for your health. How is that irritating?
Winter: Isn't that what friends are for?
Eve: You're an amazing friend Winter.
Winter: Tell your boyfriend that.
Winter: I'll hit you up another time. I'm off to lunch with Elle.

Seconds later a photo comes through of Winter with his arm around Elle's shoulders. She's looking at him confused with a smile on her face. The caption attached to it reads: How does it feel knowing I stole your best friend?

I toss my head back with laughter, refusing to feed into his petty bullshit. He knows I'm a jealous person when it comes to those I care about. Choosing peace, I set my phone aside and get back to work.

Walking into the dress shop, Elle and Aspen are already there, picking through the dresses.

"Find anything?" I ask, setting my bag on a chair.

"There you are." Elle wraps me in a hug.

I return it before hugging Aspen. "Have you been here long?"

"Not long." Aspen shrugs, returning to the dresses.

"Work kept you?" Elle asks distractedly, looking through a dress rack.

"We've thankfully had an influx of new patients which keeps me busy. I think we'll have to hire another doctor sooner rather than later." I smile. "But that's enough about work."

"That's the spirit." Aspen smiles. "What color dress are you thinking for the event?"

Delilah, the dress shop owner, appears with a smile on her face, wheeling a rack with the dresses I picked out into the fitting room.

"Eve." She gives me an air kiss on each cheek. "Wonderful to see you again. And you brought friends?"

"Of course. These are my best friends who happen to be sisters, Noelle and Aspen." I point between the two of them. "This is Delilah, the owner."

"Pleasure to meet the both of you." She gives them air kisses on the cheek too. "Did Myra already help you, or would you like me to pull a few things for you two to try on?"

"I think pulling things would be better." Elle smiles.

"Yeah," Aspen agrees.

"The three of you are so gorgeous, this will be a delight." She clasps her hands together, shimmying her shoulders. "I'll be back shortly."

"Oh, don't you need to know our sizes?" Aspen calls after her.

Delilah laughs, throwing a smirk over her shoulder. "I am very good at what I do. You'll see."

"I don't doubt her." Elle watches Delilah leave the room.

"If the dresses are anything like this–" Aspen looks through the rack Delilah brought in "–I'll give her everything in my bank account."

"That golden yellow dress would look amazing on you." Elle points at the one Aspen is holding in her hand.

Delilah reappears in the fitting room with more dresses hanging from a rack.

"Any of these will look magical on you." She smiles at Elle and Aspen.

Elle immediately reaches for the shimmering red dress, paying no mind to the rest. "Gorgeous..." She rubs the smooth fabric between her fingertips.

"Something told me red would look good on you." Delilah beams.

"I think I'm going to try on this midnight blue dress." Aspen pulls it off the rack. It has a dangerously low back that will look perfect on her. She looks at the size, smiling at Delilah. "You are amazing."

"I know." Delilah gives us a satisfied smile as we laugh. "Try them on. I'll be back shortly." She shoos us toward the dressing rooms as her eyes glitter with anticipation.

Grabbing the golden yellow dress off the rack, I head toward the dressing room and pull the curtain shut behind me. I strip out of everything but my panties, letting out a sigh of relief as I unclasp my bra. Taking the dress off the clear acrylic hanger, I already love the buttery soft velvet of the skirt. I normally wouldn't go for a yellow color for a black tie event but this looks like gold against my deep sable skin. The strapless bodice is sheer mesh with a bonded corset, giving a tasteful peek of my stomach. Velvet lines the top of the bodice and the skirt has a sexy thigh high slit.

This dress is elegantly sexy. I zip it up as far as I can before stepping out from behind the curtain.

All three of us squeal in response to our dresses. Noelle and Aspen look gorgeous.

"I knew that dress would be perfect for you. Look at the tatas on perfect display." Elle squeezes one for good measure and helps me with my zipper, making me laugh.

"You're one to talk." I grab her hip, turning her toward the mirror. "Snow won't know what to do with himself."

The deep red corset gown clings to her body as if Delilah made it for her. It has a lustrous sheen, draped neckline, straps that hang off the shoulders, and a mermaid style skirt.

"If I don't get fucked in this dress, I'm speaking to the manager." Aspen turns around, checking her ass out in the mirror in the backless, floor length dress with an eye-catching sheen. The front is halter style, coming up high on her neck and tying behind it.

"That dress is a tease," I say with a smile. "The back is so low it gives you hope that you'll get a peek of what's beneath it."

Aspen shakes her ass in response, making the fabric ripple like water as it moves over her curves. Elle and I cackle.

"I'll be upset for you if you don't get any play in that dress." Elle smacks Aspen's ass.

"Are you going with North?"

"Yeah." Aspen smiles, letting out a sigh. "But we're friends and I like being around him. I don't want to ruin it in one night and make it awkward."

"Who said it'd be awkward?" Elle pulls a pair of black strappy heels from the shelf to try on.

"I just want to be friends." Aspen readjusts the tie of the dress at the base of her neck. "It's nice to hang out with a man and not be in a fuckship situation."

"So are you not hooking up with anyone at the moment?"

"Occasionally." She smirks, shrugging her shoulder. "A girl has needs, ya know?"

"How was the weekend at Noah's parents? And what do you think of these?" Elle sweeps a stray curl out of her face after putting on the heels and lifts her dress a little to show us. "I don't know that I like how restricting this mermaid skirt is though."

"What are you trying to do?" Aspen asks, finding a pair of nude heels. "Dip it low?"

Elle answers plainly. "Yes. And I need easier access for Snow." She flashes us a smile.

"Fiend!" I toss my head back with laughter.

"I've said it once, and I'll say it again," Aspen closes her eyes, raising one palm in the air and places the other over her heart as if she's giving a sermon. "Good dick will change your life and turn you into a whole new person."

I raise my hands in the air. "Amen."

Elle falls into a fit of laughter. "I can't stand you two!"

"You're the one looking for a dress with easier access, love." I pull another red dress from the rack Delilah brought in. "Try this one on. It has a slit so Snow can bend you over."

It's very similar to the one she has on now except it has a floor sweeping train. Taking it from my hands, she disappears behind the curtain again.

"How was your weekend with Noah's parents?"

I could lie and say it was amazing, parts of it were, but the conversation with his mom put a damper on things. "Uh... it was good. Except his mom told me my fertility is declining."

Elle gasps, and Aspen snorts with laughter, trying to hold it in, but fails as she lets out a cackle.

Wrenching the curtain open, appearing in the 'easy access dress', Elle gapes at me. "She did not!"

Aspen whistles. "That's the one, sis. I'll be surprised if you two make it to the gala."

"Agreed," I add. "But you better not bail."

Elle smiles. "Thank you. I won't. Now tell us what his delusional mother said."

I give them a quick rundown of the conversation we had. "I don't want to rush into anything because society says I should have x, y, and z by a certain age."

"And you don't have to," Aspen reassures me.

"What if his mom keeps bringing it up?"

"You set a clear boundary. But you also have to ask yourself," Elle says as she grabs a pair of silver heels with thin straps, slipping one on and fastening it, "if it's something you want to deal with long term. Because if you see Noah as potential end game, his mother is also a part of that, too."

I'm not sure if Noah is *the one*. All I know is that I enjoy what we have now. While I plan for the future, it's easy to get lost in the vision and miss out on the present. However, Elle is right. I have to ask myself if I can not only accept Noah, but everything and *everyone* who comes along with him.

"Hadn't considered that," I mumble.

Delilah floats back into the room with a smile on her face. She claps her hands together. "You three look fantastic! Do you like them?"

"This dress will be perfect, Delilah. Thank you." I check myself out in the mirror again.

"You weren't wrong." Aspen spins on the spot. "This dress is perfect."

"I can't wait for my fiancé to see me," Elle says with a smile.

"You're engaged?" Delilah gasps. "Show me the ring."

Elle shamelessly holds out her hand with her brilliant smile.

"Stunning! Have you found a dress yet?"

"No. We're in the middle of moving to our home in Citrine Grove. Once that's done, I can focus more on our wedding."

"Citrine Grove is a beautiful area." Delilah releases her hand. "If you're interested, I can help you find a dress or custom design one for you."

Elle's eyes widen with surprise. "Seriously?! That'd be amazing!"

"Whenever you're ready, let me know. I'd be happy to help." Delilah gives her a warm smile. "If you're pleased with the dresses, I can get them ready for you. Once you're dressed, hang the gowns outside the door, and I'll meet you at the front of the store."

"Perfect," I say with a smile.

After we're dressed, and our gowns are hung, we walk to where the register is. "This is a gorgeous boutique," Aspen says, taking in all the décor.

Delilah's Place is a chic boutique in downtown. Baby pink and white flowers are placed around the shop as well as hanging on branches and vines from the ceiling. The ambiance is modern, yet inviting.

"How did you meet Delilah?" Elle asks as she pulls her wallet out of her bag.

I was hoping this question wouldn't come up. "She designed my wedding dress."

They gape at me, and I give them a dismissive wave of my hand.

"Stop looking at me like that. It's not that serious. I've been back since then. This isn't the first time."

It takes them a few breaths to swallow the words that were on the tips of their tongues.

"You're healing then?" Elle asks, smiling with pride.

I blink at her, not having thought about it. "Yeah, I guess I am."

"What happened to the dress?" Aspen asks, eyeing me curiously.

"I burned it."

That was healing too.

Eyes closed; I groggily feel around for my vibrating phone on the night-stand. It's one of those mornings that despite my beauty rest, I still feel like I got no sleep at all. Noah ended up spending the night at my place until he got called into work. He sent me a text around four this morning that he was going home to crash.

With my phone clutched in my hand, I stretch before silencing the alarm and bury myself beneath the covers again. Drifting off back to sleep, my phone vibrates with a text. Noah must be awake. Wiping the sleep from my eyes, I pull the covers off my head, readjust my bonnet, and unlock my phone to read the text from–

Winter: What are you wearing?

Heat warms my cheeks as my eyes widen, reading his text multiple times.

Eve: Show some decorum.
Winter: I meant for the news interview.

"That's today?" I mutter, checking my calendar. Pressing my palm to my forehead I let out a groan. The event reminder is for the wrong day, but the description of the event has the right date. That's what I get for trying to do too many things at once.

Eve: Oh. LOL. I don't know.
Winter: Nervous?
Eve: Not really. I got my days mixed up. I'm more worried about what I'll wear.

Glancing at my closet, I mentally piece together an outfit that I'd want to be seen in on TV.

Winter: What you wear should be the least of your worries.
Eve: Why do you say that?

Maybe I should've taken this interview more seriously? The reporter said it'd take less than thirty minutes. I didn't think I'd have to prepare for it.

Winter: You'll look good in anything.

Talking to him is better than a morning cup of coffee as a smile spreads across my face and my heart races.

Eve: Thank you.
Winter: Tell your boyfriend I said you're welcome. I'm doing his job with zero benefits.

I cackle, sinking into the pillows.

Eve: You have my friendship.
Winter: That's enough.
Winter: For now.
Eve: I'll see you later.

He sends me a saluting emoji in response. I stare blankly at the ceiling before sliding off the bed to get ready.

Meeting Winter in the lobby, he smiles when his eyes land on me.

"I see you found something to wear."

"Yeah." I raise my arms out to the side, looking down at my wide leg trousers cinched around my waist with a Christian Dior belt, slingback pumps, and a tight-fitting body suit. "Let's hope I don't hate how I look on TV later."

"Impossible." His eyes trail over my body from head to toe.

I smile. "You look dapper. As always." Winter's suits are always perfectly tailored. Even when he's dressed down in streetwear, his clothing fits like it was solely made for him.

He turns his smile on full wattage. "A compliment, Eve? I'm touched."

Rolling my eyes, I let out a huff of laughter. Looking through the glass doors at the entrance, I see the reporter making their way to us.

"Dr. Solis and Dr. Bradford didn't want to join us?"

"No. They said me auctioning them off is enough."

He chuckles, clearly thinking I'm joking and then stops abruptly when he realizes I'm not. "Wait... you're serious?"

The corners of my mouth tip up. "Yes. We needed something that stands out. Who wouldn't want a date with a doctor to Twisted Vines?"

"Are you up for auction?"

I tip my head back, meeting his gaze. "No. I'm just the person who coordinates."

"That's too bad."

Tilting my head to the side, I ask, "You'd bid on me?"

His eyes flick to my lips before the corner of his own tips up. "It doesn't matter. Your boyfriend will be there anyway."

The reporter finally reaches us, holding out his hand. "Hi, I'm Jordan Hawthorne."

I shake it. "Eve Valentine."

"Winter King." He shakes his hand firmly.

"Pleasure to meet you both. The interview will only take a few minutes. I think outside would be better. The design of the facility is remarkable, Miss Valentine. Would you be willing to give me a tour after the interview? I think people would love to see the inside," he says, looking around.

"I'd love to."

"Perfect. Shall we?" Jordan holds his hand up toward the entrance.

"Yes," Winter says, following him out the door.

After the interview, I give Jordan a tour and introduce him to Haven, Ilaria, and Silas. I thought Winter would leave once the interview was over, but he joins us on the tour. Not that I mind. He's a natural at communicating with people. I remember the night we met at the annual King Christmas party. Winter's mom put it on to benefit less fortunate families. My parents invited me to tag along with them to represent their dental clinic.

No one ever knows they're about to fall in love until it's too late. When I met him that night, I remember thinking he was charismatic and strikingly handsome. I didn't think anything would happen between us past an introduction until he asked me to dance. Putting my hand into his waiting one, ready to pull me onto the dance floor, sealed my fate. Even after everything that happened between us, I'm grateful he asked me for that dance.

"If you're unable to get the necessary funding, which I doubt, I'd be more than happy to do a news special. Or put you in touch with someone who can coordinate a fundraiser."

I look at Winter, realizing I've missed some of their conversation, and then at Jordan. Clearing my throat, I say, "Thank you."

Jordan pulls out his phone. "I've got to get to my next interview. Thank you both for your time. I'll see you at the charity event tomorrow."

"Pleasure to meet you." Winter shakes his hand.

I smile. "See you tomorrow."

Jordan waves, leaving Winter and I alone.

"Where'd you go just now?"

"Hm..." I look up at him questioningly.

"Just now." He points back to the hallway we came from. "You checked out. Your eyes were blank."

"Oh, nothing. I haven't eaten."

He gives me a skeptical look, raising his brow. "Your boyfriend falls for this bullshit?"

I hate that he can read me so well. "No." *Lie.*

"Right..." He draws out the word. "You walk all over him, don't you?"

"No," I say defensively. "We're partners."

"That's something business associates say, Eve. Not a couple."

I narrow my eyes at the smirk on his face. "Why do you care what I was thinking?"

"Because I could tell you weren't here. So either you enjoyed where you were more or—"

"I was thinking about the night we met."

It spills from my lips before I can stop myself. His brows knit together with confusion.

"That night, I remember you were charismatic... and okay looking."

He lets out a rumble of laughter. "Okay looking? Baby, have you seen me?"

"I'm looking right at you." *And he looks delectable.*

"Nah, give me my roses, Eve. Don't play with me."

My smile slips a little. "It's just that... Watching you talk to Jordan—you've always had a knack for charming people. I don't know." I shrug, looking away from him. "It was just a memory."

"That was an unforgettable night."

Meeting his eyes, I smile.

"Want to create another one?"

It's my turn to look confused. "What?"

"Meet me at Urbane Bites. We can sit at the bar and watch ourselves on TV."

"This sounds like a date..."

"Do you want it to be?" He smirks as I give him a bemused expression. "I'm fuckin' with you. We'll be two *friends*, having a drink, watching ourselves on TV. Or do you have to get permission from your boyfriend?"

I suck my teeth glaring at him. "No."

"Then what are you waiting for, Miss Valentine?"

I take in the smug look of victory on his face. He knew exactly what to say, and I fell for it. "Only if you buy me pasta."

"I'll have it waiting. See you at 6." He smoothly slides on his shades, leaving me wondering what the hell I'm going to tell Noah.

Pulling into the parking lot of Urbane Bites, I look at myself in the mirror. I contemplated going home and freshening up, but I didn't want to give the impression that I was looking forward to meeting with Winter. Blowing out a puff of air, I call Noelle. She picks up the video call after the second ring.

"Hey." She smiles brightly.

"Hi..." I cover my face with my hand. "I'm possibly about to do something stupid."

"How stupid?"

"Um... well, I'm sitting outside of Urbane Bites to have a drink and dinner with Winter so we can watch ourselves on TV at the bar," I rush out.

"You agreed to this?" She sounds as surprised as I am.

"He was talking shit! Asking me if I need to ask Noah for fucking permission like he's my damn daddy or some shit."

"He what?" Aspen appears on the screen.

"And your ass fell for it." Elle says. "Now look at you, conflicted in the parking lot."

"Elle!" I whine. "Come have—"

"Uh uh," Aspen cuts in, snatching the phone from her hand. "Why can't Noah save you?"

Elle cackles in the background. "I can't believe I call you two my best friends. This is mutiny!"

Pulling the phone back to herself, Elle asks, "Does Noah know?"

"No. He's at work." *I'll ask for forgiveness later. If at all.*

"How convenient," Aspen quips.

"I called you two to ask for—"

"Do you *want* to have a drink and dinner with him?" Elle asks.

"I–no–yeah... yes. I do."

"Okay... so why are you asking me for permission?"

Elle's right. Being friends with Winter is something that I didn't think I'd have, or want, to do after our split. I should've never offered him that damn lasagna.

I take a deep breath. On the exhale, I say, "Alright. I'm going in."

"Damn right you are! Never pass up free drinks and food. Have him buy a meal for Noah, too." She winks.

"I can't stand you. Bye, Elle." I laugh, hanging up the phone.

Talking to them helped me feel less stressed about this. It's only more if I make it more.

Walking into Urbane Bites, they address me by name, confirming I'm here too often. Approaching the bar, I take in Winter's broad shoulders. He's taken off his suit jacket and the sleeves of his button down are rolled up his forearm. Sliding onto the stool beside him, he turns and smiles when he sees it's me.

"Hey."

The top few buttons of his shirt are undone, exposing his gold necklaces and tattoos. Even mussed, he looks perfect.

"Hi. I—" Before I could say any more, the waiter sets a plate of chicken alfredo down in front of me and one in front of him. "Thank you," I say as I slide the plate closer to me.

The bartender appears seconds later, gently setting a bottle on the bar. "Chardonnay courtesy of Twisted Vines. Enjoy."

"Do you still come here?" I ask Winter.

"Yeah. You?"

"They know me by name—" he chuckles, "—usually I pick up the food, though."

We came to the opening of Urbane Bites together eleven years ago.

"You?" he asks.

"At least once a week."

"Much hasn't changed then?" He smiles, resting his eyes on me.

"Everything and nothing has changed."

That's exactly how I'd describe life without him. Everything changed, yet nothing changed. His absence changed everything even though I was functioning as though there wasn't a gaping hole in my chest. Life still goes on after loss whether we want it to or not. And then a breakup isn't really considered a loss. Of course I got sympathetic smiles because we were engaged, but people would immediately follow up with 'there's someone else out there'. That's easy for them to say. What happens when the person who left took the other half of your soul with them? I'm still mending the wounds from where he ripped it from my body.

Bringing his arm up, he checks the time. "Are you ready to see yourself on TV?"

Swallowing my bite, I wipe my lips with the cloth napkin. "No."

"Ready or not—" He points at the large TV mounted on the wall.

My heart races, and it suddenly feels hot in the restaurant. Setting down my fork, I'm glad I got to finish half of my pasta at least. I couldn't find my appetite with my nerves right now anyway. I'm not a shy person, but there's something about watching myself on a TV screen that makes me ridiculously nervous. Looking up at the TV, I rest my elbow on the table and rest my head in the palm of my hand.

"Tomorrow is the annual Mayor's Charity Gala, and we bring you another sponsor and business this evening," the reporter announces. "Jordan, we'll take it over to you."

Jordan, the reporter, appears on the screen, standing in front of the clinic. He gives a brief introduction and then it cuts to the interview segment of me and Winter earlier. I slide my hand over one eye and then bring up the other hand, burying my face in Winter's shoulder.

"I can't watch."

Winter just laughs.

"My voice sounds annoying! Oh my God, it sounds annoying doesn't it?"

"No." He brings his arm around my shoulders, grabbing my wrists and pulling my hands away from my eyes. He gently tips my chin up, bringing my gaze to the TV. "Look, Eve." "You're incredible, talking about what you love." His voice is a soft rumble in my ear.

Slowly opening my eyes, I watch. He's right. My eyes are alight with passion, and Winter's on my right not looking at the camera. Instead, his eyes are set on me like... I hold his entire universe. The look he's giving me on screen momentarily causes me to forget how to breathe. I can't help but wonder, does Noah ever look at me like that? Like I hold galaxies in my eyes?

My phone vibrates, pulling me from my thoughts. A text lights up my screen.

Elle: The way Winter is looking at you during this interview...
Aspen: SMITTEN!!!

I quickly flip my phone over, glancing over at Winter who has a smile on his face. Heat creeps up my neck and warms my cheeks, and I hope he didn't see those texts. The news segment isn't long, and by the end of it, I'm proud of myself.

"Thank you for inviting me here and making me watch that." I smile at him.

"Told you, you were amazing." He unwraps his arm from around my shoulder. "And for the record, I look at you exactly how you deserved to be looked at."

12
WINTER

Eve and I got lost in conversation over plates of chicken fettuccine alfredo and a bottle of wine – until her boyfriend called, asking where she was. When we pulled our gazes from one another, we realized how late it was, noticing the TV was off and the bartender was cleaning up. We were in our own world. Just like we used to be. Except, she went home to her boyfriend, and I'm going home alone.

In the silence of the car, I recount the night on the balcony at Fireside for the millionth time. When I told her I didn't mind waiting, I meant it. But I didn't think she'd get a boyfriend. The question of whether or not I should move on has been on the back of my mind. I thought the boyfriend was a front. And maybe he is. Either way, she has someone who she deems as a better option than me. A safer option. I don't blame her for guarding her heart. I royally fucked up. We both fucked up. But we're not who we were all those years ago now.

Pulling my car into the garage, my phone chimes with a text. I'm surprised to see it's Eve.

Eve: Had fun tonight. See you (and your plus one) tomorrow.
Winter: Do I get to meet the infamous boyfriend?

Shit. I have to meet her boyfriend tomorrow.

Eve: Yeah...

Winter: ???

Winter: Why the dots?

Eve: No reason.

Winter: Does he know you had dinner with me?

Eve: Does it matter?

Winter: He doesn't. Does he?

Winter: That's why your ass was runnin like Cinderella when she lost her slipper?

Eve: LMAO Shut the fuck up!

Winter: It's alright, Cinderella. Your secret's safe with me. Just remember who she ends up with in the end.

Eve: Night Winter.

Winter: Night Cinderella.

Climbing out of my car, I head inside, stripping my clothes off as I walk toward my room.

Stepping out of my pants, I hang them over the back of a chair. "Alexa, play my soundtrack." I sit on the edge of the bed in my boxers.

'Rent Free' by 6lack fills the silence in the room. Pulling out a joint, I light it and pour myself some bourbon. The thought of taking a hot shower crosses my mind until I down the bourbon and lie back on the bed. Taking a long pull on the joint, I hold it for a few breaths, blowing it out on a long exhale. I close my eyes, waiting for myself to become weightless with each hit. It doesn't take long for me to feel like I'm floating. Alexa's now playing '3:15' by Russ. She's really trying to put me in my feelings tonight. My phone chimes across the room. Opening my eyes, I rub them before peeling myself off the mattress to get it from my pants.

Reign: Hey.

A smile lights up my face.

Winter: What's up bro?
Reign: I know it's late and I'm sorry to bother you.
Winter: Never a bother. What's up? You good?
Reign: Are you still picking me up tomorrow?
Winter: Did you go to class?
Reign: Yes. I promise I did.

I know he did because I checked.

Winter: I'll be there in something extra flashy.
Reign: Sick!!!!

He'll discover soon enough all my cars are 'extra flashy' to some degree.

Winter: See you tomorrow.

Tossing my phone aside, I settle back on my bed to finish the joint. It chimes seconds later. I contemplate ignoring it, but pick it up anyway.

Aundi: You up?

I take my time finishing the joint before responding. Normally, I wouldn't hesitate to tell her to come through. I've ended most of my fuckships. They're exhausting to keep up with and not as gratifying. Aundi though... she's intelligent and gorgeous. Ironically, the last time I saw her was after the night at Fireside with Eve.

Winter: I am.
Aundi: You're not going to make me beg are you?
Winter: You know I like that shit.
Winter: But nah. I won't. I've got a long day tomorrow.
Aundi: Sweet dreams.

Attached to the message is a nude picture of her. Chuckling, I shake my head, put my phone on do not disturb, and fall asleep thinking of Eve.

I took care in choosing which car to pick Reign up in this afternoon. After narrowing it down to four, I finally picked one. The Lykan Hypersport that emulates the batmobile. Snow and North gave me shit for flying all the way to Lebanon, where they're manufactured, and balked at the ridiculous price tag. North couldn't wrap his mind around why four hundred and forty-four diamonds line the LED headlights. I don't know either, but it's sitting pretty in my garage and I can't wait to see the look on Reign's face when I pull up.

For now, I'm sitting at lunch with Snow and North. Unfortunately, Elle had an exam at school, so I've missed her half the day.

"How much longer will Elle be in her exam?"

Snow smiles at me, leaning back in his chair and takes a sip of his ice water. "Don't tell me you're not enjoying the company of your brothers."

"Honestly," North wipes his mouth with the cloth napkin as he finishes off his bite. "I didn't expect you and Elle to become such good friends."

"Despite us kissing passionately at the bar that one night—"

Snow lets out an exasperated sigh, muttering under his breath.

"She's my best friend," I continue.

"Just fuck us, huh?" North takes a bite of his wing.

"No, but you're my brothers." I wave my hand airily. "It's a given. You two have no choice but to love me."

"Unfortunate, really." Snow winks, sliding his cleared plate aside.

I kick his shin under the table, causing him to wince and retaliate by tossing a fry from North's plate at my face.

"Can you two behave? I'd like to finish my lunch without getting kicked out of the restaurant."

I let the fry assault slide for now. "Are you guys ready for the gala?"

"The one you dragged us into?" Snow finishes off his drink. "Yes."

I ignore Snow. Elle has brought him out of his shell, but he still complains about social events, even if he does enjoy himself.

"We get to meet our long lost brother tonight?" North wipes his hands clean of the wing sauce.

"Yeah." I glance at the time on my phone. "I've got to pick him up from school soon."

North smiles. "He's been good for you."

"The mentorship is for us both. Not just him."

"How did you hear about this program?"

Taking a bite of my brie and prosciutto sandwich, I prolong my response. They still don't know I go to therapy. "Something Elle and I saw online. She told me I'd be a good mentor."

Snow nods, eyeing me. "We'll go with that. For now."

When I went off the deep end, Snow got really good at identifying my tells. It got to the point he could catch me in a lie before I even finished my sentence. Now that he trusts me again, he'll subtly call it out but leave it alone because he knows now that it's personal things.

"For now." I smile, keeping track of the time on my phone. Reign said the school pick up gets pretty busy and to arrive a little early. The high school is on the other side of the city and is usually only a fifteen minute drive, but with the after school hustle it can easily become a thirty to forty-five minute commute. "I've gotta jet soon."

"He's never going to forget you picking him up in that fucking car." North chuckles, shaking his head.

"Although neither of you will admit it, because you both think it was a foolish purchase, I know the two of you salivate when I bring that car out of the garage." I can count on one hand the number of times I've driven the Lykan.

"It's aight," Snow says, crossing his arms.

"Well, if either of you boys ever want to be my passenger princess, let me know." I toss my napkin and some money down on the table.

"Fuck you." North says, letting out a rumble of laughter.

"That's the stipulation for all the shit you two gave me over that car. Be my passenger princess, and then I'll let you spin the block. Until then, enjoy the view." I slide my shades on. "Now if you'll excuse me, I've got to go pick up our long lost brother."

"I hope it gets scratched." Snow smiles, fanning some bills onto the table. "We'll see you at the gala you forced upon us."

Reign wasn't kidding. I'm fifteen minutes early and the line of cars is already out of hand. Luckily, we should be able to leave fairly quickly since I'm further up in the line. I didn't bother telling Reign which car is mine because in a line of minivans, SUVs, and family cars – you can't miss me.

A few students trickle out and then it's like someone opened a flood gate as a sea of them fill the courtyard area. I'm stoked to see Reign's reaction. A lot of the students slowly walk past with their phones pointed at the car. After a minute or two of looking for Reign through the throng of teens, I spot him. He's a little taller than most. It doesn't take long for him to find the car as I steadily move along with the line. I can't help but smile at the stunned look on Reign's face.

Revving the engine, making it growl, he and his entourage of friends look like they're losing their minds. Opening the suicide door, I greet him with a hug.

"For someone who barely speaks, you sure love attention."

Reign laughs, shaking his head. "This is fucking sick! I mean—" He slaps his hand over his mouth.

"You're good." I nudge his shoulder as the corners of my mouth tip up.

Reign's friends gawk at me and the car. He does a round of introductions to the four boys in his entourage. "This is Sam, Leon, Ian, and Julian. Guys, this is Winter."

"We thought Reign was full of shit," Julian, the short kid with the glasses, says.

"Correction," Leon raises his finger in the air. "*You* thought Reign was full of shit cause you're a hater."

Okay, I like Leon.

"Are you going to let Reign drive?" Sam, who has his locs pulled into bun on top of his head, asks.

"Nah. Not today." I shake my head. "Maybe when he gets his license and if his grades are up."

"I'll punch you myself if you squander this opportunity for the rest of us, Reign." A horn honks a few cars back. "Shit, that's my mom. How am I supposed to ride home in our minivan now?" Ian, who's almost as tall as Reign, asks.

"How bout I take a picture of you guys in front of it?"

"Not in it?" Julian asks. The warning look I give him must say enough. "Okay, that's fair."

Little shit.

Ian's mom honks her horn again.

"You better hurry."

They quickly get in front of the car, with Reign in the middle, and smile. I snap a couple pictures, before saying, "That's good. Reign can send them to you. But for now, we've got to get going, too. Nice to meet you guys."

Reign talks to Leon, Sam, and Julian. Ian stops in front of me. "Thanks for bringing my best friend back to me. It's been a long time since I've seen him excited. See you around." He slings his backpack over his shoulder and takes off toward his mom's van.

I stare after him and glance at Reign. Loss effects everyone, even if it's not the same magnitude as what loved ones experience. I'm sure for a little while there, Ian thought he lost his best friend. And maybe he did in a way because Reign isn't the same boy he was before his dad died.

His friends say their goodbyes, stealing glances at the car before they take off.

Reign lets out a satisfied sigh. "Thanks for—"

"Reign!"

I recognize Calliope's voice, turning to see her hanging out the window of her dad's truck. I wave at Vincent, her dad, who returns the wave with a smile.

"Nice car, Winter!" She grins. "Did you ask him?"

"Ask me... what?" I turn back to Reign.

"Would it be okay if Calliope stopped by your place before we head to the gala? She wants to see me."

"Do you want her to?" I keep my voice low enough for only him to hear.

"Only if you're okay with it."

"I don't mind." It will be Reign's first time at my place and I want him to be comfortable. "Did you ask Vincent?"

"No..." He looks down at his sneakers. "I thought you would."

I snort with laughter. "You thought wrong, my boy. I'll wait right here."

He slides his hands into his pockets, letting out a sigh, walking toward Vincent's truck.

"Pick your head up."

Shooting an annoyed look at me over his shoulder, he straightens his posture.

Less than thirty seconds later, Vincent is waving me over. "Are you sure you're okay with Cal joining you two tonight?"

"I don't mind. They're good kids." I nudge Reign's arm, causing him to smile. "I would've invited her to the gala, but I can only take one extra person."

"She'll be fine spending an evening with her old man. I wanted to check. I know she can bulldoze her way into things."

"It's called caring, Dad."

"I'll text you my address. If my car wasn't a two seater, she could come with us now."

"Quite the car you have there." Vincent nods toward it. "Do I even want to know how much it cost?"

"Um... probably not."

He chuckles. "Fair enough."

"Reign said he'd take me for a drive when he gets—"

"Absolutely not." Vincent cuts her off before she can even finish her sentence, and I have to swallow my laughter. "No offense, Reign. Maybe if it were something with a little less... torque."

Calliope rolls her eyes. "Whatever, Dad."

A teacher with a walkie talkie approaches us. "Sir, is this your vehicle?"

"It is, ma'am. I apologize for holding up the line. We're leaving right now."

She seems taken aback by my manners. I'm assuming she deals with angry parents and mouthy teens more than anything. "Oh–uh, thank you."

"Let's go, Reign. Vincent, you can drop her off in a couple of hours. We're going to take a drive through the canyon first and then we'll be back. You're also welcome to hang out with us too." He's only a few years older than me and we've gotten to know each other when we cross paths at True's House.

"Yeah, that sounds good." Vincent nods.

Calliope leans forward, talking to Reign. "Text me when you guys are on your way back."

"Will do," Reign says and Vincent pulls away.

Clapping Reign on the back, we head for the car. "Let's go for a drive."

Sliding into the leather seat, he grins, looking around. "This is unreal."

"What do you want to listen to?" I swipe my finger over the hologram screen, searching the music library. "It can be anything."

"Um... Hallucinogenics by Matt Maeson."

I pause with my finger hovering over the screen, giving him a side long glance. "Should I be concerned that you're listening to a song called Hallucinogenics?"

He laughs. "No. It's just a good song. You said I could pick anything."

"True." I pull up the drug song and let it play as we pull away from the school.

"Where are we going?" Reign asks as I roll down the windows.

"Quartz Pass. Have you been through there?"

"Yeah, my dad and I used to hike the trails around there."

"Same with my dad. Except it's me and my brothers now. You're welcome to come with us. We usually do something together on the weekends."

His face lights up. "I'd like that."

"I'll see what we're getting into this weekend and let you know."

Turning up the music, I let the warm breeze fill the car as we drive. Reign looks like he couldn't be happier as he looks out the window with his already unruly curls whipping in the wind. I'm not sure how I'd fair without my brothers. I think Reign really is our long lost brother like North jokes.

It takes thirty minutes to get to Quartz Pass. I've been a lot of places in the world, but Hope Valley will always be home. I love that we can go from the desert-like climate of the Valley to the lush green of the mountains. There's still some snow in some areas, but it's slowly melting as spring makes its appearance.

I've let Reign play DJ for the ride up to the pass. I pull up 'Beautiful Boy' by John Lennon. Reign gives me a shocked look.

"Are you okay?"

"Yeah... I just–my dad sang this to me when I was kid. And even as a teen... to annoy me." He smiles as his eyes gloss over. "He'd do this ridiculous dance, snapping his fingers and walk toward me... I never thought I'd miss that."

"Do you want me to change it?"

"No. Leave it." He looks down at his hands. " I was just wishing he was here to see me, this car, to meet you... wishing he was here for all of it."

"I understand your pain."

"Did your dad like this song too?" he asks, not meeting my gaze.

"Yeah. Well... my dad loved all oldies, honestly. That's all he'd play when we'd go on road trips."

He cracks a smile. "I've never been on a road trip before."

"Add it to the list, my boy." I turn the music up. "Ready to gun it?"

"Hell–I mean, yes!" He puts his arm out the window.

Putting pedal to the metal, we race through the canyon.

After driving through the pass and back, we return to my place at Sunstone Ridge. Paul, the security guard, nods as I pull up to the gate. I stop to tell him that Calliope and Vincent will be arriving soon.

"You live here?" Reign asks with wide eyes, taking in the luxury homes and sprawling green lawns.

"Nah. We're just visiting a friend."

He tears his eyes away from the window. "You're joking." He laughs once he sees the smirk on my face.

"I live here and so does my youngest brother. He's actually my neighbor."

"Will I meet your brothers tonight?"

"Yeah. We'll meet up with them at the gala."

"Have you told them about me?"

I nod. "Yep. They say you're our long lost brother."

Reign smiles, turning his attention back to the window. Following the winding road a little longer, my house comes into view. Instead of pulling into the horseshoe driveway, I pull into the garage. If I thought Reign lost his mind at the sight of the car were in now, he could possibly faint as he takes in the all the cars.

"These are all yours?"

"They are." I cut the engine.

"How much did this car cost you?"

"Three million." He looks faint. "If you pass out, I'm pulling you out of the car and leaving you on the ground until you wake up."

He blinks, laughing. "Why wouldn't you leave me here?"

"You may drool and I can't allow that."

He doubles over with laughter. "I don't drool."

"Right. Mhm. Sure." I side eye him. "Let's go inside. We have a couple of hours to get ready."

Now that he's here, I find myself nervous. The only people I've had over are my brothers, Elle, and Aspen. For all my other bullshit, I have a condo I bought when I got back to the Valley. Now I use it for when I'm too drunk to make the thirty minute drive to my place. I may be reckless and impulsive, but I'm not careless enough to bring people I *don't* care about into my home.

Reign turns on the spot. "This is really nice. You live here alone?"

"Just me."

He looks through the large, sliding glass doors. "And you have a pool?"

"I do." I chuckle. "You're welcome to come back another day and swim or chill in the theater or game room."

"You have a game room?"

I motion for him to follow me down the hall, opening the door.

Reign eagerly pushes past me. "Incredible..." he mutters.

It's a decent sized room with dark gray walls that have neon signs and retro Super Mario art. The ceiling looks like rain clouds thanks to Elle after watching some video on TikTok. The PS5 is sitting atop a console that has some figurines of my favorite game characters.

"Do you game?"

"Only at my friends' houses. I can't afford any of this stuff. Well... my grandma says *she* can't afford any of this stuff."

I can't keep my mouth from dipping into a frown. "Where does she get the money to gamble from?"

"I'm pretty sure she uses the money we get from Dad dying."

The scowl on my face deepens. "She..." Before I speak ill of his grandmother, I take a deep, calming breath and run my hands down my face. "I—" Checking the time on my watch, I say, "We've gotta start getting ready."

"Thanks for caring." He smiles.

I pat his shoulder, giving it a squeeze, and show him to one of the guest rooms, leaving him to get ready. I've yet to meet his grandma because he takes the city bus to True's House and catches a ride home with Calliope. Now, I have no real desire to meet her. Reign deserves to be a kid. He's only seventeen, dealing with issues that most adults won't have to face until much later in life if they're lucky. Instead of dwelling on his grandma, I decide to focus on making sure he has an amazing time tonight.

Calliope and Vincent arrive shortly after I get out of the shower. Dressed in slacks and a white button down, I answer the door.

"Welcome. Come in." I step aside.

"Thank you so much for having us." Vincent shakes my hand.

Calliope is looking around the same way Reign did when he first got here. "You have a really pretty house, Winter."

I smile. "Thanks. You two can hang out in the living room if you want. I'll go check to see if Reign is out of the shower." They sit on the couch and are too busy looking around to respond.

Knocking on the door to Reign's room, I wait for him to respond. He opens the door with his shirt half on. "Calliope's here?"

"Yep."

He hastily buttons his shirt the rest of the way as he follows me out into the living room.

"Reign!" Calliope exclaims. "Look at you."

He runs a hand through his damp curls, slicking them back, and it looks like Calliope may need CPR. "You look–good–nice."

Vincent is watching the exchange with a raised brow. She clears her throat looking back at him. "Right, Dad?"

"Yes. He does. You look very nice, Reign."

"Thank you, Mr. Golding." I can tell he's uncomfortable, but maintains eye contact. Good for him.

"Reign, you better finish getting ready. Our driver will be here in forty-five minutes."

"Okay." He nods, turning toward the room and Calliope follows him.

"Cal..." She slowly turns on the spot, facing her dad. "Leave that door open."

"Oh my God, Dad!" She shrieks, pushing Reign in the opposite direction. "You're making this weird. We're just friends."

I let my amusement show as they disappear down the hall. "Would you like a drink?"

Vincent lets out a puff of air with his eyes still glued to the hallway. "I think I'm gonna need it."

"What's your poison? I have bourbon, rum, tequila, wine..."

"Whatever you're having is fine. Thank you." His eyes are still on the hallway.

"I'm not sure how much you've been around Reign, but he's a respectable young man." I pour two glasses of bourbon, handing him one.

He looks at the amber liquid in the glass. "I never thought I'd be a single parent, and I'm terrified I'm going to fuck it up."

Being not much older than me, I can't fathom what he's going through, losing the love of his life and having to take care of Calliope alone. Vincent could be eighty and nothing would've prepared him to lose his wife. I feel the pain and worry in his words. Taking a seat in the chair opposite him, I down the bourbon and set the glass aside.

"You will fuck up." His eyes snap to mine. "But Calliope is going to love you regardless. We're not meant to be perfect, Vincent. I bet she already sees you as perfect anyway."

"There just such good kids. Neither of them..." His voice trails off and he knocks back his glass of bourbon. Holding the glass up in front of him, he smiles. "This is good."

"You're welcome to have more."

"No." He sets his glass aside. "That's enough for me. Thank you. I'm not much of a drinker, but I do enjoy one every now and then."

Reign and Calliope's laughter carries down the hallway.

"I'm grateful they have each other, but I wish they didn't meet because their parents are dead. They didn't deserve this shit."

"They didn't... but they'll be alright. They'll for damn sure be better off than us."

Vincent lets out a bark of laughter. "I don't doubt that for a minute."

Reign and Calliope reappear, and he's fully dressed. His usual floppy curls have been tamed by Calliope's hands and some gel. The first time we tried on the suits, he didn't have a haircut. Now that his look is complete with a bow tie and shoes–he looks confident and happy.

"Reign, you look handsome." He flashes me a smile at the compliment. "If you all will excuse me, I have to get the rest of my tux on."

"Can I show them the game room?"

"Of course."

Fifteen minutes later, I rejoin them in the living room. I'm happy Calliope and Vincent came over. She insists on taking photos of Reign and I together before we walk out the door for the evening.

Handing my phone back to me, she says, "Reign, you better take lots of pictures tonight."

"My phone," he says, patting his pockets. "I'll be right back." Calliope follows him to go get it.

"Thank you for your words of reassurance earlier," Vincent says, holding his keys in his hand.

"Any time." I nod, clapping him on the shoulder. "If you ever want to get together, let me know." The friends I did have were tied to the life that took me down a path I never want to walk again. I've chosen to surround myself with people who have my best interests at heart and uplift me, making my circle small.

"I may take you up on that offer. Calliope tells me I need to get a life."

I chuckle. "Sounds like something she'd say."

My phone chimes with a text from my driver, Saul. "Reign!" I holler. "We've gotta go."

He appears seconds later with Calliope. She beams. "Thanks for having us over, Winter."

"You're welcome any time."

"Bye, Reign. Don't forget the pictures."

"Bye, Calliope," Reign says, sounding a little distracted.

"Enjoy your evening you two," Vincent says as we head out the front door.

"You two as well."

"Our night won't be as exciting as yours," Calliope says.

"Hey! I'm exciting." Vincent nudges her arm. They laugh as they walk toward his truck.

Saul opens the door to the SUV. "Mr. King and Mr. DeLeon, you both look nice this evening."

"Thank you, Saul." I wait for Reign to get in and then climb in after him.

Pulling my phone from my pocket, I send a text to Snow and North to let them know we're on our way.

Snow: You sent Elle flowers?
Winter: You didn't? I mean her exam was pretty important today.
North: Damn. Dropping the ball Snow?
Snow: Sometimes I wonder what life would be like if you two idiots weren't my brothers.

Winter: Pretty damn terrible.

North: Unbearable.

Snow: Don't send my fiancée flowers.

Snow: Unless you tell me. So I can upstage you.

Winter: Did she like them?

Snow: I said they were from me. She loved them.

North: That's fucked up LMAO

Winter: Jackass.

Snow: The fuck would I look like? It's my responsibility to spoil my own fiancée.

Winter: Take your responsibility more seriously then so I don't have to pick up the slack.

Snow: Fuck you.

Sliding my phone back into my pocket, I glance at Reign. He looks nervous. "Are you okay?"

"Mmhmm." He nods his head, looking out the window.

"Are you sure because you look—"

"She... kissed me..." He sounds confused. "Calliope... I grabbed my phone in the room and..." His eyes meet mine. "And she kissed me."

I shift in the seat, getting a better look at him. "Is this good... bad?"

"Good... I think–I hope." His eyes grow considerably larger. "Does this mean she's my girlfriend?"

I run my hand over my mouth and chin to keep from smiling. "Did you ask her?"

"No." He shakes his head.

"Did she ask you to be her boyfriend?"

Shaking his head again, he answers, "No."

"Do you want her to be your girlfriend?"

He turns toward me in his seat. "This means she likes me... right?"

"In my experience, you don't kiss someone you don't like." Unless you're Eve. Then you kiss them and profess your love. But that's neither here nor there. This is about Reign.

"I mean... you should see the guys at school who try and get her attention."

"Why does that matter?" I quirk a brow.

"I'm not sure I'm the best match for her."

"Do you want my advice?" I rest my head against the seat, smiling at him.

"Yes, please." He leans forward, eagerly.

"Don't assume you know what's best for Calliope. It seems she's made up her mind that *you–*" I poke at his chest "–are who's best for her. That's what matters."

"Do you think she really likes me?" He has a hopeful look on his face.

I personally think she's in love with him, but again, I digress. "Another piece of advice, talk to her."

He pulls his eyes away from me and looks down at his phone, contemplating my words. "Do you have a girlfriend?"

"I don't." If Eve would stop being stubborn, maybe we could make something happen, but – *shit, I have to meet her boyfriend tonight.*

"What if Calliope and I do get together and it doesn't work out?"

I think of Brielle. "You two can be friends. I'm friends with a woman who I cared about deeply."

"Will she be at the gala tonight?"

I hadn't considered whether Brielle and Ezra would be at the gala. I'm sure they will be given they own multiple businesses. "Maybe. If she is, I'll introduce you to her and her husband."

His eyes widen. "She's married?"

"Happily." I smile. "You can be friends with girls, Reign, and the relationship can be strictly platonic. Although, I don't think that's the case with Calliope."

He rests his head against the seat, watching the city lights pass by. "Ian, the kid you met today, is my best friend. We used to do everything together. Then Dad died, and I felt like we couldn't relate anymore. Things that were fun I didn't care to do because... my world seemed gray; you know?" He turns his head to look at me as I nod before turning his attention back to the window. "The counselor at school told me about True's Circle. It took me a few weeks to decide to go, but ultimately I went because I felt like none of my friends understood where I was coming from."

"I finally went and met Calliope..." His voice trails off as a smile spreads across his face. "It was the first time I didn't feel alone since Dad died. We've become best friends. Up until today, I didn't think she saw me as more than a friend even though Ian called me a dumbass for thinking she didn't."

I let out a belt of laughter. "I have to agree with Ian."

"Now I do, too. I just hope whatever happens we'll remain friends."

"Friendship is the keystone to any good relationship, my boy. You don't gotta marry her by tomorrow."

He tosses his head back with laughter. "Am I overthinking?"

"Maybe a little, but that means you care."

"Do you want to get married?"

"I was engaged at one point."

"You were?" His eyebrows shoot up with surprise.

"Yep." Saul pulls into the art museum's parking lot.

"What happened?"

I'm not really sure how to answer this question because it's not one thing that happened. It was a multi-faceted situation. I've wondered countless times if I hadn't left, where would we be? Even if I had stayed, I think our relationship still would've ended. Neither of us were willing to give each other what we wanted. Saul pulls up to the entrance. Parking, he gets out and rounds the front of the SUV to open the door for us.

Looking back at Reign before getting out, I give him the simplest explanation I can think of.

"We stopped being friends."

13
WINTER

THE GALA IS OPULENCE at its finest. White ostrich feather centerpieces sit atop elegantly decorated tables with gold and black place settings. Beaded crystals hang from the ceiling, giving the illusion of a waterfall. Before taking a seat, we walk the red carpet to get our pictures taken. I scan what I can see of the room from where we're standing, looking for Eve, but don't see her. Snow, Elle, North, and Aspen are a few people ahead of us.

I tap Reign's arm. "Are you ready to meet my family?"

"Uh..." He swallows. "Yeah."

"C'mon." I clap his shoulder, giving it a squeeze. "They can't wait to meet you."

We walk past a few people to get to them.

Elle turns as I walk up, smiling brightly when she sees me. "Winter, you made it." She gives me a quick hug as Snow gives me a warning look.

I shoot a wink back his way. "I did. You're looking gorgeous as ever." I press a kiss to her hand.

Snow lets out an exasperated sigh, knowing I'll gladly spill the beans about the flowers if he utters a single word of protest.

"So happy you're here," he says with a bemused expression.

I pull him into a hug despite his look of annoyance. Turning to Aspen, I press a kiss to her cheek. "Stunning. Surprised you chose to come with North."

"And yet here you are..." North rests his hand on the small of Aspen's back. "Without a date."

Aspen snorts with laughter. "Thank you, Winter."

"Damn. My own brothers are the ones to hate on me tonight. It's a shame this is Reign's first impression of you." Turning to look for him, I thought he was by my side, but he's standing behind me. I pull him to my side, introducing him to everyone.

"Reign, this is Snow."

Snow offers him a dap, pulling him into a hug. "I've heard a lot about you. Pleasure to meet you."

"Thank you." Reign smiles.

"And this is, Noelle. My soon to be sister-in-law. She's somehow engaged to Snow."

"Hi." She grins, giving him a hug. "It's nice to finally meet you."

When she releases him, Reign looks too stunned to speak. I nudge him gently and he clears his throat. "That is a really nice dress," he says and Snow scowls at him.

I cover my laugh with a cough. North leans forward, looking at Snow's reaction with a smile on his face.

"Thank you." Elle turns gracefully which only causes Snow's scowl to deepen as he loops his arm around her waist, pulling her close.

"I see he has your charm," North says.

"And this," I grab Reign's arm turning him away from Elle. "Is North. Our little brother."

Reign is given another hug by North. "Nice to meet you. Glad you were able to join us."

"Thanks for having me." He smiles.

"Last, but certainly not least, is Aspen. Elle's sister."

"I see the resemblance," Reign says as she gives him a hug and a kiss on the cheek.

I would've never thought he'd be this smooth. Now that I think of it, he talks to Calliope a lot. She seems enamored with him, and I doubt it's because he's quiet.

The photographer approaches our group. "Are you guys ready?" she asks with a smile.

We step in front of the shimmering white backdrop. White and black balloons with gold decorative accents crawl up the side. Reign and I stand in the middle, back to back. Snow and Noelle are to our right while Aspen and North are to our left. The photographer gets a few photos of us as a group and then a few individual shots of us.

"Glad you came?" I ask Reign as we walk toward our table.

"I've never been anywhere this rich looking." He takes in the elaborate décor.

"I..." My words get lost in my throat. In a sea of mostly black and muted colors, Eve glows in her golden yellow floor length gown with a dangerously high slit. Staring at her laughing with her boyfriend, I run into the back of Snow.

"You good, bro?" he asks, holding onto my arm to keep me steady. Turning, he follows my line of sight. "Ah, Eve. You're gawking like a creep," he says with a smirk.

"I am not." I close my mouth, tearing my eyes away from Eve.

North looks at me, cocking his head to the side. "You have a little bit of—"

"What?" I consciously wipe my face.

"Drool," North finishes.

Reign cracks up. North and Snow follow suit. "Are they always like this?" he asks about my brothers.

"Unfortunately." I adjust my suit jacket. "Yes, they are."

"You were staring kinda hard."

"Really, Reign?" I give him a look of indignation. "I introduce you to them five minutes ago, and you're already siding with them?"

"Welcome to the family." Snow grins, patting him on the back.

North wraps his arm around his shoulder, guiding him to the table. "What school do you go to?"

Their voices fade into the background as my eyes rest on Eve. Our gazes catch from across the room. For a few seconds, she looks at me how I was looking at her before running into the back of Snow. A smile spreads across her face before she rejoins the conversation she's having with her boyfriend, Ilaria, and the doctor who I have yet to meet.

Her boyfriend looks familiar, but when I've heard Elle or Aspen talk about him, his name doesn't ring a bell. I don't get a chance to dwell on it much longer. They're making their way toward our table. I didn't consider having to sit with her and her boyfriend all evening until now. I can be cordial for a few hours, right? My eyes track the peek of her thigh I get with each step she takes. If I could just put my hands on—

"Winter." Ilaria reaches the table first. "Nice to see you again."

"You as well, Ilaria."

"Maybe we'll get to know each other after all." She takes the empty seat beside me since Reign decided to sit between Snow and North.

"I'm Silas Bradford, the other doctor at the clinic." He extends his hand, and I shake it firmly. "Sorry I missed you when you were in for the tour."

"You were with patients. That's much more important than meeting me."

He chuckles. "Thank you for being our sponsor." Silas takes the seat on the other side of Ilaria.

All that leaves is, "Eve." Not acknowledging the boyfriend on her arm. It seems she's having trouble focusing on me because she suddenly seems more interested in the décor around us. "You look—"

A hand shoots out in front of me. "Noah Kincaid."

I look down at his hand and then at his face. "Kincaid…" I mutter as my brain tries to place where I know him from.

"I know I look different." He smiles as I continue to stare at him blankly. "We used to go to school together."

My eyes widen with recognition. "Noah Kincaid. The flowers and card guy!" I glance at Eve who rightfully looks embarrassed.

I vividly remember this guy being borderline obsessed with Eve. Correction. He actually was – *is* – obsessed with her. Noah was devastated when he learned we started dating. After one of our first dates, he showed up at her house with flowers and a fucking card telling her all the reasons they belonged together. Eve could've told him to jump from a cliff and Noah would've asked which one. She let him down gently that night, but he left the valley shortly after for college.

Despite going to the same school, Noah and I didn't run in the same social circles. Makes sense he became a surgeon. He mostly kept to himself with a book in his hand while I was in every extracurricular activity time would allow. From my understanding, he knew Eve through their parents. She went to a private school, and by chance, we happened to meet at one of my parents' annual Christmas parties. Noah is the type of man who mistakes a woman's kindness for romantic interest. And here Eve is, feeding his delusion. Clearly he still heels to Eve when she snaps her fingers.

This is the guy she chose to guard her heart with. The thought makes me chuckle to myself. She raises her brow in my direction, and I can only give her a smile. I didn't see Noah as a threat then, and I for damn sure don't see him as an issue now.

"I was young and dumb." He chuckles, snaking his arm around Eve's waist. "Hopefully there were no hard feelings about that."

"No..." I shake my head. "I honestly forgot about you."

Noah clears his throat while Eve looks mortified.

I continue, "Time can clearly change a person's feelings toward another."

She talked about Noah as if he was beneath her, and now she's under him every night. There's a few beats of awkward silence before Eve speaks up.

"Where's your plus one?" She looks around.

"You came with someone?" Noah asks, a little too hopeful.

While he's definitely not the nerdy kid anymore, I'm still taller and better looking.

"I did. I'll introduce you." I smile, stepping aside. "Eve, this is Reign. Reign, this is Eve."

Reign stands, holding his hand out to her. "Nice to meet you. Are you related to Noelle and Aspen?"

Eve is momentarily stunned with confusion as she looks between me and Reign. "Uh... no."

"Could've fooled me." He gives her a charming smile. "You look great."

"Reel it in, Casanova." I narrow my eyes at him.

"How do you two know each other?" Eve asks, returning his smile.

"He's my mentor."

Eve's face softens. "Really?"

"Yeah. Winter is like…" Reign glances at me. "My big brother."

I've told him he's our long lost brother. I didn't expect him to consider me as a brother too. It's humbling to know he sees me that way. "Thank you, Reign."

"That's really…" Eve's eyes glisten, and our gazes catch. "Wonderful. I'm happy you have him."

"Me too." Reign smiles proudly.

"Allergies again?" The corner of my mouth tips up.

"Yes," Eve says, looking up briefly, blinking rapidly to gain control of her emotions.

"Babe," Noah says, startling me. I forgot he was here. "I've told you to take your allergy meds."

When Eve said people believe her allergy excuse "sometimes", she was referring to Noah's dumbass.

"Yeah, I know—I–oh, Reign, this is Noah. He's my boyfriend."

"Hey," Reign says with a half-hearted wave. I should tell him to be nicer, but how can I ask him to do something I'm not willing to do myself. "Nice to meet you," he adds as an afterthought.

"You as well." Noah nods.

"Well… now that introductions to my plus one are out of the way," I wink at Eve. "Shall we enjoy each other's company over some food and drinks?"

"I'm starving," Reign says, returning to his seat between Snow and North.

I sit beside Ilaria and am surprised when Eve takes the seat on my other side, leaving Noah sitting next to North. Honestly, it's probably for the best. Conversation sparks around the table as the waiter takes our drink orders. Snow, North, and I order bourbon. When the waiter returns with our drinks, Reign asks to try Snow's bourbon. Snow shrugs, sliding the glass toward him. I'm about to intervene when Snow shoots me a wink. If this is Reign's first drink, he's going to hate it, and I'm going to love watching him realize his mistake. Dad let us try alcohol for the first time when we were younger. All of us hated it. Now as adults, we enjoy bourbon thanks to it being Dad's favorite drink.

Leaning back in my seat with a smirk, I watch Reign peer into the glass before putting it to his lips. He slowly tips it back as Snow, North, and I watch with eager anticipation. It finally reaches his tongue, and he immediately chokes, slamming the glass back on the table as he coughs and wretches at the same time. We fall into a fit of laughter as Reign tries to catch his breath, downing his glass of water.

"You good, bro?" I ask with a smile, tipping my glass of bourbon back.

He wipes his mouth with the back of his hand. "That was disgusting."

"Lesson learned?" North asks, adjusting his glasses with a smirk.

"Yes. I don't know how you guys drink that stuff." He eyes our glasses.

"It's an acquired taste." Snow tips his glass toward Reign before taking a sip.

"You guys are so rude," Elle scolds. "Are you okay, Reign? Do you want me to go with you to the bar to get something non-alcoholic you'll actually like?"

Reign has a soda right beside him that Elle hasn't noticed. "Yeah. Yes." He stands abruptly.

"I'll join you," Aspen says.

Reign's smile could outshine the sun in this moment as they stand on either side of him, looping their arms through his, walking toward the bar. He glances at me over his shoulder, and I can't help but laugh at the look of satisfaction on his face.

"I feel like that was a setup," Snow says, eyeing Reign with Elle and Aspen.

Elle is now fixing his bow tie while Aspen puts one of his curls back into place. Reign is eating the attention up.

"Let him enjoy himself." I smile. "He doesn't get attention like this."

Reign wants what all of us want. To be seen. And right now, he has the attention of two of the most beautiful women in the room.

"I like him." North finishes his glass of bourbon. "He should come with us when we go hiking on the weekends."

My heart warms. "I've already invited him."

"Good." Snow turns his attention back to us. "Maybe you'll stop bitching about it being too early and hot and whatever else you find to whine about."

I subtly flick him off, using my middle finger to scratch my brow. Ilaria leans closer, resting her hand on my thigh. I look down at it then at her.

"Who's the oldest of you three?"

"Me. Snow is in the middle and North is the youngest."

"I love your guy's names. How did your parents decide to give you such unique ones?"

"My parents—"

Another hand unexpectedly grips my thigh. It's Eve. She leans forward giving Ilaria a fake as fuck smile. "Remember Ilaria, I told you his parents owned North Star Toys?"

Ah, this makes sense. Here I was thinking she sat next to me to protect Noah when it's to keep me from Ilaria.

"And now you and your brothers run it together?" She doesn't miss a beat despite Eve's interruption.

"We do." I nod with both their hands still resting on my thighs. You won't hear a single complaint from me. Being the cocky motherfucker I am, I lean back, draping my arms behind both of their chairs. Noah's eyes are locked on Eve's hand that is creeping up my thigh.

"What's your title?" Ilaria asks, looking at me through her lashes. Would it be wrong if I took her home?

"I'm—"

"The head of marketing," Eve finishes.

"So if I needed help with my social media..." Smiling, she removes her hand from my thigh, putting her elbow on the table and cradling her chin in her palm. "You're the man I need to talk to?"

"While I'm not a social media manager, I'm sure we can figure it out together."

Reign returns with Elle and Aspen, another drink in hand.

"Elle is also amazing at social media management," Eve says. "Right, Elle?"

"Me?" She licks her lips after taking the last sip of Snow's bourbon. "Uh... who's asking?"

"Ilaria."

"Oh, I wouldn't say I'm amazing. Everything I know I learned from Winter." Elle turns her attention back to Snow and Reign.

"You must be a good teacher."

"I am, and I don't mind giving private lessons."

Heat flashes in her eyes, and I can tell she's curious about what I could teach her. Instead of taking the conversation further, she smiles and changes the subject. "If you're marketing, what do your brothers do?"

"North is our accountant, and Snow is the CEO."

"Being the oldest, you didn't want to be in charge?"

"To get into those details," I lift my empty glass, "I'll need more of these."

"Sometimes the responsibility of being the oldest is suffocating. A gift and a curse."

For a few seconds I see a glimpse of myself in her eyes and it catches me off guard. "Yeah..."

"Would you care to dance before our food gets here?" Her eyes flit toward the DJ.

"I'd love to." Grabbing Eve's hand, I give it a squeeze, leaning closer to her. "I think your boyfriend would like his girlfriend back."

She quickly snatches her hand away as if I'm the one who placed it in my lap. Noah looks torn between saying something and keeping his mouth shut.

"Reign, I'll be on the dance floor if you need me," I say.

"Okay. Have fun." He doesn't spare me a glance, laughing about something with North and Snow.

Dancing with Ilaria, I learn we're the same age, she's also the oldest of three, and the first to attend college in her family. We have more in common than I thought we would. Her parents own a bakery called Essencia that I've actually been to a few times.

"They were disappointed I didn't want to take over the bakery. It sounds crazy, right? Immigrant parents who don't want their daughter to study medicine, but instead take over their bakery."

Holding her hand, she spins out, and I pull her back into me. "It does. Although, I know it isn't crazy for them. Did they accept your chosen path eventually?"

"Yes. When Eve, Silas, and I opened Hope's Village, that's when they finally understood my passion." She laughs, placing her hand on my shoulder as we move to the music. "Never mind the sleepless nights, countless hours of studying, and losing hair during medical school."

"People tend to only notice the success. Not the hard work that went into it. Your hair has grown back by the way."

She smiles up at me. "I've rambled enough. What about you? Do you like your work?"

"I love it. I get to work with my brothers. Don't tell them that though," she laughs again, "and carry on the legacy our dad left behind."

A solemn expression shadows her face. "I'm sorry you lost him."

"Me too. I'm grateful to have my mom and brothers, though."

"You don't have to do that, you know?"

"Do what?" I knit my brows together.

"Follow up a devastating truth with a positive. You're allowed to feel how you feel without having to say 'this fucking hurts but I still have this'. It still fucking hurts even with the positives."

For a moment, with our gazes locked, I can't find my words. Our connection is interrupted by the DJ announcing dinner is being served and the song comes to an end shortly after that. "Ilaria," I take a step back from her. "Thank you for the dance."

"My pleasure." She smiles, leading the way off the dance floor.

Returning to the table, we rejoin the conversation as we wait for our food. Reign looks the happiest I've seen him since we met. I was worried he'd be too shy to talk to anyone. Clearly my worries were pointless. He's talking as if they're his family too. Elle hands out the place cards with our names on them for the waiters to know what we ordered.

"What did you get?" Ilaria asks.

"Honestly," I unfold my napkin. "I don't remember."

"It's not just me then?" She laughs.

"Not at all. Hopefully past me chose something good."

"We can only hope."

They had us pick our entrees when we reserved the table a few weeks ago. The waiter appears with our food. From the plates that are being served, they look good.

The waiter sets a plate in front of me. "Garlic and herb beef tenderloin, roasted vegetables, and a side of gnocchi pesto," he announces.

"Thank you." Past me made an excellent choice.

After everyone's served, the conversation around the table subsides as we dig in. I'm halfway done when I glance at Eve only to realize her eyes are already on me. Well... my plate.

"You don't like it?"

She looks at her plate and then back at mine. "I didn't see the gnocchi on the menu or I would've ordered that."

"Is any Italian food safe from you?"

Smiling, she says, "No."

Stabbing a piece of gnocchi, I slowly bring it to my mouth, placing it on my tongue, and chew as she watches me. "It's delicious."

She tries to glare at me but fails, laughing. "You're a jerk."

"Oh, you expected me to share?" I take another bite of gnocchi. Looking past her, I see that Noah ordered some chicken with potatoes.

"No. It just looks good is all." Shrugging a shoulder nonchalantly, she side eyes me expectantly.

"I'll tell you what, if you give me some of your salmon, I'll give you some gnocchi."

"Deal." She smiles, making her dimple appear.

Eve slides her plate closer to me. I glance between her and the plate. "Feed me."

"What?" She looks at me and then quickly glances over her shoulder at Noah who's chatting it up with North and Aspen.

"You have a perfectly good fork in your hand. Give me a bite." I smile, knowing good and goddamn well I'm being unreasonable.

Eve stares at me for a long moment, weighing her options. I look around the table to see if anyone else ordered the gnocchi, it looks like Elle and Aspen may have, but it's already gone.

Narrowing her eyes, she stabs at the salmon with unnecessary force, making the fork squeak against the plate. "Now, Eve, I don't need that type of energy around the food I'm about to put into my body."

"You're infuriating you know that?" There's a ghost of a smile on her lips. She puts up a good front, but I know she's enjoying this as much as I am. She holds up her fork with the bite of salmon.

Feeding it to me, a small piece of salmon falls from the fork that she catches. Holding it between her fingertips, she feeds it to me without thinking. I catch her wrist, eating the small flake of salmon. My tongue brushes against her fingertips. Eve inhales sharply, and she looks as though I've zapped her. Glancing over her shoulder, I see Noah's eyes are locked onto me. *Oh well.*

"That's delicious." I focus on her again. Setting her fork down, she opens her mouth.

This moment couldn't be more perfect. "What if I changed my mind?"

"Feed me or a fork will end up in your thigh."

"You've always promised a good time." She covers her mouth, laughing. "How am I supposed to feed you now?"

"You're making me laugh!"

"I'm not making you do anything."

"Whatever. Okay." Eve takes a deep breath, regaining her composure. "Feed me."

Filling the fork with gnocchi, I put it in her mouth. When her lips close around it, my eyes flit to Noah who looks like he suddenly lost his appetite.

"You have..." Pulling the fork from her mouth, I bring my hand up between us, using my thumb to wipe some pesto off her bottom lip. I lick it off my thumb, throwing a wink to Noah over Eve's shoulder. "Some sauce."

"Oh," she wipes her mouth with a napkin, chewing. "Thank you. That was really good."

"You're welcome. You can have the rest." I slide the small plate toward her. "I just wanted you to feed me."

She gasps, playfully shoving my arm. "Winter!"

"What? The opportunity presented itself." I shrug. "Eat. Before I take it back." *And before your boyfriend has a conniption.*

"Thank you." She smiles, and I know it's the one she wears for those she loves.

Looking around the table, Elle and Aspen must've been watching us feed each other given the look of curiosity on their faces. I smile and nod in their direction, picking up my fork to finish my food. They haven't ever seen us getting along. Eve and I used to always share food, eating off each other's plates. She reinitiated that habit when she gave me that lasagna. Could I have not done it so blatantly in Noah's face? Sure. *But where's the fun in that?*

An hour later, plates are being cleared from tables and replaced with drinks, getting everyone ready for the auction. Instead of bourbon, I order a beer. When Snow receives his bourbon, Reign gives it a nasty look, making me chuckle. Eve leaves the table to get ready to auction Ilaria and Silas off.

"Good luck." I say to Ilaria, enjoying the view of her walking away.

She gives me a smile over her shoulder. Eve rolls her eyes at me, linking her arm with Ilaria. It's better for me because now I can watch both of them walk away.

Reign takes the seat beside me. "Are you bidding on anything?"

"Nah. I don't think so."

"Not even a date with Ilaria?" He smiles.

"No."

"Why?" He cocks his head to the side.

"Remember how I told you I was engaged?" He nods his head. "I was engaged to Eve."

His mouth falls open, making me chuckle. "You were engaged *to her*?" He points over his shoulder.

"I was."

"I thought you said you stopped being friends? You two looked like a little more than friends while you were eating." He nudges my arm.

Pinching my brows together, I raise my left with a smirk, wondering who the hell this kid is sitting beside me. "You're comfortable tonight."

He grins. "Anyone with two eyes could see it. I get it now though."

"Having fun with the family?" I decide to change the subject.

"Yeah. Thank you for letting me tag along."

"You're not a tag along. You—"

"Deserve to be here," he finishes.

"Ah," I pat his back. "You're getting it."

From spa packages, to artwork, and an all-expense paid weekend in Sapphire Shores–the auction is fully underway.

The auctioneer dramatically shuffles the cards and clears his throat. "Ladies and gentlemen, prepare your wallets for the final items–or people, shall I say–of the evening."

A murmur ripples through the banquet hall. Eve, Silas, and Ilaria step onto the stage. "Hope's Village wanted to create a medical facility with streamlined services for children. Before they opened their doors, parents had limited options for pediatric care. It's a comprehensive, family centered organization, aiming to meet the individual needs of each child who walks through their doors."

"Tonight they are hoping to secure funding to bring much needed services to the valley. They're offering 'A Date With a Doctor' to the coveted Twisted Vines."

The murmurs turn into a buzzing of voices. Twisted Vines is world renowned and one of the most exclusive places on the west coast. Eve is about to strike gold, and I couldn't be happier for her. The smile on her face says it all.

The auctioneer continues. "This is an amazing opportunity, ladies and gentlemen, to not only support Hope's Village, but to also get a chance to visit Twisted Vines while enjoying the company of a doctor. Up first, we have Silas Bradford who also happens to be an eligible bachelor."

Silas steps forward, and the ladies whistle and holler at him. This should be interesting. These galas never get this exciting.

"Starting bid is at ten thousand dollars," the auctioneer announces.

Reign leans closer to me. "Ten thousand dollars? For a date?"

"Yep." The bid is already at fifty thousand dollars. "The waiting list is well over a year to even get a bottle of wine from Twisted Vines. And even longer for their restaurant and resort."

"Would you wait that long for something?" Reign's eyes dart around the room at all the people bidding.

"If it's worth it, yes."

The bid ends at eighty thousand dollars. The auctioneer introduces Ilaria. "Up next is Ilaria Solis." She turns on the spot, enjoying the whistles and shouts.

Grabbing the mic from the auctioneer, she says, "I'm also single."

Laughter ripples through the audience. Should I bid on a date with her? I'm hesitant because I don't want to create a rift between Ilaria and Eve. At the same time, I shouldn't worry about accommodating Eve's feelings. I doubt Ilaria knows our history, and I'm not sure she'd want to date me once she knew. There's a difference between having once dated someone versus being engaged and planning forever with who you thought was the one. It also doesn't help they're running a business together.

The bidding for a date with Ilaria ends at a little more than Silas at ninety thousand dollars.

"You should've bid," Reign whispers, nudging my arm.

He's trying to get me caught up. "And deal with—"

Silas takes over the mic. "That's not all ladies and gents." He smiles at Eve who has a constipated smile on her face. I'm torn between laughing and being concerned. "We would also like to offer up a date with the heart of Hope's Village, Eve Valentine."

I can see her mouth, "*What?*" She tries to exit the stage, but Silas wraps his arm around her shoulders, bringing her to the front of it and Ilaria holds her hand.

"Eve is going to murder them," Elle laughs.

"This will be good for her." Aspen places her fingers into her mouth whistling loudly.

While Eve is an amazing leader, she hates being the center of attention.

Ilaria grabs the mic from Silas. "While Silas and I may be single, Eve does have a boyfriend—"

"Then he better have deep pockets!" A man shouts from the crowd.

"That's the spirit we love to hear." Ilaria grins. "This is a date with the heart of Hope's Village to Twisted Vines, how about we start the bidding a little higher?"

She hands the mic back to the auctioneer. Eve gives Ilaria and Silas a deadly look.

"You heard her," the auctioneer resumes. "Starting bid will be twenty thousand dollars."

"Goddamn," I mutter and turn to Elle. "Looks like she'll get that funding after all."

"I don't think she imagined it going this way." Elle's eyes are alight with amusement.

"No... she definitely didn't." Glancing to my left at Noah, he looks out of his depth. "You're not going to bid?"

His eyes are glued to Eve on the stage, hearing other men bid on date with her. "I–uh–yeah."

This is who she chose? "You don't have to bid, I guess."

Tearing his eyes away from the stage, Noah swivels his head in my direction. "I don't? Don't you think she'll be pissed?"

"She's not my girlfriend." I give him a nonchalant shrug of my shoulders. "I wouldn't know." *I do know.*

Eve is already pissed. By the time she gets off that stage, she'll be livid. Him not bidding will only add fuel to the already raging fire. He glances between me and the stage. The bid is already at sixty thousand. "She'll understand if you don't have the money, man..." I clap him on the shoulder.

For the first time tonight, he glares at me. "It's not about the money."

"It's not?" I splay my hand over my chest, acting as if I don't know I struck a nerve.

"No. I have Eve all the time."

Cocky motherfucker. Who would've known? "You're right. What's another night with her?" I raise my hand in the air, locking in a bid at seventy thousand.

Noah straightens up in his seat, sizing me up. He'll never get the measure because he couldn't comprehend the lengths I'll go to for Eve. *And to fuck with him.*

"Don't let him get to you, Noah," Snow says.

"Just ignore him," North adds. "We do."

Noah glances between the two of them, clearly wondering if they're serious or full of shit like me. Looking over my shoulder at them, they tip their glasses of bourbon at me with a nod. Of course they have my back. Even in bullshit. Although, this isn't bullshit. I *want* this date with Eve. Need it like the air in my fucking lungs.

After contemplating far longer than I had to, Noah places a bid at eighty thousand. "Good to know you have the money," I taunt.

"It must be nice to for you to have your daddy's money," he spits back.

"It is." While downing the rest of my beer, I raise my bid to one hundred thousand. "My dad made millions that my brothers and I have turned into billions. Can you keep up with that?"

He scoffs, sneering. "You're not good enough for her. I think deep down, all those years ago, you knew it and that's why you left. Because you were never worthy of Eve or her love in the first place."

For a split second, I imagine wrapping my hand around his throat and slamming him onto the table. That would only bring momentary satisfaction though. A slow smile spreads across my face.

"Is that what she told you?" His confidence slips a little. *Good.* "I don't know what's worse? The fact she lied to you or that you believed it."

"It doesn't matter what she told me. That's between us."

"Then when it comes to Eve and me, don't act as though you can begin to fathom what we had."

Turning my attention back to the stage, I snuff out any hope he has in this moment. "One million," I announce loudly over the buzz, causing a deafening silence to fall over the room.

Eve's mouth falls open, as does Ilaria and Silas's. The auctioneer is momentarily stunned into silence, too.

"O–One million..." the auctioneer stutters. All eyes are on me, including Noah's. I nod, signaling I meant what I said. "One million. Going once... going twice... "

I look at Noah, wishing he would try to outbid me. The auctioneer slams the gavel down onto the podium. "A date with the heart of Hope's Village sold to Mr. King."

The room erupts with applause. Smiling at Noah, I know I just started a war. Reign claps and smiles. "I thought you weren't bidding."

"She's always been worth the wait."

Noah turns his attention back to the stage where Eve is still staring at me as the auction ends. I lean closer to him so only he can hear my words. "You watched me with envy growing up. Now, you'll get to watch me take the woman of your dreams out on a date, knowing she's still in love with me."

14
WINTER

BACKSTAGE, I FIND EVE, pacing back and forth. Untying my bow tie, I pull it through my collar with a swish and pocket it as I undo the top few buttons of my shirt.

Stopping in her tracks, she turns to face me. "You!" She says, glaring. "What the *fuck* was that? A million dollars? Are you fucking kidding me right now?"

"Was it not enough?" I slip my hands into my pockets, walking toward her. "I can bid higher if you'd like."

"I didn't want you to bid! I didn't want to be up there!" She places her fingertips on her temples, rubbing them. "But a million fucking dollars, Winter? Are you insane?"

"Clinically?" I arch my brow. "No."

"Winter!" She growls my name through gritted teeth. "This isn't funny! You've made a spectacle of me. Of us."

"Do you want to take the money back?" I point my thumb over my shoulder. "If you think that'll be better then—"

I make a move to walk away, but she grabs my arm. "No! No. Absolutely not." Letting out an exasperated sigh, she looks up at the ceiling. "Silas and Ilaria would murder me if I did that."

"Then what's the problem?"

"You." She pokes a perfectly manicured finger into my chest. "You're the fucking problem."

"You've made me a problem." I grab her hand, pressing my palm against hers, intertwining our fingers, holding them up between us. "Did you think you'd tell me you still love me, and I'd let you walk away easily?" I press kiss to the back of her hand.

"You did all those years ago." Her brown eyes hold mine. "I don't understand the difference now."

"We're not who we were then, Dove."

Her breath hitches, snagging on the name I used to call her. "Does he know why you have a dove tattooed behind your ear? That it's because of me? Because of *us*." Using my fingertip, I brush her hair aside, revealing the tattoo. I gently rub my thumb over it, seeing the goosebumps pepper her skin.

"It's meaningless now." Her voice is barely a whisper.

Leaning close enough that my lips brush against her neck, I say, "I know you wish that were true. But just like that tattoo, the memories of me cling to your skin. I'm a part of you. Just like you're a part of me."

Remaining chest to chest, Eve pulls back enough to look at me. I see a glimmer of light shining through a crack in the wall she erected between us. Our eyes remain locked on each other. If anyone were near us, I'm sure they'd see sparks of electricity crackling in the air. Resting my hands on the curve of her waist, she puts her hands on my arms, and I savor the feel of her warmth against me.

We hold one another's gaze, waiting for the other to close the distance between our lips. Bringing my hand up between us, I trace my thumb along her bottom lip. Closing her eyes, she lets out a shuddering breath. The sound makes me want to fall to my knees and taste her. Eve breaks first, leaning forward. I slide my hand down the column of her throat, applying enough pressure to feel her pulse racing for me.

Pressing a kiss below her ear, I hold her in place. "Break it off with him."

"Now?" she moans.

"Preferably." Her eyes flutter open, disappointment shadowing her face. I grab her chin, holding it between my forefinger and thumb. "Oh, Dove. Did you think I'd be content being on the sidelines? That I'd give you what you need—want—while he reaps the benefits."

"No." She looks away from me, taking a step back. "I just—"

"You just..." I tilt my head to the side, catching her gaze. Pulling her back into me, I rest my hands on her waist. "What? You want me to have you in every way except the only one that matters?"

"I don't want to get hurt, Winter. I wouldn't survive losing you again."

"Eve... I hate that I hurt you. But I deserve more than fragments." I sever our connection, taking a step back.

She wraps her arms around herself, looking cold, and I slip my hands into my pockets to keep from touching her again. A silence settles over us. Before either of us can speak, Mayor Price appears followed by Elle and Aspen.

"Winter!" Mayor Price exclaims with glittering eyes. "What a bid! You two are going to be the talk of the city for ages." She doesn't seem to notice the palpable energy between Eve and me. Elle and Aspen do though, giving us both quizzical looks.

"Now, the newspaper is here and they want to snap a few pictures. Are you two okay with that? He said he'd be ready in about ten minutes."

"Yeah." Eve plasters on a smile.

"Sure." I shrug.

"Great." Mayor Price beams before flitting off.

Once she's gone, Elle asks, "Everything okay?"

"Of course it is." I give her a believable smile. "I'm going to find Reign."

"He's with Snow and North," Aspen fills in.

"Thank you." I make my way toward the stage's exit, but stop beside Eve. "You're truly a vision tonight."

I press a kiss to her temple, and it seems to summon Noah. He stops in his tracks, eyeing me. I continue on my way as if nothing happened. "She's all yours." I give him a less than reassuring pat on his shoulder.

After finding North and Snow talking to a small group, they let me know Reign went off to view the Basquiat exhibit. Weaving through the crowd of people, I stop to say hello to a few of them and accept congratulations on my bid before reaching the quiet of the art museum. It doesn't take me long to find Reign. He's sitting on a bench in front of a large Basquiat, leaning back with his hands resting on the ledge of the seat.

Sitting beside him, I let out a long, calming sigh.

"Do you wanna talk about it?" He asks, leaning forward, resting his hands in his lap.

I cock my head, giving him a side long glance. "You're barely seventeen."

He smirks. "Doesn't mean I can't listen."

"Very true." I lean forward, resting my forearms on my thighs. "There's not much to listen to though."

"Was she pissed?"

"Yes."

Reign tosses his head back with laughter, making me smile. "That's a good thing."

"How so?" I sit up, looking at him.

"A reaction means she cares, too."

I keep my eyes on the profile of his face as he stares at the Basquiat painting. "You're wise beyond your years."

"That... or I've been through some fucked up shit."

"That too." We share a laugh.

"You asked about my mother. I tried to reach out to her when I found her." He tilts his head to the side, taking the painting in from a different angle. "There was no reaction or notion that she cared. Anything from her would've been better than the radio silence I received. When people don't care, they won't waste a single breath on you."

I wrap my arm around his shoulder, pulling him into a side hug. "She didn't deserve you."

Swiveling his head to look at me, he smiles. "Thanks, Winter."

"You're welcome." I turn my attention back to the painting. "Now tell me, what am I looking at?"

He lets out a sigh. "Untitled 1981 by Jean Michel Basquiat."

"I can read." I playfully shove his arm. "What do *you* see?"

Reign stares at the painting as we sit in the reverent silence of the art museum. "I see... someone falling apart and holding it together all at once. A mess on the inside, but presentable on the outside. I see... *me*."

The night got away from me. I was expecting us to raise a few thousand dollars and go home. Of course, Winter King had other plans. A million dollars is wildly outlandish. For those who don't know Winter, it looks impulsive. However, I *know* him, and this was calculated. The only people who could outbid him – without draining their bank accounts – are Snow and North. That's how things work when you're billionaire brothers I guess. You can show up on a Friday night and drop a million dollars for a date without flinching. I'd be lying if I said my heart isn't racing at the thought.

A million fucking dollars? For time with me?

People talk about their worth in hypotheticals all the time, knowing they're priceless. However, it's entirely different when Winter King pays a million dollars for a few hours of your time and wouldn't hesitate to spend more.

This isn't only about the money or date. It's about me and Winter and all the things that have been left unsaid between us for over a decade. When I'm in his gravity, it feels like only we exist. Not to mention, I turn feral as if I have no self-restraint. No, not as if. I absolutely fucking *don't* have any self-restraint when it comes to Winter. My body still tingles with his lingering energy.

After the auction, I was ready to leave. We ended up staying a little longer for photos, drinks, and dancing. One glass of wine turned into what I am now sure was a bottle with the way my head is splitting open this morning. Squeezing my eyes shut, I feel around for my trilling phone only to realize it's somewhere in my room and won't shut up.

Noah drapes his arm across my body. "Let it ring."

He doesn't have to tell me. Closing my eyes, I easily drift back off to sleep only to have my phone start incessantly buzzing and ringing again.

"I better get it." I whimper because even talking hurts.

He responds with a light snore.

It's Saturday, what could someone possibly want today? The clinic is open for emergency appointments only, and they rarely need me. Instead of standing and possibly puking all over the fur rug, I slide off the side of the bed like a slinky and sit on the floor until the room stops spinning. My efforts prove to be pointless once I try to crawl across the room to my clutch that's lying haphazardly on the floor near the window along with my dress. The room spins and sways with any movement while an ice pick feels like it's lodged in my skull.

Reaching my bag, I ball up my dress, using it as a pillow, and grab for my bag with my eyes closed. My phone is still buzzing and ringing when I pull it out. Staring at the screen that's flooded with notifications, I blink a few times, wondering if I'm seeing double. I rub the sleep from my eyes and sit up against the wall as I unlock my phone.

I have hundreds of notifications. "What the fuck?" I mutter, reading a preview of one of them.

'The King's Million Dollar Sweetheart'. "Who the fuck?" I open the article and am met by a picture of Winter and me. My breath gets caught in my throat... or it could be puke. Either way I scramble to my feet and into the bathroom, ignoring my raging headache. I slam the door shut behind me and lock it.

I look at the picture again with shaky hands. We look like a happy couple. He's saying some smartass remark into my ear, making me laugh as he holds me close with his arm wrapped around my waist. Another notification scrolls across the top of my screen. I mean to swipe it away, but end up opening it. It's a news clip, not from the local news–from *national* news. National fucking news all because Winter fucking King decided to bid a million goddamn dollars for a date with me.

Sweat breaks out across my brow as my heart pounds, causing my stomach to flip. I grip the edges of the cool porcelain sink, dropping my phone on the ground, and puke into the basin.

This is all too much. My mind is reeling. National news? Front page of the newspaper? There were far more interesting things to happen last night, yet Winter and I have become the face of it. My phone rings. I ignore it while I finish puking. Once my stomach settles, I slowly stand up, facing myself in the mirror. I look like utter hell. Grabbing my toothpaste and toothbrush, I angrily brush my teeth. With a million questions running through my mind while my phone rings and buzzes incessantly.

Rinsing with mouthwash, I spit it in the sink and grab my phone just as it lights up with a call from Noah's mom.

"Not today, Gwen. Not fucking today." I know she's seen it. The whole world has apparently seen it. A text comes through from her seconds later.

Gwen: I was surprised to see you're trending this morning, although it isn't with my Noah.

"Your Noah?" I mutter. My disbelief turning to rage.

Shit. Noah. How is he going to take this? I pace the bathroom, tapping my phone against my palm, letting it go haywire with notifications. Wrapping myself in a robe, I quietly step into the bedroom where Noah is still sound asleep and tiptoe out to the living room to get outside to the balcony. I clear all the notifications, put my phone on do not disturb so I don't receive any more, and call Winter. It rings for an eternity before going to voicemail, making me angry. Hanging up, I immediately try again and am met by his voicemail. I let out an annoyed sigh, plopping onto one of the couches before my phone lights up with a call from him.

"What the fuck, Winter?" I seethe.

He lets out a long, drawn-out yawn, and I can tell he's stretching as if he has all the time in the world. "Good morning to you, too, Dove." His voice is gravelly with sleep.

"Don't fucking call me that!"

His chuckle resonates in my ear. "Nah. I think I'll keep calling you Dove. Or is sweetheart more fitting?"

"So you've seen the mess you've caused?"

"I don't know that I'd call it a mess."

"They've dubbed me the *King's*," I say in a mocking tone, "sweetheart."

"It has a nice ring to it, doesn't?" I hear the annoying smile in his voice.

Pressing my palm into my forehead, I groan. "Why the hell are you like this?"

"It's simple..." His voice becomes low. "Because I can be, sweetheart."

I let out a frustrated growl. "Why couldn't you have bid a reasonable amount of money?"

"Your first mistake was thinking I'm reasonable."

"You being so unbothered frustrates me." I pull bobby pins from my hair, attempting to alleviate the pounding in my head.

"What is there to do, Eve? It's already out there. We may as well find a way to enjoy it."

I lean back in the chair with a huff. "I guess..."

A second later, I'm met by the beeping of the call ending. "This son of a bitch–wait no–Carol is not a bitch. This mother fu—"

Before I can curse him to the layers below hell, my phone rings with a video call from Winter. Fantastic. I look like a crypt keeper.

"I wanted to see your face." His brilliant smile and broad, tattoo-covered chest fill the screen as he places his arm behind his head.

"I look—"

"If an insult to yourself was about to leave your lips, swallow it. You look like you had an enjoyable night out with your friends, the King... oh, and your boyfriend, I guess."

I roll my eyes. "You are so fucking arrogant. The King? For all I know, you're the one who started these salacious rumors!"

"Are you questioning my honor?" He curls his lip in fake disgust. "Do you think I, the King, would stoop so low?"

I can't help the laugh that escapes me. "Whoever wrote that article opened a can of fucking worms."

"Can you at least admit the headline is catchy?"

"And give sanction to your fuckery?" I scrunch up my face, adjusting my robe. "I think not!"

"That's fair, Sweetheart. That's fair." He nods, his basalt eyes holding mine. "Can we at least make a pact to enjoy this wave?"

There's sincerity in his eyes. He's right. There isn't much we can do about it now. It's already out there. Stressing won't make it go away. They say when a riptide sweeps you away, not to fight it. Winter reminds me of a riptide. "I'm not breaking up with Noah."

He lets out an exasperated sigh. "Eve... I'm not concerned about him and neither are you."

"I care about Noah."

"You care about him?" He gives me a bemused expression.

"I do! And I don't need to prove it to you."

He chuckles. "He's not as dumb as you make him out to be, Eve. Noah may not know for certain that you still love me, but he *knows* something."

I pick at the loops of my French terry robe. "Do you still love me?"

He sits up, leaning against the plush black headboard of his bed. "You say *still* as if I ever stopped."

Silence falls between us as I take in him and his words.

"Eve, you're not ready to hear those words from me. You're barely even ready to be around me, and I refuse to cast those words at a wall of resentment."

If he did say I love you, I'm not sure I'd believe it even if I do feel it. There's a lot of hurt that I've been harboring that has turned into resentment. It was easy to hate him when he wasn't in my life anymore because I was able to make up the narrative. Now he's here on my phone, shirtless and smiling, asking me to make a pact to set my apprehension aside and enjoy whatever comes.

I concede. "Okay. I'll try to enjoy whatever this is."

"Good, but I have to warn you, if you come at me again with your feminine wiles, I'm gonna throat chop you."

"Winter!" My cackle echoes through the morning air.

"It's wild I'm having to fight you off at every turn to stop you from kissing me," he says with a smirk.

"You make it seem like I'm attacking you."

"Damn near. Except you keep offering me scraps."

I curl my lip. "Scraps?"

"Yes, Eve. You're offering me stale crumbs while Noble Noah gets the whole cookie."

I succumb to a fit of laughter. "Did you just call me stale?"

He ignores my question. "Know that the next time you offer me anything – I'm taking it and licking the fucking plate until I've had my fill. If you thought I was insatiable back then, you have no clue what I'd do to you now. I've got ten years to make up for."

The heat in his eyes makes me swallow my laughter.

He chuckles smoothly. "Only come for me when you're ready to be devoured in all ways, Sweetheart. Until then, do your thing."

Winter is memorably skilled in making my soul sing. The first time we had sex, I swore I saw God. I had been with other guys who were well versed between the sheets, but Winter wrote the fucking book. The memories alone make me cross my legs, tightly squeezing my thighs together.

"I'll... keep that in mind."

"You do that."

"Elle is calling me," I say as her name flashes at the top of my screen. "I better answer it. Talk to you later." My tone rises at the end, making it sound like a question.

"You know where to find me, Dove."

Smiling as he says goodbye, I end the videochat and answer Elle's call.

"Want to go to breakfast or are you too big of a celebrity now?"

Now that I've calmed down after talking to Winter, I give her a lighthearted chuckle. "Yeah. Lose my number."

"Giving me up for the limelight, huh? The tabloids would love all the stories I have on you," she says in a teasing tone.

"Traitorous bitch!" She cackles at my reply. "Is it sad this is probably the most exciting thing to ever happen in my life?"

"No. You're not really a risk taker, Eve. You could use a little upheaval."

"This is more than a little upheaval." *Winter* is more than a little upheaval.

"True, but sink or swim, babe. And if I know you, you'll sprout wings and fucking fly."

I smile at her words. "Thank you for always having my back, Elle."

"Always. Now, I'm starving. Do you want to meetup for breakfast or not?"

"Yeah. Are you bringing Snow?"

"No. He's meeting up with the guys."

"Okay. Flapjacks in an hour or so?"

"See you there."

Walking back into the bedroom, Noah is snoring a little louder, making me smile as I slip into the bathroom to get ready.

After a steaming shower, I do minimal makeup, focusing on my brows and coating my lips with a clear gloss. Putting my curls into a slicked-back low bun, I pull on a pair of khaki-colored joggers, a matching hoodie, put some large solid gold hoop earrings on, and complete the look with white sneakers and a cross body bag. Noah is still sleeping when I step out of my closet. Instead of waking him, I leave a note. This is his first true day off in a while. He needs the rest. I doubt he'll be up by the time I get back anyway.

> Didn't want to wake you. I'm at
> breakfast with the girls. Take a
> deep breath before you check your
> phone. It's in the top drawer of my
> dresser. I'll bring you back a
> coffee.
> P,
> Eve

I take his phone out of his pants pocket and see that it's also filled with notifications, having missed fifteen calls from his mother. Letting out a sigh, I put it in my dresser drawer. I don't want him to wake up and see his phone before reading my note. Not that it will lessen the blow of seeing your girlfriend gracing the front page of the newspaper with her ex-fiancé. Nor will the fact that the "King" and his "million dollar sweetheart" are trending without a single mention of the sweetheart being in a relationship.

"A clusterfuck..." I mutter swiping my keys and shades off the table as I walk out the front door.

I'm met by the smell of coffee, freshly made pancakes, and the sound of applause when I step into Flapjack's Brew. This city is too fucking small. I immediately want to walk right back out, but Sunday wraps her arm around me, keeping me in place while everyone stares at me.

"If it isn't our very own celebrity."

"Sunday, please." Though no one can tell I'm blushing, my face and neck are on fire. "I just want to have breakfast with the girls."

"I understand." She gives me a squeeze. "I'm happy to see you're not too good for my pancakes or coffee now."

"Never that." I offer a smile, hoping I can eat breakfast in peace.

"The girls are this way." She guides me to a table in the back of the restaurant, tucked away from curious eyes. "Thought you'd be more comfortable back here today. And don't worry, no one will dare bother you."

"Thanks, Sunday."

She gently pats my arm, offering a warm smile, leaving me with Elle and Aspen.

"Welcomed by applause?" Aspen grins. "Next, we'll be fighting off the paparazzi."

"You make it seem like this in enjoyable for me." I ignore the waiting mimosa and grab the water, taking a gulp. "It's not."

"I imagine it's a lot," Elle says sympathetically.

"It hasn't sunk in yet, honestly." I reach for a slice of strawberry from the bowl of fruit in the center of the table.

"It'll blow over soon."

Aspen snorts. "Doubtful. I saw the video of Winter bidding a million dollars making its rounds on every social media outlet this morning. And those pictures of you two…" She does a chef's kiss motion with her hand.

"Okay, you probably hate them, but," Elle says around a mouthful of fruit, "you have to admit they are stunning."

"There's more than one?" My eyes widen.

"Yes." Aspen pulls her phone from her clutch. "Let me show you."

Holding my hand up, I shake it, cradling my face in my other hand as I let out a groan. "No, no. It's okay. I don't need to die of embarrassment today."

"I can assure you," Elle says. "There's *nothing* embarrassing about how good you two look."

"Once you're done being dramatic," Aspen slips her phone back into her bag, "you should take a peek. They really are nice pictures."

"I'll think about it." I take a bite of kiwi. "I told Winter I'd *try* to enjoy whatever this media circus brings."

"You two talked already?" Elle asks.

"I called to cuss him out."

"Naturally," Aspen snickers.

"He didn't have to bid such a ridiculous amount!"

A slow smile spreads across Elle's face.

"What?" I snap.

"Winter bid a million dollars to spend a few hours with you. Doesn't that make you get butterflies?"

"She probably crushes their wings before they can even take flight." Aspen takes a long sip of her mimosa while Elle's shoulders shake with laughter.

I gape at them. "You make me sound like a crochety bitch."

"Aye." Aspen points her fork at me with a speared peach on the end of it. "Better you say it than me."

"What do you all want me to do? Jump for joy?"

Elle takes a sip of her mimosa. "No. But it won't kill you to enjoy it. This could also be good for the clinic. Think long term. Not just how you feel right now."

I begrudgingly admit to myself that Elle is right. The clinic would've never gotten this kind of exposure without a little help from Winter's ego. More exposure means more funding opportunities for services.

Indigo appears, setting pancakes, butter, and syrup in front of us. "Morning, Eve. Would you like your coffee now or will you grab it on your way out?"

"On my way out. Thank you, Indigo."

"Sure thing." She smiles, leaving us alone again.

The sight of the fluffy, steaming pancakes makes my mouth water. Spearing one with my fork, I waste no time putting it on my plate, slathering it with butter and dousing it in syrup. While eating, we recap the night. Getting together as a group always promises a memorable time. The stack of pancakes diminishes slowly until there's nothing left.

Sitting back in my chair, I'm sated with something other than alcohol in my system. I'm ready to go back home and take a nap.

"How did Noah take the news?" Elle wipes her lips with a napkin.

I tug at hoop dangling from my ear. "He was still sleeping when I left."

"He'll be fine." Aspen waves her hand airily. "It's not like you and Winter are fucking on the side or something."

I tug at the neck of my hoodie, avoiding eye contact.

"You're not…" Elle leans to the side, catching my gaze. "Right, Eve?"

Closing my eyes, I take a deep breath. "No, things just got a little heated last night."

"You fucked him backstage?" Aspen gasps with a look of wonder in her eyes.

"No!" I hold up both of my hands with wide eyes. "We just talked and…"

Elle covers her mouth with her hands, gasping. "Did you two kiss again?"

"No! Damn," I let out an exasperated sigh, resting my elbows on the table, cradling my head in my hands. "Will you two stop jumping to conclusions?"

"Fine," Aspen says, drinking the last bit of her mimosa. "Hurry and tell us before we shout you fucked him and really give everyone something to talk about."

Elle cackles while I glare at them.

"We just talked, and I'm not gonna lie, I would've kissed him, but… he stopped me."

It's embarrassing to admit he rejected me.

"He told me this morning I offer him crumbs while, and I quote, 'Noble Noah gets the whole cookie'."

They fall into a fit of laughter that garners attention from nosy and curious patrons.

"Hush!" I hiss.

"Noble Noah!" Aspen covers her mouth, laughing. "That's perfect for him."

"Winter is good with nicknames." Elle says.

"Should've known not to tell you two shit." I swipe my glass of water off the table, drinking the rest, causing a minor brain freeze. "Do you guys even like Noah?"

"Oh, babe." Elle tries to hold in her laughter and fails. "Listen, Noah is a good guy. We're just used to Winter."

Aspen straightens up, splaying her hand across her chest. "I personally have no problem saying Noah is a fucking square." I gape at her. "But I like him well enough."

"Our opinions don't matter, though," Elle says. "What matters is that you like him."

"And you do like him... right?" Aspen asks.

"Yes." I smile. "Despite my moment of temporary weakness."

"How you haven't fucked Winter yet is a miracle of itself." Aspen shakes her head with a look of disbelief.

"Aspen!" I exclaim.

"What?" She shrugs her shoulders. "Noah is cute in like a... aw kinda way, you know? Whereas Winter...," she licks her lips, biting her bottom one, "will have you questioning your morals."

I knit my brows, cocking my head to the side. "Have you... slept with him?"

"No," she says causally with a smirk. "But you just proved my point."

Elle nudges her arm, pointing at me. "She's still thinking about that dick!"

I watch them high five each other, cackling at me. "I don't know why I even bothered coming to breakfast with you two." Despite my annoyance, the corners of my mouth tip up. I'm also relieved to know Aspen and Winter haven't slept together. Not that I'd have a right to be upset if they had.

"Also, I'm a little offended you asked if I'd slept with Winter? Do you think I'd do that to you?" Aspen asks, all playfulness gone from her demeanor.

"It wouldn't matter. We're not together and haven't been for—"

"So you do think I'd sleep with him?" Her brows knit together.

"No, but... he is good looking..." I grumble the last bit, annoyed I'm admitting it out loud.

"You *do* think he's good looking then?" A sly smile appears on Elle's lips.

"I never said he wasn't."

"Eve, just good looking?" Aspen asks with a look of disbelief. "Winter is criminally attractive."

I'm well aware of how attractive Winter is. I couldn't forget even if I tried.

"Okay, and? What do you want me to say?"

"Oh, honey." Elle clutches her chest, giving me a sympathetic look. "Don't you feel constipated pretending Winter ain't shit when we all know, and *see*, it isn't true?" She smiles innocently, batting her lashes.

Grabbing my mimosa, I take a sip out of irritation. "I *know* Winter is criminally attractive," I say in a mocking tone before taking another gulp. "In case you two forgot, I was with him for four years before *he* left. You'd think ten years would be enough time to forget someone. I'm here to tell you, it isn't. I remember the way he smells, the way his hands feel against my skin... even the way he fucking tastes."

Noelle and Aspen stare at me with their mouths agape. I continue my tirade anyway.

"It's as if no time has passed at all." I let out an exasperated sigh. "The only difference now is he's older, wiser, and yes, criminally attractive."

I tip my glass toward them before downing the other half of the mimosa, wiping my mouth with the back of my hand and setting the glass aside. "Admitting this gets me nowhere though. I refuse to get hurt again."

A long silence ensues while Noelle and Aspen study me, deciding what to say in response. Aspen speaks first.

"Girl..." She grabs my hand. "We just wanted you to admit he's fine as fuck, and you unleashed ten years of pent up frustration."

I blink at her. "I did go off on a tangent, didn't I?"

"Told you you're constipated." Elle gives me a smug smile.

We talk a while longer before heading to the front to pay. Of course the Universe thinks I haven't had enough. The King brothers, Reign included, are at the front getting coffee. Winter, of course, is looking *criminally attractive*, wearing a pair of slim fitting jeans, white air max sneakers, a baby blue hoodie, and diamond studs in his ears. Naturally he's wearing baby blue. He's always looked good in it. Winter's smile is on full display, talking to Reign. I was pleasantly surprised he was his plus one last night. From what I've heard, Winter gets around and could've easily had a beautiful woman on his arm.

Instead, he had a seventeen-year-old boy by his side who fits in as if his last name is King. I can't help but smile at the sight of them. Winter focuses on me. He says something to Reign before closing the short distance between us.

"From the way you looked earlier, I'm shocked you're up and out."

I gasp, laughing with disbelief, playfully punching his arm. "You're rude as hell."

Catching my wrist, he pulls me toward him, wrapping his arms around me, and presses a kiss to my third eye.

"Nah, Sweetheart. I'm the only one who dares to give you shit."

For a few seconds, I melt into him, closing my eyes to really savor the feeling. When I open my eyes, Sunday is standing behind the counter smiling at us. I clear my throat, hastily pulling away. Glancing around the café, all eyes are on Winter and me and a few have their phones out. I slide my shades off the top of my head and over my eyes.

"Um... this is really weird." I hug myself. "I think I'm gonna take off."

"I'll walk you out." He turns his attention to Reign. "I'll be right back."

"Hi, Reign." I smile, walking toward the door.

"You're not gonna hang out with us?" he looks at me expectantly.

"No, but maybe some other time?"

"Yeah." He nods. "I'd like that."

"Okay. Have fun with the guys."

Snow and North give me nods of acknowledgement as Winter wraps his arm around my shoulders, guiding me out the door. Looking back over my shoulder, every person in the café is staring after us.

"Winter..." I brush his arm off me. "Are you trying to give them something else to talk about?"

"They're going to talk regardless. Might as well make the gossip interesting." Draping his arm over my shoulders, he pulls me into him again.

I let out an exasperated sigh. "I have a boyfriend."

"I'm aware. Tell yourself that the next time you try to kiss me."

I try to stop in my tracks, but he keeps me in step beside him. "You're enjoying this way too much."

"You're enjoying this way too little. If you didn't have Noble Noah at your beck and call, how would this have played out?"

I would've kissed you uninhibitedly. And we'd still be having breakfast in bed right about now. "The only reason this happened is because you wanted to prove a point to Noah," I say instead, giving him a condescending sneer.

"Exactly. So, I'm not to blame, Sweetheart."

I growl with frustration, narrowing my eyes at him. "You are so..."

"So?" he asks with an annoying smile.

"So..." I cast around in my mind for the right word because I want to call him many things at the moment.

"You said that already, Dove."

"You're so damn insufferable." Pulling away from him, I quicken my pace toward my car. I stop with my fingers wrapped around the door handle. "Dammit. I was too busy being annoyed by you that I forgot my damn coffee."

He has the decency to try to hide the smile creeping across his face, failing miserably. "I can get it for you."

"And Noah's?" I cross my arms, glaring at him.

"Hmm..." He folds one arm across his chest and cradles his chin in the other hand. "What would Noble Noah do?"

"Oh my God." I let out a puff of air, raising my arms in the air, letting them slap against my thighs with annoyance while rolling my eyes.

He laughs at my displeasure. "I can get his too." Hiking his thumb over his shoulder, he asks, "Did anyone give you a hard time in there?"

Winter's soft concerned tone makes me warmer than I should be. "Um..." I clear my throat. "No. Thank you for asking."

He brings his hand up between us, caressing my cheek with his thumb. "You never did like being the center of attention. Remember when..." His voice trails off, and his smile fades. "Never mind."

He shakes his head, letting his hand drop, but I catch it.

Holding it, I ask, "Remember when, what?"

"Remember when…" He hesitates a few breaths. "I proposed to you, and it was just us two? You were so happy. *I* was so happy. And then our parents surprised us with an engagement party."

His eyes swim with emotion, and despite the heaviness vibrating between us, I laugh, leaning into his chest.

"I passed out…" My voice is muffled against his chest. "In front of everyone. It was so embarrassing."

He chuckles softly. "To be fair, there were a lot of people yelling at us when we stepped through the door."

"I was overwhelmed."

"Good thing you didn't pass out last night. I wouldn't have been there to catch you."

I tip my head back, looking into his eyes. "You'd still catch me?"

"No, Eve. I'd let you get a concussion."

I snort with laughter. "It was a ridiculous question," I say, looking down at my feet.

He gently grabs my chin. "In case there's any doubt, I'm going to catch you every time."

I get lost in his eyes. It's hard not to with the promise of his words alight in them. Blinking, I put space between us, backing away. "So… the coffee?"

"I'm surprised you didn't try and kiss me just now."

I playfully punch his arm. "Go get the damn coffee!"

"Alright, alright. I'm going. What does Noble Noah even drink?"

"Iced honey vanilla latte with oat milk."

Winter blinks at me and I can tell he's trying to keep a smile off his face.

"What?" I snap.

"Nothing." He licks his lips, nodding. "That's very fitting for him."

I attempt to swat at him again, and he jumps out of my reach, laughing. "I'll be back."

I watch him walk away before letting out a puff of air, blowing a raspberry, leaning against my car. It's a gorgeous spring morning. I close my eyes and turn my face toward the sun, letting the rays kiss my cheeks to warm them. The hangover is disappearing now that I'm full. I wonder if Noah's up yet.

I'm not sure how he'll react to the news. Noah is even tempered, but everyone has their breaking point, and this very well may be it. Before I can give it too much thought, Winter is striding toward me with two coffees in hand. A smile creeps across my face, and I let it shine instead of trying to stifle it.

"They're out of oat milk." He holds the coffees out to me.

I take them from his hands. "Really?"

"I'm fuckin' with you."

Sucking my teeth, I glare at him. "He's lactose intolerant so—"

"Damn. I should've gotten regular milk and not said shit."

"You're so evil." Laughter tumbles from my lips. "It's a pity he thinks you're honorable."

"I'm a topic of conversation for you two?"

"Bye, Winter." I roll my eyes, turning away from him to set the coffees in the cup holders in my car.

"It's a simple question, Sweetheart."

Turning to face him again, I say, "If you must know, we've talked about you twice. Once for the gala and the second time..."

My voice trails off, remembering Noah being jealous about Winter buying me coffee... and here I am again. Except this time, he's buying us both coffee.

"The point is, you're not a topic of conversation for us."

"I would be if he knew you're going to dinner with me and trying to kiss me every chance you get."

My mouth falls open. "I do not! I've had plenty of opportunities to kiss you and–you know what?" I take a calming breath. "I don't have to explain myself."

"You're right. You don't." He slips his hand around the back of my neck pulling me toward him and presses a kiss over my third eye. "But I'm happy to know I'll be the topic of conversation once he sees the headlines."

Releasing me, he takes a step back, giving me a mix of a wave and salute. "Enjoy the coffee, Dove. Or should I say tea?"

Petty ass motherfucker.

Noah is still sleeping when I arrive at my apartment, thankfully. I didn't want him to wake up and wade through the text messages and headlines before we had a chance to talk. Quietly grabbing the note I left for him off the nightstand, I crumple it up and take it with me out to the kitchen to throw it away. Letting out a sigh, I lean forward, resting my elbows on the kitchen counter, taking a moment to breathe. A walk to clear my head sounds very tempting, but I want to be here in when Noah wakes up.

As if my chaotic energy shook him awake, he appears in the kitchen, rubbing sleep from his eyes.

"Morning." He rounds the counter, pressing a kiss to my cheek. "I'm surprised you're up before me."

"I got you coffee." I grab it off the counter, handing it to him.

"And you got me coffee?" He gives me another kiss. This time on the lips. "Thank you."

"You're welcome." I can feel myself perspiring underneath my sweatsuit. My stomach feels queasy as it ties itself in knots.

"Have you seen my phone?" He takes a seat at the kitchen island.

I nibble on my lip, slipping my hands into the pocket of my hoodie. "Can we talk for a second?"

Noah stops mid-sip, letting the straw fall from his lips, giving me a curious look.

"Are you okay?" Standing, he approaches me and presses his hand to my forehead. "You're clammy. Let's go sit down and we can talk."

I let him guide me to the living room where we sit on the plush white couch. Pulling at the neck of my hoodie, I swallow the feeling of sand that's taken up residence in my throat.

"What's up?" He looks at me with concern filled eyes.

"I'm in the newspaper..."

"That's great." He smiles. "It'll be good for the clinic."

"In a way... maybe." I fiddle with the drawstrings of my hoodie. "Winter and I are on the front page. They sensationalized his bid and it sort of... snowballed. It went viral online, made national headlines, and apparently we're also a trending topic."

Noah stares at me blankly. "Who's we?"

"Me and Winter. It looks like we're a couple and–I'm sorry Noah." I look away from him cringing.

"Is that why I can't find my phone this morning?"

My headache is back with a vengeance due to my pounding heart.

"I didn't want you to see all of that before I had a chance to tell you. I woke up to hundreds of notifications... and passive aggressive texts from your mom. Noah," I grab his hand. "I had no idea Winter was going to do that. Never in my wildest dreams did I think it be newsworthy. It was just a stupid bid."

A million-dollar bid, a voice in my head whispers.

"Where's my phone, Eve?" His tone is monotonous.

Tears fill my eyes and as selfish and fucked up as it may sound, I realize I care about Noah because I don't want to lose him. "Noah—"

"Can you get my phone… please?" His eyes are on me, but it's as though he's looking through glass.

"Yeah." I rise to my feet on shaky legs.

I try not to panic as I head to my room. This is the exact reason why I've avoided relationships. I can't stand the heartbreak. Opening the dresser drawer, I grab his phone, and slowly return to the living room. He takes it when I hold it out to him.

His eyes widen when he looks at it, but he doesn't meet my gaze. Unlocking his phone, he scrolls through the messages. I want the floor to swallow me whole when he opens the article, staring at the picture of Winter and me. Shoving my hands into my hoodie pocket, I wring them.

He's gonna leave. He's gonna leave. He's gonna leave. It's on repeat in my head. *This is why you never get too close. Silly girl. Don't you remember what happened last time? You were left alone with a broken heart and missing pieces.*

Noah reads the article slowly before setting his phone on the glass coffee table. He leans forward, resting his elbows on his thighs, steepling his hands in front of his mouth. I've never seen Noah be anything other than caring, and for the most part, happy.

"You can sit," he mumbles around his hands.

Staring at the spot beside him, I choose to sit on the other end of the couch. He lets out a long low sigh, closing his eyes, and then turning his head to finally look at me.

"Are you still in love with him?"

"What?" I can't tear my eyes away from his, wondering if he can see the truth in them.

"Are you still in love with Winter?"

"No." The lie burns as I swallow the truth. "I'm not."

He studies me, tilting his head to the side. "He said something at the gala that..."

My stomach rolls. "What did he say?"

Turning his attention back to his phone, he says, "Nothing. The pictures are nice."

If my heart could leap out of my chest, it would.

"You looked gorgeous."

It settles for slamming against my ribcage.

"Eve... you know how I feel about you, right?" He reaches out for me, grabbing my hand, and scoots closer.

The ache in my chest eases a little. "I do."

"Then you know that some news articles painting a different picture than what I see in front of me, *who* I see in front of me, isn't going to change the fact that I love you."

"You..." I stare at him with a mixture of surprise and confusion. "What?"

"I love you, Eve."

"Me?"

He chuckles. "Yes. Just you. Only you."

All I can do is stare at him.

"I'm not telling you this, expecting to hear it back if you're not ready. But I felt you needed to hear it this morning, and know that I love you. I have for quite a while and will for the rest of my days."

"I love you too." The words tumble from my lips before I have time to think. "I was so scared you were going to leave."

His brows knit together with concern. "Leave? No." He pulls me onto his lap. "I just needed to see what you were talking about to understand why you looked two seconds away from passing out."

"I thought you were going to leave," I repeat. Still in shock from three little words.

"I'm not going anywhere, Eve. I can promise you that."

I wrap my arms tightly around his neck. "I love you, Noah."

My heart wonders, *Can you love two people at the same time? Do you love him or are you scared of being alone?*

He wraps his arms snugly around me, silencing the thoughts. "Love you too, Eve."

I was ready for Noah to leave. Expected him to. It feels like every time I move forward, I realize the depth of the crater in my soul Winter left behind in his wake. I'm not sure if it'll ever be healed or if the only person with the salve to heal it is the same person who caused it.

The aching in my chest subsides. It never completely leaves, it's always present, reminding me of how hurt I could be. For now, Noah's strong arms and whispered words are enough to soothe the pain.

15

EVE

SITTING AT MY DESK, Haven pops her head into my office. "Hey. Winter is here to see you."

My body stills. "Did he say why?"

Since seeing each other at Flapjack's a week ago I've been trying to avoid him. Another picture popped up online of him kissing my forehead after handing me the coffee. The story has caught on like wildfire, and I've been trying to put out the flames.

"No. I didn't—"

"Thank you, Haven," Winter says, appearing behind her, taking up the doorframe, and she steps aside. "This will only take a second."

"O... kay." She glances between us. "I will leave you two alone."

I want to say please don't, but Winter is already closing the door on Haven's curious eyes.

"If you'd answer my texts or calls, I wouldn't be here."

There's no point in lying and saying I haven't gotten them when I've been leaving him on read.

"I don't want to add more fuel to the already out of hand fire."

"Right, well. This is affecting me too. Did you ever think of that?"

I sit back in my chair as if his words pushed me. "No."

"Of course you didn't." The spicy, sweet scent of him fills my office.

"What's that supposed to mean?"

"Meaning," He rests his ankle atop his other knee, taking up even more space. "You have a tendency to only see yourself in stressful situations."

I cross my arms, scowling at him. "Excuse me. Were you not the one talking about riding the wave?"

He unbuttons his suit jacket, giving me a better view of his chest. "I was. When I thought you were going to be riding it with me." Winter shakes his head as if clearing it. "That doesn't matter. The only reason I'm here is to check on you."

"Check on me?"

"Yes. I know you don't do well with attention."

Why does he have to be so nice? It would be easier if he wasn't.

"I'm... okay. Waiting for it to fizzle out so I can have my life back. What about you?"

"Eh... I'm used to being the center of attention." He gives me a charming smile, making me shake my head. "Although," he looks off to the side, "this is different because now you're always the topic of conversation... and it hurts a little."

My breath gets caught in my throat. "Hurts?" I whisper.

"Yeah." His eyes catch mine. "Makes me wonder what could've been with us."

Winter didn't ask for this either. Constant reminders of me, him–*us*.

"Me too," I answer honestly.

We sit in silence, letting the truth settle between us. After a moment, Winter lets out a puff of air, looking around my office before settling his eyes on me. His playful demeanor slides back into place, making me smile as he stands, adjusting his suit jacket.

"Leave me on read again, and I'll give them more to talk about. See you around, Sweetheart. Oh," he knocks against the metal doorframe, "don't worry, I'd never sell our story."

"They asked you to?" News outlets have been practically begging for interviews. I've denied all but one because they're genuinely interested in Hope's Village.

"Yeah. I considered it just to fuck with Noah, but—"

"Jackass," I say with a cackle.

"—how can you tell a story that doesn't have an ending?"

His question makes me wonder if we'll ever end or if we'll always be stuck in each other's orbit.

Sprawled out on an air mattress covered in soft blankets and plush pillows, me, Elle, and Aspen are in the middle of our final girl's night in Elle's apartment. Trash reality TV is playing in the background, and music spills from the speaker. We're not paying attention to either as we talk and laugh.

"You guys!" Elle rolls over on the mattress, crushing various junk food wrappers beneath her. "I move into my *own* home *with* my future husband tomorrow!"

She haphazardly raises her wine glass into the air, a toast to herself. It's a miracle the red wine doesn't slosh over the sides. Aspen and I clink our glasses with hers.

I snort with laughter. "Did it just hit you?"

"Yes!" She gulps down the rest of her wine, setting the glass aside. "It's finally feeling real."

"So…" Aspen drops some Skittles into her mouth. "Buying the multi-million dollar home wasn't real enough for you?"

Elle rolls her eyes at Aspen who chuckles in response. "That felt real, too, but—"

"I'm kidding!" Aspen pulls her into a hug and presses a kiss to her cheek. "It's finally happening after talking about it for months."

"Yes." Elle grabs my arm, pulling me toward them, making it a group hug. "I don't know if this would be my life if you guys didn't encourage me to take that trip over Christmas."

I wrap my arms around her middle. "You and Snow would've met somehow, some way."

"Definitely would've," Aspen agrees. "He's the other half of you."

"Still." Sandwiched between us, Elle squeezes us tight. "I love you both."

"And we love you."

"Most days," Aspen adds, squealing when Elle pinches her side. "You know how I feel about mushy stuff."

"You're mushy with North," Elle quips.

Aspen rolls her eyes, letting out an exasperated sigh. "He gave me flowers. Big whoop. Besides… they are gorgeous." She smiles, and the real reaction to the gift shines through.

"He gave you flowers?" I perk up.

"Calm down. He was just being nice. You guys know North."

"We do." Elle smiles. "And he has never bought either of us flowers."

"Oh my gosh!" Aspen pushes her away, causing both of us to topple back. "They're just flowers. Not a ring!"

Elle and I crack up. "Whoa, whoa, whoa! No one said anything about a ring."

"It's what she's hoping for," Elle says through laughter.

Aspen grabs a hand full of popcorn, throwing it in our faces. "Fuck you both!" she says through a smile.

"That's really sweet he bought you flowers, though." I sit up, pulling popcorn out of my curls.

"Thanks." She takes a bite of a sour punch straw. "How are things between you and Noah since all the buzz surrounding you and Winter?"

After nearly two weeks, the buzz died down. "Uh... good." I say, still brushing popcorn off me. "He told me he loves me." A smile spreads across my face.

If their jaws could hit the floor, they would with the way they're gaping at me. They both squeal at the same time, pulling me back into a group hug. Before anything else can be said, Winter's smooth voice fills the space.

"I'm not used to this kind of welcome, but I enjoy it."

"Shut up." North pushes past him, collapsing onto the couch.

"Excuse you!" Aspen shoves him more for dramatic effect than to actually attempt to move him. "You weren't invited."

He smiles, ignoring her, and snatches the bag of Skittles from her hand. "We're leaving soon. Snow wanted to change his clothes."

"What were you guys squealing about?" Snow asks, bending down to kiss the top of Elle's head.

"Nothing," I say quickly.

"Noah told Eve he loves her!" Aspen says in a sing-song borderline whiney voice. "Isn't that cute?"

"Awww. That's sweet!" North draws it out, mocking Aspen's tone.

"That it is." Winter sits on the edge of the couch. I can't read his expression. "Did he cry after he said it?"

Snow and North crack up. Aspen tries to keep the smile off her face, but just can't help herself. I glare at her.

"What? It's true." Aspen says. "He's a golden retriever."

"There is nothing wrong with emotional intelligence," Elle says.

"Of course not, Elle." Winter places his hand over his heart, bowing. "You're right."

"Will she say anything you won't agree with?" Snow asks.

"No." Winter shrugs. "She's one of the smartest women I know."

I can't help but to wonder who the others are and if I'm one of them. *It doesn't matter.*

"Can't be mad at that answer." Snow heads toward the bedroom. "I'm gonna go change."

Elle pops up, following behind him. "I'll be back."

"Aye!" North points his finger at her. "I'm starving and trying to get out of here, but your precious husband insisted on changing clothes."

Winter glances at his phone. "And we have to pick up Reign in thirty minutes."

Elle holds up her hands. "Geez! I can't talk to my husband?" They both stare blankly at her. "Fine. Fine. I'll hurry him up."

"They need a chaperone sometimes I swear," North sighs.

"That's how it's supposed to be, old man," Aspen says. "Anyway, where are you guys going tonight?"

While they chat, I get up to grab a bottle of water from the fridge. The apartment is almost bare. The TV, couch, and a few other items are being sold and picked up tomorrow. Everything that they're keeping is already at their home or on the way there. Grabbing a bottle of water, I close the fridge, and lean against the counter, taking a drink. Winter enters the kitchen, leaning against the counter opposite of me. He rests his hands on the ledge of it, causing his watch and rings to glint.

"What was your response?"

I gulp down my mouthful of water, nearly choking, and wipe my mouth with the back of my hand.

"To what?"

He crosses his arms, drawing my attention to his muscles, and crosses his legs at the ankles.

"To him professing his undying love."

Taking my time to respond, I set my bottle of water aside.

"I told him..." My voice trails off, hesitating a few seconds. "I love him too."

We hold each other's gaze for what feels like minutes. I'm sure it's only a few seconds. Agonizing seconds. *Why the fuck do I still care after all this time?* My heart races, and my stomach flips, making me feel lightheaded and nauseous. I feel a trickle of sweat trailing down my back, but I can't look away from him. Whatever emotions he's feeling, he doesn't give them away.

Pushing off the counter, he stands in front of me, causing me to tip my head back to look up at him. "I'm curious."

"About?" I swallow.

He cocks his head to the side, raising a brow. "Do you go around telling everyone you love them?"

This wasn't the response I was expecting. I open my mouth to say something, but it's so dry, nothing comes out.

"Let's go, Winter!" North hollers from the living room.

"Told you I'd hurry him up," Elle says proudly.

Winter steps away from me, turning his back without another word. I reach out for him.

"Winter..." My fingertips brush his arm.

Facing me again, his usually warm brown eyes are icy, making him look devoid of emotion. He slowly looks down at my hand as if he finds it offensive. Snatching it away, he doesn't spare me a glance as he heads for the front door.

If I don't care, then why does this hurt so fucking much?

Winter

Therapy days have become ritualistic. I visit dad, have a pre-therapy session with him. Then I drive to therapy and sift through my emotions with Dr. Maddox acting as the sieve, helping me break them down so they're not so heavy. Afterwards, I keep my phone on do not disturb, grab something to eat, and then go home to decompress.

Except today, there's a deviance in my ritual. My steps slow as I approach Dad's grave. I'm surprised to see Snow standing in front of his headstone. I come to a halt, trying to decide if I should give him space and come back after therapy.

Without turning, he says, "I'm sure we spend the same amount of time here, yet this is the first time we've been here together since—"

"The funeral." I close the gap between us, standing beside him, shoulder to shoulder.

"Yeah." His voice is barely audible.

We stare at Dad's headstone, getting lost in thoughts of what once was and what could've been. Snow shrugs out of his jacket, throwing it on the grass, and sits on top of it. I do the same. We both plant our feet on the ground, hooking our arms around our knees.

"How often do you come?"

A smirk tugs at my lips. "Enough for me to know the groundskeeper by his first name."

"Casper?"

"Isn't his name ironic?" I chuckle.

Snow smiles. "I thought he was messing with me at first when he introduced himself."

"Same!

"He's friendly, too."

We both sing the Casper theme song, leaning against each other, laughing. "I want to watch that movie now."

"Me too. Dad would be proud we've clearly never grown up."

"Never that." I hesitate before asking, "What's on your mind that you're visiting Dad?"

"Everything." He blows out a puff of air, running his hand over the expertly trimmed grass. "I wish he could meet Noelle."

"He would love her. Like we all do."

"I know. What brings you here?" He leans back, pressing his palms into the earth, stretching his legs out in front of him.

I sprawl out on the grass, laying on my back, watching the clouds lazily float by. "I always come here before therapy."

He doesn't need to look at me for me to see the smile on his face. "I knew you weren't meeting up with someone." Joining me, he lies on his back, letting out a sigh.

"What did you think I was doing?" A cloud passes by that resembles a teddy bear.

"I don't know. Just assumed whatever it was you wanted to keep private and you'd tell me when you were ready."

"You trust me again?" I watch him out of the corner of my eye.

He shifts, turning his head to look at me. "With my life."

I smile, returning my gaze back to the sky.

"How's it going?" he asks. "With therapy."

"Good. Great, actually."

He chuckles. "You sound surprised."

"I am. I know you've encouraged me to go on multiple occasions, but I wasn't ready until now."

"I feel that. What changed?"

I take a deep breath, linking my hands together, bringing them behind my head. "I was... my father's son. He led. I followed. Then he died, and I became CEO and the head of our household. The responsibilities were never ending. I was a fiancé, expected to walk down the aisle when the foundation I stood on for so long was demolished to dust. Finally, to really drive the point home that I didn't have a clue who I was, I became an addict and gambler.

"I've been countless versions of myself but have known none of them. So I kept burning everything down around me until the ash settled and I could see I never got to know myself. Just me. Winter." I place my hand over my heart. "Not the oldest son, the big brother, the CEO, the fiancé, the fuck up, the womanizer... just me. I'm trying to figure out who *I* am."

Snow doesn't say anything for a few beats. The only sound is the breeze rustling through the leaves.

"After you left, I was terrified every time the phone rang with an unknown number it was someone calling me to tell me you were dead."

"I'm sorry."

"No, I'm sorry you thought you had to carry all of that alone."

The hole that's been in my chest, *my soul*, for countless years gets a little smaller, making it feel tight. Emotions lodge themselves in my throat as my eyes sting with tears.

"You know you're not alone, right?" Snow holds up his hand between us and I wrap mine tightly around his. "I always got you. Through everything."

His eyes become glossy like my own.

"Love you," is all I can manage to say around the emotions.

"Love you, too." He squeezes my hand again before letting it go.

We sit in a comfortable silence, lying on our backs over Dad's grave watching the clouds overhead.

"Maybe Dad thought we needed to talk today." Snow says after a few minutes.

"Yeah. I'm glad you're here."

"How do you feel after talking to your brother?" Dr. Maddox asks, sitting in the chair across from me.

Our sessions are feeling more like I'm talking to an old friend than to someone I pay to talk to for an hour.

"Light." I smile. "When I went off the deep end, I created a rift between us. I knew without a doubt he loved me, or he wouldn't have been there, but I could also see the disappointment in his eyes, too. The resentment..."

"Why do you feel there was resentment there?" His elbow rests on the seats plush arm with his hand fisted underneath his chin.

"Because he took on the burden I refused to bear. The life I have right now is because of him. He's sacrificed and lost a lot. And I wasn't there for him. When his fiancé died..." The familiar sting of tears pricks my eyes, and I tip my head back, swallowing the lump in my throat. "Instead of showing up for him, I asked for money to get more drugs and out of a gambling debt."

Trying to stop the tears is useless, so I let them fall, staring up at the ceiling. I hear Dr. Maddox moving around and hear him place a box of tissue on the glossy wooden end table beside me. Grabbing one without looking at him, I wipe the tears from my face.

"Have you two talked about this?"

"A couple of times." My voice is barely a whisper. "He could tolerate me being elusive, the gambling, and even the drugs, but that – showing no regard for him losing his fiancé – was what caused the biggest rift between us. Snow has always been there for me and..." My voice trails off, regret sitting on the tip of my tongue.

A brief silence ensues, Dr. Maddox letting me sit with the intrusive thoughts before he speaks. "Winter."

I wipe my nose with the Kleenex, crumpling it in my hand, and look at him.

"Has Snow forgiven you?"

"Yes."

"Then *you* need to forgive yourself. Holding onto the pain of the past as a punishment to your present self is only going to keep you anchored to the guilt."

Leaning forward, I rest my forearms on my thighs. "I used to think forgiveness was simple."

"And now?" Dr. Maddox raises his brows with a smile tugging at his lips.

"Now." I let out a heavy exhale. "I realize how strong the roots of guilt are and how deep I have to dig to excavate and remove them."

"You're doing the work, showing up for *yourself* every day *is* doing the work, Winter. Maybe you need to figure out a symbolic way to let go of your past mistakes."

"What do you mean?" I tilt my head to the side.

"Do you have a fireplace?" I nod, furrowing my brows, wondering where this is going. "Okay, what you could do to symbolically release is take strips of paper and write down your past mistakes on them. For example, 'not being there for Snow' could be one. Write all those mistakes out on those strips of paper and then burn each individual one. As it burns, imagine your guilt burning away with the paper, giving you space to start anew."

I press my lips into a thin line, unsure if something as simple as that can possibly help me release years of guilt. "Will that really help?" I raise a skeptical brow.

Dr. Maddox smiles. "It's all about your intention. Are you willing to forgive yourself, Winter?"

"Yes."

"Then it doesn't hurt to try."

Instead of using the fireplace at my house, I take the forty-five minute drive to Garnet Falls. I have a secluded, small one bedroom cabin that I bought shortly after getting out of rehab. Initially, I spent a lot of time alone because I was disassociating when I was around others. I was learning to cope without the high of drugs and the rush of gambling.

It was difficult. When I was in rehab, I felt as though I was in this safe bubble with the perfect environment. After I completed the program, it felt like I was being thrust back into the world, and all coping mechanisms I learned in theory went out the window. It felt like another form of rehabilitation minus the perfect environment. I tried the support groups, therapists, counselors, meditation, sound baths... whatever it was – I tried it. It all worked in some way. The problem was, at the end of the day, I was still alone. Instead of facing that, I filled the void with acceptable vices.

Alcohol and women. Heavy on the women.

As with most bandages, they work for so long before you have to tend to the festering wound beneath. I'm learning to get comfortable with being uncomfortable, which means facing myself.

I considered doing this 'symbolic release' with Snow and North, but decided it's best to do it alone. It's for me after all.

Pulling into the graveled driveway, I cut the engine, climb out, and grab the leather duffle bag along with the cooler from the backseat. I went back and forth about spending the night since I have an event for work tomorrow, but I felt solitude and fresh air would do me some good.

Stepping into the cabin, I take a deep, relaxing breath and set the duffel bag down on the deep seated, overstuffed gray couch. The whole cabin is smaller than my living room and kitchen at my house. For all the excess I have in other spaces, there's none of that here. Where a TV would sit is a bookcase filled with worn books, board games, puzzles, and framed pictures. This space is a sanctuary for me.

Ten steps later, I'm standing in the kitchen, equipped with a stove, microwave, fridge, and minimal counter space. I set the cooler filled with shrimp, baby potatoes, smoked sausage, garlic, corn on the cob, butter, lemon, and an onion on the counter. Grilled shrimp sounded good tonight. Heading through the backdoor, I light the grill, letting it heat up while I get everything ready. Once everything is prepared and seasoned, I put the shrimp on skewers, setting them aside on a plate. I dump the potatoes and corn onto some tinfoil, fold it shut, and toss it onto the grill. This meal reminds me of Dad. When we'd go camping, or to our family cabin, it was something he'd make.

While it cooks, I grab my duffel bag and head to the room. It has a king size bed, fitted with deep teal linen sheets, taking up most the space. Setting the bag on the bed, I change into a black sweatsuit and some sneakers I don't mind getting dusty. I pull the hood up and dig into the bottom of bag for the notebook and pen I'll use to write down things I want to let go of. Maybe I'll fill up the entire notebook I chuckle to myself.

I turn the shrimp and potatoes over before heading toward the firepit. It's the only thing I invested in besides the purchasing and upkeep of the cabin. I wanted a nice fire to sit beside underneath the stars. No matter how hot it is at home, it gets chilly here at night at the cabin. While dinner cooks, I crack open the notebook and start writing what I want to let go of.

For a moment, my stare is as blank as the paper. I'm hesitant to trudge into painful things. There's an extensive list of moments I've been holding onto out of guilt. Putting the pen to paper, I let out a sigh and start writing.

Not saving Dad.

I still wish I could've saved him despite knowing it was medically impossible. Survivor's remorse.

Being angry with Dad for dying.

Why the fuck did he leave me with an astronomical amount of responsibility and expect me to be able to handle it?

Not being able to carry the family legacy according to plan.
Leaving my family to figure it out without me.
Leaving Eve without a word.

I think about this every single day. *Every. Fucking. Day.* The decision to leave wasn't right, but while I was floundering, it felt that way. Eve wasn't willing, or ready, to meet me where I was. I didn't want to be saved. I just wanted her to sit with me. To know she was by my side would've been enough.

Taking a deep breath, I let the pen fall onto the notebook, running my hands over my face. "Fuck." I mutter, setting the notebook and pen aside to check on the food.

Peeling back the foil, my stomach growls in response to the potatoes and corn. Grabbing a fork, I try a piece of potato. It's soft and ready to eat. I step inside, getting the shrimp, and put it on the grill. Once it's done, with a nice color, I plate the food, and take a seat near the firepit to eat. The only noises around me are the birds, the lake a few yards away lapping against the shore, and the wind whispering through the trees. Eating, I welcome the peaceful silence.

I'd love to bring Reign here. I'm not sure if his grandma would let him spend the night with me though. And she'd have every right to be skeptical, we still haven't met. I've met everyone else's parent or guardian. She has yet to stop by True's House or be home when I pick up or drop off Reign. For all I know, she may not even care. I hope it's not for the sake of Reign. When I ask about her, he's not too eager to divulge details either. I trust if there was something going on, he'd tell me. If not him, Calliope more than likely would.

After I'm done eating, I head inside to wash the dishes. My phone rings from my bag in the room. I contemplate getting it, putting the clean dishes in the strainer. Deciding to ignore it, I head back outside and light the fire in the pit as the sun disappears behind the mountains. Grabbing the notebook, I continue my list.

Wasting seven years of my life.

People will try and flip it to say that they were lessons I needed to learn. There was absolutely *nothing* to glean at the end of a line of cocaine or empty pockets from gambling. It was an ugly time I'd wish upon no one. End of story.

Not being there for my brothers.

I failed both of them, missing countless moments and leaving them in their grief. They say not to jump in the water after a drowning person, unless you're trained, because they can cause you to die too. I didn't want to drown them.

Worrying Mom after losing Dad.

Mom and I have an amazing relationship now. I know she loves me unconditionally even though I'm not proud of the shit I've done. Not once when I was going through it did she say she was disappointed in me. The only words ever said were 'I love you'. That made the teeth of guilt hold onto me tighter. I wondered often why I was living like no one loved me. Now I know it's because then, I didn't love myself.

Tapping the pen against the notebook, I reread what I wrote. It's not as long as I thought it'd be. Not being able to think of anything else, I start to tear the sentences into individual strips. When I think of another.

Taking so fucking long to forgive myself.

I tear it free from the notebook. The fire is blazing with embers crackling in the air. It's dark outside now and stars are twinkling in the sky. Looking down at the strips of paper in my hand, I feel like something needs to be said. So I talk to the person I always do.

"Dad... after ten years, I still don't know if you can hear me. I like to think that you can. Hopefully you can't see what I've gotten into." I laugh to myself. "And if you have, in spite of it all, I hope you're still proud of me. Losing you was... violent. It felt like someone took the air from my lungs and told me to breathe. The pain and the fear that gripped me was unrelenting.

"I'm sorry I couldn't save you. I know it's ridiculous to apologize for an inevitable, but..."

The memory of me realizing CPR wasn't working plays in my head, taking me back to the moment he slipped away like smoke in a breeze.

"I tried, Dad." Hanging my head, I look at the strips through blurred vision. "I'm in therapy now. Don't tell Snow, but he was right–it helps."

Sniffing, I wipe my nose on the sleeve of my hoodie. "The whole reason why I'm out here in the woods, talking to the stars as if they're you, is because my therapist encouraged me to let this shit go. All this guilt, anger, and grief–none of it is doing me any good.

"And in some fucked up way, over the years it's become a crutch. Something for me to fall back on and say 'See, this is why I am the way I am'. The hurt and pain can be just as addicting as the high of all the good things."

I shuffle the papers in my hands. "I'm not sure whether you're proud of who I've become, Dad, but I'm proud of me. There were countless times I could've slipped under, faded away, and I didn't. I held onto the slivers of hope that someday, somehow things would get better. I know nothing's perfect, but the life I have now is pretty damn close."

Taking a deep, cleansing breath, I shift my gaze to the fire. "Letting go of the emotions I've been tied to, in some way, means I'm letting go of you too. Just know that I'm letting go, not forgetting you... love you, Dad." Placing my hand over my heart, I look up at the stars, closing my eyes, and stand under the night sky until I'm ready. Opening my eyes again, I read the first strip of paper.

"Not saving Dad." My voice is barely above a whisper, holding onto the paper a few seconds longer before tossing it into the fire. The flames catch it, turning it to ash. I wasn't expecting watching the paper ignite and incinerate to be satisfying. It brings me a release in an inexplicable way. There's something about naming the mistakes that have kept me tied to the past and then watching them go up in smoke. It's... *freeing*.

I continue naming, tossing the paper into the flames until each strip is lost in the fire. Watching the flames burn bright, I tip my head back, letting out a sigh.

"I'm not my past nor my mistakes." I whisper the mantra to the night sky, allowing myself to believe it.

Hearing the rustling of leaves, I snap my head forward. I've been out here countless times and have only seen cougars and bears wandering. My heart rate quickens at the thought of either animal being only feet away. I strain my eyes to see something, anything, in the dark, densely wooded area of the cabin's perimeter. Hearing a twig snap, I'm about to book it inside when I see antlers.

"What the fuck is that?" I mutter. From the outline, it's too massive to be a deer or even an elk. It finally steps out of the trees, revealing itself as a... moose. I'm stunned for a few moments, placing my hand over my heart and then my lips turn up into a smile. They were Dad's favorite animal because he thought they were funny looking in a whimsical way. In fact, a stuffed moose was one of the first toys he sold when North Star

Toys opened its doors. The flames from the fire cast a warm glow over the moose. I can tell it easily towers over my six-four frame. Having never seen a moose in the wild, I'm not sure what to do other than stand still and watch it.

It inspects the ground, eating foliage, apparently oblivious to my presence. Shifting my weight, my leg brushes against the chair I was sitting in, causing it to make a sound loud enough for the moose to turn its attention toward me. We stare at each other, both frozen on the spot. After a few breaths, the moose lets out a huff air, making it look like smoke is coming from its nose in the crisp night air, acknowledging me. Staring for a few seconds longer, it must decide I'm harmless and continues eating leaves and twigs from the ground.

I have to agree with Dad, moose are whimsical—in a gigantesque way. Tonight, I'm going to choose to believe that Dad somehow guided this moose here to let me know he's with me. And always has been.

16
WINTER

WALKING INTO NORTH STAR Toys, I head for Noelle's office. I meant to be here earlier, but decided to have a slow morning to myself. Slept in, took a plunge in the frigid lake that was better than any coffee, showered, had breakfast, and then came straight to the office. A reset was much needed. The only thing I *have* to do today is attend the influencer luncheon with Noelle.

Looking down at my phone, I knock on her door, more out of courtesy than necessity, and enter without waiting for a response. Finishing out a text, I look up and am surprised to see Eve, but keep my face neutral. I forgot Noelle invited her to the event a few weeks ago. This is the first time I've seen or talked to her since the night at Elle and Snow's apartment. Our gazes collide for a split second before I focus on Elle.

"Afternoon, Miss Mistletoe." I take a seat on the leather couch near the windows. "Are you ready?"

"Hi Winter..." Eve says.

I nod without looking at her. "Eve."

"Did you just get back?" Elle smiles, linking her fingers and resting her chin on the back of her hands.

"I did. Miss me?"

"Terribly." She presses the back of her hand to her forehead, clutching her chest. "Couldn't carry on without you."

Laughter tumbles from my lips. "You deserve an Oscar."

She bows in her chair. "How was the cabin?"

"Refreshing." I feel Eve's eyes on me. "I'll tell you about it some other time."

I respond to a text from Brielle. She sent me a picture of what the event setup looks like. We wanted something laid back and fun. "Did Brielle send you the picture of the luncheon setup?"

"Amazing, right? Everyone's going to love it."

"Are you ready?" My eyes momentarily flit to Eve who is looking at me expectantly.

"Yes." She snaps her laptop closed at the same time Snow enters her office, rounding her desk to give her a kiss.

"Wrapped things up early. Glad you're back." Snow smiles in my direction. "North already left to pick up Aspen."

"Replacing me with Snow?"

Elle snorts with laughter. "Yes, I can still ride with you if you want."

Snow displays his annoyance at how easily Elle agrees with me. "Nah. I don't need Snow crying."

"Can't have that," Elle says, nudging Snow's arm playfully. "Eve, are you ready?"

"Uh... I only brought a two seater today," Snow says. "Did you not bring a car Eve?"

"No. I was going to ride with Elle... and Winter." She mumbles the last part.

"I'm sure you can still ride with him." Elle smiles at me brightly. "Or take my car."

I leave it up to her to decide. Eve looks between Elle and I, settling her eyes on me. "Do you mind if I ride with you?"

Shrugging, I say, "It doesn't matter, but we better get going or we won't make it to Fireside in time to greet the guests."

"Perfect." Elle clasps her hands together. "We'll see you guys there."

Snow gives me a look as if to say he doesn't make the rules. Standing, I motion for Eve to walk in front of me. Before I can take two steps, I feel tugging on my suit jacket. For a moment I'm ready to give Snow a slug bug, but realize it's Elle.

"Be nice," she whispers.

Eve is already out the door, walking down the hallway toward the elevator.

"I am."

Both she and Snow give me a look, knowing I'm full of shit.

"*I am*," I say with a little more emphasis. "I haven't said anything to her to be anything other than nice."

"Exactly." Elle pokes my side, causing me to move away from her.

Snow laughs, wrapping his arm around Elle's waist.

"I don't see why it matters. She has a whole ass boyfriend!" I whisper yell.

"She thought you two were friends!" Elle whisper yells back. "And then you got all weird after you found out about Noah professing his undying love."

I snort, causing Eve to glance at us over her shoulder.

"Be nice!" Elle says when Eve turns back around.

"Al-fucking-right." I adjust my suit jacket, buttoning it.

"Aye." Snow swats my arm. "Don't curse at my wife."

Letting out an exasperated sigh, I say, "Alright," through gritted teeth.

Elle gives me a triumphant smile that I don't return. I step into the elevator first, leaning against the back wall. Eve enters, standing beside me clutching the handle of her bag in her hands like I may snatch it. I suppress an audible sigh because why is she crying to Elle about me not talking to her? It's not like she's reached out either. And above all of that, *why the fuck does she care?* She's in love with Noah, allegedly. I still think the whole thing is bullshit, but I was gonna let her rock and be happy. This woman is infuriating. Wants me but doesn't fucking want me and then cries when I'm not on her ass. *Spoiled fucking brat.*

Looking up, I see Elle eyeing me in the reflection of the elevator doors. Bringing up my hand, I scratch my eyebrow with my middle finger, making her laugh. Snow and Eve look between us. I keep my face stoic, licking my lips in an attempt to keep a smile at bay. A few seconds later, the elevator dings and the doors slide open.

"See you guys there." Elle intertwines her hand with Snow's, leaving Eve and I alone.

"I'm this way," I mumble, looking over my shoulder to see if she's following behind me.

Reaching my car, I open the passenger door for her. Contrary to Noelle's accusations, I am still a gentleman. Eve slides into the front seat, and I close the door behind her. Getting in, I press the start button, latch my seatbelt, and put it in reverse. When I place my hand behind her seat to back out, her eyes are on me. I can't hold it in any longer, putting the car into park.

"What are we doing, Eve?"

"What do—"

"You're far too intelligent to play stupid." I unbuckle my seatbelt, cut the engine, and shift in my seat to face her. "You heard me the first time, *what* are *we* doing? You tell me you love me, then you go out and get a boyfriend, and now you're hurt over me not talking to you for a few days."

"I'm not hurt," she defends.

"Okay, then what are you?"

"I thought you were mad."

I tilt my head to the side, resting my arm on the steering wheel. "About... what?"

She tucks her hair behind her ear, looking down at the leather straps of her designer bag. "Noah."

I raise my brows, chuckling. "Oh."

My chuckle turns into a laugh. Eve stares at me like I've lost my mind. Sighing, I catch my breath.

"Do you honestly think..."

I trail my fingertips up Eve's arm, grazing my fingers along her collarbone, watching goose bumps pepper her skin. She inhales sharply when I reach the hollow of her throat.

"That Noah..."

I continue sliding my hand up the supple skin of her neck, stopping at her chin.

"Holds any weight..."

I trace her plush lips with the pad of my thumb.

"In my life when it comes to you?" I ask, slipping my hand around the back of her neck. "I regret to inform you, Sweetheart, he doesn't."

I pull Eve toward me, crashing my lips into hers. For a moment she stills but just as quickly melts into the kiss. I tease the seam of her lips with my tongue, coaxing her to open, and she does. The taste and feel of Eve is maddening and exhilarating. She fists the lapels of my suit, giving just as much as I take, molding her mouth to mine. If there are moments I could save for eternity, it'd be these fleeting ones with her. When she allows herself to indulge with me instead of expending all of her energy proving a point no one believes. Eve leans into me, into the kiss... into *us*. Did she truly forget how we feel together? Lightning touches with thunderous feelings.

My ringer slices through the charge of our kiss, severing our connection. Eve pulls away, eyes wide, looking stunned with desire dancing in her eyes. I smile, letting the phone ring, and reach out to run the pad of my thumb along her bottom lip.

"I needed a reminder of how you feel."

She keeps her eyes on me, unblinking.

"I've gotta get this." Starting the car, I answer the call as it connects to Bluetooth. "Hey, Mom."

"How's my boy?"

I glance at Eve who is still staring at me. "Close your mouth and put your seatbelt on."

She finally blinks, clamping her jaw shut, scowling at me as she reaches for her seatbelt.

"Excellent." I wink at Eve.

"Are you with someone? I only wanted to check in."

"I'm with Eve." I can see her gawking at me out the corner of my eye as I pull into traffic.

"Eve?" Mom echoes. "As in *your* Eve?"

"Yes. *My* Eve."

Eve crosses her arms, raising a brow, challenging my words with a look. I'd kiss her again to prove my point, but I'm too busy weaving through traffic.

"Hi, Eve," Mom gushes. "How are you honey?"

She shoots me a murderous look before responding. "I'm good, Carol. How are you?"

"Oh, it's so good to hear your voice. What are you and Winter doing together?"

I'm petty, making a V with my fingers and sticking my tongue between it.

Eve gasps, swatting my arm. "I – um – we –"

I laugh silently while she struggles to find her words.

"Noelle invited me to the influencer luncheon, and I had to ride Winter–"

Eve chokes on her own words, looking mortified, and I wheeze with silent laughter. She covers her face with her hands, shaking her head.

"I had to ride *with* Winter because Snow was driving a two seater. And now I'm wondering why they didn't just take her car." She mumbles the last sentence to herself.

Elle wanted to meddle today. I won't complain because I got to taste Eve again.

"Those boys and their cars." I can hear the eye roll. "I'm happy you and Winter are back in each other's lives."

"Me too," Eve says, swapping her glare out for a smile. "What are you up to today?"

"I'm going to have lunch with some friends and then I'll go Salsa dancing this evening."

Eve looks at me as if verifying whether or not Mom takes Salsa lessons. I nod, saying, "She does."

"Carol, you're going to have to teach me how to dance Salsa."

Mom chuckles. "You'll have to have Winter bring you to my place here in Sapphire Shores."

That's highly unlikely. I'm not naïve enough to think because we shared a world-tilting kiss that she's going to drop her stand-in boyfriend and run off into the sunset with me. At this point, I'm not expecting her to give me another chance. I can't help but wonder how far things would've gone between us had my phone's ringer not clouded that moment.

"Yeah... I'll think about it. I'm pretty busy with the clinic right now."

"No rush, honey. I know you've got your own life now." Sadness flickers across Eve's face. "I'm happy to hear your voice and to know you're doing well. I won't keep you two. Winter, call me tomorrow morning, okay?"

"I will, Mom. Love you."

"Oh, and post pictures of the luncheon. Your father would be so proud of all you've done, Winter. Love you."

Mom ends the call and music plays through the speakers. Eve looks out the window, watching the city pass by. I can tell she's lost in thought.

"I didn't mean to put you on the spot."

She tears her gaze away from the window. "No. It was really good to hear her voice." There's a smile on her lips that doesn't reach her eyes. "She was like a second mom."

"I'm sure she still sees you as her daughter."

Eve laughs softly. "It's been a while, Winter. I doubt she still sees me that way."

"You can doubt all you want, but I know that Mom will always consider you family."

She considers me for a moment before turning her attention to the window, pressing her fingers to her lips. I let the music fill the silence between us and leave her to her thoughts for the rest of the drive to Fireside. Pulling into the parking lot, I notice she's still tracing her lips when I park beside Snow's car.

"You kissed me," she says when I turn off the car.

"I did." Climbing out, I round the back and open the door for her. "But don't worry," I say, taking her hand to help her out. "It won't happen again."

Her heels click onto the ground as she slides out of the car, looking up at me. I put my hand on her waist to keep her steady. "Why?" slips from her lips before she can stop herself.

I smile, tugging her toward me, and shut the door behind her. "Because, Sweetheart. Next time, you're going to beg for my lips to touch yours."

The hitch in her breath lets me know my words affected her the same way my kiss did.

To my amusement, Eve tries to keep her distance, using Noelle and Aspen as a shield. It's fine with me because I know the tingle of our kiss still lingers on her lips. The luncheon is well underway, and it's been a blast getting to know our guests, eating, and playing games together. It was Elle's idea to fly the influencers in for an exclusive welcome luncheon. Instead of just being faces on a screen and words in an email, it's given us an opportunity to build a relationship with each other.

There are five micro influencers, who have less than ten thousand followers, and the rest fall in the middle, with only one having over a million. Elle and I decided that followers couldn't be a major deciding factor when someone with less can be far more engaging. Despite the tedious task of going through all the applicants, after meeting those we chose, I know we have an amazing team. The youngest kid, Bonnie, is five years old, and I'm surprised she's able to contain her personality in her body. I watch her drag Dominic, her dad, toward the inflatable "Wacky

Slide" with its large hills. Her brown eyes are alight with excitement and her afro puffs are tied up in sparkly rainbow ribbon. Dominic looks like he's ready to crash. I chuckle to myself, walking beneath the large colorful balloon arches toward the drink table.

Travis is our oldest influencer. He's 18, but his parents are here anyway, talking to Elle and Snow. They thought our offer was a scam because they didn't believe their son could make any money "dancing" on social media. They obviously don't watch his channel because he does reviews and is honest, engaging, and intelligent. He wants to pursue the influencer lifestyle while they expect him to choose the more traditional route of college. This is his first major contract, so hopefully after this event, and seeing it's real, they'll support his passion a little more.

Reaching the drink table, I smile at Charlie, the quietest of the group. Her reserved demeanor is a stark contrast to her animated online personality.

"Are you enjoying yourself, Charlie?"

Her eyes widen, making her look like a deer in headlights. "Uh... yeah. I am... I guess," she adds as an afterthought.

"You guess?" I raise my brow, chuckling.

Pressing her palm to her forehead, she tries to hide behind it. "I didn't mean it like that."

"No offense taken. There's a lot," I wave my hand through a stream of bubbles, "going on here."

"It's not the venue. The décor is amazing."

Grabbing a glass, I place it under the spout labeled "lemonade" and fill my cup, asking, "Care to talk about it?"

Charlie looks around, taking in all the colorful décor that's content creator worthy. She knits her brows together, frowning over her green eyes. "It's just... I don't think I fit in. I mean look at everyone else."

She looks down at her t-shirt, jeans, and Chuck Taylors with a disappointed expression. I look around too, trying to see what she does. The other kids are dressed to the nines in the latest fashion. While they look nice, I can guarantee that the majority of their parents picked out their outfits. But when you're fifteen, fitting in matters.

Sipping the lemonade, I grab a cookie from a nearby tray and take a bite. "Do you know why you're here, Charlie?"

She shrugs, crossing her arms. "Because my parents said I should monetize my following."

I chuckle. "You don't want to make money?"

"I do. I just... like getting online and talking about stuff that I love. It never occurred to me that I could make money, you know? Sure, people send me stuff, and if I get to it, I review it, but I didn't think anyone would pay me. It's all new I guess." She lets out a sigh.

"That's understandable." I nod.

"So..." she says after a beat. "Why am I here?"

"Because you stand out. We didn't invite you here to fit in."

Charlie considers me a moment before saying, "I never thought of it that way."

"Be yourself and enjoy it. No one here is expecting you to fit in."

She visibly relaxes, smiling at me. "You're pretty cool, Mr. King."

A chuckle rumbles in my throat. "I'll take that compliment. Enjoy the party."

I excuse myself, weaving through the arcade station and passing the ball pit to get back to the table. Taking a seat, I'm pleased to see Charlie is no longer a wall flower and is talking to the other guests.

Elle slides into the seat between Snow and me. "We've done a good job, Winter."

I tap my bright yellow cup against her pink one. "That we did, Miss Mistletoe."

"What are you going to call me once I marry your brother?"

"*Mrs.* Mistletoe."

She laughs, playfully swatting at my arm.

"Nah, I'll call you Mrs. King because you deserve that title after pepper spraying Snow."

"Shhh!" she hisses, holding a finger to her lips. "He hasn't brought that up in a while."

"Doesn't mean I've forgotten, Snowflake," Snow says on the other side of her.

"Look what you've done, scarred my brother for life with your malicious attack."

"Elle was just waiting for the day to use that can of pepper spray on someone," Aspen chimes in.

"Just wishing a motherfucker would, huh, Elle?" North asks.

"I was not! You guys make it seem like I was power crazed."

"If I remember correctly," Eve says, "you *did* say you hope you actually got to use it."

"Oh, she used it alright," Snow says, giving her an appraising look.

"This evidence is damning, Elle." I click my tongue, shaking my head.

"Snow," Elle says, "aren't you going to defend my honor or something?"

He looks at her then at the rest of us. "I'll allow it."

Elle gasps, looking betrayed, causing laughter to ripple around the table. She knows Snow doesn't have a problem putting anyone in their place when it comes to her. We talk for a few more minutes amongst ourselves before we make our rounds with our guests again. Even Snow, who is the most anti-social of us all, is enjoying himself. I never could've imagined Snow jumping into a ball pit in a tailor made suit, hand in hand with Elle, and a few of the other guests like he is today. North and Aspen are kindly giving some reprieve to Dominic and Tosha, Bonnie's mom. Brielle gave them something a little stronger than lemonade, and now they're taking a moment to themselves at their table.

By the end of the luncheon, everyone is acting more like friends than strangers. Tomorrow, Elle and I will give them a tour of North Star Toys. We're the only Black owned toy company in the United States that manufactures its own toys. Tours are open to the public during the summer months by reservation only. When we first offered tours, people came in masses. Initially, Snow wanted to stop offering them because they were overwhelming for our employees and facility. Instead, I suggested reservations because the tours attract people from all over the world. It allows us to manage crowds and offer a more unique experience.

After our guests collect their swag bags, the cars arrive to take them, and their families, back to the hotel. We wave them off and head back inside to help break everything down for the rental services to pick up. I stop in my tracks, surprised to see Aundi standing at the hostess station, talking to Ezra.

"I'll be right there," I say to Elle, glancing at Aundi.

Elle nods, following Snow and North back out to the balcony.

I reach Aundi right when she finishes paying for her food, and she nearly runs into me when she turns around. Taking a step back, she looks up at me, and a slow smile spreads across her face.

"Winter."

"Aundi." I wrap an arm around her waist, giving her hug and press a kiss to her cheek. "What are you up to?"

"Grabbing food." She holds up the brown paper to-go bag with *Fireside* printed on it. "I have a meeting with some investors from New York, and my office is five minutes from here. What about you?"

"We had an event." I point over my shoulder at the balloon arches. "It just ended."

"It looks like it was fun." She smiles.

"Honestly, it was. Had I known your work is nearby, I would've invited you."

"Not like we're really talking about life when we're together."

"Yeah..." I nod. "You have a point. Do you want to hang out later? Maybe grab something to eat?"

She's in the middle of sliding the strap of her purse up her shoulder when I ask, and it slips from her fingertips, jostling the drink carrier she's holding in her hand.

"I can help you." I take the bag of food and the drinks.

"You want to... spend time together?"

"Yes." I use my free hand to slide the strap of her purse back onto her shoulder. "If you'd like. I understand if you—"

"I thought this was a hook up situation." She motions between us, raising a perfectly arched eyebrow.

"Or we can do that."

"No..." Aundi laughs softly. "It's just you've never expressed interest in hanging out before."

"I wasn't interested in hanging out before because I wasn't available emotionally. I just needed a release." Aundi doesn't flinch at my words, but they grab Ezra's attention who's suddenly more interested in our conversation than doing whatever he supposedly was at the register.

"And now you are?" She crosses her arms.

"Honestly, I'm working on it. I've been on a... journey back to myself so to speak. That's why I haven't been around as much."

Aundi's brown eyes scan my face almost as if she's trying to tell whether I'm full of shit or not. After a few breaths, she smiles as she says, "Dinner is a good place to start. Pick me up at my place." She takes the food and drink from my hand. "Thank you, but I got it. See you tonight."

The cocky side of me didn't expect her to say no. While the parts of me that I'm still getting to know knew she had every reason to.

"I'll be damned." Ezra whistles, interrupting my train of thought. "Winter King respectfully asking a woman on a date? Looks like I owe Brielle a hundred bucks."

"Owe me what?" Brielle joins us at the hostess station.

"Your lover boy here just asked someone out on a date."

"Finally!" she exclaims.

"Finally, what?" Elle asks, arriving with the others following behind her.

"Winter asked someone out on a date," Ezra gladly fills them in.

"A date?" All of them say as if singing in rounds. Eve's voice is a little higher than the rest.

The urge to punch Ezra in the face is strong. He gives me a smug smile, draping his arm over Brielle's shoulder.

"Yes." I look at them. "Why is that so fucking shocking?"

"I mean," Snow says. "It's you."

"Snow!" Elle reprimands him.

"You haven't gone on a date in t–"

I give North a lethal look, cutting him off.

"Don't mind them, Winter." Elle loops her arm through mine, guiding me toward the door as she shoots Snow and North daggers with her eyes. "They have to be assholes before they can be happy."

"Enjoy your date!" Ezra calls after me as I walk out the door with Elle, flicking him off over my shoulder.

"Who are you going out with and when?" Elle asks, genuinely interested so I tell her.

"Tonight with Aundi. She's the only woman you've ever seen at my place aside from you and Aspen."

"Oh!" Her eyes widen with recognition. "She's gorgeous. I got a good vibe from her. Almost as tall as you too, isn't she?"

"In heels, yes. She's six feet or just under six feet, and yes, she's fucking gorgeous."

Elle smiles at me. "I'm excited for you, and I hope you enjoy yourself tonight."

"Thanks, Elle." I wrap her in a hug when we reach our cars, prolonging it just to annoy Snow.

I give a hug to Aspen and say bye to North and Snow before turning my attention to Eve, who is standing off to the side. "Ready?" I open the passenger door for her.

She hesitates for a few seconds before placing her hand in mine, sliding into the front seat.

Rounding the car, I get in and ask her, "Where did you want me to take you?"

"To my place."

"Alright, put it in the GPS."

I slow to a stop at Fireside's entrance and wait for her to finish putting in her address. After a second, the GPS pulls up the map, telling me to turn right.

Eve pulls her phone out, checking it before sliding it back into the bag. "Carol was right," she says. "Your dad would've been so damn proud of you today."

I glance at her out of the corner of my eye as I pull onto the road.

"Although, I doubt there's ever been a moment he hasn't been proud of you." Looking at me, she smiles.

"Thank you, Eve." Swallowing hard, I attempt to dislodge the lump in my throat.

"It was good to talk to your Mom today."

"Even though I put you on the spot?" I smile at her.

"Yes." She laughs softly.

I rest my arm on the center console, leaning closer to her, gripping the steering wheel with one hand. "She'll ask about you every now and then."

"What do you tell her?"

I hike up my shoulder. "That you seem happy."

Her eyes remain on the scenery whipping by.

I rub my hand over my beard, asking, "Are you?"

"In many ways," she says as her gaze meets mine. "Yes."

"And the other ways?"

"Eh…" She blows out a puff of air. "The other ways are complicated."

"Are they? Or are you making them complicated?"

She sucks her teeth, giving me mean side eye.

I straighten up, leaning away from her. "Aye," I smile. "I know how it gets in that pretty little head of yours."

Her eyes narrow.

"Pretty *big* head?"

Eve gasps, gaping at me. "Screw you, Winter."

"Shit, I wouldn't stop you if that's what you want." I let my eyes wander over her before focusing on the road again.

She tilts her head to the side, crossing her arms. "Aren't you going on a date later?"

I wish Ezra would've kept his fucking mouth shut. Although, I guess this is what I get for shamelessly flirting with his wife in front of him for years.

"It's dinner." I don't even know if Aundi would call it a date.

"Do you date?"

"Not for romantic reasons." The GPS announces our destination will be on the right.

"Is tonight for romantic reasons?"

I slowly drive down the tree lined street, coming to a stop in front of her brownstone that has barrels of daisies sitting by the front door. "You don't get to ask me that." I put the car in park, taking my foot off the brake.

"Oh," she scoffs. "But you can kiss me?"

"You're right." I place my hand over my heart, bowing as much as my seatbelt will allow. "Please give Noah my deepest apologies." I take my shades off, setting them on the dash. "That's if you tell him."

"I wouldn't have anything to tell him if you—"

"Did you tell me no?"

Silence.

"Did you push me away?"

Silence.

"Did you pull away?"

More silence.

"I think when you kissed me the first time, you didn't expect to feel anything, and instead, you felt *everything*. It terrified you to realize that after all this time–after all the pain and hurt–your heart still belongs to me."

Her brown eyes war with mine, hating and loving me at the same time. Eve laughs bitterly, severing our connection. "Something belonging to you doesn't mean you know how to take care of it."

I let her words sting, knowing she's right. There were a million different ways I could've handled myself back then, and I chose all the wrong ones. I take a deep breath, considering her words. I can acknowledge she's right while honoring the fact that I deserve to be seen too. Last night, I made a conscious decision to forgive myself. To release myself from my past mistakes.

Remembering that freeing feeling, I say, "I didn't even know how to take care of myself back then, Eve."

She gives me a side long glance, her eyes shine with tears.

"I don't tell you this to diminish the damage I caused, but I'm not who I was over a decade ago. At some point, you've got to free yourself from the past for the sake of yourself. Fuck everyone else. Shit, who knows, maybe I never was the one for you, and it's Noble Noah after all."

She snorts with laughter, wiping her nose with the back of her hand.

"But that's something you're never going to know if you don't allow yourself to."

Eve looks down, rubbing the leather strap of her bag between her fingertips. Above all, I want Eve to be happy even if it isn't with me. She deserves that and so do I. Noah steps out onto the stoop, wearing some scrubs, looking ready to save the damn day. He squints, trying to see into the car even though I have the darkest tint legally allowed. *Dumbass.* Okay, I may have to work on letting her be happy even if it isn't with me. Eve looks at Noah, letting out a sigh.

"Well, damn. Don't keel over with excitement at the sight of him."

She laughs, shifting her gaze to me. "Enjoy your date."

Opening the door, she slips out of the car without another word or glance. I watch her walk up the sidewalk, climb the stairs, and step into Noah's arms.

I imagined Aundi and I would go to a swanky restaurant, sip some wine, and eat overpriced mediocre food. Instead, I'm wearing an apron with paint speckled hands, laughing and thoroughly enjoying her company. When I picked Aundi up, she led me to a sketchy looking warehouse downtown. It looks like a place a serial killer would call home–and had me questioning what the fuck Aundi is into–until we stepped inside and got the opposite.

In this seemingly dilapidated building, there are thousand dollar art pieces and sculptures. It's a newer gallery that offers art nights to the community. Aundi saw a ready-to-paint ceramics night and signed us up.

Looking at her vase, she turns it side to side. "Do the circles look like nipples to you?"

"What?" I chuckle, looking at her vase. "Actually..." I tilt my head to the side. "They kinda do. Maybe you shouldn't put the dot in the center?"

"You're right." She fills in the circle with sky blue paint. "Are you enjoying yourself?"

"I am. Can't say I wasn't a little worried when you led me here, but I figured if I got a good enough head start, I'd be alright."

Laughter tumbles from Aundi's lips, filling the space between us. "If I knew you were scared, I would've told you where we were coming."

"And let you see my fear?" I suck my teeth. "Never."

"It's been a while since I've laughed like this." She sighs, catching her breath.

"What do you do in your free time?" While Aundi and I have a sexual relationship, we don't have much outside of that. At least until tonight I thought we didn't.

"Honestly, not much. Most of what I do is to distract myself from missing my daughter."

I stop painting my mug, meeting her gaze. "Can I ask—"

"Why doesn't she live with me?" She verbalizes my question, and I nod. Aundi sighs, continuing to paint as if she's trying to find her words. "My ex-husband and I let her decide who she wanted to live with. I don't blame her, you know?"

She briefly glances at me before dipping her brush into the paint. "Our whole life is back in Seattle. Her friends, grandparents, school... all of it is there. So when I moved out here, she didn't want to leave that behind. Shit, neither did I, but I also didn't want to keep doing the same thing either. I didn't want to be stagnant."

"How old is she?"

"Noor is thirteen. When she was here last weekend, she said she wanted to come live with me since she'll be starting high school." A smile lights up her face. "I'm not trying to sway her, but I really hope she does. I've missed her terribly."

"Kudos to you for giving her a choice. A lot of parents would say what it's going to be and that's final."

"It's difficult to let Noor make her own choices. Her dad and I never want her to feel like she has to choose between either of us. The divorce was hard enough already. We want Noor to know, wherever she goes, she'll be loved and supported."

My innate curiosity wants to know what led to her relationship ending in divorce, but I don't want to unknowingly poke at an old wound by asking her.

Smiling, I say, "I admire you, Aundi."

"Thank you." She continues painting her vase. "Now, what does Winter King do in his free time?"

Focusing on my mug, I attempt to create a gradient effect with hues of blue to mimic the night sky and answer her question. "Work, spend time with family, and volunteer at True's House."

"That's the community center for kids, right?"

"Yeah. I'm a mentor there."

"Really?" She raises her brows with surprise. "For some reason, without ever having seen you interact with kids, I know you're amazing at it."

"I like to think that I am." A chuckle resonates in my chest. "It's been just as beneficial for me as it has the kid I've been hanging out with."

"What made you decide to volunteer?"

Squeezing shimmering gold paint onto the pallet, I grab a new brush and dip it into the gold to paint the stars onto my mug. "I needed something outside of myself. At that point, seemingly I had it all while also having nothing at all. There was no depth to my life. So... I dove in."

"I know we don't talk a lot when we're together–" I let out a huff of laughter, meeting her gaze "–but I can tell you've changed, and I'm happy for you." Aundi's lips curve into a smile.

"Thank you."

She holds her vase up, turning it side to side. "I think I'm ready to take it to the kiln."

"It looks amazing. I love the design." There's a mandala, made of white and navy blue dots, blooming on the side of the vase.

"Thank you. I love yours too." She points at my mug.

The top half is a dark blue, almost black, that fades into a lighter blue further down the mug. I add a few more stars before setting my paintbrush aside. "This was a lot of fun. It's been awhile since I've done something like this."

"Now that you know it's not a serial killer's home, you can attend more classes." She slides off the stool. "And maybe we can even come here again together?"

Matching the smile on her face, I say, "I'd like that."

17

EVE

Kissing Winter cracked open a trove of emotions I've struggled to keep buried. Each interaction with him pulls a brick from my already crumbling exterior. The other day, he knocked down a whole wall when his lips crashed into mine. Even if I could rebuild it, I wouldn't. I've been hiding behind the safety of the fortress I built long enough. Maybe it's time to let a little light in.

"Are you okay?" Noah asks with his chopsticks teeming with noodles, suspended halfway to his mouth.

"Huh?" I look down at the carton of rice and chopsticks in my hand, realizing I was lost in my thoughts. Scooping some up, I take a bite. "Yeah. Just tired."

Noah studies my face for a few seconds, looking unconvinced. "You seem... distant lately."

Plucking up a piece of General Tso's chicken, I pop it into my mouth to prolong my response. How do I tell him I'm daydreaming about a kiss that didn't come from him?

"There's a lot to do at work." Not a total lie. "Hiring new therapists, buying the equipment, and the community day. I'm not sure why I planned that now."

He chuckles, a smile to replace his concern. "Because you care about the community and know it's an amazing idea."

After attending the influencer luncheon, I felt inspired to do my own event. I want to host a community day at Hope's Village with the intention of making it an annual event. It would be an opportunity for people to see the clinic, meet Ilaria, Silas, and the therapists, and for the community to learn about what services and resources are offered.

"I hope there's a good turnout. We're putting a lot of money into this."

"A million dollars isn't enough to cover costs?"

Giving him a look of indignation, I nudge his leg with mine. "Doesn't mean I want to spend it immediately."

"I'm kidding. When is the night at Twisted Vines?"

Noah won't call it a date. It's "*the night*".

"Next Saturday."

"How do you feel about going with Winter?"

I inhale a piece of rice, coughing erratically, lurching forward as I gasp for breath.

Noah pats my back. "Maybe try chewing next time."

I shoot him a glare. "Thanks. I'll keep that in mind." Grabbing the glass of perspiring ice water, I gulp down a few swallows, letting out a breath of relief. "Uh... It's Winter. We get along well enough."

A little too well.

"Besides, Ilaria and Silas will be there too."

"It should be a fun night for you all." There's a snide undertone in his voice.

Placing my hand on his arm, he looks at me. "Thank you for being understanding."

"Of course." His features soften as he lets out a sigh. "And I hope you guys have fun. Do I wish it were me going with you instead of Winter? Yeah, but Hope's Village is more important than my pride."

Guilt pricks my heart. Noah has been with me through it all, offering me patience and understanding. I know I can be difficult, and he's effortlessly scaled every one of my walls, joining me in the mud instead of trying to pull me out of it.

For the first time in over a decade, I realize it's time to let go of what once was and embrace what could be. Leaning forward, I catch Noah off guard, pressing a kiss to his lips. He momentarily freezes before threading his fingers through my curls, tugging me closer.

All windows are down, sunroof open, with music blaring through my car's speakers. I sing the last lines–terribly out of tune–before turning it down to a respectable level to avoid side eye from the neighbors. I pull into my parent's half circle driveway after considering grabbing lunch from somewhere else. It's been over a week since I hung out with them last. I smile, parking behind Fox's 1991 forest green Range Rover that I have no doubt he will take to his grave. He has another car but is faithful to his first love. To Fox's credit, he's kept it in tip-top shape, and I'm sure it runs better than a brand new car off the lot.

Sliding out of my car, I smooth my hand over my hair to tame my mermaid waves that were whippin' in the wind. I start for the front door, pausing when I hear faint music coming from the backyard. Following the noise past the open garage, my heels click along the concrete. I walk under the blooming garden arches that Mom is proud of, and step on the steppingstones leading into the backyard. Our handprints and milestones are imprinted on them. From baby feet imprints to important dates, such as graduations, my parents have documented them all in the form of steppingstones. I hope to do the same in my own backyard one day. I step on the stone with Mom and Dad's handprints, displaying their anniversary date, before my heels sink into the blanket of green grass, making my way toward where Mom is kneeling near the rose bushes.

Placing my hand on her shoulder, she jumps, and a smile spreads across her face when her gaze meets mine.

"Hi, Honey!" She places her hand over her chest. "I thought you were Jude and I was ready to swat you."

"He's that bad today, huh?" I look around the yard and see Dad tending to the hedges toward the back.

"When is he not?" She pulls her gloves off her hands, wiping them on the apron tied around her waist. "Sorry I missed your text. I would've had something ready for you to eat." She rises to her feet, getting ready to head inside.

"I didn't text, Mom. I just wanted to see you and Dad."

She stops in her tracks, turning to face me.

"And get something to eat," I add as an afterthought. "But I can manage on my own."

Mom presses a kiss to my cheek. "There should be some chicken noodle soup in the fridge, if Jude hasn't inhaled it." Chances are high that he has. My stomach grumbles at the mention of it.

"Don't you love having all of us home again?" I ask, letting my amusement show.

Mom cracks a smile, letting out a huff of laughter. "Depends on the moment."

"I'm going to eat and then I'll say hi to Dad."

"Okay." She pulls her gloves back on, adjusting her sun hat.

Mom and Dad love tending to the garden. They take great pride in having the nicest one in the neighborhood. Heading inside, I let out a sigh of relief as the cool air hits my skin. It's not quite scorching summer weather yet, but it's warm enough to make you want to sit near a fan.

I enter the kitchen, pausing when I reach the fridge. My gaze slides over the pictures hanging on it. Wedding announcements, birthdays, and thank you cards litter the door. Mom will put anything on the fridge. My whole body reacts when my eyes land on the picture of Winter and I that was on the front page of the newspaper. Of course Mom cut it out and put it in the center of the fridge. The picture transports me back to that night and the always palpable energy between us. Every time I think I'm moving away from him, something pulls my attention, and feelings, back to him.

I grab the picture, lifting it up, unsurprised to see the picture of Noah and I beneath it. Rolling my eyes, I sigh heavily, letting go of the picture, and pull the fridge door open. I rummage around inside of it until my hands land on a small, square container holding the chicken noodle soup that's been stuffed into the back. Pulling it out, I read Jude's name scrawled across the top.

"Finders keepers..." I mumble, taking the lid off, putting the glass container in the microwave.

When I turn around, I nearly jump ten feet in the air at the sudden appearance of Fox. "Jesus! Announce yourself!"

He laughs at my startled expression. "Why, when you give me this reaction?"

I shove his arm. "Jerk."

"How do we live in the same city now and I don't see you any more then when I was away?"

Leaning against the counter, I rest my palms on it. "Maybe because we both have adult responsibilities. You could always be like Jude and randomly stop by my job to bring me coffee."

"He does that for you?" Surprise laces his tone.

"Yeah." I nod. "A few times a week."

"Damn." He pulls a bottle of water out of the fridge. "I never would've thought you two would be close."

"Our relationship has aged like fine wine."

Fox chuckles. "What are you doing here, anyway?"

"Came to see Mom and Dad and find some food."

His eyes land on the lid with Jude's name taped to it. "You know he's gonna blame me, right?"

"Will he?" I give him a bemused expression. "Is he even home?"

"Nah." He twists the cap off the water, taking a sip. "He just left to go meet up with Aspen."

I tilt my head to the side, nodding. "Interesting..."

"Are they a thing?"

"Honestly, I don't know. Jude has forbidden me from talking to her about their friendship."

Fox lets out a belt of laughter. "The punch from that girl is still tender after all these years, huh?"

"I didn't know she'd take it to the extreme." I hold my hands up shrugging.

The microwave beeps, opening the door, I pull the steaming chicken noodle soup out. My mouth waters as I grab a spoon and take a seat at the kitchen island.

After I savor a bite, I turn my attention back to Fox. "How's the new job?"

"Good." His eyes light up like they always do when he talks about his work. "It's been a lot of fun."

"That makes me happy to hear. I know you love your travel."

"I still do and will, but that nomadic lifestyle clashes with some of my dreams."

"Which are?" I dip my spoon into the soup, letting the broth flood it, and sip it off.

"I want roots. Dating was also non-existent. I didn't have the time for anything more than random hookups. It's fun at first until you're sitting in the most breathtaking places and have no one to share it with."

"I can imagine that being a little depressing. Especially if you want to share it with someone."

"Yeah, and I missed you guys."

"Awww! You love me?"

"Sometimes." A smile tugs at his lips.

He turns, opening the fridge, and rummages around for something to eat. After a few seconds, he straightens up with a container of fruit. He glances back at the fridge door and then back at me.

"What's up with you and Winter?"

"Nothing..." I shove a bite of noodles into my mouth. "Why do you ask?"

"Because..." He sits on the chair beside me. "It's clear there's something still there between you two."

"Regrets?" I look at him with a smile.

He chuckles, taking a bite of strawberry. "You regret being with him?"

"No," I say honestly without hesitation. "I don't think I ever could in spite of what he did."

Fox falls silent, eating his fruit, probably mulling over my response. He's the easiest to talk to in the family. The most intuitive. Fox has a gentle, welcoming nature about him with a strong zest for life. It's near impossible to not spill your secrets to him.

"Have you—" He pauses, taking a bite of cantaloupe. "I know the way he left was sudden and traumatizing…"

"Yeah…" I fill my spoon with more soup. "You sound like you have something to say about it though?"

"It's just…" His gaze meets mine. "No one leaves like that for the fuck of it."

"People do it all the time."

"True." He pops a blueberry into his mouth. "But do *you* honestly feel he left just for the fuck of it?"

This is a question I've asked myself a million times. It's a hard one to face because I knew Winter well enough at the time to know he wouldn't do something as drastic as that purely for the "fuck of it". Acknowledging that means I have to acknowledge the reality that I wasn't really there for him when he needed me most. I've gone back over every memory I can recall with a fine tooth comb and I was doing everything I could to help him after his Dad died. Maybe it wasn't enough? I'm not sure what more I could've done differently if anything at all. After all this time, I still don't know what I did or didn't do to make him leave. Or if it was anything to do with me.

"No." I say as I put the last bite of chicken noodle soup into my mouth.

"Maybe you should talk to him. Because energy like that," he nods toward the picture of Winter and I on the fridge, "is a once in a lifetime type of thing."

I finish the rest of my soup in silence, ruminating over his words.

After taking the longer route back to work to clear my head, I drop my purse into the chair near the door and plop down at my desk. Leaning back in my chair, I stare up at the ceiling, decorated with vines and flowers, letting out a long sigh.

I didn't tell Fox I spent two years begging, pleading, and crying to Winter for an answer. The pain of losing him has never really dulled. It's like having shrapnel buried in my chest. It doesn't go away; you just get used to it. Sometimes I do wonder what life would've been like if I had said "yes" to Noah all those years ago instead of Winter. One thing I know for sure is that I'd be a stranger to heartbreak. My phone rings, pulling me from my spiraling thoughts.

I reluctantly get up to pull it out of my purse, seeing it's a number I don't recognize.

"Hello."

"Hi. This is Sasha from Twisted Vines. Am I speaking to Eve Valentine?"

"Yes." I sit back down in my desk chair. "You are."

"Great. I'm calling to confirm the upcoming charity dinner dates."

"The six of us are scheduled for next Saturday night at—"

"Actually–" she cuts in "–I'm calling because we need to split the dates into two nights."

"Oh..." I straighten up, leaning forward, resting my elbow on the desk, and cradle my chin in my hand. "Okay."

"Yes, we apologize for the inconvenience—"

"Not a problem," I lie.

"We don't have the capacity to fit all of you into one night."

"Understandable." When a waiting list is years long, and your colleagues betray you, I guess this is to be expected.

I hear her fingers fly across a keyboard, followed by a momentary pause. "Friday, I have Winter and Eve. Saturday, I have Ilaria, Silas, Melody, and Bradley."

I clutch my phone tighter. "Um, is there any way to switch them around. Maybe Winter and—"

"Unfortunately," Sasha cuts in again. "We can't. We only have room for one extra couple on Friday night and had to get approval for the extra two couples on Saturday."

"Right..." My uncertainty drips from the word. "Okay. Yes. Friday and Saturday." It makes no sense trying to compromise with her when they're already clearly going out of their way to accommodate us.

"Perfect!" Sasha says brightly. "Twisted Vines is happy to have Hope's Village as our guests."

"Thank you." I return her sincerity even though it feels like an ice cube is slowly making its way down my throat.

After ending the call, I tap my phone against my forehead, trying to think of a way to get out of going on this date with Winter. I'd accepted my fate when I thought I'd be with Ilaria and Silas, but now Winter and I alone? It's no longer a night out. *It's a date.*

Ilaria knocks on the doorframe, thankfully interrupting my spiraling thoughts. "C'mon in," I respond dejectedly.

"Why so solemn?" She takes a seat in front of my desk, making herself comfortable, sipping on her iced tea.

"I just got off the phone with Twisted Vines—"

She perks up. "Do not tell me they canceled our reservations!"

"No." I shake my head. Although, that would've been ideal for my own selfish reasons. "Still scheduled for Saturday."

Ilaria relaxes again. "Okay, so why do you look sad?"

"Because... I'm not joining you guys on Saturday."

She gasps. "Why not?"

"Winter and I will be going on Friday. By ourselves."

Her shock morphs into excitement. "You get to be alone with Winter King? Hope Valley's very own billionaire bachelor. I'd *die* to—"

"He was my fiancé, Ilaria."

She chokes on her iced tea. "Excuse me?"

I nod against the silence.

"You were *engaged* to Winter King?" I nod again. "I thought a million dollars was a little outlandish, not that you're not worth it."

She gives my hand a reassuring squeeze even though I know she meant no harm with her words. "But I wasn't going to pretend to know what a billionaire does with more money than I'll ever have. It all makes sense now." Her eyes meet mine. "You know he's still in love with you, right?"

"Winter?" I say dumbly as if he isn't the topic of conversation. "No he's not."

She tilts her head to the side, giving me a knowing look. "Eve, please don't insult my intelligence."

I let out an exasperated sigh, running my hands through my hair. "Maybe he is, which means I can't go on this date–night out–with him."

"The only way..." Her brow furrows as her voice trails off. A smile slowly spreads across her face. "The only way I see this being a problem is if the feelings are mutual?" She annoyingly wags her brows at me.

"They're not."

"Right." Laughter tumbles from her lips. "I can't believe you let me flirt with that man in front of you!"

I crack a smile. "I didn't want to come off as the jealous ex."

"If Winter was my ex-fiancé, I'd be jealous too."

"Ilaria!"

"What?" She gives an innocent shrug of her shoulders. "You can't deny that man is other worldly level of fine! His smile alone is enough to—"

I give her a dismissive wave of my hand, turning on my computer. "I'm not having this conversation with you."

Ilaria's enjoying my discomfort a little too much. "Alright." She lets out a long, low sigh. "Well since you have no feelings for him, the date on Friday should be fine."

I'm so fucked. "Yep, it should be."

"Great!" She slaps her palm against my desk, standing and heading for the door. Before leaving, she turns back around. "For the record, nothing ever happened between Winter and I."

"It wouldn't have mattered if it did," I say without looking up from my computer.

"I wish I could be as delusional as you, girl." She gives me a smile before disappearing down the hall.

Noah pulls up to Elle and Snow's new place. They wanted to have a nice dinner instead of a traditional housewarming party. Getting out of the car, Noah appears on my side seconds later and opens the door for me. I slide my hand into his as he helps me out. I'm fixing my hair in the window's reflection when an innately familiar voice rumbles behind us.

"Noah and Eve. How are you two this evening?"

Turning around, I inhale sharply when my eyes land on Winter. He's decked in black from head to toe. The fit is casual but he alone elevates it. Even the diamonds glinting in his jewelry are black and he clearly has a fresh fade. He flashes me a brilliant smile.

"Good," Noah answers for the both of us.

Winter doesn't take his answer for the both of us. "You look nice, Eve."

"Thank you." I look down at my bodysuit, that's nearly the color of my skin, and wide leg linen pants. "You too." My eyes widen, realizing I didn't stop myself. I can feel Noah's eyes on the side of my face, but I make no effort to meet his gaze.

"You think so?" Winter asks.

Thankfully, before I can answer, a car pulls up that grabs Winter's attention. Seconds later, a woman steps out who looks like she walked straight off the runway. She's dressed in white, complimenting Winter's outfit nicely as he plants a kiss on her cheek. I wonder if this is the woman he went on a date with. Winter's giving her his attention as if she's the center of his world. They're talking when they get closer to Noah and I. The woman's deep brown eyes meet mine, and she gives me a warm smile.

"Aundi, this is Eve and her boyfriend Noah."

She extends her perfectly manicured hand, and I take it.

"Nice to meet you." I match her smile. Aundi is gorgeous. She has flawless ochre skin with jet black hair that's pulled into a perfectly messy bun sitting atop her head and full lips.

She shakes mine and Noah's hands. "You as well. Sorry I'm late." Her attention slides back to Winter.

"You're right on time," he assures her, gently squeezing her arm before resting it on the small of her back. "But let's get inside before Snow and Elle talk shit."

Aundi laughs, and unsurprisingly, it sounds like a pretty melody. Winter grabs her hand, interlacing their fingers. My eyes hyperfocus on their linked hands. Are they a couple? Noah wraps his arm around my waist, pulling me closer to him, pressing a kiss to my temple. Warmth spreads through me as I smile up at him. I have no reason to be concerned with who Winter is dating.

But I am.

Just another reason he and I have no business going on a date together.

I didn't think our group would grow past Elle, Aspen, and me so quickly. Nor did I think it'd include the King brothers. Yet here we – including Wilder, his girlfriend, Luna, Brielle, and Ezra – are, gathered around the outdoor fire pit sitting on the lavish couches that line the conversation pit nestled in Snow and Elle's backyard. The mountains and the setting sun provide the perfect backdrop to our evening. I haven't talked much to Winter and Aundi. Not that I need to interact with them to see the ease they have around each other. Maybe she'll be good for him.

"I'll be back," I whisper to Noah.

He turns his attention away from North and Wilder, focusing on me. "You okay?"

"Yeah. Just need to go to the bathroom."

He gives my hand a squeeze as I stand up and falls back into conversation with North and Wilder.

"Where's the bathroom?" I ask Elle.

"Down the hallway, turn left, and there's a half bath just off the laundry room. Do you want me to go with you?"

"No." I place my hand on her shoulder. "I can manage."

"Okay. Call me if you get lost."

Shaking my head, I snort with laughter, holding up my phone. "I'll send an S.O.S. text."

Aspen and I were giving her shit, saying it'd be easy to get lost in their house. It's big, yet cozy. Walking down the hall, I pull my phone out of my back pocket, and reply to texts from Mom, Dad, and Jude. Fox is the one who doesn't say anything unless he has to.

"Heads up, Sweetheart," Winter rumbles as I bump headfirst into his brick of a chest, causing my phone to clatter to the floor. He wraps a hand around my arm, keeping me steady.

"Shit." I look up at him. "Sorry. I didn't see you there."

Bending over, he picks up my phone. "You wouldn't have with your eyes glued to your screen," he says teasingly, placing it in my hand.

"Thanks."

Winter's eyes travel down my body, looking me over from head to toe. "My pleasure. Where were you going before you crashed into me?"

"Bathroom..." He's still close. His spicy, subtly sweet cologne, invades my senses.

"Nature calls." Winter steps aside, holding his hand up as if leading the way, and a smile tugs at my lips.

We hold each other's gaze as I walk past. I turn my attention to my feet once there's distance between us and I round the corner. "Oh, Winter." I stop abruptly, turning to face him. "Did they call you from Twisted Vines?"

"No..." He closes the distance between us again. "Why?"

"They changed the date. It's Friday instead of Saturday."

He slides a hand into the front pocket of his jeans. "Just me and you?" Winter takes another step toward me.

"Yeah... if you don't want to go I—"

"Why wouldn't I want to go?" He cuts my excuse short.

I shift my weight to my other foot. "Aundi."

"Why would she be a problem?" His eyes search my face for the truth.

"I just thought... well, since she's here that—" I take a step back because he's intoxicatingly close, "—you two are together."

"Nah," he says simply.

"Oh… if you're busy Friday night then—"

"Then I'll clear my schedule," he finishes for me.

The look in Winter's eyes lets me know he isn't going to let me get out of this damn date.

"I can't go to Twisted Vines with you."

"Can't or won't?" He cocks his head to the side, seeing through my bullshit.

I let out a puff of air, deflating against the wall. "Why do you want to go on this date with me, Winter?"

Amusement lights his eyes. "Did I or did I not bid a million dollars?"

"Yes, but—"

"I expect a date, Eve. Miss me with the bullshit excuses of you can't." He waves his hand aside as if flicking them away.

"It's not my fault they changed the date last minute." I give him a nonchalant shrug of my shoulders. "I'm busy that night and can't go."

He chuckles, looking off to the side as he licks his plush bottom lip, smoothing his hand over his neatly trimmed, close cropped beard.

"Are you?" I cross my arms, nodding my head. "Bet." He leans against the opposite wall, crossing his arms, matching my stance, looking far more formidable. "You don't have to join me."

"I know I don't." We hold each other's gaze in a stare down. I break first, turning away from him to head toward the bathroom.

"You don't have to join me, Eve." His voice fills the hallway. "But you *will*. Especially when I tell Mayor Price I want my money back."

I feel the blood rush from my head to my feet, leaving me lightheaded. Slowly turning to face him, he's looking at his nails.

"You wouldn't dare."

A million dollars means Hope's Village is sustainable. We can focus on what matters – the community. And now he's threatening to take that away from me over some meaningless date.

He pushes away from the wall, standing at his full height in front of me. "I'd love for you to try me, Eve." His eyes scan my face.

He looks around, seemingly disinterested in my refusal. "Listen. I've let you run long enough." He plants his palm on the wall near the left side of my head. His gaze collides with mine. "I've come to collect, Sweetheart, and I want *every* fucking thing."

I swallow. I'm not ready to be alone with Winter. I don't trust myself to be alone with him. One would think not much could happen in a public space, but they haven't met Winter King.

His other palm plants on the other side of my head, caging me in. "Either come on a date with me or I pull funding."

I glower at him.

"The options are simple, Eve."

"This is controlling and manipulative and—"

"Fair," he says, cutting me off. "It's fair. You honestly didn't think my generosity came with no strings attached, did you?" He plucks up a stray curl, brushing his fingertips against my collarbone and then he has the nerve to flash his smile at me.

"You're an asshole," I scoff.

"No, no, Sweetheart. Just how I've always given you what you want, now you will give me what I want." He takes a step closer, keeping his hands on the wall, staring down at me. "After all this time you not only want me, but you need me too."

"I don't need you," I grit out. "I haven't needed you."

He brings his hand up between us, gently cupping my chin, dragging his thumb along my bottom lip. "Lies sound pretty spilling from your lips. I wonder if my name will still sound the same."

"*Will?*"

"Yes. Will." He says it with such confidence as if he knows we'll end up tangled together again. Or maybe we never quite untangled ourselves. "Clear your schedule, Eve." His voice is a low rumble. "And try to drop the attitude because I'd hate to have to fuck it out of you."

My breath hitches.

"I'm not sure Noah can survive that."

Footsteps carry down the hall. I push away from the wall only to have Winter's hand wrap around my throat, applying light pressure as he pushes me back against it. Before I can think, blink, or breathe his lips are on mine. My heart races with panic while the feel of him keeps me rooted in the spot, reveling in his touch. I bring my hands up, fisting the sides of his t-shirt as his tongue slips into my mouth. He takes another step toward me, keeping our connection, and presses his hard body into my soft curves. Just when I settle into the kiss, he pulls away, resting his forehead against mine.

"Friday, Eve." He says it as a promise.

I nod with my eyes still closed. *Pathetic.* He steps back, leaning against the opposite wall and pulls his phone out. I feel like sliding down the wall but keep my shaking knees locked to prevent it. *Stand up!* I yell at myself.

"Friday, what time?" he asks as Noah rounds the corner.

"There you are." His eyes flit to Winter.

"Sorry to keep her," Winter says as if he didn't just have his tongue in my mouth. "She was letting me know our *date*," he says, stressing the word, "will be on Friday."

Noah's brows dip into a frown. "Friday?"

"Yes." I lick my lips, hoping my lipstick isn't smudged. "They called me today to let me know they had to move some things around to accommodate us all."

"Oh..." Noah says.

"What time should I pick you up?" Winter has absolutely no regard for Noah.

"I hadn't planned on..."

Winter's eyes have a challenge in them as if daring me to argue.

"Um... four thirty? We have to be there by six and it's a little over an hour's drive so..." I am unequivocally fucked.

"I'll be there." Winter pats Noah on the shoulder. "Good to see you again, man."

He leaves Noah and I alone. "So just you two, huh?"

"Yeah. Yes." I stumble over my words. Still dizzy from Winter's kiss.

"I'm a little relieved he has a girlfriend now."

"Girlfriend?"

"Yeah. Aundi. Why else would he show up with her?"

"Oh, they're not—" I cut myself off. This has been the first time he's mentioned the date without looking tense. "Yeah. Cute couple. I still need to use the restroom."

"I'll wait for you."

"Okay," I say over my shoulder, shutting the door behind me. Once it's locked, I slide down it, letting out a shuddering breath. My heart is still racing from being in close proximity to Winter. I take a few deep breaths, reeling my feelings in. That motherfucker really needs to stop kissing me.

18
WINTER

WILL I PULL FUNDING if she doesn't show up? Absolutely. Do I enjoy being the bad guy? Thoroughly. If Eve has made me the villain, I will gladly play the part. There was a time when I would've made the impossible possible for her. I still will. Except now, I need the energy reciprocated.

I've thought about us being together again, wondering what it'd be like. I'm not sure Eve will be able to let go of the past she clings to as if it's a life vest. It's a sobering thought. Maybe we'd both be better off moving on. That idea sticks only for a few seconds before my stubbornness knocks it out of the way. If she gives me a millimeter, I'm taking everything. Eve has been all I've wanted since the moment I met her.

My eyes connect with hers from across the room, pulling me into her gravity. Pretty women are everywhere, but none of them have ever made my heart stutter with a single look. It's not her undeniable beauty but the way she carries herself with graceful confidence.

Even after she severs the connection our eyes made, I feel like I took a dip in her aura.

"Aye, man. Are you listening?" Snow bumps my arm. "Dad needs us on stage for the speech."

I will myself to look away from the mystery woman. "Speech?"

"Yes. Where'd you go just now?" His brows knit together. *"Are you nervous or what?"*

"I was..." My voice trails off as I glance back toward the woman, but she's gone. *"Damn."*

"You good?" Snow places his hand on my shoulder.

"Yeah... I just saw – never mind." I shake my head. *"Let's go on stage."*

I follow behind Snow. North is already up on stage with Mom and Dad.

It's our parents' annual Christmas party. One of the biggest events of the year for Hope Valley. This year, Dad wanted me to give the speech since I'm next in line to be CEO. He plans to retire sooner rather than later, and I'm more than happy to take the reins. Dad wraps me in a hug.

"You got this, son. I'm so proud of you." He kisses my cheek before returning to the microphone.

I join Mom, Snow, and North, giving each a hug, feeling proud of my family.

Dad takes a minute to introduce me, even though everyone in the room knows us, and steps aside, handing me the mic. My nerves grip me for a few short seconds, adjusting my suit jacket, I take a deep breath, and begin my speech. Midway through, my eyes connect with the same warm brown eyes that left me curious.

My voice trails off, entranced by a simple look. Her lips twitch, giving me a smile, raising her brows as if saying *"continue, idiot!"* I clear my throat, tearing my eyes away from her, and finish my speech. I'm not even sure what I said, but it must've been good with the round of applause that breaks the silence. I smile, putting the mic back on the stand. Now it's time for food, drinks and dancing.

I track her movements through the crowd until she disappears around a marble column, guessing she's heading toward the bar. My dad claps me on the back.

"Beautiful speech, son. I know no matter what happens, our family's legacy is always in good hands with you boys."

"Always." I return his enthusiastic smile.

"Come." He wraps his arm around my shoulders. "There are a few people I'd like for you and your brothers to meet."

We follow him as though were his entourage. These introductions are more for my dad to talk shit with his friends then anything. As soon as we're introduced, I hang back with Snow and North.

"What are you two getting into after this?" North sets his empty glass on a servers tray as they pass by.

All three of us look each other. "Are you trying to run on 2K?" we ask in unison, leaning against one another, laughing.

"My place?"

"Yeah. North and I will bring beer and snacks."

"Sounds like a—"

Dad places his hand on my shoulder, gently pulling me toward him. "This is my oldest son, Winter."

"Wonderful speech," the tall gentleman says, extending his hand. "Cole Valentine, and this is my wife—"

"Vivienne Valentine." She holds her hand out, shaking mine. "Pleasure to meet you."

"Thank you for joining us tonight."

"We wouldn't miss it." She pats the back of my hand.

Dad introduces Snow and North, exchanging pleasantries. I'm not sure what the Valentines do, but if there at this party, it means they're affluent. I look around the crowd, wondering where Mom went. People are drinking, eating, and talking. The dance floor is slowly filling with people. Turning back around, I'm met by Mom and the woman I wasn't sure I'd see again. Their arms are linked, and they're talking as though they've known each other for ages. I rack my brain, trying to recall having met her. I doubt I'd forget if I have.

The woman unloops her arm from Mom's and stands between Mr. and Mrs. Valentine, a spitting image of her mom. Her brown eyes collide with mine, and I swear I see myself in the depths of them.

"There you are." Vivienne wraps her arm around the mystery woman's waist. "Where are your brothers?"

"Fox is at the bar." Shifting her gaze to her mom, she steals glances at me out of the corner of her eye. "And I don't try to keep up with Jude."

She was captivating from across the room. Up close, I'm enthralled. Her crimson colored dress looks to be made of silk, clinging and rippling over her body. Loose waves of brown hair brush against her collar bone. Bringing her hand up, she gently sweeps one curtain of hair over her shoulder. It's a mundane gesture pulling a heated response from me as I watch her breasts swell against the fabric as she moves. I look only for a fraction of a second. Long enough for her to notice.

Great, now she thinks I'm an ogling creep. Instead of looking disgusted, the corners of her plump lips turn up into a small smile. She takes a deep breath, making the fabric of her dress tighten again. Okay, she's fucking with me now.

"Oh, forgive me." Vivienne splays her hand across her chest. "This is our daughter, Eve."

Why have I not met her before? I wonder to myself.

"You haven't met the King sons." She points at us, saying our names. "This is North," he smiles and nods, "Snow," he tips his glass toward her, "and Winter, the oldest." I extend my hand.

She looks down at it as if it might electrocute her. I flash her a smile, and she slips her hand into mine. Her palms are soft, and her fingers are long and delicate with crimson-colored tips. The connection is brief, but it's enough to send a bolt of electricity through my bloodstream.

"A pleasure," I say, releasing her hand before I drag her out of here. "Do you dance?" I ask instead.

Eve glances at the band on the stage. "Are you asking me to dance?" That same small smile with a hint of temptation and mischief sits on her lips.

"Will you dance with me?"

"I'd love to."

I take her hand in mine, leading her toward the dance floor. The live band has been playing Christmas songs for the better part of the evening. Now that people are wanting to be on the dance floor, they're playing a mix of current hits and classic Christmas songs. Reaching the center of the dance floor, I coax her closer to me until her body is pressed flush against mine.

"How come I've never met you before?" I place my hand between her shoulder blades, trailing it down the column of her spine, resting my palm against the small of her back.

Her lips part, taking a deep breath as if she's been asked this question a million times. "I went to Alexandrite Academy."

"The all-girls school?" I can't help raising my brows with surprise.

"The one and only."

There's only one girl's school near here, and it's four hours away. Senior year, my friends and I took a trip there for the weekend, resulting in a few girls getting expelled. "I went there through my sophomore year and then begged my parents to let me go to a public school. They settled on private, Garnet Prep. After that, I went away to college. Long story short, we wouldn't have had time to cross paths."

"Has the private education paid off?"

"Yes. I plan to apply to medical school once my pre-requisites are out of the way." I stop moving to the music, looking down at her. "What?"

"That's impressive." I move with her again to the beat. *"Congratulations."*

"You're easily impressed then." She cocks her head to the side, raising her brow.

"Quite the opposite actually."

"Do you say that to all the women?"

"No. Just you." I chuckle smoothly. *"I mean it, congratulations."*

Her face softens. *"Thank you, but don't celebrate prematurely. I have to wait until I get in... if I get in."*

I'm silent for a beat.

"You're staring..."

"Yeah... I'm confused."

"About?"

"Don't you think what you're currently doing is worth celebrating?" She alone, as she is in this moment, dancing with me, is worth celebrating.

"I—" Her brown eyes hold mine, but they're looking at me differently. As if seeing me clearly for the first time. *"—hadn't thought about it. I... guess you're right."*

"Small steps lead to great things, Eve. Don't forget that. In fact," I grab two flutes of champagne off a tray passing by, handing one to her. *"We're going to celebrate you applying to med school right now."*

Even though she rolls her eyes, a smile lights up her face.

"To you." I raise my glass. *"All that you are and have yet to be."*

Her smile slips as she stares into my eyes.

I clink my glass against hers. *"Chug it."*

Her eyes widen. *"Chug it?"*

"Yes, Eve. Chug. If my calculations are correct, it's been awhile since you've had real fun with all the hard work you've been putting in."

She hesitantly raises the glass to her lips. I mimic her movement, waiting for her to take the first sip. After a few breaths, she tips the glass back and so do I. Once the golden liquid is gone, she wipes her mouth with the back of her hand, coughing, and then falls into a fit of laughter. The sound is rich and smooth, like being wrapped up in a well-worn blanket. I smile, watching her, getting lost in the sound.

Eve presses her hand against her head, squinting. "That is going straight to my head. If I puke later, I'm blaming you."

Another server passes by. I set our empty glasses on their silver tray. "Then we better enjoy ourselves until that happens."

Eve and I dance and talk as if we're old friends. There's an ease with her. It's refreshing that she's not fawning over me because of my last name. Genuine relationships are far and few between when your family is as affluent as ours. It's a gift and a curse. The friends I did have moved away and went off to college. Some have even started families. I'll be twenty-one in a month. I'm barely ready to consider taking over the family business let alone starting a family.

"I need water," Eve says, fanning herself. Sweat shimmers over her skin, giving her a dewy glow.

I take her hand, leading her toward the bar and order us both waters. "Are you enjoying yourself?"

She smiles, displaying a dimple on her left cheek. I've noticed when she genuinely smiles, a smile that lights up her whole being, that little dimple appears like a reward.

"Thoroughly." The bartender hands us our water. "But all we've talked about is me. Tell me about you. Who is Winter King?" She sweeps her hair over her shoulder.

I take a few gulps of water, eyeing her over the rim. "As pretentious as this sounds, I'm used to my reputation preceding me."

"If you would've led with that, I would've refused to dance with you."

I let out a rumble of laughter. "I wouldn't have held it against you."

"C'mon," she says, smoothing her hand over the lapel of my jacket. "Who are you without your last name?"

Her touch leaves a warmth in my chest. It takes me a few breaths to gather my thoughts. Without my last name? Shit... who the fuck am I without it? "Honestly speaking, I've never considered it. Everything about me is about my family's legacy."

"Everything?" She gives me a disbelieving look. "I believe your life is deeper than a Google search."

"You've Googled me?" I flash her a smile.

"No." She straightens up, clearing her throat. "Let's start somewhere else. What are you doing after this?"

"Going home to play video games with my brothers."

"Really?" A look of surprise is on her face. "You're not going home with anyone?"

"Are you asking me to take you home?" I cock my head to the side.

"N-No." She stumbles over the word. "I just thought since—"

"I'm fuckin' with you. Casual hook ups aren't my thing."

Eve sets her empty glass aside. "Do you have a girlfriend then?" Despite sounding nonchalant, I pick up on the hint of disappointment at the possibility that I might.

"No." A flicker of relief crosses her face. "Boyfriend?"

"Nope." She shakes her head. "The last guy I dated didn't like my ambition. Kind of turned me off from dating."

"What do you mean?" I pinch my brows together.

"He wanted an educated trophy wife to be on his arm, and I am so much more than that."

"You are."

Her brown eyes snap to mine. *"What?"*

"You are so much more than that."

"You barely met me."

"I don't need to know you, Eve, to recognize your worth."

Her plush lips part as she looks at me. Before she can speak, someone bursts the bubble we've been in since we met.

"Hey, Eve." It's a man's voice.

Turning in the direction of it, I come face to face with a kid that I went to school with. It takes me a moment to recall his name. *"Noah?"*

"Winter." He holds his hand out, waiting for me to shake it. Despite my annoyance with his interruption, I'm a gentleman and shake his hand.

"Eve and I were just getting to know each other." Hopefully he'll get the fuck on.

No such luck. *"Oh, Eve and I have known each other for years."*

"Is that right?" I ask in a deflated tone.

Eve giggles, trying to mask it by clearing her throat. *"Did you need something, Noah?"*

His eyes ping pong between us before settling on Eve. *"Uh... I came to ask Eve for a dance."*

"Oh..." She groans, looking down at her feet. *"I've been dancing with Winter and these heels are giving me hell. I'm going to find my parents and head home. Maybe next time?"*

"Of course." There's disappointment in his tone.

"You should've told me your feet hurt. We could've sat down and talked."

"You're a great dancer. It's worth the temporary discomfort." I kneel down on one knee in front of her. *"W-What are you doing?"*

"Taking your shoes off." I grab her ankle.

She pulls it out of my hold. *"I can't walk barefoot in here."* Her eyes dart around the room.

"You're with me, Eve. You can do whatever the fuck you want. Now, may I have your foot, please?"

I hold out my hand, waiting for her to place her perfectly manicured foot into it. She does, hesitantly. Eve sucks in a sharp breath through her teeth when I free her from the shoe. Indentations from the straps coil around her foot. I brush my fingertips over them. A soft moan slips from her lips, causing a smile to appear on mine. Her eyes snap open when she realizes the noise she made.

"I didn't mean—"

"I'm never one to judge." I slip her other shoe off, brushing my fingertips over the indentations. This time instead of moaning, she mashes her lips together. I chuckle, rising to my feet and am startled Noah is still in our bubble. Ignoring him, I hold my hand out to Eve.

She wiggles her toes. "That feels much better."

"Glad to—"

"Do you want to get together this week?" Noah interrupts, talking to Eve.

"Sure, Noah." She gives him a dimpleless smile. "It's good to see you."

Eve loops her arm through mine, ending the conversation as we leave the bar and weave through the crowd.

"Are you two—"

"No." She cuts me off. "He's mistaken my kindness for interest."

"So, if I ask you for your number, you'll give it to me?"

She stops in her tracks, a few feet away from her parents. "Yes."

I dip my hand into my suit jacket, pulling out my phone and hand it to her. Her fingers swiftly tap across the screen. She hands it back to me a few seconds later with a smile on her face. A smile that makes her dimple appear.

"A dove?" The emoji is beside her name.

"Yeah. They represent good things... peace, love, romance, and they're beautiful."

All things that could easily be associated with her.

"I like that." I tap my phone against my palm before sliding it back into my pocket. "Thank you for the dances and conversation."

"Any time." She glances over her shoulder at her parents who are now waiting on her. Eve tugs on the lapel of my suit, pressing a kiss to my cheek. When she pulls away, our lips are a breath apart from each other. I'm tempted to close the gap, but don't. While her beauty is undeniable, I really want to get to know her.

"I'll text you later, Dove."

She gives me a brilliant smile. "I've never had a nickname before. My name is too short."

"I think Dove is fitting."

"C'mon, Eve, honey," her mother calls.

"Coming," she says over her shoulder, focusing on me. "Bye, Winter."

"Bye, Dove."

I blink to fingers snapping in front of my face. "There you are."

"What?" I clear my throat, straightening up in my chair.

"Did you hear anything we said?" North asks.

"Yeah." I try to sound convincing, looking around Snow's office as if I'll find a clue. They look at me, silently calling my bullshit. I rub my eyes with the heels of my hands, letting out a sigh. "Nah. I didn't."

"Are you okay?" Snow asks with concern on his face.

"I am. There's just a lot on my mind."

"Someone." North interjects. "Some *one* is on your mind. It's about time you stop pussyfooting around her."

"I'm not pussyfooting."

"Mmm..." Snow grunts, pursing his lips.

"I'm not." I shrug defensively, looking between the two of them. "She has a boyfriend."

"She has a *distraction*."

"When the fuck did you become a relationship guru, North?"

"Anyone with two fucking eyes can see you're pussyfooting." He adjusts his glasses. "And I have four."

Snow and I snort with laughter.

"What am I supposed to do?" I ask honestly. "I can't add prison to my list and kidnap her."

"Apply pressure and don't let up," Snow says.

"I already have. I told her I'd pull funding if she didn't go on this date with me."

"Damn." North chuckles. "Ruthless."

"For fuck's sake. First I'm pussyfooting and now I'm ruthless?"

"I think you're going about it the right way," Snow says. "You're letting her come to you instead of forcing your way into her life."

"You don't think taking the money back is forcing my way?"

"No." Snow shrugs nonchalantly. "It's a contractual agreement. You were the highest bidder."

"He made sure of that," North says.

"Aye." I point at him. "Being a billionaire is a beautiful thing."

At the end of each week, we have a meeting just us three. It helps us keep the company, as well as ourselves, on track. This company was never meant for only one of us. Each of us brings something invaluable to the table. I know Dad would be proud of the three of us. Not solely because of the company, but also because of the men we've become.

Later in the afternoon as I'm walking out to my car, I send a text to Eve.

Winter: Ready for tonight?
Eve: Unfortunately, JLo.
Winter: LMAO See you soon, Dove.

Chuckling to myself, I slide into my car. This is going to be an interesting evening.

19

EVE

AFTER ALL THIS TIME, he still calls me Dove. I thought he was ridiculous at first for giving me a nickname right after meeting him. Truth is, I loved it the moment it rolled off his tongue. And I still do.

Letting out a frustrated sigh, I sit on the floor of my closet. Clothes are strewn all around me, courtesy of the tornado of my indecision. I've told myself I don't care what I wear tonight. Yet here I am, considering going shopping with the few hours I have left before Winter arrives. There's a lot of things happening that I never thought would happen again. Going on a date with Winter is number one.

"Still can't decide?" Noah steps into the closet, leaning against the dresser in the center of it.

"No." I pick up a black leather Prada pump with a block heel, debating on whether I should wear them.

"Does it really matter what you wear?"

"Yes, Noah." I sigh, annoyed with his attitude over the past week. His agreeability came to a screeching halt when he realized Winter and Aundi aren't dating. "It matters what I wear."

"You're treating this like a date."

"How else am I supposed to treat it?" I decide to go through my closet again. There's no time to run to the store *and* deal with Noah's bullshit.

"I don't know... maybe like you already have a boyfriend. You've been in your closet for hours, dressing up for him."

My hand hovers over a jade green outfit I forgot I ordered. I stop, turning slowly to face Noah.

"Who the fuck said it's for him?" I say with a sneer. "Clearly you know nothing about me if you've failed to realize I *always* put a lot of thought into what I wear." I scoff, rolling my eyes, turning back around to get a better look at the outfit.

"Do you still have feelings for him?"

"No," I say flatly, pulling the outfit out, noticing it has a light shimmer to it. This might be the one. "If I don't go, we don't get the funding the clinic desperately needs."

"I've never known you to be desperate."

His words burrow under my skin, making my blood boil. "Fine, Noah. Donate a million dollars, and I'll stay home with you and stroke your ego."

It's a low blow, but he deserves it for all the shit he's been giving me over this fucking dinner. He pins his arms across his chest falling silent.

"You're making it seem like I intentionally changed the plans or that I even want to go tonight." *You do.*

"I'm sor—"

I hold up my hand, too annoyed to hear an apology. "You can let yourself out. I've got to get ready."

I brush past him, setting my outfit and heels on the chaise near the window in my room. Grabbing my phone from my dresser, I head to the bathroom, locking the door behind me so Noah can't follow me in to apologize. Hopefully he leaves. I can only imagine how he'll act once Winter gets here.

Sometimes I wonder if Noah is with me because he loves more or if I'm just his prize after all these years. Maybe a mix of both? Pushing those thoughts aside, I turn on the shower and strip out of my clothes. I grab my phone, connecting it to the speaker and scroll for a song. Before I can find one, a text comes in from Winter.

Winter: What are you wearing tonight?
Winter: If I remember correctly, green is your color.

Letting out a sigh, I tip my head back, accepting I was dressing for him after all.

Eve: I already picked out an outfit without your input.
Winter: It's green isn't t?
Eve: ...
Eve: Yes.
Winter: Can't wait to see you.

The butterflies ignite, threatening to take flight. *Calm yourself, girl.* Instead of responding, I put on Still C U by Jessie Reyez and get into the shower.

An hour and a half later, I'm staring at myself in the mirror, applying a nude lip color. Leaning back, I stare at my lips, wondering if I should add a bit of gloss to them. I grab my phone to check the time, realizing I still need to put the outfit on and hope I don't change my mind... again. Taking it off the hanger to put it on, I know I made the right choice. The set is made out of a gauzy, light material that gives it an airy summer vibe. I pull on the high waisted, wide leg pants, wrapping myself in the crop top with bell sleeves, criss crossing the strings around my waist to secure the fabric covering my breasts. The pants are long enough that I'll need higher heels to keep them from dragging on the floor.

I catch a glimpse of myself in the mirror when I step into my closet. Winter was right. Green is my color. I grab some white patent leather Prada platforms with a chunky heel. My phone rings with a text where I left it on my bed.

Winter: On my way.

My heart races. Oh my God this is *happening*! How the fuck did I go from not talking to my ex-fiancé to going on a date with him? I focus on getting my shoes on because I definitely don't want to invite him inside. For jewelry, I choose small gold hoop earrings, stacking rings and necklaces to elevate the look. Finally, I spritz on some perfume. Tousling my loose curls in the mirror one last time, I smile.

I look fucking good.

Grabbing a small purse, I shove my phone and lip gloss inside. When I reach the living room, I'm startled by Noah's voice.

"You look gorgeous." He gets up from where he was sitting on the couch.

"I thought you left."

"I didn't want to leave things on a shitty note."

"Then don't bring a shitty attitude into my space and it won't." I turn my back to him, grabbing my keys out of the bowl on the mantle.

"I know I've been an ass this week and I'm sorry."

"In the future, if you're not comfortable with me doing something, tell me instead of letting me follow through with it and making me the bad guy."

He closes the gap between us, wrapping his arms around my waist, pulling me into him. "I thought I'd be okay with it... until I wasn't."

"Do you think I'm going to ride off into the sunset with him?" I tease, attempting to lighten the mood.

"Anything is possible, Eve."

I place my hands on either side of his face, making him look at me. "I'm not going anywhere, Noah."

I'd never do to someone else what Winter did to me. No one deserves to endure that pain.

"I'd rather be here with you then going to Twisted Vines. Actually..." I bite my bottom lip, looking off to the side. "I'm not gonna lie and say I'm not excited to finally be going to Twisted Vines, but I wish it were with you."

He laughs, burying his face in my neck. "That's fair. I can't blame you."

I press a kiss to his cheek. "I lo—"

The doorbell interrupts our moment. My stomach drops to my feet. "I'll get that."

Noah drops his hands to his side, releasing me. I see the muscle in his jaw flex as he takes a barely noticeable deep breath. "Of course," he says with a hint of bitterness in his tone.

I feel like a hypocrite, telling him he has nothing to worry about when I've crossed the line with Winter more than once. Better yet, Winter has crossed the line. Not that I did anything to pull myself back over it. I'll take those moments with him to my grave.

I will my feet to move toward the door. I let my hand hover over the knob, taking a deep breath before opening it. Winter's back is to me. When he turns to face me with his brilliant, signature smile, I feel like I've forgotten how to breathe. Winter straddles that fine line of being ruggedly handsome and beautiful at the same time. He's wearing a green linen suit that's a few shades darker than my outfit with a cream colored shirt, unbuttoned of course to show his chest and tattoos, and a cream colored, silk pocket square. Layered gold necklaces gleam on his neck, amplifying his rich sepia skin. The rest of his jewelry is gold too. Like mine. We both have a deep love for the finer things in life. Something I miss.

"For you." He holds a stunning bouquet out to me, made up of white and pink daisies, baby's breath, and yellow roses.

I take them from him, unintentionally brushing my hand against his. "You remembered?" My guard slips.

"I'd never forget."

Tears sting my eyes. "Dammit, Winter." I stomp my foot, looking away from him. "They're beautiful." I say, looking up at the sky, blinking back the tears.

From our very first date years ago, he's always given me flowers. Even after we started living together, if we were going on a date, he'd give me a bouquet. Specifically, with pink gerbera and common daisies because they're my favorite. He's given me hundreds of bouquets, and I never stopped being surprised or loving them. Not even now.

"Thank you." I give him a genuine smile.

"Of course. Are you ready? You look radiant by the way."

"You're striking, as always." I smooth my hand over the lapel of his jacket, forgetting Noah is here.

I quickly remove my hand when I hear Noah's voice behind me. "Hey, Winter."

"Noah." Winter gives him a mix of a salute and a wave. "Terrible you can't come with us tonight."

My eyes widen, giving Winter an *"are you fucking kidding"* me look. He smiles at Noah in response.

"I'll be here when she gets back."

"Valiant of you." Winter is clearly unphased. "Ready, Dove?"

"Dove?" Noah asks, confused.

If this bouquet wasn't so pretty, I'd smack Winter over the head with it.

"My apologies." Winter places his hand over his heart, bowing slightly. "Old habits die hard. Are you ready, Eve?"

"Yes," I say, wanting to leave this uncomfortable conversation behind. "Let me put these in some water first."

Before I can turn to head back inside, Winter takes the bouquet from my hand, giving it to Noah. "Be a gentleman and put these in some water, won't you? We've got to hit the road to be on time for our date."

Noah stares at the bouquet for longer than necessary. "No problem." He takes them, holding them tighter than I'd like, but I keep my mouth shut.

"Thank you." I smile at Noah. "Um... well, we better get going."

Winter holds his hand out to me and I take it. Before I can take a step toward him, Noah pulls me back, cupping my chin, bringing his mouth to mine with my hand still in Winter's. I don't know what to do with myself other than succumb to the kiss and hold onto Winter. After a few *very* long breaths, Noah breaks our connection.

"Love you," he mutters against my lips.

The words are on the tip of my tongue until I see the look in his eyes. His love isn't for me right now. He's using it as an attempt to put Winter in his place.

I blink. "Yeah. See you tonight…" I pull away from him, heading down the steps, stopping halfway down. "Love you," I add as an afterthought over my shoulder.

Noah gives Winter a smug smile, seemingly satisfied with my dejected response.

"Let's go, Dove." Winter tugs on my hand, and I follow him to his car. He opens the door for me, helping me into the white leather seat.

When he gets in the driver's seat, the spicy, sweet scent of him wraps around me. I inhale deeply, closing my eyes as he starts the car.

"Damn." He brings the car to life and *Are You That Somebody* by Aaliyah pours from the speakers. "Noble Noah isn't taking this well, huh?"

"Would you?"

"This never would've happened with me. I just know he's sliding down a wall in distress right now."

"Winter!" I can't help the laughter that bubbles up in my throat. "You're so fucking arrogant."

"Me, personally?" He pats his chest. "I'd be *siiiccckkk*–crying, screaming, and throwing up–if some guy like me came to pick up my girlfriend. We'd fight on sight!"

"Why are you like this?" I ask through laughter.

"Should we turn around and go get him?" He hikes his thumb over his shoulder. "I'm sure he could eat out back or something."

"Stop being an asshole and drive!" I point at the road, trying to wipe the smile off my face.

"I could always have Snow or North do a wellness check if—"

I playfully swat his arm. "Focus on the road. Noah is fine, but you won't be if you don't shut the fuck up."

"Alright, I'll stop *if* you make me a promise."

Folding my arms, I turn slightly in the seat to get a better look at him. "What?"

"To have fun with me tonight. Let your guard down a little bit." A silence falls between us as I consider him and his words. "What do you have to lose?"

"Myself." I answer honestly.

Coming to a stop at a light, he reaches out, rubbing his thumb against my cheek. "Is that such a bad thing?"

"With you? Yes." I swallow, torn between wanting to relish his touch and pull away. As always, I stay.

His eyes search mine. "What if it's not?"

Everything—my heart, soul, and mind—have been stuck in the past. I'm having a hard time reconciling with the Winter I knew and the man asking me to let my guard down. Fox's words resound in my head – *because energy like that is a once in lifetime type thing.*

"Okay. I'll let my guard down... only for tonight."

He smiles, merging onto the freeway. "That's all I need."

Twisted Vines is a small, family owned vineyard nestled in the hills of Hope Valley with majestic views. From the moment we traveled up the charming, winding dirt road, I knew we were in for an experience. So far we've experienced pinot noir, chardonnay, sparkling wines, and they brought a 1992 vintage cabernet sauvignon out of their vault for us to try. I'm grateful when they lead us toward the restaurant because I drank quite a bit of the vintage wine instead of sampling it. I promised Winter I'd have a fun time with him tonight, and I'm going to follow through. Not that there's a dull moment with him to begin with.

The restaurant is dimly lit, giving it a moody, intimate ambiance. The well-worn stone flooring and walls remind me of the cellar we were just in. Greenery hangs from the ceiling and pictures displaying the history of Twisted Vines decorate the wall. The hostess leads us to a table at the back of the restaurant.

Winter pulls my seat out for me before taking his own. Looking around, I now see why we had to come alone. Fitting a group of six in this small space with other guests would be a tight squeeze. Even Winter looks too large. He shrugs out of his jacket, draping it over the chair. The motion causes his cologne to waft my way as if I needed to inhale more of him right now.

"Your waiter will be right with you," the hostess says with a smile.

Winter thanks her and turns to me as she walks away. "Is it everything you'd hoped for?"

"It's much more. I didn't realize wine could be so delicious."

"I saw you drinking that last sample like you were in the Sahara desert."

I clap my hand over my mouth, stifling a laugh. "It was good, okay?"

"I could tell." His teeth look like they're glowing when he smiles with the dim lighting and the flicker of the candle sitting atop the table. "We'll get a bottle before we leave."

"Winter, you don't—"

He holds up his hand. "Save the modesty for your boyfriend. I don't want it or need it."

I grew up with money. Then I met Winter and learned what it meant to not have to consider it.

"In case you're wondering, I still love being spoiled." I say.

He chuckles low and smooth. The sound vibrates in my own chest.

The waiter appears at our table with a carafe of water. She grabs the glasses, filling them up. "Hi, I'm Morgana. We do things a little differently here at Twisted Vines."

I glance at Winter who's also giving her a quizzical look. "At most places, you order your food first. Here, we lead with wine." She sets a short menu of wines on the table. "When you pick one out, the chef makes a meal that compliments your wine choice."

"That sounds amazing." My excitement bubbles.

"The menu is seasonal with the vegetables grown here in our garden and meat sourced from local farmers. I'll give you some time to pick out your wines." She leaves us alone again.

When I look at Winter, he's staring at me with a smile on his face. "What?" I pick up the glass of cool water, taking a sip.

"Nothing." He picks up the menu. "It's good to see you happy."

"Oh..." I set my glass aside, tucking my hair behind my ear. "Thanks."

Watching me a few seconds longer, he turns his attention back to the menu. "What are you getting?"

"Choose for me."

Raising his brow, his eyes meet mine. "Really?"

"Yes." I nod. "I wanna see what you pick out for me and if I like it."

He leans back in his seat, tilting his head to the side, causing the pale green diamond studs in his ears to glint. Only Winter would have diamonds to match his outfit.

"Are you going to talk shit if you don't like it?"

"Relentlessly."

He lets out a deep rumble of laughter. "This feels like a setup."

"It's not. You told me to have fun and now look at you being hesitant."

"Alright. I'll order for you." He sets the menu aside.

The waiter reappears before I can respond. "Are you ready?"

"Yes." Winter grabs the wine list, looking over it one more time. "She'll have the pinot noir, and I'll have the cabernet sauvignon, please."

"Perfect. I'll be right out with your selections." She takes the wine list, leaving us alone again.

"I didn't think we'd ever be doing this again." I motion between us.

He leans forward, resting his forearms on the table. "I was waiting for you to cancel last minute."

Resting my elbows on the table, I fold my hands under my chin. "Would you have let me?"

"No," he says without blinking. "I would've loved for you to try and call my bluff though."

"You really would've pulled funding?"

"In a heartbeat. I meant what I said, Eve. I want every fucking thing."

His words travel straight to the spot between my thighs. I clear my throat, smoothing my fingertips down my neck. I'm grateful he can't see my blush. The waitress returns with our wine, saving me from Winter's consuming gaze.

The wine reminds me of rubies, swirling in the glass. I bring it to my lips, taking a slow sip, letting the flavors sit on my tongue before swallowing. I taste cherry with savory herbal notes and hints of strawberry and cocoa. The blend makes me want to dive into the glass.

I lick my lips, holding the glass up in front of me as if it's magic. "This is delicious."

Winter gives me a satisfied smile. "I knew you'd like it."

"You did good, Mr. King." I tip my glass toward him before taking another sip. "How's Reign?"

Winter's face lights up in a way I haven't seen before. "He's great. Passing his classes and helping a couple days a week after school at Cru's."

"That's amazing. He's flourishing then?"

"Yeah, he is." He takes a drink of his wine, licking his lips. "I'm not sure if it's me making a difference or if he's healing."

I knit my brows together. "Do you think he'd be doing what he is now without you?"

"Honestly..." His eyes meet mine. "No. He's like watching a flower bloom. I pour good things into him, he soaks it up, and he grows. Reign needs that. Deserves that."

I grab his hand from across the table. "You deserve that too."

A flicker of what used to be passes between us. The now broken and frayed string that used to tether us to one another feels like a live wire with our intertwined hands as the conduit. His touch reminds me of home. I startle, pulling my hand away when the waitress reappears.

"For the pinot noir," she says. Setting a plate in front of me, she tells me what's on it. "We have chicken linguine with figs and goat cheese."

Looking at Winter, he's smiling at me, knowing my love for pasta.

"And for the cabernet sauvignon, we have beef bourguignon with garlicky panko gremolata and pomme puree."

"Delicious." Winters smiles with his eyes still on me.

"Enjoy." She sets fresh glasses of wine down before leaving us alone again.

I clasp my hands together, staring at the pasta like it's the love of my life. "I'm about to demolish this."

"I can see it in your eyes." He pulls his silverware free from the white cloth napkin. "I've yet to meet someone who loves pasta as much as you do."

"I'm not sure that's possible."

"Do you remember the first time we tried to make it?"

I snort with laughter, unwrapping my silverware. "It kept crumbling! I was so frustrated you finally went to the store to buy some."

"You were on the verge of tears."

"I was hangry and out of my mind. It looked easy as hell on YouTube."

"Everything looks easy on there, Dove." He takes a bite of his food, savoring it as he briefly closes his eyes. "Have you tried making it since then?"

"You mean have I tried torturing myself since then?"

He chuckles.

"No. I haven't."

"Try this." He holds his fork out to me with a little bit of everything on it. I don't hesitate.

The flavors melt onto my tongue as he pulls the fork from my mouth. "That's delicious. Here." I twirl some noodles onto the fork. "Try mine."

"The first bite for me?"

"Yes. After my first bite, I'm not sharing."

He opens his mouth, taking the bite. Chewing slowly, he nods his head. "That's good. The fig sounded questionable."

I laugh.

"But it complements the flavors of the pasta and goat cheese." Taking his fork, he dips it in the pasta.

"Excuse you." I gape at him. "What the hell are you doing?"

"Eating." He grins, twirling another bite onto his fork.

I watch him through narrowed eyes as he takes another bite.

"Delicious." He wipes his mouth. "How are things at Hope's Village?"

Looking down at my plate, I push some of the noodles around with my fork before wrapping up a bite. "I'm doing a thing that was inspired by you."

"By me?" He has a fake look of surprise on his face. "The very man you hate?"

I take a sip of wine. "Not hate. Simply an aversion." I thought hating Winter would be easier until I realized I wasn't capable.

He lets out a rumble of laughter. "Like a fucking allergy?"

"Exactly." I point my fork at him.

"At least it's not a life threatening allergy."

"That remains to be seen..." I say in between bites.

The corner of his mouth tips up into a sly smile. "Tell me about your thing."

I launch into details about the community day. Winter listens to me with rapt attention.

"Will you come to it?"

He pauses with his wine glass halfway to his mouth, surprised. "On behalf of North—"

"No." I shake my head, holding his gaze. "On behalf of Winter King."

"I'll be there." He smiles. "As long as you jump in the bounce houses with me."

I snicker. "Deal."

"Did you want me to take you home after this?" He's already cleared his plate and only has a few sips of wine left.

"How about a walk through the vineyard instead?" I'm not sure how long we've been here, but I know I'm not ready for it to end.

"I'm down for whatever with you."

My shoes dangle from Winter's fingertips as we walk across the vineyard's lush grass that's too soft to not be barefoot in. The sun is getting ready to set and the wind has picked up, providing a light, fresh breeze. I've had a question on the tip of my tongue since he picked me up. Deciding I may not have another opportunity, I let it tumble from my lips.

"Winter..." He shifts his gaze to me. "Can I ask you something?"

"Anything."

I stare down at my feet, sinking into the grass, trying to gather the courage I had seconds ago. Stopping in my tracks, I meet his gaze.

"Why did you leave?" Tears unwillingly sting my eyes and a lump forms in my throat. "I want to hate you so fucking badly but I can't. I've tried. Now here we are, together again, like no time was lost and... fuck... why did you leave?"

It's more a of a plea than a question.

His eyes are filled with anguish and torment as he looks into mine. Bringing his hand up between us, he wipes the tears from my cheeks.

"It was all too much, Eve." His voice is barely a whisper over the wind.

"I was there." A fresh well of tears form in my eyes as my voice cracks. "I-I *begged* you to come back."

Winter looks away from me, turning his face toward the sky. His onyx eyes look bottomless when they meet mine again.

"You were trying to fix my grief, Eve, looking at me as if I was a puzzle with a few too many missing pieces. I felt alone. You were pushing for that fucking wedding even though I tried to reason with you that I wasn't ready. I just needed time... for you to sit with me..." A tear streams down his face, and I can feel my poorly mended heart cracking all over again. "And you couldn't do that."

His words pierce my heart, creating a tightness in my chest. This is truth I wasn't ready for. I played out countless scenarios in my head. Never once considering that *I* pushed him away.

"I thought things would get better. Even at your lowest–you were my everything. If I could've freed you from your pain I would've. I thought the wedding..."

The lump in my throat becomes painful and my words get buried beneath it. "I'm sorry, Winter," I whisper, reaching up to wipe his tears. "I'm so sorry..."

"Me too." His eyes swirl with emotion.

I can tell he's hesitant to believe my apology. I don't blame him. Holding his gaze, he looks away from me. I wait for him to say something. Anything. He doesn't. Turning away, I take a deep shuddering breath, wondering how I failed the man I love so badly? Without thinking, I walk with no clue where I'm going. I feel like I can't breathe, needing space before I ruin things again trying to fix them. I think he needs space too because he doesn't follow or try to stop me.

20
EVE

WITHOUT LOOKING BACK, I walk until I can no longer feel his presence. That's when I let out a sob, letting the pain I've kept locked away bubble up and spill from me. Winter physically lost his dad, and I emotionally lost him. I thought if we focused on the wedding, starting our lives together, that we'd both have something to look forward to. It seemed like the perfect distraction. Except I lost sight of him, focusing too much on the future. I was desperate to get to a point where grief wasn't eclipsing our life. My efforts only pushed him further into the void that already held him captive. I believed if he got the right help, everything would be okay.

I don't know why I feel the need to fix things. It was the main reason I wanted to become a doctor. Helping people is a passion of mine. I'm just not sure when the passion turned into a savior complex. Even now, I had to walk away from Winter because my mind instantly launched into ways I could fix what broke between us. I'm not sure I can undo the damage I caused.

For once, instead of trying to fix it, I sit with it. I sink onto the grass, hugging my legs to my chest. I didn't want to ruin our evening, but I couldn't hold the question in any longer. It's one I've been asking from the moment he left. As painful as it is, I now realize why he didn't talk to me. I know even if he told me then what he just told me now, I wouldn't have heard him. I thought I could turn the red flags to green.

The worst part of all this is that Winter felt alone even *with* me by his side. Looking back, his grief scared me because it consumed him. Being a fixer, I over compensated, thinking if he went to the right therapist, support group, or took the right meds he'd feel okay.

I pushed and pushed and fucking pushed.

None of that mattered because all he wanted was for me to have his back–to sit with him.

I rest my forehead on my knees, taking deep breaths. I blamed Winter for everything because it was easier to do then examining my own faults. I've always been blind to them. I look up when I feel a water droplet land on my hand. Rain clouds above match my mood.

Fantastic. I left my shoes with Winter and this isn't the best outfit to be caught in the rain in. Letting out a sigh, I swipe the tears from my cheeks with my fingertips. I don't make a move to get up despite the large, cold rain drops landing on me. I don't mind a little rain. I'm also not ready to face Winter.

My choice is made for me when I hear the roll of thunder in the distance. I jump to my feet, fear gripping me. I can handle rain, but I refuse to be in the middle of a thunderstorm by myself. The sky splits open, dumping rain. My clothes cling to my body, leaving little to the imagination I'm sure, and my feet grow numb with every step between the chilling rain and wet earth. Another crack of thunder followed by a flash of lightning causes me to yelp and break out into a run. *Fuck this.* I can't really see between the droplets of water clinging to my lashes and how hard the rain is falling.

I hear my name in being called in the distance. Winter can't be far. I didn't pay attention to my surroundings when I walked off. Of course,

I didn't think I'd get caught in a torrential downpour with thunder and lightning. My heart pounds in my chest more from fear of being electrocuted then from running. Winter comes into view, and I almost start crying again from relief.

I launch myself at him, wrapping my arms around his neck and my legs around his middle.

"I got you," he mutters in my ear. "You're safe."

"We're gonna die." I bury my face in his neck.

I feel his chuckle resonate against my chest that's pressed to his. "No, Dove. It's about three miles away."

"Three miles too close." Another whip of thunder rumbles followed by lightning. I wrap myself around him tighter. "Please get me inside. Or let's go home, please."

I'm sure I look like a wet cat clinging to him, refusing to let go.

"Loosen your arms a little so I can breathe."

"I'm sorry." I give him some slack.

His hands palm my ass, hiking me further up his body before he walks. I try to ignore the feeling of his large hands sliding from my ass to my thighs. It's like trying to ignore the thunder and lightning in the sky.

"You okay?" he asks, wrapping an arm around my waist while his other hand grips my thigh.

"Yes." *Because you're here.*

Noah doesn't understand – nor does he try to – my fear of thunderstorms. He thinks it's silly because I'm an adult. Even though I tried to explain to him how Fox and Jude locked me outside in the middle of a thunderstorm. Lightning struck a tree in our yard, causing a few large branches to fall off. It scared me half to death; I was ten and didn't ever consider lightning could kill until then. I've been terrified ever since. I think it scared our parents too because Fox and Jude were grounded for months afterwards.

"We're almost back to my car." I don't want to drive in this weather, but I also don't want to be out in the open, exposed. "I've gotta put you down to get my keys from my pocket."

I reluctantly unravel myself from him, putting my feet on the ground. He quickly dips his hand in his pocket. I look around and there aren't as many cars in the parking lot as there were when we first arrived. Were we the only ones who didn't get the thunderstorm memo? Opening the door, he waits for me to climb in. Once the door is closed, and Winter's safely in the driver's seat, I let out a sigh of relief. He starts the car, turning on the seat warmers and heat. Before he can put the car in drive, there's a knock on his window that causes me to jump.

It's someone dressed in a rain poncho, holding the hood of it on their head against the rain and wind. They tip it back a bit, and I recognize it's our hostess.

"You can't leave," she shouts over the rain.

"What?" My eyes widen.

"Why?" Winter asks.

"There are downed trees and a powerline on the road back to the main one. They won't be able to clear it out tonight for you guys to leave safely."

Winter cuts the engine. "So what are we supposed to do?"

"Can you please come inside and we can talk about accommodations?"

"Yes, of course. I'm sorry to keep you out there." Winter climbs out of the car and rounds it to open the door for me. He must see the worry in my eyes because he says, "It's going to be okay."

I put on my shoes and then we dash across the parking lot and into the safety of the restaurant. The hostess shakes her poncho off before hanging it up. Winter wraps his jacket around me.

"My name is Kiersten, by the way. Are both of you okay? It's terrible out there." Her eyes scan our bodies, lingering a little longer on Winter.

He wraps his arm around my shoulders, giving me a tight squeeze. "Yes. What accommodations were you speaking of?"

"We have our bed and breakfast, and due to the thunderstorm, we had a few cancellations. Our plan is to pave the road leading to and from the vineyard closer to the end of summer to avoid situations like this."

"Were we the only ones who didn't know about this thunderstorm?"

"No, it was a surprise for us too. The national weather advisory didn't send out a flash flood warning until a couple of hours ago."

I didn't think our walk was that long. "Flash flood warning?"

She gives me a sympathetic smile. "I assure you, are safe here. Just not on that road. There were a few other guests who will be staying the night as well." She turns her attention back to the screen. "Okay, I just had to check what room it was. You'll be in number nine."

It finally sinks in. "We're spending the night together?" I look at Winter.

He smiles. "Looks that way, Dove."

Alone? All night? With him? The man I already struggle to keep a safe distance from? This evening just keeps hitting me with surprises left, right, and center. None of them seem to be good.

"This way." Kiersten smiles, leading us back outside. Except this time there's a walkway.

I stop in my tracks. "I need my bag. It has my phone."

Winter holds it up.

"Oh. Thank you." I take it from him.

We continue following Kiersten. A house that I didn't notice before comes into view. It's more like a mini mansion then a house. Green vines creep up the sides of it, giving it an enchanting look. Warm lights glow in the windows now that the sun has set. Maybe staying here won't be so bad after all. I imagine the views from the rooms are breathtaking.

Reaching the front door, Kiersten opens it and warm air envelopes us when we step inside. A fire crackles in the stone fireplace in the corner.

"You'll be in good hands," Kiersten assures us. "I've got to get back to the restaurant. There were some more guests I need to take care of."

"Yes, of course," Winter says.

"Thank you for accommodating us," I say.

She gives us both a smile and a wave before disappearing again. We're promptly met by another employee.

"Hi." He gives us a warm smile. "I'm Amir, the innkeeper."

"Nice to meet you." I return his smile. "I'm Eve and this is Winter."

"Despite the circumstances, I'm glad you two can stay with us tonight. You'll be staying right this way." He holds out his hand, signaling for us to follow him. "It's our biggest room with the best view."

Okay, maybe *all* the surprises aren't bad. I take in the spacious room decorated in warm, neutral colors with a large canopy bed wrapped in gauzy white material dominating the space. Windows are opposite of it, providing the best view just like Amir said. We follow him through the suite. There's a living room with plush seating, decorated in cozy blankets and pillows. I let out a gasp when he shows us the bathroom with the large claw foot tub set in front of a large window with another beautiful view. All I can think about is getting naked and soaking in it.

"If there's anything you need, please do not hesitate to let me know. We've also provided you with some fresh clothing. It's not the quality

I'm sure you're accustomed to, but it's the best we can do given the circumstances."

"Thank you for even providing us with dry clothing," I say.

"Of course. I'll leave you to it and get our other guests checked in. Hopefully you're able to enjoy the rest of your evening." Amir smiles before leaving us alone.

I pretend to be more interested in the room's decor, avoiding eye contact with Winter, suddenly hyper aware of his presence. Unsure of what to say after his truth before the rainfall.

"Why don't you take hot bath so you can warm up?"

I turn to face him. "What about you? Aren't you cold? Do you want to get warm together? Because I'm—" I smack my palm against my forehead, closing my eyes, realizing how it sounded.

Winter chuckles and it echoes of the bathroom walls. "I know what you meant, Eve. Take your time. Besides, that outfit is holding onto you for dear life."

"What?" I look down, realizing my pants have rips at the waistband and bottom. Whipping around, I look in the mirror to see my makeup is running down my face and there's a tear on my left shoulder. "I look like I walked through hell! Oh my gosh!"

"You look like you got caught in a thunderstorm. I'll be out here." He grabs the door handle, getting ready to close it behind him.

"Winter..." His eyes meet mine. "Thank you for saving me."

"I didn't save you, Dove. You saved yourself. All I did was carry you."

My nose stings as tears prick my eyes. I think of how much hatred I've harbored toward him over the years when he has every reason to hate me too. But he doesn't. Winter caters to me with tenderness as though I'm still his. He closes the door behind him and I let out a deep sigh.

"What a fucking night..." I mutter, turning on the hot water to fill the bathtub.

Grabbing my purse, I unzip it and pull out my phone. There are several missed calls and texts from Noah. My thumb hovers over the call back button, dreading his response to me having to spend the night with Winter. There's not much I can do about it. I'm not going to die trying to get back to him. My phone has three percent battery left. That's enough to call Noah and talk to him for a few minutes. Sitting on the edge of the tub, I quickly press the button to call him back before I change my mind.

"Hey, Babe. There you are. I was checking in because I saw there was a thunderstorm near Twisted Vines."

I'd believe him except he's never cared about me during thunderstorms before. "Yeah... I'm okay. Winter—" I cut myself off. He doesn't need to know anything about him. "We have to stay the night," I blurt out.

"What?" I feel the ice in his tone.

"The road to get here is a dirt one and a few trees—"

"You guys were supposed to leave hours ago. What kept you?"

I didn't want to leave. My phone beeps, letting me know my battery is low.

"When we got here, they gave us a tour, plus wine tasting, and then we had dinner. That took a while..." My voice trails off.

"That sounds like the perfect date," he says cynically.

"It—what do you want me to do, Noah? We couldn't leave even if we wanted to."

"No, but you could've left earlier," he shoots back.

I really can't argue that point, but I do anyway. "You're being unreasonable."

"I'm being unreasonable? Me, Eve? I'm being unreasonable because I don't want you to spend the night with your ex-fiancé?" He scoffs. "Are you at least in separate rooms?"

"Well..."

"For fuck's sake." I can tell he's struggling to contain his annoyance with me. "You're sleeping together?"

"No! We're not sleeping together! They only had one room and—"

"Fucking convenient." He spits at me. "For all I know Winter fucking King moved heaven and earth to cause this to happen."

"Oh, please, Noah. You sound ridiculous. Not even the workers at Twisted Vines knew about the thunderstorm."

"What I want to know is what you two were doing that you couldn't leave earlier? Because I call bullshit on dinner and a tour taking that long."

I tell him the truth. "We were talking."

"Talking? Catching up on—"

"What was I supposed to do? Sit in fucking silence all night?"

"You weren't supposed to fucking go!" he shouts. "I don't understand how you deluded yourself into believing that I was okay with this when I clearly wasn't. Honest to fucking God, Eve, would you be okay with me going on a date to a vineyard in the goddamn mountains with my ex-fiancé?"

No. I'd want to murder him like I do now. "First of all, check your tone with me, Noah. Second of all, you could've used the tone you're using right now when you were in front of me."

"You're conveniently oblivious to everything as long as it doesn't affect you. But if it's anyone else, fuck them right? They'll just have to get over it."

His words cut deep because I know he's right. Winter said the same thing in much nicer words not even hours ago. The tears well up in my eyes again.

"It's–I didn't–I'm sorry."

Noah lets out an exasperated sigh, falling silent for a few breaths. "I don't know if I can do this, Eve..."

"What?" My phone beeps again. "S-So what are you saying?"

"I'm saying that I don't know if I can do this. It's blatantly clear my feelings aren't valid. You do whatever the fuck you want first and then ask for forgiveness later. I don't—"

"What are you saying?"

"I don't want—" My phone dies before he can finish his sentence.

"Fuck!" I shout, looking at the black screen. Letting out a frustrated growl, I set my phone on my thigh, staring up at the ceiling as I grip my frizzy curls. Everything is dumping on me like the rain pouring from the sky. I'm cold and exhausted. Maybe it's a good thing my phone died because I can't think of anything good to say to Noah right now. There's a soft knock on the bathroom door.

"What?" I snap.

"Um... are you good?"

I stare at the ceiling for a few blinks, not wanting to answer because I feel the threat of tears. "Yep," I respond curtly.

It's quiet, and I think he's left until I hear his voice again. "Do you want me to believe that? Because I can if—"

In spite of it all, I laugh.

"Can I come in?" he asks as the door slowly opens, and Winter appears with his eyes covered.

"I'm not naked... yet."

"Damn." He drops his hand, smiling. "Ruining my hopes and dreams."

"You need bigger dreams."

"And you need to turn off that water." He points at the tub that is dangerously full.

"Shit!" I jump, lunging to turn it off. When my hand touches the handle, I see my phone slide off my thigh and into the tub.

"No!" The shock quickly turns into despair. I slide off the edge of the tub, onto the floor, and cry. Burying my face in my hands, I let it out.

I feel Winter sit beside me. As badly as I want to stop crying, I can't. He doesn't say anything, just sits with me. After some time, I feel him wrap his arm around my shoulders, pulling me into him.

"My intention wasn't to make you cry, Dove." He thinks this is about earlier and a part of it is.

"It's not that–I mean it was–it is..." I take a shaky breath. "There's a lot I wasn't ready to handle today."

"Want to talk about it?" He smooths my wet curls away from my face.

I shake my head, resting in the crook of his arm.

"Okay." He kisses my temple. "Do you want me to sit with you?"

"Yes." My voice cracks. He tightens his arms around me as we sit on the bathroom floor.

We stay like this until I start shivering. "You should take a bath," Winter says gently, slowly unraveling his arms from around me. The cold seeps into my bones without his touch.

He turns around, plunging his hand into the water to pull the plug from the drain. I hear my phone rattle around in the bottom when he grabs for it, pulling it out a few seconds later.

"We can ask if they have some rice if you want?" He holds it up, giving it a hopeless look.

I shrug, hitting the rock bottom of the fucks I had to give. "I don't really care at the moment."

He sets it on a towel that's off to the side. "You can use mine if you want."

I imagine calling Noah from Winter's phone. He'd figure out a way to get here downed trees and powerlines be damned. "No, it's okay. Thanks though."

Now that the tub is drained, he turns the knob, filling it up again. Grabbing a few bottles off the tub's tray, he reads the labels before setting them aside and twisting the cap off one that looks like a mini wine bottle. I watch him pour it under the stream of water. Bubbles froth a moment later, and the scents of honey and lavender fill the air. It puts me in the mood to sink into the tub again. The water reaches the perfect soaking level, and he turns it off.

"Take your bath. I'll be right out there."

He stands and I catch his hand from where I'm still seated on the floor. "Thank you, Winter."

He squeezes my hand, giving me a smile before slipping his out of mine and disappearing through the door. I wipe my face, getting to my feet, and quickly strip out of my damp clothes. As soon as my toe hits the hot water, my body relaxes. I slowly steep myself into the bubbly foam and feel myself fully relax as I slip beneath the surface.

I sit until the water gets lukewarm. Standing, I grab the detachable showerhead, rinsing off again, and get out. There's some leave in conditioner on a tray with other sample size bath products that I rub through my coils that smells like vanilla. After I coat my hair, I check in my bag to see if, by luck, I have a hair tie. I find one in the zipper pocket and pull my curls into a bun. Finally, I pull on the white t-shirt that has "Twisted Vines" printed on the front and the soft sweats with the Twisted Vines logo emblazoned on the hip. Stepping out into the living room area, I swallow hard when I see Winter is only wearing a towel wrapped around his waist.

He looks up from his phone. "I couldn't stand the feel of that wet suit any longer."

"I don't blame you." I avert my eyes, trying to look anywhere but his chest and that coveted V.

"Your nipples are pierced?" His eyes are glued to my chest.

I glance down and you can see the barbells and my nipples straining through the shirt. "Nope. Just an illusion."

He chuckles, shaking his head. "Smartass. How long have you had them?"

"Mmm... about eight years I think."

"They look good."

"You haven't even seen them." I cross my arms over my chest.

"I've seen enough to know." He stands and my eyes dip to the substantial bulge noticeable through the white towel. "I'm a man with feelings, Eve. Show some respect."

I suck my teeth, laughing. "Oh, please! You were just staring at my tits."

"I'm not respectable though, Sweetheart."

"Go take your bath instead of walking around here like a desperate thirst trap."

He grins, looking me up and down as he walks past on the way to the bathroom. Seconds later I hear the shower start. Winter has never liked baths. He thinks it's gross to sit in your own "filth" even if you're washing off afterward. I find a ridiculously soft robe folded on the end of the bed and slip it on. Settling in front of the fireplace, I stare out at the star lit night sky.

This place beat my ass today, but I can't deny how beautiful it is. Noah creeps into my head. I'm not sure I'd call him even if my phone was working. I wish he was honest from the beginning instead of pretending everything was okay only to blow up on me. It feels reminiscent of Winter and me. Noah's words repeat in my head – *you're conveniently oblivious to everything as long as it doesn't affect you.*

In both instances – with Winter and Noah – I was getting what a wanted. Or I thought I was. With Winter, I wanted a wedding, and with Noah, I wanted a boyfriend who'd dote on me no questions asked. My needs were met because I demanded it while their needs... I either ignored them or didn't want to see them. I've had other relationships before. None of them being as serious as the relationships I've had with Winter or Noah. Truthfully, I love Noah. However, after what he said to me, I'm not sure it's in the way I convinced myself it was. Maybe he's right? I am deluded.

Winter steps into the living space in light gray sweats and a white t-shirt that matches my own, and it brings my train of thought to a screeching halt. I'm taking the picking of gray sweats for Winter personal, because who the fuck consciously does that, knowing the power they possess? He pulls the towel off his head and I watch his muscles strain against the white t-shirt.

"Feel better?" I ask in an attempt to shift my focus.

He grabs the other robe off the end of the bed, pulling it on. "Much. What time is – wait you don't have a phone." He grabs his off the coffee table. "It's nine. Do you think it'd be a dick move to order food or something?"

"It's a bed and breakfast. I'm sure they have other guests. Plus, I'm hungry." I smile innocently.

"Ahhh." He nods his head. "That makes sense. Leave me to look like the dick."

My smile slips. "That's not what—"

"I'm kidding. I know I'm an asshole." He snatches the menu off the table, setting it on my lap. "Let me know what you want."

"While the food was good, I'm in the mood for junk food."

I scan the menu, relieved to see it's more relaxed offerings such as burgers and chicken tenders. "Spicy black bean nachos and an order of chicken tenders with a side of ranch, please." I hand him back the menu.

"I love that you've never been afraid to eat in front of me."

I quirk a brow, tilting my head to the side. "Other women don't?"

"Nah. Not really. They'll eat, but you thoroughly enjoy your food."

"That's the purpose of it... besides nourishment of course. Besides, you've heard me fart before, so does it really matter?"

He struggles to keep the smile off his face. "You're so unlady like. Deplorable, really."

"You still ate my ass..."

He lets out a belt of laughter. "Eve Marie Valentine! I am a gentleman. A man of honor. How dare you accuse me of such filthy acts – " I side eye him " – that I fully intend to commit again."

I cover my face with a throw pillow. "Winter."

"Don't act shy now. You're the one who brought it up." He focuses on the menu again. "Do you want to share the nachos and chicken or are you being selfish?"

"We can share." I set the pillow on my lap.

"Bet." Winter gets up, heading toward the phone on the desk. It takes him less than a minute to order. "They said thirty minutes."

He lays beside me, turning sideways until his head is in my lap, resting on the pillow.

I stare at him. "You're treating this like a slumber party."

"We're here already." He grins up at me, looking devastatingly handsome. "Might as well."

"Might as well..." Instead of fighting the urge, I sink my fingers into his curls. He groans, making me smile. "Feel good?"

"Yeah." I can see his eyes rolling behind his eyelids. "You feel good."

I watch him enjoying my touch, nibbling my bottom lip, trying to decide if I want to talk about earlier or not. "Noah broke up with me..."

He startles me, clapping his hands. "About fucking time. I had a hunch this would be the event to finally push his ass over the edge."

I lean back, cackling. "You're going to hell!"

"You'll be there too so I'm good, Dove."

"You don't even care if I'm sad or not?"

"I know you're sad. Despite not wanting to see it, I can tell you care about him."

"I do..." I admit softly.

"Can I ask you something?"

"Yeah." I continue messing around with his hair.

"Do you love him?" His eyes slide up to my face. "And answer honestly."

"Yes, although... he called me deluded today... said I was conveniently oblivious to things. And I think maybe he's right."

"He's one to talk. Noah convinced himself you were over me because you were under him."

"I thought I was over you too."

"You're both oblivious then." I suck my teeth, glaring at him. "I never tried to fool myself into believing I was over you. The only thing I ever knew with a certainty was that I wasn't getting over you."

"Maybe you're right." I let out a sigh.

"What set him off to speak his mind now?"

"That we're going to be in the same room together."

"You never told him about us kissing then?"

"Us?" I look at him like he's crazy. "You kissed me."

"And you liked it, Katy Perry."

I open my mouth to respond, instead laughter tumbles from my lips. Leaning forward, I rest my head on Winter's chest as I laugh. "You're ridiculous."

Before I can pull away, he wraps his hands around the back of my neck, interlocking his fingers. My laughter immediately dies down when our eyes meet. It's clear what he wants and for the first time in what feels like forever–I give to him uninhibitedly.

21

WINTER

Eve closes the small gap between us, pressing her lips to mine. Before, the kisses felt fevered – rushed – but this one is slow and intentional. I follow her lead, opening my mouth when her tongue teases my bottom lip. Sitting up, she shifts her body, straddling me. When our hips connect she lets out a soft moan that I swallow. I let my hands roam over her body, caressing her curves and squeezing the soft, supple parts of her. Slipping my hand under her shirt, I play with her nipples like I'd been wanting to do since I saw they're pierced. She bites my lip, grinding against me as she hums with pleasure.

"I've missed that fucking sound..." I mutter in her ear.

She rubs her soft center against my hard length. I play with her nipples with one hand while I slip my other hand into the waist of her sweatpants. She gasps when my fingers glide along her warm wetness. I tease her clit with my fingertips, wondering if she still tastes the same.

A knock at the door interrupts our moment. Eve groans, collapsing onto my chest.

"The food would come now," she mutters.

I chuckle at her disappointment. "We have all night." As badly as I want her, I don't want to rush into anything when she's fresh off a breakup and we haven't had a chance to really talk.

"You're right. I'll get the food." She sits up, and I pull my hand out of her pants, tasting her on me. Her eyes widen.

"I don't know why you look shocked, Dove. Hopefully I'll get a better taste later."

I watch her stumble to her feet, causing me to chuckle as she heads for the door. A few seconds later she reappears, wheeling a cart with the food sitting on it.

"They sent a bottle of wine for our troubles." She holds it up, wiggling her brows.

"It'd be impossible not to enjoy this place with the endless flow of alcohol."

Eve giggles, taking the top off the food.

"I'm gonna wash my hands real quick. You can start eating without me."

"As if I was going to wait on you." She shoves a chip smothered in black beans and avocado into her mouth.

"I knew I should've ordered my own food with your bottomless pit you call a stomach."

She gapes at me as I laugh my way to the bathroom. When I reenter the living room, she's eating while searching for something to watch.

"Any suggestions?"

I sit beside her. "Nah. I'm fine with your company."

She turns it off, taking a bite of her chicken tender. "Good. I hate searching for something to watch."

"Why were you looking then?" I shove a nacho into my mouth.

"Habit." She shrugs. "Noah and I usually watch something while we eat."

"Ah." I nod my head. "How long were you two a thing?"

"Officially?" She licks some ranch off her thumb. "A few months. Randomly hooking up? Eight... almost nine years."

That means he was there for her when I wasn't. Knowing I did it to myself doesn't mean I don't feel an inkling of jealousy at the thought of him swooping in to save the day. Even if that is his annoying nature.

"That long? That's longer than we were together."

"Yeah..." she says softly. "I guess it is."

Eve and I officially got together after our first date a week after we met. She moved in with me a couple of months later. Our parents questioned if we were moving too fast. It didn't feel that way for us. Everything felt right with her. I proposed to Eve on our third anniversary. We set our wedding date to be on our four year anniversary. Dad died six months before we were set to walk down the aisle. I disappeared a couple of months later.

"What about you?" She interrupts my thoughts. "Any girlfriends?"

"Not officially. I had a thing with Brielle for a while. She was the closest I ever got to another relationship after you."

"Ezra's Brielle?" Her eyes widen.

"Yep. Her."

She gawks at me. "I can see it, but it's also clear Ezra is her other half."

"Yeah." I take a sip of my water. "We were never meant to be, although I enjoyed the time we had."

"So you're still not dating Aundi?" She tries to sound nonchalant.

"Just friends... with occasional benefits." Aundi and I used to hook up almost daily. Now that we've become genuine friends, it's more about enjoying each other's company. I don't mind the shift. "Were you hooking up with anyone else before you settled on Noah?"

"Settled?" She snorts with laughter.

"What else would you call it?" I dip a piece of chicken into the ranch.

"Safe." Her eyes meet mine.

"That's a good word for Noah. Do you want to be safe though?"

"Well... I don't want to get my heart broken if that's what you're implying."

"That tells me what I need to know."

She raises her brows, letting the straw she was sipping on fall from her lips. "Oh, yeah? And what's that?"

"You never gave him your heart to break."

Looking into the glass, Eve traces her finger around the rim. "Clearly I had every reason not to."

"I think you create reasons that you're willing to stand beside until you see them manifested."

She cuts her eyes to mine. "I don't understand. Do you want me to be with Noah?"

"I want you to be happy." I place my hand over my heart. "And I mean that with everything that I am."

"For fuck's sake..." She tuts, looking away from me, fanning her eyes. "Is every word from your mouth perfect today?"

"I have my moments." Picking up the bottle of wine, I grab the corkscrew. "Shall we have a glass of wine with our luxurious meal of nachos and expertly fried chicken tenders?"

She rewards me with a dimpled smile, picking up a wine glass.

Later that night, Eve is sitting between my legs, leaning back against my chest, while we watch the final remnants of the thunderstorm from the balcony. Light rain is still falling minus the rolling thunder and flashing lightning. A large down comforter we pulled off the bed is wrapped around my shoulders, enveloping us both. We've been seamlessly slipping between comfortable silence and easy conversation.

"Are you happy you came?"

"Aside from running away from your truth bomb, my clothes being ruined, being broken up with, destroying my phone, and crying uncontrollably, yeah," she says on a long sigh. "I've enjoyed myself."

"Twisted Vines really fucked you up, huh?"

"Dragged my ass and left me for dead."

I try to tamp down my laughter and fail miserably. "Your edges still intact?" I make a show of turning her head side to side.

"Get your paws off me!" She swats them away.

"Ow!" I shake my hand. "Those nails are weapons."

She hisses like a cat holding them up. "Don't fuck with me."

I wrap my hand around her dainty wrist, examining what are supposedly nails. "Seriously, these should be illegal." They're decorated with intricate designs and gems that I'm surprised fit on such a small space. "What are these? The talon special?"

Eve slides further down my chest, cackling. She wrenches her wrist from my hold. "They're the fuck you up special if you don't stop talking shit!"

"I don't doubt you." She makes herself comfortable again against me. Warmth spreads through my chest with her body pressed against mine. "Did you want to go inside?"

She's silent for a few seconds, seemingly weighing her options.

"Yeah," she says, yawning. "I guess."

I pull the blanket off my shoulders and wrap it around her as if she's a burrito. Standing, I throw her over my shoulder, causing her to squeal.

"Shhh..." I palm her ass, holding her in place. "You'll wake our neighbors."

Stepping into the suite, I slide the glass door shut behind us and make my way to the bed. Once I'm close enough I toss her on it like she's sack of potatoes. "Dropped you like today dropped your ass."

Eve is laughing so hard it's silent except for a squeak every couple of seconds. I pull off my shirt while she collects herself. When my eyes land on her again she's smiling at me. I know today was hard on her. I didn't want to tell her she wasn't there for me when I needed her most. If I kept it, the only feelings I'd be protecting would've been hers. I didn't expect Noble Noah to break up with her over the phone hours later to pour additional salt in the wound I reopened.

But in this moment where she's lying on the bed with a brilliant smile on her face, looking at me, I know she's happy. I grab a pillow from the bed. Despite our tryst earlier, I don't want her to feel pressured into doing anything with me.

"Where are you going?"

"The couch." I grab another blanket from the bed.

Her brows dip with confusion. "Why? We can sleep together." She covers mouth. "I mean share the bed."

"Technically we'll be doing both if I sleep here." I tilt my head to the side. "Are you sure you want that?"

"Yes. Yeah. I do."

We stare at each other while I weigh the options. It'd be less complicated if I slept on the couch. But I don't think she wants to be alone tonight.

"Alright." I toss the blanket and pillow back onto the bed, sitting beside her. "I... um... I think we'd both be better off if we didn't have sex tonight. I want you – so don't get stuck in your head – but not like this. You're hurting and processing. Normally I'd say dick is the answer–" she snorts with laughter " –but for now I'll be whatever else you need me to be."

She sits up, pressing the softest most tempting kiss to my lips. "Thank you for holding space for me... even when I don't deserve it." Shifting her body, she moves so she's in front of me. "Winter, I'm sorry I wasn't there for you when you needed me."

Eve's eyes don't waver from mine. I'm not sure how long we stay like this as our souls recognize it's in the presence of its other half.

"I wasn't angry with you initially. It was a crushing sadness. Eventually that sadness shifted to bitterness and then to anger. I was lost, Eve. There were no lights on for a very long time."

Reaching out, she caresses my cheek. "What happened to you, Winter? You became a ghost and then you reappeared again out of thin air. Where'd you go?"

"Snow didn't tell you?"

She shakes her head. "No. He'd only tell me that you were okay. Never anything more."

I knew this moment would eventually come. I consider my time after Eve, until I returned home, to be my darkest. "I'll tell you, but let's get comfortable first, because it's a long story."

I get the lights, and she tucks herself in beside me, slinging her leg across my waist and resting her head on my shoulder.

Winter's deep, calming voice fills the room. "When I left that night, I only meant to be gone for a few days. A couple of weeks at the most. After seeing North and Snow, I went for a drive, trying to clear my head. I wanted to call you and tell you... but I didn't know how to express what

I'd already told you countless times. There was water in my lungs, and I could feel myself dying."

Each word feels like an ice cube sliding down my throat, lodging itself in my stomach. The heavy feeling of dread settles into my bones. This moment isn't about me, though. It's about him telling me the answers I've been needing for a decade. I wasn't there for him then, but I can be here for him now. Instead of interrupting with an apology, I let him speak.

"One moment I was contemplating what to do, then I blinked, and I was crossing the state line. That's the first time I remember disassociating."

I don't want to interrupt him, but I have to ask. "What's disassociating?"

"It's when you feel completely detached from everything around you, even your body. You know those dreams where you're watching yourself?"

"Yes."

"That's what it feels like except I couldn't wake up."

The closest state line is three hours away from Hope Valley. My heart drops at the thought of him driving in that state of mind alone. "That's terrifying."

"It can be. It's a mix of terror and relief sometimes. At that point, I didn't have a name for it. It just felt like I lost pieces of time. My mind put me on auto pilot."

"What did you do when you realized you'd driven that far?"

"You called me." My breath gets caught in my throat. "I pulled over, had my thumb hovering over the button to answer, but I couldn't bring myself to talk to you. I didn't want to go to therapy. I didn't want to take the fucking meds. I didn't want to see the look of disappointment in your eyes every time you looked at me. I didn't want to pretend to be okay."

Tears slip from my eyes, rolling over the bridge of my nose, and onto Winter's chest. I can feel the pain and confliction in his voice as if he's back on that road, staring at my name on his screen, knowing I won't understand.

"I... losing Dad was more than I could handle. We were so close." His voice cracks. "And then watching him die, watching everything I knew slip away, altered me in a way I couldn't fathom."

Bringing my hand up, I touch his cheek that's cold and wet. Sitting up, I wipe the tears from his face. I didn't think it was possible for my heart to break anymore but it does. He grabs my wrist, pressing a kiss to my palm, and then gently pulls me back onto his chest.

"Even though I was spiraling, I had no right—"

"You had every right."

"No, I had no right to hurt you, Eve."

"But I hurt you..." I whisper.

He's silent for a few breaths. "Can we agree that *we* were wrong?"

"Yes," I say as he kisses the top of my head. "Where did you end up?"

"Vegas. Sin city. Spent some time there. Got a nasty addiction to cocaine and gambling. I'd travel, but always ended up back there like it was a vortex."

"Did you... were you using before you left?"

"No. I was drinking more, though."

Part of being oblivious, as Noah so poignantly put it, was that I convinced myself part of Winter's problem was that he was drinking more. Again, I was focused on the wrong thing.

"If it weren't for Snow, I wouldn't be here. I'd been using cocaine long enough, I never thought I'd overdose until I woke up in the hospital with

Snow sitting beside me. I thought I died. I should've died." Those words make my stomach roll. "Shit, I wanted to."

"Don't say that," I whisper.

"I didn't care what happened to me then. I haven't felt that low since."

"How did you..." My voice trails off trying to find the right words.

"Get clean?" He fills in for me. "Snow gave me an ultimatum. I could continue on the path I was on, but he'd sell everything. North Star Toys, our childhood home, my shares of the company–everything. He was done and didn't see the point in trying to keep our legacy alive. North had Snow's back and was ready to sell everything too. Or I could return home with him and get the help I needed. He and North would run the company until I was ready to step in.

"Since I'd been sober for at least a couple of days, my mind was clear. I kept seeing Dad and remembering how proud of me he was. That made me choose home. I was left with a lot of responsibility when he died, but I had no intention of squandering it."

"That's why it felt like you just reappeared one day?"

"Yeah. How did you... know I was back?"

"I saw you running with Snow one day at Opal Park. It felt like I'd seen a ghost. I didn't recognize you at first but I'd never forget you. I left when I realized you weren't a figment of my imagination."

"Sounds like me every time I saw you."

I can't help but laugh. "We were both avoiding each other."

"Neither of us knew what to do."

"How long have you been clean?"

"Five years. I relapsed twice in the beginning. Finally got it together and have kept it together... for the most part. I still enjoy a joint or an edible, but when have I not?"

My shoulders shake with laughter. "Good question."

"I've learned other ways to sort through the mess in my head. Swimming, hanging out with people who make me feel good, volunteering, therapy... all of those things that seem small have the biggest impact."

"I'm grateful you're here, Winter." I wrap myself around him a little tighter.

I never knew what a best friend was until I met him. It's beyond someone being there for you the most. A best friend is a soulmate. Someone you don't ever have to wear a mask for, and regardless of how much time has passed, it feels like no time has passed at all.

"I can honestly say now, me too." I hear the smile in his voice.

"This whole time I thought you ran off to start a new life. I remember wondering where you went and who you were with... and if you were happier without me. I'd rather you have been happier without me then having to endure what you did."

"If I'm being honest, I've only truly been happy within the past few months, getting to know myself."

A smile spreads across my face. The heartache is eased by a bit of peace. "I know I've been a raging bitch—"

"No comment," he mumbles.

I jab his side. "–but underneath all of that, I hoped you got everything you wanted because you deserve it."

He's silent for a few breaths. "I knew you liked me."

I suck my teeth, attempting to roll away from him, but he keeps me glued to his side. "Aht, aht. I finally have you where I need you, and you got me fucked up if you think I'm going to let you slither away."

"Slither?!" I bury my face in his chest, laughing. "I fear to know how you see me through your eyes."

"You're my heaven and hell because without that duality I wouldn't have you, and I want nothing less than all of you."

I slide my body on top of his, melting onto his chest. He grabs the blanket, pulling it over us, and wraps me up in his arms. I kiss his neck, settling into him, feeling grounded by his embrace.

22
EVE

I FELL ASLEEP ON Winter's chest. When I open my eyes, he's already awake, scrolling through his phone.

"How long have you been up?" I mumble, closing my eyes again.

"A few hours."

"What?!" I pop my head up, trying to move, but his arm is wrapped around my waist with his hand palming my ass. "Don't you have to pee? You could've woken me up."

"I'm comfortable." He keeps scrolling through his phone.

I rest my head on his chest again, listening to his heartbeat. "When did you become a morning person?"

"Since rehab. The early hours are the quietest. Except," he sets his phone aside, "it's not morning anymore."

"What time is it?"

"Noon." Again, I try to move but it's like trying to push against a brick wall. "It's okay to rest, Eve. You can't save the world today anyway." He puts his hand on my head, gently guiding me back to his chest.

I relax into him as he massages my neck. Freeing my curls, he sinks his other hand into my hair, massaging my scalp. *Heaven* is the only word that comes to mind. Winter knows me well. He may not know my new habits, but he knows the ones that make me who I am. Every day I hit the ground running and don't rest until I fall into bed at night. Leisure isn't really in my vocabulary unless I carve out time for it. Which I rarely do. That doesn't mean I don't take care of myself because in between all that I like to be pampered. But sitting down and resting? Being still? Not something I'm accustomed to. For now, I allow myself to be a lady of leisure.

"Do you want brunch?" His voice vibrates against my ear pressed against his chest.

"That sounds good." My stomach growls in agreement. "No wine though."

"Yeah. Don't need you leaving here an alcoholic." He picks up his phone, scrolling for a bit before rattling off brunch options. We order baked ham and cheese rolls with a honey mustard glaze and orange juice.

"It's been awhile since I've had breakfast in bed."

"What?" He sets his phone aside. "Even with Noble Noah at your beck and call?"

"No. He didn't worship the ground I walked on."

He sucks his teeth. "You know good and well that's bullshit."

"He didn't." I shrug. "Noah is nice, sweet, charming–all of that–but romantic wise..." My voice trails off.

Noah is everything good, except he does lack in the romance department. He often assumes I want grand gestures when really it's the little things. A cup of coffee, cuddling, talking about anything and everything, holding my hand while driving, kissing me on my third eye, breakfast in bed... it's the little mundane things that I crave.

"Noble Noah isn't a romantic?"

"Not really... he's very literal."

"Eve, he's a surgeon."

"Okay, and?" I pick my head up, looking at him.

"He's meticulous. I'm sure he likes things a certain way, rarely deviates from a plan, and knows exactly where he'll be in five years. Of course he's sweet. He's a fucking nerd."

My mouth drops open.

"C'mon, Sweetheart." He nudges my chin with his finger, closing my mouth. "That's not shocking. As I was saying, I'm sure his experience with women is limited to you and few others he's picked out who remind him of you."

"Winter. That's creepy as hell. Don't say that."

"Have you seen his other girlfriends or partners?"

I have and now that Winter mentions it, they sort of have resembled me.

"They're a wannabe version of you, huh?" The corner of his mouth tips up.

"What does that have to do with anything?"

"Meaning you are his first and last. You're his prototype."

"You're making him sound weird, and he isn't." At least he didn't seem like it until he pointed this out.

"All I'm saying, Dove, is sweet doesn't necessarily translate to romantic." He traces his finger along my cheek bone. "Can he even make you come?"

There's a flame flickering in his eyes.

Not like Winter can. I know that for a fact. It's one that's impossible to forget. "What does that have to do with being romantic?"

"There needs to be passion, longing... an intense craving that can be temporarily placated but never truly satiated." He gently grabs my chin. "That's the root of romance. I know I could have you every moment for the rest of my days and it'd never be enough."

I kiss him. Hard and fevered. As If I can drink those words and let them seep into my bones. Winter grabs the back of my neck, holding me in place. My tongue meets his, lighting me up like a live wire. He switches our position by flipping me onto my back. I wrap my legs around his waist and slip my hand into his sweats. My fingertips wrap around his length and a guttural groan spills from him into my mouth. I stroke him. He breaks the kiss to rest his forehead against mine and watch me. After a few strokes, he catches my wrist.

I scowl at him, and he chuckles. "How often do you receive without expecting to give?"

Sitting up on my elbows, I nibble my bottom lip as I contemplate his question. "Not often."

He presses kisses along my jaw, down my neck, and lifts my shirt to tease my nipples, tugging on the rings.

"Then sit back, spread them legs, and let me take care of you," he whispers in my ear.

Keeping my eyes on him, I slowly lower myself down to the bed as he kisses his way down my body. When my head hits the pillow, all I can see are his eyes locked on mine from between my thighs.

"Lift your hips." *I listen.*

He grabs the waistband of my sweats, dragging them over my hips, down my thighs, and off my legs. I keep my knees together until he leans to the side, meeting my gaze.

"Be a good girl. Spread 'em for me. Nice and slow." He smooths his hands along the outside of thighs.

I slowly slide my feet across the bed, spreading my legs. Winter inhales sharply, and I fear if he breathes on me, he'll send me into oblivion. It's been so fucking long. Too long.

"Do you want me to take care of you?" He rests his hands on my inner thighs, massaging close to my center, tantalizing but not giving.

I shake my head yes, laying back against the pillow.

"That's not an answer, Eve. Use that pretty mouth."

"Yes—on me—your mouth..." This man has me all flustered. I don't even know how to speak. Sitting up on my elbows, I lock eyes with him. "Eat my fucking pussy, Winter."

"There's my girl."

Slipping his hands under my ass, he pulls me toward him. He flattens his tongue against my center, slowly, torturously, dragging it along my wetness.

"Fuck..." I breathe out. My body twitches as I grip the sheets.

He does it again, this time going lower, lapping at a part of me only he's ever touched. Gripping my thighs, he pushes them further apart, shoving his whole face in my center. I grab the back of his head, holding him in place as if I can push him deeper as he dips his tongue into my wetness.

Winter always eats, leaving no crumbs.

"Shit," I pant. "Right. Fucking. There."

There's a knock on the door that we both ignore. I'd become violent if he stopped right now. I'm past the point of caring or even thinking as he draws circles with his tongue around and over my pearl. My toes curl, and involuntary cries of pleasure spill from my lips. Winter grunts and groans like I'm the fountain of youth and I'm giving him life. He slips one finger... two fingers... three fingers into my wetness. I tighten around him, gripping them as he pleasures me.

All the passion, longing, and craving he talked about is hidden in his tongue. I'm sure of it. As sure as I am about this release that's going to pull me under. With the flicks of his tongue and the depth of his fingers–I shatter for him. Arching my back, I grab around the bed for anything, something, to hold onto. My fingers find the pillows and my nails scratch against them as I grip them, crying out with pleasure. Winter sits up, making a slurping sound as he does. He keeps his fingers buried in me and rubs his other fingertips back and forth over my clit until he opens the floodgates. Leaning forward, he sticks his tongue out lapping up my release like I'm a water fountain. The satisfied smile on his face, the way I can't stop coming, and the decibel of my moans create the sweetest symphony.

When he finally, slowly pulls his fingers out of me, my voice is hoarse, and my body is humming with pleasure. I melt into the bed not daring to move, savoring this moment. Winter brings his hand up, rubbing my release onto my lips. I open my mouth, letting him dip them inside, sucking them. He sucks his bottom lip between his teeth, watching me.

There's another knock on the door. "Are you still hungry?"

I nod my head yes with his fingers still in my mouth.

He pulls them out. "For food, Eve."

"Oh," I let out a satisfied sigh. "Yeah. That too."

He shakes his head with a smile on his face. "I'll get it."

"Good." I turn on my side. "Because I wasn't going to volunteer."

Before I can snuggle up with a pillow, Winter makes me yelp when he smacks my ass. "What the hell?" I whine, rubbing my cheek.

"With a perfectly smackable ass, I'd keep that attitude in check if I were you."

I raise my brow in in his direction, curling my lip.

"Or fuck around and find out."

I grab the blanket, covering myself before I respond. "The food is going to get cold, Win Win."

He narrows his eyes in my direction as I cackle into the blanket.

"What'd I tell your ass about calling me that?"

I try to stop laughing but end up snorting instead. I've seen Winter embarrassed on one occasion, and one occasion only, when his mom called him Win Win in front of me. I personally thought it was cute. It's a childhood nickname given to him by Snow when he was little and wouldn't say his full name. Winter's hated since it was first uttered. Snow and North used it to agitate him when they got older, and his mom used it as a term of endearment.

He takes a step closer to the bed, I yelp, hiding my head under the blanket. "Keep talking shit, Eve."

I hear him pad to the door. Giving him zero opportunity to smack my bare ass again, I quickly pull on my sweats before he returns. When he returns, he tracks my hands as I tie the strings.

"Wise choice." He takes the top off the food, revealing the ham and cheese rolls, glistening with the honey mustard glaze.

"Ohhh..." I groan. "Those look so good."

He sits beside me on the bed, picking one up, and holds it up to my lips. When I open my mouth to take a bite, he snatches it away, taking the first bite instead.

I smack his arm. "Win Win! Give me a bite!"

"You're definitely not getting a bite now." He shoves the whole thing in his mouth and pulls the plate out of my reach.

He presses his palm against my forehead when I reach for it. I collapse against his chest instead, laughing. My soul has missed this level of comfort and vulnerability.

"Are you going to behave yourself?" He holds the plate away from me.

I sit up, clasping my hands, and place them in my lap. "Yes. I will." My stomach growls. "Please feed me."

"Manners, Dove?" The corners of his lips turn up. He holds one of the rolls up to my lips again, giving me a bite this time. I try to take it from his hand, but he pulls it away. "Let me feed you."

"Just shove the whole thing in my mouth," I say around the bite.

"The whole thing?" He raises his brow.

"The whole roll."

Winter licks his lips, biting them to keep his amusement from showing.

"You haven't grown up yet?" I give him a bemused expression.

"I'll never grow up."

"Clearly." Leaning against the headboard, he sets the plate in front of us. I don't even bother trying to reach for one. Winter holds another roll up to my mouth. "Why do you insist on feeding me?"

"Who else do you share food with?"

"No one." I chew my bite slowly. "Just you."

"That's why."

Struggling to keep the smile off my face, I say nothing in response as he feeds me another bite.

Later in the afternoon, Winter pulls up in front of my place. Leaving Twisted Vines was bittersweet. Everything fell apart and into place all at once. Winter and I never discussed what we could be. We were in the moment of us. That's all I needed.

Winter gets out of the car, appearing on my side, and opens the door. I take his hand and get out. I grab my shoes from the floorboards. Holding them up, I look at the white leather covered in mud with regret. Winter bought me a cheap pair of flip flops from the gift shop. We look like spokespeople for Twisted Vines. The only thing that comes to mind at the moment is a hot bath and sleep. I'm grateful it's the weekend and I don't have to worry about interacting with others.

I climb the steps and unlock my front door. Looking at Winter, he smiles.

"I'll let you get some rest. Did you want me to take you to get your new phone?"

I smack my palm to my forehead. "That's right." The peace and quiet of being disconnected has been nice. "Um... I can go by myself. I'm sure you have other things you'd rather do today then chauffeur me around."

"I'd actually enjoy that." He leans against the wrought iron railing.

I blow out a puff of air, looking away from him, wondering if I'm falling back into him too easily? How can you fall back in if you weren't ever out?

"Can you give me a few hours? Pick me up around..." I click my tongue. "Six-ish?"

"Six-ish it is."

Pushing away from the railing, he closes the distance between us. I tip my head back to meet his gaze. He gently wraps his fingers around the hollow of my throat. Winter applies just enough pressure to pull me toward him so we're only a breath apart. He slides his hand up my neck, cupping my chin, and brings his lips to mine. My eyes flutter shut. If he asked me for my last breath, it'd be his. I drop my bag on the step, wrapping my arms around his neck, needing to be flush against his body.

He pulls away, resting his forehead against mine. "Unless you want company, I suggest you go inside and get ready so I can see you again in a few hours."

"You're not bad company."

"Imagine that. Eve Valentine doesn't hate me after all."

"Shut up." I push at his chest, and he catches my wrist, pulling me back to him.

He kisses my lips and then presses a kiss to my third eye. "See you later, Dove."

Before I can protest, Winter slides down the railing like a child, grinning when he gets to bottom, and jogs to his car. I watch him pull away from the curb, waving with a dopey smile on my face before heading inside. Closing the door behind me, I lean against it. I really hope this doesn't wreck me.

After a scalding shower, a much needed nap, and some food–I'm getting ready for Winter to pick me up. Looking in the mirror, I blow dry my still damp twists, hoping my hair cooperates. I prefer to wear it down because ponytails and buns give me headaches after a few hours. I really need to get braids so I don't have to fuss with it for a while. Thinking I'll text Elle and ask her if she'll have time this weekend, I search around for my phone, only to remember it's not working. I squeeze my twists to see if they're dry and of course one of them is being stubborn. Letting out a sigh, I continue blow drying.

Once my hair is dry, it doesn't take me long to get ready. I do my brows, apply some mascara, and put on some sheer butter gloss. I'm in the middle of taking my hair down when I hear a knock on my door. My heart races at the thought of inviting Winter into my space. I give my arms a rest and head to answer the door. Glancing at the clock, I'm surprised Winter is half an hour early. I swing the door open.

"Win–" My voice falters when my eyes collide with Noah's.

"You're back." I'm confused by the happy expression on his face. "I've been trying to call you since we talked yesterday." He steps around me as if this is our shared space. Wrapping his arm around my waist, he tries to give me a kiss that I dodge.

"Yeah." I push against his chest and out of his hold. "My phone fell in the bathtub."

"Seriously?" He gives me a disbelieving look. "Or did you just block me?"

I suck my teeth, instantly annoyed. "Yes. Seriously." Knowing I don't need to prove anything to him, but also wanting to put him in his place, I grab my phone off the coffee table and hand it to him.

He tries to turn it on and of course nothing happens. "You should've put it in rice."

"It was under water too long." *Because I was having an emotional breakdown.*

"How did it fall in the bathtub?"

I press my fingertips to my temple, massaging it. "Are you here to pick up your stuff? Because I'm—"

It's his turn to look confused. "Pick up my stuff?"

"Yeah." I wrinkle my nose, trying not to roll my eyes at the question that is so stupid it doesn't deserve an answer.

"Are you breaking up with me?"

"Noah..." I gape at him, resting my hand on my hip. "Be serious right now."

"I am and you keep looking at me like I've grown two heads."

"You," I point at him. "Broke up with me!" I point at my chest. "You said you didn't know if you could do this!"

He steps closer, grabbing my hands. "I'm sorry for the things I said. I definitely didn't break up with you."

"Noah..." I pull my hands from his.

"I'm sorry, Eve. I was just – you and him, the history, it's a lot. He's everything I'm not."

"You're right. He's everything you're not."

Noah flinches.

"Did you ever stop to think that maybe that's what I loved about you? That you aren't anything like him."

The tightness in his body dissipates, he looks at the floor, rubbing the back of his neck. "No. I didn't," he mutters.

"Noah..." I wring my hands together, pacing the floor.

My throat feels dry, knowing I can't be with him anymore. I thought we could work. And we did. But that's all we did was–*work*. I'm sad for our relationship to be over. He's been a part of my life for so long that I never stopped to imagine what it would be like without him. It's not fair to treat him like a security blanket that I can fall back on when other things fall apart. Noah deserves someone who is going to love him without reservations. I placed unrealistic expectations on him from the start, hoping to a fill a void that he didn't create nor could he ever fill.

"Are you okay?" He surveys me with concerned filled eyes.

"We need to talk," I blurt out before I lose my nerve.

He lets out a defeated sigh as if he can feel the inevitable coming. "This can't be good."

Nibbling my lip, I force a smile. "It's not necessarily bad either... depending on – well, let's just sit." I motion toward the couch, sitting first.

He gingerly sits beside me as if the cushions are prickly. "Let me first say, I apologize for the things I said yesterday. I didn't mean them."

I look down at my hands in my lap. "You meant them. You just feel bad for saying them."

"I really do love you..." he says softly.

"I know you do. And I love you too, but—"

"Ah." He nods. "The infamous 'but'."

"It's not in the way you deserve, Noah." Leaning forward, Noah rests his elbows on his thighs. Unsure of what to do, I awkwardly pat his back as if I've never touched him in my life. "If we stayed together, we'd both be settling."

He scrubs his hands down his face, letting out a deep sigh. "After all these years, I thought I finally had you."

I've lost count of how many times Noah has asked me to be his girlfriend. He asked me shortly after we met when we were kids and then countless times in between. When Winter and I split and he came back in my life, all I could offer him was sex and company. I should've known that wouldn't be enough for Noah. Then Winter and I were suddenly in each other's lives again. When Noah asked me for the infinite time to be his girlfriend, I said yes without hesitation. I thought maybe my avoidance of relationships all these years was my problem. Not that I was still deeply, madly, and unequivocally in love with Winter. Despite knowing that fact after seeing him at Fireside, I still gave Noah what he's always wanted– me.

Noah trusted me with his heart, and I've been as reckless with it as Winter was with mine. I tried to tell him over the years that I wasn't good for him. Because whether or not I acknowledged it, I knew I wasn't going to love him to the bottomless depth I love Winter. His name is fitting because he froze my heart in time only to thaw it out again to beat for him.

"It's selfish of me to admit, but I thought we could work." Tears sting my eyes. "I really did. You've always been there. You've always been perfect. So please don't think it's anything to do with you. It's all me... as cliché as that sounds."

He smiles, laughing lightly. "I could never see you as cliché, Eve."

I look down at my hands through blurry vision. "You'll find some woman who lights you up and makes you feel whole."

"I—" he begins but is interrupted by a knock on the door.

I inwardly groan. There's no doubt that's Winter. I was hoping to avoid adding insult to injury for Noah.

"Were you expecting someone?"

"Mmhmm..." I hum a little too high pitched, nodding my head. There's no way they can avoid seeing each other. Although, I doubt Winter will care.

"I can get it." He tries to get to his feet.

"No, no. Sit." I wrap my hands around his wrist, pulling him back down. "I can get it. Um... just a sec."

He looks at me with confusion. I give him a fake as fuck smile, getting up to answer the door. Walking toward it, I try to envision how this will go down. I thought Noah and I were broken up. Seeing him today was not in the plans. Reaching the door, I open it and am met by a forever delicious looking Winter and the scent of him wraps around me.

"Hey..." His voice trails off as his eyes roam over me. "Are you ready or...?"

"I—um—Noah stopped by and—"

"You invited him over before talking to me?" Noah asks from behind me.

I squeeze my eyes shut, cringing. When I open them again, Winter is trying, and failing miserably, to keep a satisfied smile off his face.

"A pleasure to see you too, Noah. I came to pick up your—oh, wait—that's right. You broke up with her."

My eyes grow as large as the moon. I can't do anything but stare at Winter and hope to God Noah doesn't—

"So we get into one fight and you sleep with him?" Noah scoffs.

I suck in deep breath, glaring at Winter before I turn to face Noah. "No. I didn't sleep—"

"Did you tell him about breakfast?" Winter asks and I whip around, glaring at him. "All organic, homegrown, with the most refreshing drinks. Like a natural spring. I can still taste it on the tip of my tongue."

Winter is so nasty. And I'm no better.

"What does he mean by that, Eve?" Noah asks behind me, clearly understanding the jist of the innuendo.

"Nothing," I say in a sing song tone. "Nothing at all."

"Did you sleep with him?" Noah demands.

"How does this matter now?"

"Because you were just pretending to care about my feelings." Noah looks as if I flipped a switch in him. His eyes that were full of understanding moments ago are now filled with betrayal and hurt.

"I do." I turn away from Winter. "If I didn't, I wouldn't have bothered talking to—"

"Obviously you weren't going to bother with anything since he's here."

Exasperated, I throw my arms up into the air, letting them slap against my thighs. "What do you want, Noah? For me to chase after you? For me to grovel at your fucking feet for a fight you caused? You told me you didn't know if you could do this." I motion between us. "And expected me to not feel some type of way about that. Shit, maybe my heart wasn't fully in this, but at least I never jumped ship."

"No. You didn't because you were never on the same ship as me in the first place."

His words sting like he meant for them too.

"You know what?" Noah scoffs. "You two deserve each other."

"You've known that, too." Winter's voice pierces through the silence. "Yet, here you are, getting your heart broken unnecessarily."

"Shut the fuck up, Winter," Noah snaps.

My eyes bounce between the two of them, waiting for the eruption to happen.

Winter chuckles low and smooth. "My apologies. I'll let you have your moment since that's all you've ever had."

Noah's eyes are cold, his nostrils are flared with his hands fisted at his sides. I can see the pulse in his neck from where I stand only feet away. There's a silence for only a moment before his eyes slide to mine.

"You know he was an addict, right?"

He takes a step toward me. I'm not sure if he's trying to be intimidating or threaten me, but I'm annoyed he even thinks he can step to me.

"He's going to fuck you and leave just like last time. It seems that's all your worth, anyway."

Surprisingly, I'm the one who erupts. I cock my hand back so far, Noah's head snaps to the side when it connects with his face. The silence following is deafening. He grabs his jaw, and I'm hoping I dislocated it. My hand is already throbbing.

Leaning to the side, I match his stance so our eyes are level. Faint red lines from my nails appear on his left cheek. When Noah's eyes lock onto mine, his are full of anger while mine are full of venom.

"You know you're a bitch, right?" I ask, mirroring his movements as he straightens up, working his jaw. "And to think I actually felt sorry for you. Don't you ever fix your mouth to say those words about me or him again. Do you understand?"

Noah glares at me as if he could ever dare to match my energy. He tries to avert his gaze from mine, rising to his full height. That isn't a problem, I stand on my tiptoes so I'm eye level. "I asked you a fucking question. Do you understand?"

He scoffs, running his tongue across his teeth. "Yes."

"If you go low, I will go lower and bury you. Never doubt that, Noah. I tried to keep this amicable. Keep my name," I point at my chest, "his name," I point at Winter, "and anyone else's name," I wind my hand around like it's a tornado, "that I love out of your fucking mouth."

Noah's look is mutinous. He gives me a tight nod before turning and flinching when he sees Winter blocking the doorway. Noah pauses, clearly wondering if he should dare walk past Winter.

He steps aside, holding his hand up to lead Noah's way out. Noah stays rooted in the spot for a few more seconds before daring to walk past him. Of course, Winter stops him, putting his hand on his chest.

"Let this be a reminder that *my* girl could beat your ass if she wanted to." He lets him past, but stops him again by putting his hand on Noah's shoulder. "If I hear anything, a peep, whisper–*anything*. I will break your fucking hands."

Winter gives him a formidable look before letting him go and slapping him on the back. "See you around, Noah."

I collapse onto the couch once Noah climbs in his car and leaves. Winter comes inside, shutting the door, and sits beside me. I hiss when he picks up my hand, inspecting it.

"Let me go get some ice."

He gets up, heading toward the kitchen. I hear him rustling around before he reappears a few minutes later with a small baggy of ice and a kitchen towel. He wraps the towel around the baggy, picks up my hand again, and places it on my swollen skin.

I wince. "Thanks."

"You know," Winter rests his head against the couch, "I'm proud of Noah for finally finding his balls."

"Do you take anything seriously?"

He scrunches up one side of his face in thought. "A few things. You, my family, and a few friends. But I'll never take Noah seriously. I bet you he'll apologize once he calms down."

"Doubt it. He was *angry*." Seething may be a better word.

"I would be too if I found out you were another man's breakfast. Broken up or not."

I cover my mouth with my free hand, cackling. "I said nothing! You had to start in with a crappy innuendo."

"I personally think I said it beautifully. Noah..." He cringes, tilting his head side to side. "Not so much."

"I'm gonna be honest... I wasn't expecting Noah to have an ounce of asshole in him."

Winter moves the ice pack around my palm. "You're his villain origin story. I bet this kicks off his man whore phase."

"I've corrupted him." I cover my face with my palm.

"He'll be alright. Enough about him, though. How's your hand?"

I flex it slowly and am met with a dull ache. "Sore. But I'll be okay. I shouldn't have hit him."

Winter presses a kiss to my palm. "Thank you for defending my honor."

He kisses his way up my arm like he's Gomez Addams. "That shit was sexy as hell."

He whispers in my ear. "Got my dick hard."

I feel his tongue slide across my neck. "Winter!" I holler, shoving away from him.

He leans back against the couch with a smile on his face. "All I'm saying is, seeing and knowing you have my back after thinking you didn't is... a beautiful feeling."

I lean closer to him and press a soft kiss to his lips. He wraps his hand around the back of my neck and kisses me a few more times before letting me go.

"I'm always happy to show you that I'm in your corner."

I'm ashamed to admit I never considered Winter wants to be treated with the same tenderness he so freely gives me. He wants to be soft with *me*, and that's an honor.

"I know that now. Did you still want to get a phone?"

"Dammit. That's right." I sit up. "Let me grab my shoes and bag."

"Uh... Dove." He grabs my wrist, pulling me back toward the couch. "Come here for a second."

"What?"

He turns me to toward the large gold, ornate mirror that sits in the corner of my living room. Half of my hair is still in twists. I clasp my hands over my head as Winter chuckles. "I forgot I was doing my hair! Give me a few and—"

"Sit." He throws a pillow on the floor between his legs. I stare at him, and he pats the pillow. "C'mon."

I listen, making myself comfortable between his legs. "What are—"

My question ceases when I feel his hands in my hair, gently unraveling the twists. For as big as his hands are, his touch is delicate. I glance at the mirror in the corner, taking in his side profile. Winter concentrates on my hair as if there's no other place he'd rather be. I bring my knees to my chest, hugging them as he works in silence. His eyes catch mine in the reflection. The corners of his lips tip up before he turns his attention back to my hair. I've learned that the most intimate moments rarely involve being naked with another. Not physically anyway.

They're the moments I can uninhibitedly be myself. When my soul sighs with relief knowing it's in the presence of someone who fully accepts me. Flaws and all. I can name all the people I feel that sense of belonging with. Winter is one of them. He feels like home.

My vision becomes blurry, and a tear slips down my cheek. I let my eyes slide shut in hopes that I don't turn into a blubbering mess. Instead, I relish in his touch and attention. I'm not sure how long it takes or if my hair even looks good. For once–*I don't care.*

All that matters is Winter is my soft landing, my safe space. I hope I'm his too. I want to be his.

Fox was right. This is a once in a lifetime kind of energy, except I'm a lucky girl and am experiencing it twice with my soulmate.

Winter sink his hands in my hair, massaging my scalp, and then fluffs it up before saying, "Perfect."

I wipe a few stray tears from my cheeks before turning to face him. "Thank you."

He pulls me toward him, kissing my third eye. "Of course."

We end our evening together at Carnelian Park, walking hand in hand. It's a little alarming, yet comforting, how seamlessly Winter and I go together when we're not working against each other. I forgot how easy we can be. Maybe that was our issue all those years ago. Our relationship had been easy and seamless until it wasn't. When things became rough and unpredictable–so did we.

Winter's steps slow when we reach the large fountain in the center of the park. He pulls me in front of him, wrapping his arms around my shoulders, and rests his chin on my head. I place my hands on his forearms, staring at the dancing water mesmerized. Nothing has felt right in so long that the past two days with Winter have felt like a dream. It's a head rush. I haven't had time to overanalyze and think of the ways this could fall apart. However, there is one thing I know for sure.

"Can I be honest with you about something?" I tip my head back, trying to meet his gaze.

"I always want you to be honest. Even if you don't think I'll like it."

That's exactly what worries me is that he won't like it. I shift my gaze back to the fountain, hoping I find the right words. "I don't know what we are right now. I only know I'm enjoying it." He squeezes me a little tighter. "But... we're not who we were and I want to get to know you–*us*–now. I want to take things slow even if we are soulmates."

I don't want to jump back in without knowing how to love him as he is now. While my love for him is true, we can't pick back up where we left off over a decade ago as if nothing happened. Neither of us are who we were then, now.

Winter doesn't respond. I worry I said the wrong thing. Turning around in his arms, he unravels them and pulls me toward the fountain's ledge, coaxing me to sit on his lap. He wraps his arms around my waist and buries his face in my neck, inhaling deeply. After a moment he sits up, staring at the illuminated water dancing around in the fountain before focusing on me.

"On our way to the gala, Reign asked me what happened to us."

"What did you say?"

He grabs my hand, rubbing his thumb against the back of it. "I've been asked that question a million times. I always gave any answer but the real one. When Reign asked me I was honest. I told him we stopped being friends."

"Relationships are friendships, but everyone treats them like partnerships. I'm not sure when or where we fucked up but we did." Winter cups my chin, rubbing my cheek. His eyes are intense and full of purpose. "I'm willing to do whatever it takes to not only be with you but also be your best friend again."

My heart stutters in my chest, and suddenly I feel crazy for asking to take things slow. I crash my lips onto his and wrap my arms around his neck like I'm never letting go. *Because I'm not.* He responds with the same voracity. Threading his fingers through my hair, pulling me flush against him. A moan slips from my mouth to his.

We get lost in this moment until someone whistles, reminding us we're not alone. Winter gives me a few more chaste kisses before his eyes meet mine.

"Let's take it slow. I want to take you on dates. Spoil you, show you I'm about it, and that you deserve it. I want to learn you."

"I may have spoken too soon." I wrinkle my nose. "Do we really wanna take things slow?"

A chuckle resonates deep in his chest. "Yes." He kisses my neck. "I like to savor things. Especially you."

"How can I argue with that?"

23

EVE

BREEZING INTO FLAPJACK'S BREW, my heels click across the tile flooring as I head toward the outdoor patio. It's a relief to *not* have all eyes
on me walking into any establishment after gracing the front page of
the paper with Winter. Sunday smiles and waves to me from where she's
talking to a table of people. Stepping through the patio doors, Noelle
and Aspen wave me over to a table tucked off to the side.

"Hey." I give them both a hug before taking a seat, slinging my bag
over the back of the chair. When I turn around, Aspen is looking at me
with narrowed eyes. I glance at Elle who is too busy typing out a text to
notice her sister is giving me third degree burns.

"Something on your mind, Aspen?" I pick up the glass of cool water,
taking a sip, holding her gaze.

Aspen tilts her head to the side, scrutinizing me, gliding her tongue
across her teeth as if sizing me up. She leans forward. "Who are you
fuckin' because I *know* it ain't Noah. That glow–" she dramatically waves
her hand in the air over my body "–is demon dick glow."

Elle's eyes snap toward me at the same time I choke on an ice cube.

"Aspen!" I wheeze, coughing erratically.

"Who are you fuckin'?" She enunciates each word, leaning back in her
seat while I fight for my life, waiting for the ice cube to melt.

Elle gasps. "Wait... the date!" She snaps her fingers. "You and Winter—"

I hold up my hand, taking a long sip of water. Setting my glass aside, I catch my breath as the coughing subsides. "It's a long story."

"Then you better talk fast. I only have a half hour lunch," Aspen says.

Before I can dive into what happened, we order our food. We haven't seen each other since my date with Winter over the weekend. We were supposed to meet Monday evening for dinner, but Aspen picked up an extra shift, Elle ended up having a night in with Snow, and Winter took me out on our first date... again. That's how I know they're my soulmates. We can go days without talking and still remain close.

I tell them about the date to Twisted Vines being both amazing and disastrous. From Winter and I talking about what happened to us, the thunderstorm, to Noah finally reaching his breaking point, breakfast the following morning, the mistaken break up and the real break up, and finally–Winter and I deciding to take things slow. Noelle and Aspen both stare at me with rapt attention, startling when the waitress sets our food in front of us.

"What's today? Friday? We've been on two dates already this week and," I unwrap my silverware, freeing the fork from my napkin, "I'm happy."

It takes them both a moment to realize I've got nothing more to say as I dig into my Caesar salad.

Elle finally blinks. "We don't see you for a week and you have a whole new life? Winter didn't utter a single word about this either."

I snicker, taking another bite of salad. "It's not like we're announcing an engagement or something. We're not even officially together."

Aspen sucks her teeth. "Yeah you are. You're just not labeling it yet."

Instead of responding, I take another bite. All I want is Winter. We don't need a label to confirm that fact. What matters is that we're going at our own pace, enjoying discovering each other again.

"Noah finally had enough of your shit." Elle takes a bite of her sandwich. "Good for him."

We all stare at each other, falling into a fit of laughter. "Can't even be mad at him," Aspen says.

"I was mad at what he said. Not him." I take a sip of water. "Is it weird I'm proud he has an ounce of asshole in him?"

"No." Elle shakes her head, swallowing her bite of food. "It may sound heartless, but he needed that experience."

"Not heartless," Aspen says. "I think he mistook his obsession with you for love. Not to say he didn't care about you. Noah was so enamored with you, he ignored all the neon, flashing signs that led you back to Winter's arms... and dick."

I gasp, letting out an ugly cackle.

"I mean c'mon, Elle is marrying his brother for fuck's sake. It's kismet."

Winter also believes Elle and Snow meeting was kismet. I didn't think that'd apply to us too.

"Never thought we'd be dating brothers," Elle says, flashing a smile in my direction.

"Or that you'd kiss both of them." Aspen pats Elle's arm.

Elle chokes on her bite of sandwich.

I scrunch my face up with confusion. "I'm sorry... *what*?"

"What?" Aspen says looking between Elle and me, cringing, becoming more interested in her soup.

"Did you say kiss?" When and how did she ever kiss Winter?

"Um... it's a really funny story." Elle scratches her neck.

"Hilarious," Aspen adds, forcing a laugh.

"Humor me." I lean forward, resting my forearms on the table.

Elle clears her throat, sitting up straighter, and tucks her braids behind her ears. "It was so long ago I hardly remember." She bats her hand in my direction, waving it off. Checking her phone, she says, "Would you look at the time. I have—"

"Noelle, did you kiss Winter or not?"

She looks at me, holding my gaze before dropping her shoulders, cringing as she closes her eyes. "Eve, it was after the breakup. It was one kiss. I didn't have a clue who he was, just that he was good looking—"

"You can say that again," Aspen fills in.

"You're not helping!" Elle glares at her. "It was at the bar that one night. He kissed me to make Malcolm jealous. That's it."

"Winter was the guy you kissed who vanished at the bar that night?"

No wonder we didn't cross each other's paths all these years. We went into stealth mode every time we did. I saw Winter a handful of times, and I always thought I would know exactly what I'd say. Each time, I'd think about it, watch him from a distance like a stalker, and then lose my nerve. Until Noelle introduced Snow as her new boyfriend. Then I was angry because I couldn't avoid him anymore.

"Yes," Elle answers.

I pick up my fork, taking the last bite of salad, and lean back in my chair. Swallowing, I look at her.

"Are you mad?" She asks wearily.

"No. I fucking hate Malcolm. Winter obviously made him regret losing you with the way he chased you through the bar after."

Aspen snorts with laughter. "I forgot we had to whisk her away from his desperation."

"He was screaming my name." Elle palms her forehead. "May sound strange, but I'm so damn grateful he cheated on me. Now I have Snow and you have Winter again."

"Funny how life works out." Aspen raises her glass in the air.

"Well, I'll be damned." Elle and I toast our glasses to hers. "I do have something to thank Malcolm for after all."

I spent the afternoon looking at a few houses with Jude and Fox. Jude is hoping to move out of our parent's house as soon as possible. Especially since he'd like to have a dating life. He really liked one of them and is going to put in an offer. Mom texted me on the way home to ask if I wanted to meet her at the mall to go shopping. She and Dad are going to visit her parents in Arizona in a few weeks and wants some new outfits. Retail therapy is always a good idea to me. Plus, now that Jude and Fox are home, me and Mom don't get as much alone time as we used to.

"Does this mean you two are dating?" Mom asks, after telling her Winter and I are talking again.

She pulls a blouse off the rack, trying to sound casual even though she now has a bright smile on her face. Saying Mom adores Winter is an understatement.

"Yes." I grab the blouse from her hand, putting it back on the rack. "Mom, that's ugly."

Her shoulders shake with laughter. "I only wanted a closer look."

I scrunch up my face side eyeing her. "Looking at it on the rack is close enough."

She continues to peruse, picking better options. "I'm happy to hear you and Winter have reconnected again, honey." She gently squeezes my arm. "How are you feeling about it all?"

"It feels... easy. Almost too easy. Like maybe I'll get comfortable and then the floor will disappear from under me."

"Hmm..." She loops her arm through mine, patting my arm, exiting the store and heading toward another one. "I understand why you feel that way, but are you responding as who you are now? Or who you were back then?"

As I contemplate her question, she steers me into a different clothing store. "Both."

She's silent for a beat. "You can't guard your heart and expect love to find a way in, Eve."

Mom always tells me what I *need* to hear, not what I *want* to hear. Winter and I agreed that we both messed up. I'm torn between feeling like I don't deserve him and cautiously loving him because what if he leaves again?

She stops walking, turning to face me. "I'm sorry if my words upset you. I—"

"No, Mom. They didn't. You're right. I needed to hear that."

"Dad said he told you about the time he left me." She sits on a bench in the shoe section of the store.

"He did." I sit beside her. "Which I couldn't believe."

She chuckles, patting my leg and grabs my hand, holding it. "In a way, it was for the best."

I lean back a little, giving her a side long glance, scrunching up my face. "How was having your heart broken good?"

"Because," her brown eyes meet my own, "we grew up. Came back to each other as adults, not children under the influence of others. We knew what we wanted without a doubt. Our love never faded, only intensified. It was stronger... unshakeable."

"Intensified is a good word for it." Winter and I have been full tilt since the date at Twisted Vines. I knew it was going to change everything between us. "How did you forgive Dad?"

She lets out a long, low sigh with a wistful smile on her face. "He kept showing up for me and didn't stop. I gave that man absolute hell for months–" I lean into her, laughing. "–and regardless, he kept showing up, letting me know he was there no matter what."

"That sounds like Winter..." I look off to the side, thinking about how I blamed him for years, not willing to look at myself.

Mom gently grabs my chin, bringing my gaze to hers. "Eve, you've got to let go of the past and show up for him. Just like he's showing up for you. Don't let what happened ruin what has yet to be."

Leaning forward, I kiss her cheek. "Thank you, Mom."

She wraps me in a hug.

Instead of going out tonight, Winter and I decided to have a night in at my place. We took edibles, ate a plate of wings and fries, and now we're on the couch, with my head resting in his lap, binge watching X-Files. I look up at him, remembering the conversation I had with Elle and Aspen. He feels me staring at him, meeting my gaze.

"What's on your mind Miss Valentine?"

Sitting up, I lie across his lap, propping my head up on my hand. "I'm curious as to whether or not you were going to tell me you kissed my best friend?"

He lets out a rumble of laughter, sliding his hand down his face. "She told you?"

I nod my head. "She did. Well Aspen did, and then Elle confessed."

"Were you mad?"

"Nah." I lay my head in his lap again. "I fucking hated Malcolm. I would've kissed her myself if I was there just to leave him wondering if we were having an affair behind his back the whole time."

"I would've loved to see that."

Looking up at him, I raise my brow.

"Not in that way," he says. "Unless..."

I jab his side.

"I'm kidding."

"I bet you are." He stretches his arm out over my chest, rubbing my arm. A few minutes later, the X-File's episode ends.

"Do you want to watch something else?"

"Sure," I say not wanting to move away from him.

He slides his hand from my arm to the sliver of skin showing where my shirt has ridden up, swiping his thumb back and forth. I feel my nipples harden. It's been two entire weeks since we've engaged in any type of sexual activity. When I said I wanted to take things slow, I didn't realize he'd withhold dick from me. Tonight may be the night I beg for it.

Sitting up, I fold my legs under me so I'm kneeling beside him, and press my lips to his. I hear him set the remote aside, abandoning his search. He rests his hands on my waist, and I deepen the kiss, dipping my tongue into his mouth. I slowly slide my hands over his chest and abs, reaching his belt. When he feels me trying to unhook it, he grabs my wrist, pulling away.

"Winter," I whine. "Let me have my way with you."

"I thought we agreed to take things slow." Amusement lights his eyes.

"And we can." I straddle his lap, winding my hips. "With me on top of you."

He wraps his hands around my waist, stopping my movements.

I let out an exasperated sigh. "At least let me see it and say hi."

Winter snorts with laughter. "You've never said hi to it before. Why start now?"

"Because it's been ten years." I reach for his belt again. "And I want to get reacquainted."

He grabs my wrists, holding them up between us.

"This is cruel and unusual punishment. If you knew how horny I was right now, you—"

"I want you to show me."

"What?"

"Show me how horny you are for me, Eve." Slipping his hand under my shirt, he toys with my nipple. "Let me watch you play with yourself until you come."

"Will you be joining me?"

He wraps his hand around my throat, pulling me toward him, kissing me. "Of course."

Winter doesn't have to tell me twice. I stand, pulling off my pants and panties in one swift motion. He has an impish smile on his lips.

"Shirt too," he says. "I want to see all of you."

I quickly pull it over my head, turning on the spot, giving him what he wants. Winter smacks my ass, making me giggle. It's been far too long. I lie on the opposite end of the couch, spreading my legs, loving that his eyes are only for me.

"Now I want to see all of you." I slip my hand between my legs, drawing slow circles around my clit.

Winter stands, pulling off his shirt, exposing his abs. My eyes are glued to his hands as he drags his belt through the loops. When he hooks his hands in the waist band of his jeans and boxers, I hold my breath.

"Keep playing with your pussy for me." I didn't realize I'd stopped, and listening, I strum my finger over my center. "That's my girl."

Winter takes his pants off as a reward. The sight of him alone, hard for me, is enough to push me over the ledge I'm already teetering on. He sits on the couch, sprawling out, slinging one arm over the back of it, wrapping his other hand around his length. I want to sit on it. Bounce on it. Help him reach his release. Winter strokes his hand up and down. I watch with greedy eyes, rubbing my clit harder. Needing to feel full, I dip my middle and ring finger into my wetness.

He groans with his eyes trained on my hand, in a trance as he strokes himself. I've never been one to take direction well. I sit up on my knees and wrap my hand around Winter's. For a moment I think he's going to stop me, but he moves his hand, letting me hold his shaft. I rub my thumb over the glistening tip, eliciting a guttural moan from him. Leaning forward, needing a taste, I lick off his arousal before wrapping my lips around him.

"Bring that ass over here," he commands, bringing his legs up.

I spread mine apart, making room for him to lay down.

"Did I tell you to stop?"

"No." I lick my lips, biting the bottom one.

"You need to learn how to listen. Now bring that ass over here and sit on my face.

"I'll listen to that." I position myself over his mouth, with my own hovering above his dick, licking it before I suck on it.

"Mmm..." he groans, smacking my ass. "I know you will." Wrapping his arms around my hips, he pulls my center down onto his waiting tongue, giving me a jolt of pleasure.

I moan around him in my mouth, sucking harder. He palms my ass cheeks, squeezing them, spreading me open. I tighten my hand around him, jerking as I suck, and moving my hips, gliding across his tongue. It's been two weeks since the last time he had a taste of me and my first time tasting him in over a decade. I suck on Winter as if my mouth and tongue can prove how badly I've missed him. I've missed everything. The way he tastes, smells, feels, smiles, laughs – everything.

Curling my toes and sliding my feet underneath him, spreading my thighs as far apart as the couch will allow, I feel a tidal wave building in my core. He circles his tongue around my clit, once, twice, and the third time is the charm. I nearly choke, losing my sense of self as I unravel for him. Winter tightens his arms around my waist, keeping me in place, licking and sucking up my release.

He replaces his mouth with his fingers, slipping them inside me. I tighten around them. Winter grabs my hair, tugging on it. My only intention right now it to suck the soul out of him. And I do. Tightening my grip, hollowing my cheeks, sucking hard and slow, I watch his toes curl.

"Shit," he hisses. "Eve..." My name spills from his lips like a plea.

I quicken the pace, brining him closer to the edge with each bob of my head. When my hand finds his balls, massaging them, he pulls my hair, thrusting his hips forward, groaning. My mouth fills with his warm release. I don't let up, swallowing what I can, maintaining the hard, slow sucks. The way he's panting sounds like I'm taking everything from him. Eventually, I slowly drag my lips off of his length. Licking up the rest of the release I couldn't catch, watching his dick twitch in my hand.

"Fuck," he says hoarsely. "I don't know if I should be embarrassed or impressed I was about to tap out if you wouldn't have gotten off of me."

Smiling, I sit up, and he slides his fingers out of me. Turning around, I lie on top of him, wrapping my arms around his middle, and pressing my cheek to his chest.

"I thought you said you wanted to watch."

"I had a front row seat and thoroughly enjoyed the view. You know those rollercoaster rides where you get soaked at the end?"

I cackle, burying my face in his chest.

"Eve's Tsunami Punani has a nice ring to it, don't you think? Or wait, Eve's Garden?"

Trying to control my laughter, I rest my chin on his chest, looking up at him. "I missed you."

He hooks his arms underneath mine, sliding my body up his until our lips are level. Threading his hand through my curls, he guides my mouth to his, kissing me. Pulling away enough to talk, he mutters, "I missed you too, Dove."

24
WINTER

THERE'S AN EASE TO my life lately that I haven't felt in a long time. I used to have it together on the outside while being a mess on the inside. Now my outward appearance matches the energy I'm feeling inwardly. Things are manageable where only a few months ago they were becoming unbearable. Instead of grinning and bearing it, I'm doing the work, feeling it all without getting stuck in the emotions. It's overwhelming at times, especially when I feel two polar emotions at once. Happiness, genuine happiness, has been something I've been getting reacquainted with. I panicked when I was feeling happy and in the moment, only to find myself starting to disassociate in the same breath.

Disassociation had only happened for me when I was feeling a negative emotion. It was jarring to have it happen when everything feels right. Dr. Maddox reassured me that I'm not losing my mind and that I'm learning to rewire my response to large emotions. It doesn't happen every time I'm happy, and usually I can catch myself and stay in the moment. That's progress I will celebrate. Before, I couldn't control it. I'd slip out of my body, not knowing when I'd feel like myself again.

Dr. Maddox has taught me ways to "stay in my body" when I feel it happening. Grounding techniques have been what work best for me. I try to immerse myself in the moment by tuning into what's around me. I'll acknowledge what I can see, hear, touch, smell, and taste if there's something for me to taste. I remember months ago when I first sat down in Dr. Maddox's chair. And now, you couldn't pay me to miss an appointment.

"I'm seeing my ex-fiancé... again," I confess.

Calling her an ex feels foreign since Eve has never felt like one. We've been spending most of our free time together since the night at Twisted Vines.

Dr. Maddox sets his pen down, adjusting his thick, black-framed glasses, and takes a sip of water, staring at me over the rim. He sets it back down gently, resting his hand on his chin. We stare at each other. This happens when I'm waiting for him to ask the probing questions and he's waiting for me to elaborate. He knows me too well.

"It's not bad," I press on. "It's actually been... amazing. We're not together. We're just exploring who and what we are now. Because all we know is then."

"Is that satisfying for you? The exploring while not being together."

"Does it matter?" I rub my palms against my thighs. "We agreed to take it slow..." My knee bounces.

"The question remains the same, Winter. Is this relationship, the agreement, satisfying for you?"

"It's..." My voice trails off. I've thoroughly enjoyed the past month with Eve. Each time after seeing her, I find myself wondering what it'd be like if we were *truly* together again. If we weren't just standing on the ledge, waiting to free fall back into us. "I left her. I understand her apprehension."

Dr. Maddox holds my gaze, waiting for me to tell the truth like he knows I inevitably will.

I suck in a deep breath. "Okay... Alright. I wonder if me leaving is always going to be looming between us. I fucked up. She knows that. I know that. I feel like we're taking it slow because she still hasn't forgiven me and is trying to decide if she even can. And if she can't..." It's not even something I want to think about but I press on. "I worry what that will mean for us. Well, I know what it means. It means that there is no us. And that is an excruciating possibility."

I fall silent, feeling like I'm saying too much but I can't stop myself.

"I love her. I love her so fucking much my soul aches. Which sounds dramatic, I know, but it's true. It was torture watching her for months with someone else. Even though I knew she belongs with me. And now..." I sit up throwing my arms out to the side. "I have her but I don't really have her. So no... it's not satisfying."

I collapse back against the couch, staring up at the ceiling. Eve, herself, will always be enough. She has been since the moment I met her. Over the past month, I've tried to convince myself that having fragments of her is enough. My soul can't accept that. I want every single fucking piece like I said. The problem is, I don't know if I deserve those pieces. Why trust me again when I'm the reason she fell to pieces in the first place?

"Winter," I shift my gaze to his. "You deserve to have your needs met, too."

My vision unexpectedly blurs. I turn away from him, balling my fist and pressing it to my mouth. I squeeze my eyes shut, willing the tears not to fall. They do anyway.

"When we were together," I croak. My voice is barely above a whisper. "I poured so much into her I never stopped to see if she was pouring into me too. Not to say that she never did, but when I really fucking needed her it was like she needed me to get back to who I was before Dad died. At first she was understanding, but it got to a point where she was trying to push me out of my grief. I felt like Eve couldn't care for me in the way I cared for her."

A truth bomb I never wanted to detonate. Eve has her apprehensions and I have mine too. I'm not naïve enough to think we'll never experience rough patches again. Knowing that they're inevitable and that she couldn't support me back then has me hesitant. I try to remind myself we're different people now. However, I know better than most that you don't know what's to come until you get there. Being there for someone when things are easy and staying when things are difficult are two entirely different things. I don't expect her to carry or fix me. All I need to know is that she's with me.

"You both abandoned each other?"

"Yes." Leaning forward, I snatch a tissue out of the box sitting on the coffee table between us, and I wipe my face and nose. "Physically and emotionally."

"Have you forgiven her?"

I shift in my seat, putting my elbow on the armrest and press my palm into the side of my face. "Maybe a little too easily."

"Forgiveness is never easy."

"It just wasn't serving a purpose." I hunch a shoulder. "It took me years to fully let it go. Now that we're back in each other's lives those old feelings have resurfaced."

I fall silent and Dr. Maddox takes it as his cue to speak. "There's layers to healing, right?"

I nod.

"I'm not sure that anyone is ever fully healed. If someone claims to be–I call bullshit."

Smiling, I look down at the tissue in my hand.

"It's unrealistic to expect to never have a trigger ever again. However, it *is* realistic to be able to manage your emotions when those triggers are pushed. There's power in being able to name what we're feeling. Because if something is mentionable it's manageable."

The last sentence sticks in my brain. "I like that. If it's mentionable it's manageable."

Dr. Maddox smiles. "It's a watered down version of a quote that Mr. Rogers said."

"I used to love that show. Fuck... now I feel old."

"If you feel old, I'm ancient."

I laugh, running my hand down my face. "Didn't mean to insult you."

He waves his hand airily, dismissing my apology.

"You've taught me a lot, Dr. Maddox. Thank you for helping me name things so they're manageable. Thank you for seeing me."

Momentarily, he looks stunned. Dr. Maddox removes his glasses, wiping under his eyes and pinches the bridge of his nose. He takes a few breaths, slides his glasses back on, and smiles when his eyes meet mine. "You're doing the work, Winter. Thank yourself."

Instead of going home to be alone like I normally do after a therapy session, I decide to meet up with my brothers instead. I pick up Snow and North first. Reign isn't done with school for another hour. He begged me to check him out early. I would've if he hadn't have skipped a class last week. It was his accounting class that Reign claimed he doesn't need because he's already ahead in the class and knows what he's doing. I had North put him to the test, and sure enough, anything he threw at him, Reign was able to solve. Despite being impressed, am I going to let it slide? Hell no. He'll finish out his day and then he can hang out with us.

I pull up to Elle and Snow's house, parking behind North's car. Elle pulls out of the garage as I get out of my own. She stops, rolling down the window to reveal she's with Aspen.

"We're just waiting on your Eve." Elle slides her shades down her nose, looking at me over the frames.

"She's not mine." *Yet.*

"But she will be. You two are so fucking annoying." Aspen rolls her eyes, looking in a small, round handheld mirror as she applies lip gloss. "Eve belongs to you whether she wants to admit it or not and vice versa." She points her lip gloss at me.

"Are you supposed to be blowing up her spot like this?"

"Please." Elle waves her hand dismissively, scoffing. "We say it to her damn face."

I wish I was as confident about us as they are. I'm not sure where I expected Eve and I to be right now. Further than where we currently are is for sure. We still haven't had sex. That's not for lack of trying on Eve's part. I'm the one holding out. I don't want physical intimacy to get in the way of our emotional intimacy. Our attraction to one another has never been a question. That's a given. One of my favorite things is lying in bed with her at night, talking about everything and anything without sex being a thought or expectation. That level of intimacy is what my soul craves.

Elle pulls me from my thoughts. "Oh, there's your future wife now." She points toward the road.

I turn to see Eve pull up beside my car. There hasn't been a time since I met her that she doesn't take my breath away when I catch sight of her. Eve steps out of the car, braids flowing in the wind with the afternoon sunlight kissing her sable skin.

She's my definition of perfection.

"Hey, you." She wraps her arms around my middle, looking up at me expectantly.

I give her what she wants, pressing a kiss to her lips. "Hey, Dove." I dip my head a little lower, inhaling her scent of jasmine and vanilla.

She places her hands on either side of my face, cradling my head. Her brown eyes search mine. "Are you okay?"

"Yeah." I can tell she doesn't believe me by the way she squints her eyes. "I had therapy today. You know how that shit goes."

I don't really mention therapy. Not because I'm ashamed, but because it's mine. It's personal. I don't want to go to therapy and then come home to hash it out further. I've created the boundary of whatever I spill on the couch, I leave there. The whole purpose is for me to unload. Not to pack it up at the end of the session to unpack at random.

Eve presses onto her toes slightly, kissing me. "Did you want me to go to your place after we're done? I won't try and jump you. Promise. Just aggressive cuddling."

"I'll always want to aggressively cuddle you."

She gives me a dimpled smile. "I'll text you when we're done, okay?"

"If I'm not home, let yourself in. I'm not sure what trail we're hiking."

"C'mon, wrap it up you two," Aspen hollers from the car. "We've got places to be."

"Just a minute!" Eve exclaims. "I'll see you tonight."

"Hurry up and kiss so we can go!" Elle yells.

"Tonight." I wrap my hand around the back of Eve's neck, pulling her toward me, and kiss her. She melts into me like she always does with my touch. For dramatic effect, and to leave her breathless, I dip her and kiss her like she's giving me my last breath.

Aspen and Elle squeal. "You guys are so cute it's disgusting!" Aspen fake retches.

I help Eve stand upright, break the kiss, and turn her around, smacking her ass. She jumps, looking back at me as she walks to the car.

"Tell Reign we'll take him out soon," Elle says.

"Will do." I give them a mix of a wave and salute as I head inside to find Snow and North.

I check the living room first to find North asleep on the couch with a book splayed over his chest and his glasses halfway down his face. North goes through glasses like underwear. For as money conscious as he is, I'm surprised he doesn't wear contacts. I fix his glasses, set the finance book on the coffee table–no wonder he's asleep–and kiss the top of his head. No matter our age, he'll always be my baby brother.

Walking through Snow's house as if it's mine, I find him in his office. It reminds of the one Dad had in our childhood home. Floor to ceiling bookshelves, dark mahogany wood with a muted shine, deep, rich colors, leather accent chairs, and a fireplace in the corner. I plop down in one of the chairs, letting out a loud, announcing sigh.

Snow looks up from where he's sifting through papers, glaring at me, and then acts as if I'm not here.

"I didn't realize you were working from home today."

"I wouldn't be..." he says distractedly. "If work would leave me alone. Wilder sent some paperwork that needed to be signed. You know I like to see things in my hands."

You'd think the man doesn't have a desktop, laptop, or tablet with the way he stays printing digital things off.

"We have to leave in an hour."

"I don't think—"

"If I ever hear you're blowing off Elle for work I'm going to throat chop you and then put you in chokehold."

He drops his pen on the desk, letting out an exasperated sigh, and then leans back in his chair. "How the fuck did Dad do it? Run the company, have a solid relationship with Mom, make individual time for each of us boys, and not lose his shit? Typically, I don't give a fuck because I just power through. But now it's not just me. It's Noelle too, and I never want her to feel neglected because I stupidly made work my life and don't know how to switch it off."

Snow really has to be struggling for him to talk to me like this. We used to talk about everything until I fell into the deep end and couldn't be there for him like he needed me to be. I feel we're slowly getting back to the space of being each other's confidant. I just wish it never got fucked up in the first place.

Standing, I move from the couch to the chair in front of his desk. "Then give me the other reigns so the load isn't so heavy."

He slowly lifts his head, meeting my gaze. "What?"

"The marketing department is a well-oiled machine. It wouldn't be hard to find a replacement for me. Work wise. Personality, you'll be hard pressed."

He scoffs, leaning back in chair.

"That way you're not alone, and we can share the responsibility."

Snow steeples his hands, resting his chin on his fingertips as he looks at me. There's a long moment of silence that I let him have while I grab his best bottle of bourbon and pour myself some. I tip the glass toward him as a salute before taking a drink.

"You'd do that for me?"

"I'd do anything for you, Snow. You know that. I'm a little offended you're even asking."

"I'm sorry." He scrubs his hands down his face. "I... it's that you haven't really shown any interest in sharing the responsibilities."

"Because I knew I wasn't ready then. I wasn't going to be able to support you in the way you needed. I'm sure I would've been a hinderance. Now I'm ready."

"You've never been a hinderance."

Those unexpected words burrow into my soul and heal a piece of me that's been needing my brother's love. I look down at my hands through blurry vision and pinch the bridge of my nose in hopes I won't start crying. It doesn't work.

"Fucking sap." Snow snatches a Kleenex from the holder on his desk and hands it to me. There are tears in his eyes too but he blinks them away before they have a chance to fall.

"Shut the fuck up." I take the Kleenex from him. "Ass."

"Are you sure about this?"

"Wouldn't offer if I wasn't. Plus, I don't think Dad ever meant for one of us to run the company alone. Dad was the face of North Star Toys, but Mom was always by his side. He was never alone, and you won't be either."

Snow gives me genuine smile. "Alright. We'll work out the details and make it official."

I stand, holding my arms out to the side. "Bring it in."

He raises his brow, giving me an incredulous look. "You're serious?"

"Either give me one or I'll force myself on you."

"That sounds like abuse."

"It will be. I'm waiting." Snow stares at me for a few more breaths before reluctantly getting out of his chair. He rounds his desk, looking me up and down every step like I'm insane. Eventually, he hugs me. "Hug me like you love me, motherfucker."

He tightens his hold, I'm sure in an attempt to squeeze the life out of me, but I don't care. "Sometimes you just need a hug from your brother."

Eventually, Snow relaxes, giving me a real hug, and even pats my back. "Love you," he says with nothing but affection in his voice.

"Love you, too."

"What the hell is going on?" North asks from behind us. "Did someone die?"

"No, asshole," Snow says giving me a half-hug as he motions for North to join us.

"Is this a setup?" he asks skeptically as he inches closer.

"No, but we will jump you if you don't join us," I reassure him.

"How many times do I have to tell you violence is—"

Snow and I grab him by his shirt and pull him into the hug.

Reign is waiting with Calliope and Ian on the curb of the pickup line when we arrive. I purposely arrived later because I learned the first time that the pickup line is an adult form of hell. Reign doesn't mind. It gives him more time to spend with his friends and Calliope. They officially started dating the day after the Gala because he wanted to ask her to be his girlfriend in person.

"Is that his girlfriend?" North asks. He's only seen her in passing, but hasn't been formally introduced. Vincent is off on the weekends and likes to do things with Calliope. She's only been to my house a handful of times and each time, North hasn't been there.

"No. Just a girl he's holding hands with," Snow says sarcastically.

North smacks the back of his head, and Snow retaliates by turning around in the front seat and smacking him.

"If you fuck up my leather seats, I'm gonna fuck both of you up. Sit your overgrown ass down, Snow."

"He's a fucking opportunist," Snow claims, glaring at North, who's wearing a smug smile, in the mirror.

I pull into a parking space and get out so I can say hi to Calliope and Ian. Since I picked Reign up the first time, I've encouraged him to invite Ian over on the weekends. He's an awesome kid, and Reign shines a little brighter when he's around. I have yet to meet Reign's grandma, but according to him, she doesn't like him having anyone over to their house when she's not there. And she's never there. I almost told Reign it's not like she'd know. Instead I was an adult about it and told him he could invite his friends to my place. As a result, my house has become a hangout spot. All I care about is that Reign is flourishing. We all get out and head toward Reign and his posse.

"Winter!" Calliope gives me a hug.

"Hey, Winter." Reign smiles, bumping my fist.

"Hey. You ready?"

"Absolutely." Reign picks his backpack up off the ground and slings it over his shoulder.

"Wait!" Calliope holds up her hands. "I made something for you, Snow."

"What?" Snow's eyes widen.

She throws her backpack down on the ground, and pulls out a small, neatly wrapped box. I know what it is, but look clueless when Snow turns to me for help.

Calliope places it in his hands with a bright smile. "Nothing big. It's just a thing I do." She looks unsure of the gift now due to Snow's lack of reply. I nudge him.

He clears his throat, staring down at the box. "Thank you, Calliope. This is very thoughtful of you."

"You don't have to open it now if—"

Snow is already tearing open the packaging, causing her eyes to light up. While he opens it I shift my focus to Ian. "Sorry you couldn't come tonight."

He rolls his eyes, pushing his curly red hair out of his face. "My mom said maybe next time."

"There's always tomorrow."

"Hopefully she lets me go tomorrow. She says I need to focus on school a little more since we're nearing the end of the year."

"That's what I tell Reign, too."

"I missed one class," Reign grumbles.

Ian's mom pulls up in her minivan, honking. "For God's sake woman!" he grumbles, grabbing his bag. "Hopefully I'll see you guys over the weekend."

Ian gives Reign a fist bump and Calliope a wave before running toward the van.

I turn my attention back to Snow who is slipping on the bracelet Calliope made him.

"The round beads are onyx and the cubes are genuine lava rock."

"You made this?" Snow turns his wrist from side to side, looking genuinely impressed. I swear I also see a glimmer in his eye that he quickly blinks away.

"Yep." She nods proudly.

"Thank you, Calliope. I love it."

"You're welcome." She turns her attention to North. "Hi. I'm Calliope."

"North." He shakes her hand. "Nice to meet you."

"You too. Sorry I didn't make anything for you."

"Don't worry about it. Beautiful bracelet you made, by the way."

"Thank you. I love making them."

"Alright, Reign. Let's go so we can get you home at a decent time."

He turns to Calliope, saying his goodbye. North, Snow, and I pretend to be more interested in each other to give them their privacy. However, I am a child and can't stop myself from whistling when he kisses her. Reign's ears turn a crimson color, and Calliope buries her face in his chest.

"Grow up." Snow pushes me toward the car.

Calliope's dad pulls up seconds later, and Reign puts a respectable distance between them. Vincent waves at us from his truck as we climb into my Range Rover. Reign climbs in a few seconds later, avoiding eye contact with us. I start the engine.

"Reign." I look at him in the rearview mirror.

He watches Calliope and her dad pull out of the parking lot. "Yeah?"

"You get to choose where we go hiking today."

"Really?" His eyes finally meet mine, and I nod. "Moonstone Canyon. I used to go there with my dad all the time."

"Perfect," is all I can manage before emotions choke me.

Snow lightly punches my arm, giving me a knowing look, and turns on some music.

There isn't a trail in Hope Valley that we didn't hike with our Dad. I know everyone thinks boys are mama's boys, and we are, but we adored our Dad. He was loving, patient, and always showed up for us and our Mom. Thinking back, I can't remember a time he wasn't there for us. No matter how big or small the event or achievement. Then one day, he wasn't there anymore at all. I wouldn't wish losing a parent on anyone, especially not Reign.

That's why I took it upon myself to make sure his first trip back to Moonstone Canyon without his Dad is fun and memorable. Before leaving the valley, we stopped by the grocery store to get burgers, hot dogs, potato salad, corn on the cob, and stuff to make s'mores.

The hike was almost an hour. We had to take turns lugging the food and drinks up the steady incline. It was worth it to see the elation on Reign's face. He built the fire and even cooked the food. It's been fun to watch him in an element he loves.

Now we're sitting around making s'mores as the sun sets behind the mountains.

"Are you doing anything this summer, Reign?" North puts a marshmallow over the fire.

"Probably not." He hunches his shoulder. "I got into a summer art program in Paris, but I don't think I'll be able to go."

"Wait... hold on. Rewind." I knit my brows, cocking my head to the side. "You're going to casually drop that you got into a summer art program all the way in Paris?"

"For real," Snow chimes in.

Reign concentrates on piecing together his s'more. "It's not like I can go. I don't have a passport, and my grandma isn't going to pay for it. I don't even know why I applied," he says softly.

"You applied because you know your art is amazing." North points his flaming marshmallow at Reign.

"Put that shit out before you burn one of us, Smoky the Bear." I nudge the skewer out of the way. "He is right though."

"None of you have even seen my art to say that." Reign takes a bite of his s'more.

"We've seen the passion and the way your eyes light up when you talk about your art," Snow says. "We don't need to see it when we can feel it."

"Exactly." I pat Reign on the shoulder. "Do you want to go to Paris? Tell me more about the program."

"It's two week intensive program for high school students. They'll take us on tours to museums, art studios, they'll have lectures, and of course I'll get to paint." Reign's excitement is evident even though he's trying to tamp it down. "It's at the beginning of August. Ian got accepted for film."

"Is he going?"

"Oh, yeah," he says around a bite of s'more. "Ian's parents will pay for anything that will enrich him. They think he spends too much time in front of his TV and computer."

"You didn't answer his question," North says, lighting another marshmallow on fire.

"I said Ian is going and—"

"No," Snow cuts in. "Winter asked you if you want to go to Paris?"

Reign falls silent again for a few breaths, staring at the fire. He takes a deep breath looking at me. "Like I said it doesn't—"

"It's a yes," North blows out his marshmallow, "or no question."

"Yeah. I wanna go," Reign says it as though he feels guilty for wanting something he thinks he can't have.

"Alright. We'll figure out your passport and—"

"No," Reign says holding up his hand. "Nope. I'm not a charity case. You guys have done enough, and I'm not going to take anymore from any of you."

North adjusts his glasses, curling his lip. "Charity case?"

"I thought you said we are your brothers..." Snow looks sullen. I remember him doing that face when we were kids and he wanted us to feel bad for him. Well played, brother. Well fucking played.

"You are!" Reign reassures him, looking distraught by the sudden change of Snow's demeanor. "It's just that – I don't know. I don't want you guys thinking I'm a leech or something."

"You're our little brother," I assure him. "You'll always be a leech."

Reign cracks a smile while North looks affronted.

"Damn. That's how you feel?" North asks.

I ignore North's hurt feelings and address Reign's concerns. "We don't view you that way. You rarely ask for anything. And when you do ask for something, it's small."

"Yeah. Like a pizza. You know we're billionaires and you asked for a pizza!"

"I was hungry..." Reign says matter-of-factly, sliding off the makeshift seat, and sits closer to the fire.

A few weeks ago we were out and Snow asked him what he wanted and his response was a pizza. We had just left the electronic store and Snow was sure he'd ask for something from there. It made all of us chuckle when we realized he truly wanted a pizza. And he really did because he ate a whole pie by himself.

"Point is, if you want to go to Paris, we'll make it happen for you."

I'd really love to know where the money Reign gets from his dad's death is going. It's definitely not used for him or anything he needs. I noticed his clothes were a little too small, and Calliope let it slip that his grandma kept promising she'd take him shopping. She never did. I waited a couple of weeks to see and his clothes just seemed to be getting smaller. Instead of taking him shopping, I had Eve, Noelle, and Aspen take him under the guise they were going for themselves. Reign didn't question them buying stuff for him in the mix of them buying things. All three women are persistent, and I'm not sure he can tell them no. We'll have to work on that.

"Can I think about it?" Reign gives me a side long glance.

"Not if you're thinking of every reason as to why you supposedly don't deserve to go."

Reign ignores me, pulling his knees to his chest, watching the fire. I give him a few seconds to respond and then pick up a pinecone, launching it at his back.

He whips around, and sees the pinecone lying behind him. "What the–did you just throw this at me?"

"No. It was North."

North looks up from his s'more he's piecing together, confused by the mention of his name. "Wha—"

Reign chucks the pinecone at North's chest.

"Aye!" North looks at the pinecone resting in his lap. "What was that for?" He sets his s'more aside and chucks the pinecone back at Reign.

He ducks, and it hits Snow instead. Even though he's been watching the whole thing, Snow acts like North hit him intentionally. He takes it as an opportunity to fuck with North, picking up two pinecones, throwing them at him.

"Hey!" North holds up his arms in front of his face. "Those things hurt, fucker! Why are you throwing them so hard?"

I try not to laugh at the chaos I unlocked and pick up a pinecone and chuck it at North. "Language! There are children present."

"Are you counting yourself as a child?" North asks, grabbing a pinecone and throwing it at me. It hits me square in the forehead. Everyone stops, looking at me, and North looks like he's watching his life flash before his eyes.

"A headshot, North?"

"It was an accident." He backs up.

"Was it? Because that felt pretty calculated to me." I move so quick; North doesn't have time to block himself from the pinecones I launch in his direction.

All hell breaks loose as it turns into every man for himself as we run through the woods like three of us aren't grown adults. Reign is laughing so hard he's falling every couple of steps, but his aim remains impeccable as he hits Snow on the back of the head with a rather large pinecone. Snow turns around with murder in his eyes, looking for the culprit while Reign and I laugh behind a tree trunk. We don't hear North sneak up on us, blowing up our spot, pelting us with pinecones and acorns.

"Bro, what the fuck?" I crawl behind a tree, joining Reign. "Where the hell did you find acorns?"

North is in the middle of cracking up when Snow hits him on the side of head with a pinecone. When he tries to run away, his foot catches on a fallen branch. Snow abandons the use of forest items and grabs North by the ankle. He kicks Snow's shin so hard he lets go, grabbing his own leg in pain.

"You better fucking run asshole," Snow says through gritted teeth.

"Fucking hell," I sigh exasperatedly, knowing this just turned into a real fight. "We've gotta save North."

"We?!" Reign asks, looking at an angry Snow.

"Yes. We." I grab him by the arm, pulling him behind me as we run after Snow and North.

North is bolting back to the campsite with Snow following close behind him, shouting expletives. I take a short cut with Reign, winding through trees and jumping over rocks until we cut in front of Snow by a few feet.

"Stay out of it, Winter!" Snow shouts.

I ignore him. That's Snow's problem. He wants to fuck around until he finds out and then takes it seriously. We reach the campsite before him, but North is nowhere in sight. Snow comes barreling in a few seconds behind us.

"Where is he?"

"I don't—"

We turn toward the sound of rustling trees, and North appears in the clearing like a deer in headlights. Snow takes off toward him with Reign and I following close behind. He reaches North before us, grabbing him by his t-shirt, getting ready to punch him. I tackle Snow before his fist can connect. Reign tries to grab me by my shirt to keep me from tipping over the edge of the hill.

It's no use. All four of us tumble over the side. Hitting grass, rocks, and brush as we begin our journey down. Everything is a fucking blur. We hit each other and everything else in between. The hill didn't seem this high at the top. If someone is watching, I know they're laughing their asses off at us.

"My fucking glasses," North hollers.

I laugh so hard I start wheezing. This happens every single time, and he still wears them boldly. Eventually, we come to a rolling stop at the bottom. That's when the pain sets in. Everything hurts. The only thing I can do is stare at the darkening sky and contemplate why I keep hanging out with my brothers. Lifting my head, I feel a pain in my neck, and twist it side to side, cracking it. Snow and North are moving, but Reign is not.

Panic grips me so tightly I feel the adrenaline seep into my veins. "Reign!" I scramble toward him. "Reign!" He's a few feet away from us.

My panicked voice sets Snow and North into action. What if he hit his head on a rock? Or broke his neck?

Looking at him, I'm afraid to touch him. His eyes are closed and he looks too peaceful. We all crowd around him. "Reign..." I gently touch his arm.

"Is he—" Snow begins.

Reign rises up like the fucking undertaker, scaring the shit out of us all. We scramble backwards while he laughs hysterically. I clutch my chest, breathing deep, trying to calm down.

"You little shit!" Snow shouts.

Reign holds up his hands. "I'm sorry." He tries to swallow his laughter. "I'm sorry. It was the perfect opportunity."

"If I wasn't so relieved you're alive, I would kill you," I say with my heart still racing.

"Three times. Because all of us are going to get our licks in." North squints at him.

Reign ignores our threats, standing up, and brushing himself off. We all follow suit. North aimlessly searches around for his glasses before letting out a sigh and standing beside us. Now that we're at the bottom, the hill looks much steeper.

I clap Reign on the back. "You know what this means right?"

"What?" He looks up at me as I wrap my arm around his shoulders.

"You're officially a King brother now."

His smiles grows as Snow wraps his arm around his shoulders too. North wraps his arm around mine.

"Which means..." Snow begins.

"The last one up this hill is carrying all that shit back to the car," North says.

Reign looks confused for half a second as we take off, running up the hill. He follows behind us, laughing. I don't think he's gives a fuck if he has to carry it because he's found a home in us.

25
WINTER

MOM IS VISITING FROM Sapphire Shores for the weekend. Eve wanted to be here, but her grandparents are visiting and tonight is their last night, so they're having a dinner. Since Snow and Noelle just moved into their new place, Mom wanted to have a celebratory dinner with all of us. We miss having her near. I also understand why she wanted to move. It's where she and Dad built a life together and where she lost him – and the life they built. We still have each other, of course, but it's not the same without Dad here. I'm grateful we're still close-knit despite what we've been through as a family and individuals.

Mom wraps me in a much needed hug, making all worry and stress melt away. I pick her up off the ground, hugging her back just as fierce.

She swats my arm. "Winter Cole King! Put me down!" I'd believe the sternness in her voice if she wasn't laughing.

"Alright." I let her feet touch the ground, giving her one last squeeze. "It's just so good to see you."

Cradling my face in her hands, she gives me a warm smile. "Always good to see you, too, son." She loops her arm through mine, guiding me toward the backyard where Snow, Noelle, North, and Aspen are. "Now, let's eat while we all catch up."

👑

Spending time with family is always rejuvenating for me. We may see and talk to each other every day, but there's nothing like us being together. Especially with the addition of Noelle and Aspen. They fit in like they were always meant to be a part of our family. We made lemon garlic chicken skewers, corn on the cob, and Mom made her infamous potato salad. It's been a fun evening of enjoying each other's company and good food.

Snow nudges my arm, handing me a beer. "Should we do the announcement now?" he asks low enough for only me to hear.

"Yeah."

We wanted to tell Mom in person that I'll be running North Star Toys alongside Snow. North had no interest in joining us. He's happy crunching numbers, ensuring our money is always right. We've tried to keep the position change under wraps since Mom is still good friends with the majority of the people at the company. We told the necessary people and will make a company-wide announcement Monday morning. We didn't even tell Noelle. Had we not gone private last year, I'm not sure this move would've been possible. Especially with my track record. The board gave Snow a lot of shit when they caught wind of my reckless behavior. He silenced their worries by working hard and keeping the company afloat while I went under. North came up with the idea to start quietly buying shares so that we could truly own the company again and not just be the face. Finally, last year, between us three and Mom, we owned the majority of shares and were able to buy everyone else out, allowing us to go private.

I remember Mom cried when we told her we owned it again. Before we started buying the shares, the company wasn't following the dream she and Dad had. She never said it disappointed her, but she didn't have to because we could see it in her eyes. Now I can only imagine her reaction when we tell her about me finally deciding to run the company alongside Snow.

There's only six of us, but Snow stands, clinking the side of his beer bottle with a fork like he's speaking to a room full of people. The chatter around the table dies down as he clears his throat.

"Winter, North, and I have an announcement to make," Snow says. Mom turns her attention toward us, setting her wine glass aside. "I'll let Winter tell it."

Mom, Noelle, and Aspen are looking confused as I stand beside Snow. I pull North out of his seat, making him stand with us. With me in the middle, I wrap an arm around both of them. It's only family, but I'm still nervous.

"I thought losing Dad was going to be the end of our family. It felt like the end of me. At least the version of myself I knew at that time." I look to my brothers who're giving me encouraging nods. "When Dad left the company to me, I misunderstood what he meant. He didn't leave the company solely to me. He left it for *us*." I pull Snow and North a little closer. "Which is why I'll be joining Snow as COO."

Mom gasps, covering her mouth as she looks between the three of us. Noelle claps along with Aspen who whistles in celebration. North and Snow give me hugs before letting me go. Mom gets up, rounding the table and gives me a tight hug.

"I'm so proud of who you are, Winter."

"Thank you, Mom." My voice cracks. "I always need to hear that."

After another round of drinks in celebration, Mom asks me to go on a walk with her around the garden. North and Aspen are getting ready to take off while Snow and Noelle are cleaning up. Mom and I step onto the lush, green grass of the backyard and head for the garden. Elle told

Snow she wanted a garden like she were in a fairytale, and he gave her exactly that. It's like stepping into a storybook.

"I know your Dad is happy." She smiles at me wistfully. "You boys have turned into such fine men."

"Thanks, Mom." I kiss her cheek.

"How are you feeling about this shift?"

"Anxious," I answer honestly. "In a good way. I finally feel ready."

Healing is interesting. You don't think all the personal excavation you're doing is working, questioning if it's even worth it, and then you're met with something you used to run from. Instead of fleeing, you face it, *knowing* you can take it on. You realize you're talking to yourself a little nicer, know you deserve better, and are worthy of a life created around your own narrative.

Mom stops in front of the rose bushes, turning to face me. "I've always been proud of you. Even when you thought I shouldn't be. I hope you know in here now," she places her hand over my heart, "that our love, *your* family's love, has never been contingent upon your actions. We love you, Winter. Always have and always will." She smooths her hand over my back, patting it, before pulling me along the garden's path again.

I walk beside her in silence, processing her words while she stops smelling the various kinds of flowers.

After a few minutes, the only words I can find are, "Thanks, Mom."

She smiles, gently touching the peonies. "How are things with your Eve?"

I sit on a stone bench in the center of the garden. "I should've never left her. I'm not sure she'll ever truly forgive and trust me again."

Mom plucks up a pale pink peony. "That's one idea." She sits beside me. "Or, have you ever thought maybe *she's* afraid of messing things up?"

"Eve?" I knit my eyebrows together, turning my lips downward. "No."

"Just because she stayed doesn't mean she's guiltless. You've struggled to forgive yourself, what if she's experiencing the same emotions now that she knows *why* you left?"

"I didn't consider that." Leaning forward, I rest my forearms on my thighs.

"You were so busy blaming yourself that you haven't realized others could be blaming themselves, too." She pats my back before standing again. "Just something to consider."

Transitioning from the marketing department to management has been hectic to say the least. It's been a long fucking day. The transition was supposed to be smooth. Like dipping my toes into water. Instead, it feels like I'm being waterboarded. I used to think Snow didn't have any patience. I'm realizing I'm the one who's never had it to begin with. Snow, the grump, had to tell *me* that I'm being too crass with people. Now I know why he was stressing. It's meeting after meeting, issue after issue, followed by more meetings, and a lot of shit that could've been a fucking email.

Snow handles it all with grace. You'd never be able to tell that he was stressing in his office only weeks ago. Despite being the big brother, I find myself looking up to him often. While it may be stressful now, I know once I get a good grip on the reins, I'll do well. Above all, I'm happy with my decision to work alongside Snow. To his dismay, I offered Noelle the position as my assistant. She happily accepted. Especially since she can work remotely when she wants and around her school schedule.

Looking around my desk for my phone, I pause when my eyes land on the last picture of me, Snow, and North with Dad. This week has been hard for reasons other than role adjustments. There isn't a moment I haven't thought about Dad, what he'd do, or wouldn't do, and what life would be like if he were still with us. My sadness is presenting itself as stress. It's putting me in a headspace I try to avoid at all costs, but the only way to avoid it would be to not take on the new position. I've spoken with Dr. Maddox three times this week. If it weren't Friday, I'd be calling him a fourth time.

At the end of the sessions I always come to the same conclusion: I'm exactly where I need to be. I know I've made the right move for myself. When Dad used to talk about me taking over the company, it always felt like a "someday" thing. And when "someday" came around, I thought Dad would still be around to help me navigate this role. Dad isn't here, but Snow is and he's been amazing this week with helping me learn the ropes. Underneath the sadness is this untamable happiness that I get to do this alongside my brother.

I see my phone on the table near the window. Getting up, I grab it and call Eve.

"Hey, Baby." She answers on the second ring, focusing the camera on her. I'm not sure how I've held out this long when she looks the way she does. "Did you call just to stare at me?" Her plush lips turn up into a smile.

"And if I did?"

"I'm not gonna complain." She cradles her chin in her hand, batting her lashes. "You know I love your attention."

"Can I give you all my attention tonight?"

"As much as I'd love that, I can't. Fox has that event at the museum tonight, remember? Since Mom and Dad are out of town, I want to support him."

"That's right." I rub my eyes with my free hand, pinching the bridge of my nose. "I forgot."

"Are you okay?" Her brows furrow with concern.

"Yeah. I just wanted to hang out and decompress. But Fox needs your support." It's his first event as the director. I'd want my family there too.

"You can always come with. Fox would love to see you."

"Thank you, but I think I'm gonna go home and chill. I'm fucking tired."

"Do you want me to stop by after?" she asks, still looking at me with concern.

"You're always welcome at my place. Let yourself in whenever you're done."

"I'll see you tonight."

"Tonight." I smile, trying to not let my disappointment show.

We end the call at the same time Snow enters my office.

"Ready for another meeting?" he asks a little to cheerily for my taste.

"Must we?"

He wraps his arm around my shoulders, giving me a squeeze. "Unfortunately, yes. The good news is at least I'm not sitting in them alone anymore."

The smile on his face makes all of this worth it.

I let out a sigh of relief, driving down the tree-lined winding road leading to my house. North waves me to me as I drive past his place and I honk my horn in response. The one neighbor who would've complained about the noise, Ms. Lexington, finally croaked. She had an issue about everything. Trash bins, grass length, guests, and would even complain if someone was driving in the community too late. When her house finally went up for sale and a young, new family moved in, we may or may not have had a block party in celebration.

Pulling into the garage, I park and sit in the silence of my car. After a few minutes, I grab the brown paper bag from Buds & Roses off the front seat and climb out. The only thing on my mind is taking a shower, eating an edible, and laying on the bed in my boxers. That thought leaves my head when I step through the door.

Rose petals are scattered across the floor and tea light candles light the path. A glass of bourbon and a note sit atop the entryway table. I toss my keys and the bag onto it, picking up the note.

Drink Me.

I recognize Eve's neat handwriting. Holding the note, I grab the glass of bourbon and follow the path of rose petals. They lead to the dining room where music is playing. The table is set for two with wine glasses and a bottle of wine from Twisted Vines. After a long day, expecting to come home to an empty house, this is a welcomed surprise. Setting the note down on the table, I loosen the top few buttons of my shirt, and step into the kitchen.

Eve is dancing around with a glass of wine in her hand. Splotches of flour are on her arms and face. She tucks her braids behind her ear, causing them to be dusted in flour too. Singing along to Jessie Reyez with her whole chest, she sways to the beat with her eyes closed, taking sips of wine between words. For a moment, I just watch her because it's rare she lets go. And here she is in my space, carefree and happy. When her eyes open, they widen when she focuses on me.

"You're home?" She glances around at the clock.

"I am."

"Shit." She presses her palm to her forehead. "I thought I had enough time to make dinner and get ready before you got here." Eve dusts off her t-shirt with a knot tied at the bottom and her skirt. "You know how I get when I cook."

"I do." Eve knows how to throw down in the kitchen but she is a chaotic cook. There are too many ingredients strewn across the counters for me to decipher exactly what she's making. "Aren't you supposed to be at an event supporting your brother? Not covered in flour, dancing around my kitchen."

"I was... but I felt like you needed me a little more tonight." She shrugs her shoulder, biting her lip. "I made that pizza you like. Fresh made dough and sauce, with basil from Mom's garden, and the homemade mozzarella."

Closing the distance between us, I rub my thumb over a flour spot on her chin, wiping it off. She looks up at me with her deep brown eyes and all I see is my future in them.

"You did all of this for me?"

"Yeah. You deserve it... and so much more."

"Eve..."

"Yeah?" Her eyes flit to my lips.

"I love you. I never stopped loving you."

Her eyes become glossy. "I fucked up really bad, Winter..."

"What do you mean?"

"I wasn't there for you when you needed me." A tear slips down her cheek. I wipe it away. "I'm so sorry. If I could go back, I would've listened instead of pushing. I've been worried I'm not capable of giving you what you need and—"

"Eve." I hold her face in my hands. "You're all I need. Just you. It's always been just you. The rest will fall into place. We'll figure it out together."

"You still want to be with me?"

I don't know whether to shake her, kiss her, or both. "I loved you then. I love you now. I'll love you always."

"I love you too. Then, now, and always."

Eve crashes into me or I crash into her. I'm not sure, but it doesn't matter because she's in my arms. I want to feel her. *Need* to feel her. Gripping Eve's thighs, I wrap her long legs around my waist, carrying her to the dining room table, ready to have a feast. I haphazardly move everything out of the way, ignoring the sound of glass and silverware hitting the floor. Laying her down on the table, I break our kiss to explore the rest of her body with my lips and hands. I slide up her shirt, nipping at her supple nipples, teasing the rings, before sucking one into my mouth.

She dips her fingers into my curls, tugging. The sensation makes my dick jump. Giving her nipples ample attention, I gently tug on the rings with my teeth before trailing more kisses over her stomach. Reaching her skirt, I fist it, sliding it up her hips. I sink to my knees, looking up at her.

"No panties? You came over here to offer yourself up," I grip her hips, pulling her to the edge of the table, "didn't you?"

"Yes," she says breathlessly.

Knowing Eve came here with the intention of giving herself to me makes my mouth water with desire. I run my tongue along her wetness, getting every drop before it goes to waste. Eve cries out, spreading her legs further apart. She looks like my last meal, kneading her breast and teasing her nipples while I eat her pussy. This sight alone has me teetering on the edge. I flick, lick, and suck on her pearl until she starts shaking like her soul has been raptured. She hums my name as she moans, unraveling for me.

I drink from her oasis until she nudges my head away.

"Tapping out?" I lick my lips, wiping my beard, training my eyes on her. "I told you I want every fucking thing. Are you not going to give it to me?"

Her eyes are heavy lidded when she opens them, watching me unbutton my shirt, unfasten my belt, and drag it through the loops.

"I asked you a question." Unbuttoning my pants, I pull them down with my boxers. She bites her lip as I grip my dick, stroking it, waiting for her answer. I step out of my pants and boxers, kicking them aside.

Grabbing her ankle, I pull her closer to the edge. Eve lets her legs fall open. I tap her sensitive clit with the tip of my dick, making her moan.

"What are you going to give me, Eve?"

"Everything." Her voice is hoarse from saying my name.

"Good girl. Guide me in."

I grab her thighs, keeping her legs open. She sits up on her elbows, reaching between us to wrap her hand around my length, lining me up with her center. I inhale sharply when the tip dips into her warmth. I watch myself disappear inch by inch, stretching her out. Eve closes her eyes, breathing deep.

"Too much?" I sling her leg over my shoulder, keeping the other in my grasp while I bring the thumb of my free hand to her clit. Rubbing slow circles around it, I feel her relax.

"Yes... no... I don't care." Eve tips her head back. "You feel so fucking good," she groans, lowering herself back onto the table, letting me take over.

I ease into her, relishing in the sensation of her tightly wrapped around me. Holding Eve's waist, I bury the rest of me in her, stealing her breath. Leaning forward, pressing my chest to hers, I wrap my hand around her throat.

"Take it all, Sweetheart," I mutter in her ear, thrusting my hips forward, fitting snugly in her walls. "It's been too long."

Eve cries out, sliding her hands up my back, wrapping them around my shoulders. I welcome the sting of her nails digging into my skin as she holds onto me. Giving her time to adjust, I keep my thrusts slow and deliberate. She presses kisses to my face, neck, and chest. Eve relaxes her legs, unhooking them from behind my back, and opens them wider.

Sitting up, I press my palms into the backs of her thighs, making her knees touch the table with her feet resting on my shoulders. Eve slides her hand down her body until she reaches her clit, rubbing slow circles that match my thrusts.

"I've always loved watching you play with this pretty pussy." I admire how beautiful she looks beneath me. The way she's open for me, the bounce of her breasts, and the way my name sounds spilling from her lips.

Eve's eyes slide shut. I slide my hand up the column of her throat, resting it below her jaw, applying light pressure.

"Keep those brown eyes focused on me," I say as she opens them. "I want to watch you take it. I want you to see what you do to me."

She lets out a guttural moan, still playing with herself, focusing on me. All I see is love for me, illuminated in the depths of her deep, velvety brown eyes.

"Winter..." she pants. "I'm gonna come."

"Don't stop playing with that pussy." I hook her legs over my shoulders, gripping her waist, plunging into her hard and deep.

Eve lets out a needy moan, coming for me. I pick up the pace of my thrusts, causing the table to scrape across the floor. The tension that's been building is pulled taut, ready to snap.

"Shit, tell me where to cum, Eve." I ask remembering under the thick sex-filled haze I'm not wearing a condom.

She opens her legs wider, saying, "In me."

Eve Valentine will *always* be my undoing. I let out a husky growl, listening to her command, spilling into her. My hips stutter to slow stop. Leaning forward, I collapse on top of Eve, listening to her heart slamming in her chest. She trails her fingers up and down my back while we come down from our euphoric high.

"Thank you for showing up for me," I say, sitting up on my forearms, looking down at her.

She puts her hands on either side of my face. "Thank you for giving me another chance after giving you so much hell."

I let out rumble of laughter. "Finally accepting you're a stubborn brat?"

"I said hell. Not anything about me being stubborn."

"Same difference." I shrug.

She swats my chest, looking affronted. "And to think I made you a homemade–fuck–the pizza!" Eve pushes me off her with surprising strength, scrambling into the kitchen with her ass and titties out. I follow her, pulling on my boxers, and round the corner as she peers into the oven. She places a hand over her heart, letting out a sigh of relief.

"I never turned it on." Pulling it out, she turns on the oven, and leans against the counter, waiting for it to heat up.

I grab a couple of paper towels and run them under warm water. Turning toward Eve, I kneel in front of her while she looks confused.

"What are you—" She falls silent, watching me clean up the post-sex mess dripping down her thighs. When I'm almost done, she softly says, "I forgot what it's like to be tenderly cared for." Looking up, she covers her face with her hands, sniffling. "I feel stupid for crying over you cleaning cum off my thighs."

I lick my lips, trying not to laugh. "You're not stupid." I press a kiss to each thigh once I'm done and stand in front of her. " I'm sorry no one's been taking care of you how you deserve. I'll always be happy to remind you how loved you are." I kiss the center of her forehead and throw the paper towels away.

"You've always been gentle with me."

"You deserve it." I wipe an escaped tear from underneath her eye.

"I don't know about that…" She looks off to the side. The oven beeps, alerting us it's warm. Eve turns to grab the pizza, but I place my palms on the counter, caging her in. Her eyes meet mine.

"Have you been beating yourself up this whole time?" I furrow my brows with concern. "Is that why you wanted to take things slow? Because you thought you didn't deserve to be with me?"

She swallows hard, looking at my shoulder, avoiding my gaze. "I don't."

"Eve—"

"You left because of *me*, Winter." She points at her chest.

"Do you want me to be upset with you?"

"No–yes–I don't know." She shrugs, rubbing her hand along the back of her neck. "I think you're forgiving me too easily. You'd already forgiven me before we saw each other again that first time at Fireside. I should be groveling or something. Begging for your forgiveness and all you've given me is… love."

"I mean… if you want to get on your knees and beg, who am I to stop—"

"Winter!" She shoves at my chest.

I catch her wrist, holding onto her hand, intertwining our fingers. "It wasn't just you. Yes, the way things were going between us was *a* reason but it wasn't *the* reason. I'd just lost Dad, was severely depressed, my family was falling apart, I was expected to run a company only weeks after his death – everyone needed something from me. I felt suffocated. It'd be unfair, and too easy, to place the blame on you."

"I'm sorry I wasn't there for you even though I was right beside you." She rubs her thumb against the back of my hand.

"You tried to be there. In your own way."

Eve did her best at the time. Just like I did. No one can say for sure what they would've done in our situation because everyone interprets the same experience differently. At the time, *we* did our best.

"Yeah… I guess you're right."

"I am right because I loved you then, like I love you now, and always will."

"I love you too." She presses a soft kiss to my lips, pulling away with a smile, resting her forehead against mine. "I was so pissed when I saw you at Fireside and every emotion came rushing back as if no time had passed."

I chuckle, giving her another kiss.

"That's when I realized I didn't have a clue of the depth of the love I have for you. And I doubt I'll ever discover it. So all I can do, and want to do, is keep loving you."

Wrapping my hand around the back of her neck, I bring my lips to hers, kissing her slow. Eve has always been the only woman for me. I've known it since I met her at that Christmas party, I knew it when I left, and I know now it will always be her. Eve loops her arms around my neck, making her body flush against mine. She moans desperately into my mouth when she wraps her leg around my waist and feels my reaction to her touch. The oven beeps again, invading the tension building between us.

"That damn pizza." She pulls away. "Should we eat first?"

"Yes." I palm her ass, squeezing it, and then smack it. She lets out a mix of a yelp and a giggle. "Because I'm kidnapping you and keeping you in my bed all weekend. I hope you didn't have any plans."

"You're my only plan." She kisses me again.

26

EVE

RUBBING MY EYES, I pad through Winter's house, wearing his t-shirt, trying to remember where I left my phone Friday afternoon when I got here. I'm not sure what time it is. But judging by the way the sun is assaulting my eyes through the windows, it's still early. All I know is it's Monday, and I spent the entire weekend with the man I'll forever be hopelessly in love with. I'd spend today with him too if Hope's Village Community Day wasn't happening this week. Despite my meticulous planning, there's still a lot to be done and confirm before Friday.

I find my phone sitting on the spotless kitchen counter. My cheeks warm with embarrassment, realizing someone probably heard me moaning Winter's name while they were cleaning and I was getting railed. I cautiously look around, feeling a small bit of relief that we seem to be the only ones here this morning. Being too loud was the least of my worries this weekend. Actually, I didn't have a single worry.

It was me and Winter. In our own world. No TV. No phones. Just us. We made love, fucked, talked, slept, ate, and thoroughly enjoyed each other's company. Swiping my phone off the counter, I head back up to his room. I check the time to see it's half past five and that I have missed calls and texts. I didn't tell anyone where I was going because I didn't think I'd be with Winter all weekend.

Reaching his room, I shut the door behind me, and climb in bed beside him. Winter pulls me closer until my head is resting on his chest with his arm wrapped tightly around me. He kisses the top of my head and then his breathing slows again as he drifts off to sleep. I lie still, basking in this love-soaked moment. A moment I never thought I'd have again. Afraid if I move it will fade away like a dream does when I wake. I press my ear to his chest, listening for his heartbeat and interlace my fingers with his, grounding myself.

This is real. I close my eyes, feeling tears pool in the corners of them. Being next to him isn't enough. I sling my leg across his middle, sliding on top, and press my chest to his, resting my head in the crook of his neck. Winter wraps his arms around me, holding me tight.

"What's on your mind, Dove?" he rumbles, his voice deep, gravelly, and comforting.

"Nothing."

"It's too early to be lying."

I smile against his neck. "Nothing's wrong. I'm happy. Unbelievably happy... I hope all this is real."

He pinches my ass, making me yelp. "Not a dream, Sweetheart."

I bite his neck in retaliation.

"You trying to start something?"

Instead of responding verbally, I bite him harder.

I'm on my back with my hands pinned above my head before I can blink. I become acutely aware of the tingling between my thighs. Winter may have the upper hand, but I'm still going to talk my shit.

"Is this supposed to be intimidating?" I look up at him.

"No." He trails his other hand over my body. "I want you soft and wet for me."

Sliding his hand under my shirt, he cups my breast, kneading it. "Just like you are now."

He teases my nipple, making an involuntary moan slip from my lips. "But you love when I take control because your only expectation is to come for me like you're about to do." Winter wraps his hand around my throat.

"What's your job, Dove?" He pulls my shirt up, giving himself a perfect view of me.

"To come." I spread my legs for him and he momentarily frees my wrists to line himself up with my center, keeping a firm hold on my throat.

"Where are you going to come?" He presses the tip into my wetness, closing his eyes as he does. When he opens them again, his blazing focus is on me.

"On your dick."

He groans, hooking my legs over shoulders. "Good girl." Winter slams into me, making my eyes roll back in my head and my hips buck to meet his thrust. "Too much?"

I shake my head "no" as much as his hand will allow. He leans forward, pressing a kiss to my lips. When he sits up again, he plunges into me.

Sometimes I want slow and sensual. Right now, I want him to fuck me like he hates me. And he does. His thrusts are deep and relentless. The pressure of his hand around my throat heightens the pleasure of his strokes. I let my knees fall open, welcoming every inch of him.

"You look perfect taking all of me." He watches his length slide in and out. "I want to go deeper."

Deeper? As if I wasn't already filled to the brim with pleasure, he releases my throat and pulls out, grabbing my leg, and flips me onto my belly. His strong hands grip my hips, pulling them up, putting me on my knees. Winter plunges into me from behind, and I cry out.

"Oh, God..." I sound needy as fuck but couldn't care less.

A deep chuckle rumbles in his chest. "No, baby. Just me. Say my fucking name." He grabs my braids, wrapping them around his wrist, pulling me back toward him.

"What's," he buries himself inside me, "my," pulling out, he growls, "fucking," I grab the headboard as he slams into me, "name?" he commands. "Say it."

"Winter!" I moan his name.

Bringing his mouth to my ear, he wraps his free hand around my throat while the other holds my hair. "And who do you belong to?"

"You," I say desperately. "Always."

"Even your last breath belongs to me, Eve. Just like I belong to you."

Winter sinks into me. He slides his hand down my body, finding my clit, and massages it. I press my ass into him, spreading my legs further apart. He keeps my hair wrapped around his wrist, using it to guide me up and down his shaft. Each thrust of his hips brings me closer to my climax. The tingling starts in my toes, radiating through my body.

"I wanna drown, Eve," he whispers gruffly in my ear. "Give me your oceans. Come on this dick, Sweetheart."

My breath hitches when I feel myself falling over the ledge. I free fall into him, into us, giving him all of me. I slip under the tidal wave of release. Winter keeps the pressure on my clit, diving deep, riding the wave with me. Instead of giving in, I match his thrusts, throwing it back. He fucking moans for me, holding onto my hips like that will keep him from falling. Pressing my palms into the headboard, I bounce on him, making him topple over the edge, saying my name.

"S-Shit, Eve..." he hisses, palming my ass cheek.

I move my hips, taking all he has to give me. When I know he doesn't have a drop left, I slide off of him, slowly lowering myself onto the bed.

Winter lies beside me, pulling me into his arms, and presses a kiss to my shoulder. "What we have will always be real, Eve."

Winter insists on taking me to work this morning. I didn't have any work appropriate clothes at his place, so he came to mine to get ready with me. It took longer than usual because neither of us could keep our hands to ourselves. I watch him pull a pair of gray slacks over his thick, muscular thighs and have to momentarily leave the room to compose myself since apparently I'm feral. It's pointless. When I reenter my bedroom he's rolling up the sleeves of his button down, revealing the veins in his arms.

"Slut," I scoff. "Who wears gray slacks to the office?"

Winter lets out a belt of laughter. "You can't even see anything." He looks down at his crotch, shaking his leg, trying to make the very noticeable print disappear. "It's my dick, Eve. What do you want me to do?"

"Not wear gray slacks like you're unaware of the power held within the fabric."

"Okay, you're making it sound like if you unzip them it'll take you to Narnia."

"Close enough," I mutter, applying lipstick.

"No one is looking at my dick but you, Dove. And what? You think because your little ass hugging pencil skirt is past your knees it's appropriate?"

"It's not my fault you're insatiable." I pop the cap back onto my lipstick, blowing him a kiss in my vanity mirror's reflection.

Winter stands beside me, leaning forward so our faces are level in the mirror. "I'm gonna need you to write a reality check and remember who was on their knees this morning."

My mouth falls open and he presses a kiss to my cheek.

"We're gonna be late. Are you ready Miss Valentine?"

I glare at him a moment longer before freeing my braids from the bun they're in. "Yeah. Are you gonna buy me coffee?"

"Would I be your boyfriend if I didn't?"

Butterflies explode in my chest, making my heart beat erratically. Winter's *mine* again.

Flapjack's Brew is packed with the morning rush. Instead of waiting in the insane drive-thru line, we head inside. I loop my arm through Winter's, resting my head against his shoulder while we wait. He's on his phone, answering emails, texts, and calls he ignored for me over the weekend. Things have become busier for him with his new role alongside Snow at North Star Toys. I'm proud of Winter for stepping into it even though I know it isn't easy. The King brothers were close with their dad, but Winter was practically his shadow. They were always together. Even when he died, Winter was there.

And now, over a decade later, he's stepping into a role he dreamed of with his dad. It's bittersweet. I've tried to be there for him as much as I can without hovering. I'm learning to sit with him when he needs it instead of trying to make things go away. Sometimes things never go away. They just become easier to bear when you have someone by your side who's a witness to what you're going through. So I let him know each day I'm here and that I see him.

Winter orders our coffees and we move to the side to wait for them. There's already someone at the counter, grabbing their drink. When they turn around, Noah is face to face with us. His eyes land on me and he has to wrap his other hand around his coffee to keep it from slipping from his fingertips.

"What's up, man?" Winter asks. Not missing a beat.

Noah's eyes dip to our intertwined hands. He nods his head in my direction. "Eve." And then brushes past us.

"Told you he'd regret what he said."

"Shut up." I nudge his arm, turning around to find Noah still watching me. He gives me a small smile, pressing his back to the door, and slips out of it. I let out a sigh, turning my attention back to Winter. "Am I bad person?"

"Noah Kincaid, possibly the sweetest person in Hope Valley, has you questioning if you're a bad person?"

"Winter…" I groan, feeling even worse. "I should've never dated him."

"Noah is a genuinely nice person, but he's not stupid. He knew, just like you did, that whatever you two were doing wasn't a real relationship. Noah accepted what you gave while you tolerated him."

I nibble my lip, knowing Winter is right. Noah's parting words were hurtful, but I'd feel spiteful too if I were him. I don't have much time to think about it when the barista calls Winter's name. He grabs our order, handing me my drink along with a cranberry orange scone. I take a bite of the warm pastry and close my eyes as the flavors melt onto my tongue.

"Let's go, Sweetheart. Snow wants to go over a few things with me before our first meeting of the day."

I see the dread in his eyes. "Do you need me to send you motivational messages to make the meeting better?"

"Anything from you makes everything better."

It's been near impossible to get any work done. My brain can't focus. Well... not on what I need it to. I keep thinking of Winter even though we've been texting all morning. I'd love to say it's the newness of our relationship. That would be a lie though. I've always been a little – a lot – obsessed with Winter. From the moment we met at the Christmas party, he was on my mind like a tattoo. I was drawn to everything about him. Looks, personality, his smile, the cadence of his voice, his cologne – *everything*. In my opinion, he's a good obsession to have.

Keeping true to my word, I'm sending Winter motivational messages. My version of motivational messages anyway. Since he wanted to talk shit about my "ass hugging" pencil skirt. I sent him a picture of my ass being hugged by said skirt. With the text attached saying:

Eve: To make your meeting easier. Or harder...
Winter: You're really trying to get me caught up in these gray slacks today?
Eve: You chose them. Not me.
Winter: I'll take you to Narnia later.

I cackle, making Haven peek into my office with curiosity. They make it seem like I never enjoy myself.

Eve: Please never refer to it as taking me to Narnia again.
Winter: It sounded better in my head.
Eve: Do you want to come with me to my parents' for lunch?
Winter: Yeah. I'll meet you there though. I have a packed morning.

Eve: Okay. See you in a few hours.

I set my phone aside when I hear a knock on the doorframe. Looking up, I'm met by Ilaria's large brown eyes and warm smile.

"Come in." I wave her in with my hand. "What's up?"

"I have a little down time." She slides into the chair in front of my desk. "Thought I'd see who has you looking like a ray of sunshine before noon."

"Am I not always a ray of—" Ilaria cuts me a look. "You make it seem like I never smile."

"You have a beautiful smile that I've never seen this much in the eight years I've known you."

To be honest, my cheeks hurt from the dopey, love-drunk look I've had on my face since Friday afternoon. I can't help but be happy when everything *finally* feels right.

"Winter and I are together again."

The pitch of Ilaria's squeal makes me plug my ears. She jumps up from her seat, rounding the desk, and wraps me in a tight hug. "I'm so happy for you two! I don't know why your crazy ass gave that man the run around for so long."

I curl my lip side eyeing her when she lets me go. She smooths her hands down my shoulders, patting them. "It doesn't matter now because you're together again."

Haven appears in the doorway. "Ilaria, your ten o' clock is here."

"Okay." She clasps her hands together, bouncing on the balls of her feet. "Eve and Winter are together again."

Haven lets out a squeal that rivals Ilaria's. "Will you two keep it down?" I hiss. "We don't want to scare the children."

"Where's Silas?" Haven peeks her head out into the hallway. "Silas." She whisper yells, disappearing down the hallway, reappearing with him in tow a few seconds later. "Guess what?"

Silas looks around the room, utterly confused. After a beat, he says, "I won the bet, didn't I?" A smile spreads across his face.

"A bet?!" I give them all a look of indignation.

"I was the only one who was in your favor by the way," Silas says. "You two both owe me ten dollars." He points his finger at Haven and Ilaria.

"What was the bet?" I gape at them.

"Ilaria and I thought you'd give him a little more hell before getting back with him," Haven says casually. "Silas said you're not an idiot and would be back with him sooner rather than later."

"Oh?" I pin my arms across my chest, leaning back in my chair. "So you two thought I was an idiot?"

"All love." Ilaria flashes me a smile, patting my shoulder. "But anyone, and I mean *anyone*, could tell you two were going to be together again. It was just a matter of when."

"I didn't know the three of you found my love life so interesting."

"Please! C'mon!" Haven exclaims. "Winter King is–*was*–one of Hope Valley's most eligible bachelors. And that million dollar bid. How could we not be interested?"

"Speaking of money, Rosaline owes me ten dollars, too," Silas says.

"The new therapist?" My eyes widen. "She's not even from here. How would she—"

"We caught her up to speed." Ilaria nods proudly. "We were all very invested."

I point my pen at her. "You need to be invested in your patients."

"Understood, boss." She gives me a salute paired with an unapologetic smile and disappears out the door.

"Out of my office. Both of you." I sweep my hands toward them.

"Alright, I'll let you get back to laughing with your boyfriend." Haven wisely slips out the door.

"Hey, Eve." Silas slips his hands in his pockets. "I'm happy for you. I know I'm quiet, but you're one of my dearest friends. You deserve all the love and happiness."

Silas rarely says anything. He talks more to his patients then he does to adults. I hold his gaze for a few breaths, feeling the lump in my throat and the sting in my eyes.

"Thanks, Silas."

He nods, giving me a smile before heading out the door.

I manage to get some work done before heading to my parent's. We hired a speech therapist a few weeks ago, and now we need an occupational therapist. I narrowed it down to a few potential candidates. Ilaria and Silas need to take a look at their resumes before I reach out and schedule interviews. As angry as I was with Winter for making that million dollar bid, I'm grateful. We're going to be able to provide the best possible services to children and families in Hope Valley. My chest swells with pride at the thought.

The smell of lime and cilantro hit my nose when I step into my parent's house. It's no surprise that I find Mom and Dad in the kitchen, cooking side by side. Now that they're both retired, they do practically everything together. I admire their love and relationship and am lucky I got to witness it growing up. Even if I did think their kissing was disgusting.

"Mom," I give her a kiss on the cheek. "Dad," I give him one too.

"Hey, honey." Mom smiles.

"Do you want to eat out in the garden?" It's a beautiful day.

"I'd love to. What did you guys make?"

"Some mini chicken quesadillas. You know Fox loves these. He'll stop by later."

"Thank you for still feeding all of us."

"Wouldn't have it any other way," Dad says, pulling some of the mini quesadillas off the skillet.

Jude appears in the kitchen. He stops, looking me up and down in disgust. I do the same to him. I'm not sure how long it goes on before he laughs, pulling me into a hug. "Busy weekend? I tried calling Friday night to tell you I got the house."

"You did?! That's amazing! Finally moving out of your parents' place. I'm proud of you."

He glares at me before the corners of his lips turn up. "Thanks. Me too. I can finally date again."

"Telling women you live with mommy and daddy wasn't working for you?"

"Anyways!" Jude announces loudly. "I was on my way out. Aspen is going with me to get some things for my place."

"That's sweet of her..." I've been so wrapped up in my own shit, I haven't checked in with the girls like I normally do. I wonder if she and Jude—

"We're not dating. We're not anything. Just friends."

"I didn't say anything."

"I saw those rusty ass wheels turning in your giant noggin."

I punch his arm.

He groans, holding his shoulder. "I was kidding. Damn. You've been working out?" He squeezes my arm.

"With Winter a couple of times a week."

"What about Winter, honey?" Mom perks up at the sound of his name.

"Nothing, Mom. We've just been working out together."

"He always has taken such good care of you."

"A really nice man," my dad adds.

"Except for when he—" Jude begins and swallows his words when I cut him with a look.

"If you want me to stay out of your business, I suggest you stay out of mine."

He purses his lips, pulling me into a hug. "Love you, dear sister."

"Uh huh. Have fun with Aspen."

He presses a kiss to my cheek, leaving me alone with my parents.

"It's ready, Bug." Dad holds a platter of mini quesadillas in one hand and guacamole in the other.

I follow them into the backyard, grabbing the cups and plates off the counter. Mom carries a pitcher of freshly made strawberry lemonade. I'd probably starve if it weren't for my parents still cooking for us. There's nothing like a home cooked meal made with love by your parents. They set the quesadillas, guacamole, and lemonade onto the table. I set the table while they take their seats. My phone buzzes in my purse that's slung across my body. Taking a seat beside Mom, I check to see who text me.

Winter: I'm here.
Eve: We're in the garden. Use the side gate.

Winter appears soon after he reads my text. Looking at Winter is akin to someone squeezing my lungs. Breathe. I remind myself. He looks perfectly disheveled with his top few buttons undone and his relaxed demeanor. Getting up from my seat, he wraps his arm around my waist as I press a kiss to his lips.

"Dove..." he mutters against my temple. Winter leans down giving a very shocked Mom a kiss on the cheek. "Vivienne." Dad stands, giving him a bear hug, clapping him on the back. "Cole."

"Son," Dad takes his seat again, "you can always call us Mom and Dad. Glad you can join us for lunch."

Mom is staring between Winter and I as though she's witnessing something so beautiful she doesn't want to utter a single word and ruin the moment. She presses her palms together, bringing them to her mouth, looking like she's saying a silent prayer of thanks. Next time she tells me I'm being dramatic – I'm going to tell her to look in the mirror again. Her eyes gleam, resting on me.

"You're Winter's Eve again?"

Memories of our engagement party flood my mind. Since he proposed close to Christmas time, the theme was "Winter's Eve". Our parents, specifically our moms, spared no expense. It was a night to remember. I still consider as one of the best nights of my life.

I look at Winter, grabbing his hand, threading my fingers through his. "I've always been his."

27

EVE

HOPE'S VILLAGE COMMUNITY DAY lands on the first Friday of summer break. My worst fear was that no one would show up. It's now shifted to not having enough water and food for everyone. It feels like everyone in the Valley is here. Today also decided to be our introduction to summer weather, creeping close to the hundreds. With all the activities, and cooling stations, I don't think anyone is noticing the heat. It's been non-stop since the event started at noon.

It's been reassuring to see the community pull together to make this day possible. The local pediatric dental clinic is here, offering free fluoride treatments, Flapjack's Brew is providing drinks, and Fireside is making mouthwatering barbecue. It's like a mini carnival with all the bounce houses, games, and entertainment.

Ilaria and Silas stand on either side of me. "You've done good, Eve." Ilaria wraps her arm around my shoulders.

"I hope you're proud and not nitpicking." Silas nudges my arm.

Becoming a doctor was a dream of mine since I was a kid. I remember lining up my stuffed animals, pretending they were sick, and taking care of them with brightly colored band-aids, homemade concoctions, and a lot of love. Everything I did academically was with my future career in medicine in mind. When I finally made it through pre-med, I applied to some colleges back East, a few on the West coast, and to the medical school here. I was crushed when the first letters I received were rejection letters. It made me question whether a path in medicine was for me, until I got an acceptance letter from Hope Valley University of Health Sciences. I was ecstatic. I still remember celebrating with Winter after opening up that letter.

A dream was coming true at the same time my life was about to come apart at the seams. Everything unraveled when Winter left. Me, my mental health, school... I lost my job and moved back in with my parents. Everything piled on, weighing me down until I couldn't breathe. I was in med school for a year before I dropped out and let myself drown for a little while.

Eventually, I went back to school, taking a few classes to see how I felt. That's when I met Elle. Things were slowly looking up again. I got a job as a receptionist at a doctor's office, thinking I'd eventually return to medical school one day. Instead, I became the office manager after working there for a couple of years when the previous manager retired. They told me I was the perfect candidate given my medical background and were willing to pay for additional classes to help me be successful. It put me on a path to where I am now, standing between Ilaria and Silas after opening our very own clinic. While it isn't what I had planned, I love it. I enjoy being behind the scenes and creating a facility that provides the best care with compassionate doctors.

"Not today." I wrap my arms around them. "I'm proud of what we've built."

"You've built," Ilaria corrects. "Silas and I threw the idea out there and you ran with it."

"We wouldn't have our own practice without you, Eve. Take your flowers."

"Alright." I squeeze both of them. "If you–"

"Speaking of flowers…" Ilaria says.

Winter's presence is commanding without having to announce himself. My eyes land on him as he weaves his way through the crowd, holding a large bouquet of flowers wrapped in burlap, tied with a green silk ribbon. It feels like a movie where everything else fades away and it's just me and him despite all the commotion going on around us.

Reaching me, he slides his hand around the back of my neck, bringing his lips to mine. "Sorry I'm late."

"You're here. That's all that matters. Thank you for making time for me."

"Always." He hands me the bouquet of daisies, roses, and baby's breath. After giving me all his attention, he links his fingers with mine, saying hi to Ilaria and Silas. "How's the event gone so far?"

"Amazing," Silas says.

"Couldn't have done it without our Eve." Ilaria wraps me in a half hug, giving me another squeeze.

"She's pretty damn amazing," Winter agrees, making me melt under his praise.

"We're gonna go do some rounds. Make sure everything's running smoothly." Silas nudges Ilaria's arm. "We'll catch up later," he says, leaving us alone with Ilaria walking in step with him.

"I need to get these in some water. They'll die in this heat."

I lead the way into the clinic, letting out a sigh of relief when the cool air hits my skin. Stopping in the break room, I grab a vase from a bouquet of flowers my parents got me when Hope's Village first opened, filling it with water. I carry it into my office and set the flowers in it. I'll be taking them home with me later this evening anyway. Turning around to face Winter, he's drawing the blinds. My heart rate quickens, knowing what time it is.

"Can I steal you for a bit?" He shuts the door, locking it.

"You can steal me for forever if you want."

"Forever?" He stands in front of me, kissing my neck.

"Yes. Forever."

"Mmm..." Winter lets out a deep, throaty moan pressing his body into mine, guiding us to the piece of wall between the door and window. "Then, now, and always."

I crash into him, scaling up his body, wrapping my legs around his waist. He holds me up, pressing me against the wall. Winter bites my bottom lip, soothing it with a kiss before dipping his tongue into my mouth.

"Why are you wearing jeans today?" He tugs at the waist, unfastening the button.

"I didn't realize you'd be needing easy access."

"I always want you wrapped around me." Peeling off the jeans, he steps back, admiring the lingerie I'm in. "No..." He shakes head, plucking up one of the dainty straps hugging my hip, making it snap against my skin. "You're wearing these for me."

"*I'm* all for you."

Winter hooks his thumbs in the straps of my panties, sliding them off, clutching them in his hand. His blazing basalt eyes lock onto mine.

"You know you have to be quiet, right?"

Anticipation ricochets through my body when he grazes his fingertips against my skin.

"How do you plan on keeping me quiet?"

Placing his hand on my hip, he tugs me closer. "For the sake of not traumatizing the community, you'll need something to silence the moans that are about to spill from those lush lips of yours. And the only thing we have are..." he holds up my panties, letting them dangle from his fingertips, "these."

The excitement that ripples through me makes goosebumps pepper my skin. Winter understands my desire to be dominated. Past partners were either too worried about their own release or I didn't trust them enough to allow them to put their hand around my throat. With Winter, I open my mouth, waiting for him to slip the panties in.

"Always so eager to please me, Sweetheart." He unbuckles his belt, pulling down his pants and boxers just enough to grip his length in his hand, taking it out. I moan when he slides the tip along my wetness. "But I'll save these for the right moment."

Gripping my thighs, he hoists me up, pressing my back to the wall and entering me in one swift motion. I bite his shoulder, eliciting a growl from him. Winter hits the spot that sends pleasure through me with each thrust of hips.

"I wanna watch you play with it. Can you play with yourself for me?" His voice is gruff, borderline begging.

How can I not give him what he wants? He holds me up, maintaining the rhythm while I reach between us and give him what he needs. Letting my head drop back, Winter wraps his hand around my throat, applying just the right pressure. Just enough to heighten the pleasure pulsing through me. I wrap my legs tighter around him when my body tingles on the verge of release, welcoming each thrust.

"Winter..."

"Yes, Sweetheart?" He grips my thighs tighter, going deeper.

"I'm coming..." My body tenses, tightening around him, before letting go. A sharp cry spills from my lips before Winter stifles it stuffing the panties in my mouth. I bite them as the pleasure overwhelms me.

"Good girl, come for me."

I shatter for him. My eyes roll back, sliding shut, and Winter grips my thighs tighter to keep me from slipping. This is the first time we've ever done this, and at the height of my climax, I hope it isn't the last. My muffled cries fill my office. Winter hooks his arms under my legs, spreading me further. I grip his shoulders, needing something to hold onto.

"You're fucking perfect," he groans. And as if he needs to prove his point—he comes.

I clasp my hands around the back of his neck, moving my hips to ride his release, feeling him spill into me. He shudders, moaning. Winter's moans are my kryptonite. I move my hips until I'm sure he has nothing left to give me. Winter keeps me pinned against the wall, resting his head in the crook of my neck, catching his breath. I keep my arms and legs wrapped around him.

After a moment, he pulls away, looking at me with the panties still in my mouth. Winter cups my cheek, swiping his thumb across my lip. He gently sets me on my feet, pulling the panties free, replacing them with his lips, sliding his tongue into my mouth. We kiss until we hear movement outside my office door. I pull away first.

"I have to get back out there."

He grabs Kleenex off my desk, cleaning me up, tossing them in the trash when he's done. I reach for my panties, and he hides them behind his back.

"These are mine, Sweetheart."

I gape at him.

"Keep your mouth open like that and I'll shove them back in there and bend you over that desk." He nods toward it.

Grabbing his chin, I kiss him, sucking his bottom lip into my mouth, nipping at it with my teeth. "Promise?" I mutter against his lips.

"Put your jeans on before I really do steal you for the rest of the day."

"Winter, do you know how uncomfortable it is to wear jeans with no panties?"

"No." He pulls his pants up, fastening his belt, with them still clutched in his hand. "But I imagine you're about to find out."

"Win Win..." I whine, standing with my ass out. "Give me my—"

"You're definitely not getting them back now."

"If I didn't find this sexy—"

"But you do." He hands me my jeans.

I snatch them from his hand while he leans against my desk, crossing his ankles, watching me pull them on. He kneels, helping me into my sneakers, and ties them for me. Straightening up, he holds my gaze, sliding my panties into the breast pocket of his jacket, and patting it.

"Thank you for trusting me." He slides a braid out of my face, tucking it behind my ear, pressing a kiss to my third eye.

"Unfortunately for me, there isn't a thing I wouldn't do for you."

"Anal?"

"Yeah..." I draw out the "h". "That's *still* a hard pass. I'll let you eat it though." Winter isn't even into anal. The time we tried it was because I asked and despite preparation and patience–it wasn't our thing. Apparently he hasn't forgotten the experience either.

He lets out a belt of laughter, wrapping his arm around my neck as we rejoin the event.

Noelle, Aspen, Snow, and North show up together, including my family. They brought more gifts and flowers for Ilaria, Silas, and me. Not only are we supported. We are deeply loved. This community day has given families an opportunity to get to know us in a way they wouldn't have through office visits. It's safe to say the event is a success. Over a thousand people came, and once we sort through new patient information, we'll be at a point where we have a waiting list until we can hire another pediatrician. The crowd has thinned, and some of the vendors are packing up or have left. Winter slips his hand in mine, pulling me along behind him.

"You made me a promise, Sweetheart." I think he's going to take me back to my office, but instead he pulls me toward the bounce houses. "Did you think I'd forget you said you'd jump with me?"

A smile spreads across my face. "No."

"Good, because—"

"Eve." A familiar voice says my name.

Turning in the direction of it, I stop in my tracks when my eyes land on Noah. "Hi..."

Winter turns around when I tug on his hand. Seeing who it is, he closes the distance between us, wrapping his arm around my waist.

"Noah. How are you, man?" I don't get how Winter is so unbothered.

"I'm okay. Thanks."

"Are you sure?" He doesn't look it. The breakup hit him hard. His mom did send me some nasty text messages. It felt good to finally tell her to go fuck herself and block her number.

"I just wanted to apologize to you, Eve. For the things I said. It wasn't right. And you too, Winter."

"Don't worry about it." Winter pats his shoulder. "You were angry. What I said still stands, though." He laughs but it isn't playful.

"No. I'd never—"

"Thanks, Noah." I give him a hug. He wraps his arms around me until Winter clears his throat. "I'm sorry for slapping you."

"I deserved it." Noah hangs his head.

"No." I gently touch his arm. "You didn't, and I'm sorry."

He smiles.

"Can I give you some advice?" I ask.

"Sure..." He looks skeptical.

"Whoever ends up being the one for you, keep your mom out of your love life. Call a friend, write in a journal, or talk to Henry. But for the sake of you and being happy, tell your mom as little as possible."

He chuckles, rubbing the back of his neck. "Yeah. I learned that with you."

"Good. You'll be alright, Noah. Take care of yourself."

"I will. Bye, Eve." He nods at Winter before leaving us alone again.

"Alright, Heartbreaker, let's go!" Winter continues on our path toward the bounce house.

"You're going to hell!"

Flipping me over his shoulder, making me laugh uncontrollably, he says, "I'm taking you with me."

28

EVE

ARRIVING AT WINTER'S PLACE, I let myself in like he told me to. He had to head back to the office to wrap up a few things before the weekend. We were thinking of getting together with everyone at Fireside. Instead we decided to have a chill night at home. I'm grateful for the success of the community day, and now I'm ready to relax. Setting my keys on the counter, I pull my phone out of my purse to text Winter.

Eve: Home.

Winter: I'll be joining you in an hour or so.

Eve: X-File marathon?

Winter: Sure thing, Scully.

Winter: Do you want me to pick something up to eat?

Eve: Yes! Surprise me. I'm going to take a soak in your big ass tub.

Winter: It'll cost you a nude.

Eve: You're charging me?! The love of your life! The woman of your dreams!

Winter: You can be all those things and still show me your titties.

Eve: You already have my panties. What more do you want?

Fixing my bag on my shoulder, I climb the stairs to his room, toss my stuff on the chaise, and kick off my shoes.

Winter: Every fucking thing Eve. Then, now, and always.

Staring at the text, his words make my heart thrum. Every day since we chose each other again, I've wondered if I'm living in a waking dream. He loves me deep, even when I'm not sure I deserve it. The only thing I can do is admit my faults, show up for him–us–and choose him every single day. It's been a long time since I've felt calmness within myself. My life was in order, but my heart wasn't. The person who shattered my heart is the only one who could mend it. Despite trying to fight it, I knew I wouldn't feel whole again until Winter put the piece he took back into place, his love being the medicine.

Turning on the water for the tub, I strip out of my clothes. Winter and I can fit in it comfortably without getting water everywhere. I love filling it up with scalding water, salts, and soaps and sinking into it up to my neck. Winter likes the water to be lukewarm because he's "not trying to boil". Is there any other way to take a bath though? After pouring in all the stuff that smells good, I take the picture for Winter. Being petty, I cover my nipples with my forearm and fingertips, sticking my tongue out with my mouth wide open.

Winter: Teasing me?
Eve: Never.
Winter: Wait till I get home.
Eve: Either way the situation works in my favor. See you in a bit.

Connecting my phone to the speaker, I turn on some music, and slowly slip into the water, stretching out my arms and legs. Once the line of bubbles reaches my neck, I turn off the water, closing my eyes, and soak. Every thought leaves my brain, relaxing into the bath.

I'm not sure how much time has passed, waking with a jolt when water goes up my nostrils. Sitting upright, coughing and sputtering, I grab for a towel, knocking the speaker into the water. Thankfully it's waterproof. I set it upright and flip the drain for the tub as though it did something to me.

Annoyed with myself for nearly drowning, I stand, wash myself off, and get out of the tub before I kill myself. Checking the time, Winter should be home anytime now. I pad into his room, finish drying off, and apply some lotion before putting on my clothes. Oversized sweats with a t-shirt is my favorite cozy clothes combination. I pull the Twisted Vines shirt over my breasts and stomach, pulling my braids out of the neck. The shirt has sentimental value now.

Climbing onto Winter's bed, I bury myself under the comforter, sending him a text.

Eve: Chicken fettuccine alfredo sounds good.
Winter: LOL that was the plan. I'm leaving in 5 minutes.
Eve: And one of their cucumber lemonades with a dash of tajin.
Eve: Oh and the peanut butter cheesecake.
Winter: Anything else your highness?
Eve: That will be all peasant.
Winter: I got just the thing to wash your mouth out with.
Eve: Please, sir. I am a lady.
Winter: Of the night?

"Of the night..." I mutter to myself, rereading his text, gasping when it clicks.

Eve: You are so disrespectful!
Winter: I noticed there's no denial on your part.
Eve: Get me my food.
Winter: LOL see you soon.

Exiting out of our texts, I open up my reading app to dive into a romance book that Elle recommended. I make myself comfortable. A little too comfortable. After a few chapters, my eyes feel heavy again. I'm fighting to keep them open. While today was fun, it was busy. I'm more exhausted than I thought.

Waking up, I'm confused. My phone is resting on my neck, and it's dark outside. Winter should be home by now. Why wouldn't he have woken me up? Pulling the blankets back, I grab my phone and head downstairs. When I get to the bottom, it's dark aside from the light on in the kitchen. Looking at the time, Winter should've been home hours ago. It looks like he hasn't been home at all. I check our texts again. Still the same one he last sent and no missed calls. Maybe he's with Snow and North? I send him a text.

Eve: Hey. I fell asleep. Did you already come home?

I call his phone. It rings and rings, eventually going to voicemail. Hanging up, I immediately try again. And again. And again. Getting his voicemail every time. My panic simmers. I take a deep breath. This isn't happening again. He wouldn't do this to me. Not again. Not now. I pace the kitchen, chewing on my nail, trying again. Voicemail.

"Shit," I mutter. "Don't panic, Eve. He wouldn't leave you." *Or would he?* A little voice whispers in the back of my mind. Noah did say he'd do it again. That's why his words hurt so much because Winter leaving again is a very real possibility. One I haven't wanted to voice out of fear it may come true. A lot of good that's done me. I take another deep breath, calling Noelle.

"Hey, babe."

"Hi." My voice doesn't sound like my own.

"Are you okay?"

"Yeah, yeah. I'm fine." I sound a little more convincing. "What are you and Snow doing tonight?" Despite the panic gripping my throat, I try to sound casual. I don't want to sound crazy for nothing.

"He got home a little while ago. We'll probably just hang out at home. North and Aspen just left to go meet up with some friends. What about you guys?"

"We're just gonna hang out here. Watch some X-Files."

"Oooo! Spooky Dick Mulder!"

"Who has spooky dick?" I hear Snow ask in the background.

Even though my stomach is in knots, I laugh.

"Mulder from X-Files." Elle says matter-of-factly.

"How would you know?" he asks. "And why would you want spooky dick? Is that a kink?"

Noelle lets out an exasperated sigh. "I can just tell. Use my imagination. Have you seen the X-Files? They call him Spooky Mulder, but he's always getting play. So his dick probably makes you levitate or – you know what? Mind your business. This is between me, Eve, and Mulder. Anyways, babe."

"Thanks Elle." Hearing her antics eases the worry a little. "And thanks for coming today."

"I'm so damn proud of you, Eve. I love you."

"Love you too." Tears sting my eyes. I squeeze my eyes shut, refusing to cry. "I won't keep you from Snow. Enjoy your night. I'll talk to you tomorrow."

"I'm not sure if it'll be enjoyable now that he's side eyeing me over the spooky dick comment. If it's any consolation, yours makes me levitate too."

Snow mumbles something inaudible in the background. It must've been dirty, the way she's giggling.

"Text me later. Love you." She hangs up.

Resting my elbows on the marble countertop, I cradle my head in my hands, taking a few calming breaths. Winter definitely isn't there or with North. Where the fuck could he be?

"You're overreacting. You're overreacting. You're overreacting," I repeat as if saying it will make the anxiety subside.

I try Winter's phone again. Still no answer. I send him another text.

Eve: Can you at least let me know you're okay?

The knots in my stomach tie themselves tighter, making me feel sick. I rush to the sink, dry heaving until my vision becomes blurry and I can't breathe. Leaning over the sink, I gasp for air. Once the feeling subsides, I make my way back upstairs, trying Winter's phone again. There has to be a reasonable explanation as to why he's not home nor answering calls and texts.

There has to be because I refuse to believe history is repeating itself. Even if the little voice in the back of my head is whispering *I told you so.*

29
WINTER

THIS WEEK HAS BEEN less stressful as I settle into my new title as COO of North Star Toys. When Mom comes back in a few weeks, we'll have a celebration party. By that time, it'll be a little over a month since I stepped into the role. For now, the only thing on my mind is going home and spending the weekend with Eve. I was so proud of her today. When I found out she didn't finish med school, I felt a lot of guilt. Forgiving myself doesn't mean I'm absolved of regret. From the moment I met her, that was her dream. Then I left and fucked up both our lives. She's assured me it wasn't my fault. That she could've finished if she wanted to. Her words were sincere even though I struggled to believe them. Until today. The passion and happiness that lit up her eyes let me know she's exactly where she *wants* to be.

Walking out of the office, I feel around in my pockets for my phone, wanting to turn the ringer back on. I've had it on silent due to meetings. Untangling it from Eve's panties, I see Reign is calling. I quickly answer it, noticing I've already missed a call from him.

"Hey—"

"Winter?" His voice sounds strangled and scared.

My steps slow as I walk to my car. "Are you okay? Where are you?"

There's a brief pause, and I'm ready to say his name again when he speaks. "No. I didn't know who else to call and—"

"Are you at your house?"

"Yes." He sniffles.

"Do you want me to pick you up?"

"Please," he says, and it sounds like a plea.

"I'll be right there." I jog to my car, getting inside. "Do you want me to stay on the phone with you while I drive?"

"Yes."

My phone automatically connects to the car when I start it. Backing out, I ask, "Do you want to talk about it?"

His response is a cry. A cry that makes my heart constrict. It sounds desperate and hopeless. I've heard it before, coming from myself, my brothers, and mom. It's a cry of grief. The one you let out when you realize the nightmare is a reality. It grips you so tightly you feel like you'll never break free, everything pulling you under at once. My vision becomes blurry, and I swipe at my eyes, feeling his pain in each sob.

"I'm here. I'll be right there. I promise."

Reign cries the entire car ride. When I pull onto his street, he's sitting on the curb between his house and the neighbor's, holding his head in his hand. I stop, getting out. When he hears my footsteps, he looks up at me through his curtain of curls. I don't have a chance to get a good look at him before he launches himself at me. Reign holds onto me tightly.

"Hey." I wrap my arms around him. I smooth his hair back, but he refuses to look at me. "You're okay."

He's not, but I'll do everything to make sure he is. I hold him while he cries. Unsure of what else to do or say. I'm not sure there is anything I can do to make this situation better. His sobs slowly turn short gasps of air as his tight hold on me loosens. After a few minutes, he pulls away. That's when I see it. His eye is beginning to bruise and there's a cut on his cheek. He flinches when I reach for him. I take a step back balling my hands into fist.

"Reign, who hurt you?"

He won't look at me. "M-My grandma."

Turning away from him, so he can't see my anger, I run my hands down my face, taking a deep breath.

"She kicked me out."

"What?" I snap and he jumps. "I'm sorry." Holding my hands up, I squeeze my eyes shut, failing to calm myself down. "What do you mean she *kicked* you out?" I ask a little softer.

Reign shoves his hands into his pockets, anguish shadowing his features. He takes a deep breath, looking at me, before his eyes meet the ground again. "Ian wanted to go out this weekend..."

I can barely hear him so I take a step closer, feeling a small bit of relief when he doesn't flinch. Instead of asking questions, I wait for him.

Less than a minute later, the words pour out of him. "I asked her for money because Ian wanted to go to the movies and arcade. She said she didn't have it. She never has it. It's always next week or 'You're living here for free with no job, what more do you want?'. I didn't take that as an answer this time. I asked her about the money. Dad's money. The money we–*I*–get from his death. She said it goes to bills to keep the lights on and a roof over my ungrateful head.

"I'm not a fucking idiot though. She's at the casino too much for the money to be going to anything else. Dad used to get after her for spending all of her social security checks there. He took care of everything for us. Supported her and me. I asked her about gambling. She said I had no right–and maybe I didn't–but life has been hell without Dad, Winter."

Tears fill his eyes again as he looks at me.

"Even when I was angry with Dad, I couldn't be for long. But over the past few months, there's this storm," he places his hand on his chest, "this rage that has been building. It's not so much at him. It's at the situation. I know I'm not difficult, but grandma thinks I am, so for her– that's what I'll be. I told her I was going to get an inquiry about the money. See if it could be put in a trust for me or something. Anything so she couldn't get ahold of it. And she snapped. She smacked me."

"Smacked you? Is this the first time?"

He shakes his head, keeping his eyes on the ground. "No. She was spewing hateful shit. That I ruined Dad's life. If it wasn't for me, he'd still be alive and she wouldn't be stuck with me."

"Reign." I take a step toward him and he meets my gaze. "You know that's not true, right?"

He shrugs, looking away from me.

"I never met your Dad, but in the pictures I've seen, you were his world. If anything, you were the best thing to ever happen to him."

I hate that he's experiencing this. That his grandma is making him question his dad's love. I wish I could carry all of this for Reign.

"Yeah... maybe you're right. All I know is I can't be here anymore." He keeps his eyes on his sneakers. "I've got nowhere to go and—"

"You can stay with me," I blurt out with zero thought. I'm not sure if he can. I don't know what the protocol is for a situation like this. Whatever it is, I'll move heaven, hell, and mountains to make sure he's okay and keep my word. "If you want..."

"With you?" He smooths his hair out of his face, getting a better look at me, gauging to see if my words are sincere. "You're serious?"

"Yes." Despite being nervous–it feels right. "Let me make some phone calls first, okay?" I glance at his house to see a woman's face disappear behind the curtain. "Your grandma's still here?" My blood is back to boiling.

"Yeah."

"How long have you been out here?"

"A few hours."

The temperatures have only been climbing today, and she locked him outside in this heat. "A few—" My jaw ticks. I open the passenger door, starting my car, and turn the air conditioner on full blast. "Get in. I need to make a few calls."

Giving me a skeptical look, he glances at his house before climbing in. "I tried to get my stuff, but she won't let me."

"Don't worry about that. She'll let me." I shut the door, pull my phone out, and call Snow.

"What's up, bro?"

I lean against the front of my car with my back to Reign. If he thinks Snow is bad when he's angry—I'm worse. "I'm going to commit murder. I hope you have bail money."

"Uh... I do, but is there another route this situation can take? Where are you?" I can hear he's in his car. He hasn't made it home from work yet either.

"Reign's house. And it's taking everything in me to not bury his grandma in the backyard." She peeks out of the curtain again as if she feels my menacing mood.

"I need to know what happened because it's going to be difficult to get you off a murder charge."

I tell him everything that Reign told me about the money, verbal, and physical abuse.

"Jesus Christ..." He mutters when I finish talking. "I shouldn't encourage murder, right?"

"One of us has to be the voice of reason. I was hoping it'd be you."

"I'm kidding. Sorta. Let me call Saint. I'm not sure if he's on duty today, but if he's not, he'll send someone else so you can go in and get Reign's things. You need to call Hudson and make sure it's okay that you take him. I'm sure he's more familiar with situations like this and will know what's best."

"I'm not leaving him here, Snow. I told him he could come with me already. I can't do that to him."

"I know. I know. We'll figure this out together, alright?"

"Okay." I take a deep breath.

"Do not go in that house without Saint. We need this to be as clean as possible for Reign."

"For the sake of Reign, I won't do anything stupid."

"Okay, I'll hit you back. Call Hudson. Oh, and text me Reign's address."

Before calling Hudson, I check on Reign. He's sitting with his head resting on the window, staring at his house.

Opening the door, I say, "Give me a few more minutes, okay?"

He nods, not saying a word or looking at me. I close the door, sending a text with the address to Snow and call Hudson, explaining the situation.

"This is terrible," Hudson says. He sounds how I feel. "A few things need to happen. A police report needs to be filed. It's late in the day, but you can still apply for emergency custody given the circumstances. That's only a temporary order. There will be a hearing date given. Are you wanting to become his legal guardian?"

I look back at Reign who's still staring off into nothing. "Yes. If he'll have me. I don't know what the fuck I'm doing but I'll do my best."

"That's all he needs. I know a few family lawyers if you need a contact."

"Thank you, but we have a team. No offense. There's no room for error."

"I was hoping you'd say that. I've seen too many cases where kids are put back into broken homes because the family can't afford proper legal representation."

My phone beeps alerting me of another call. "That won't be the case with Reign." *Hopefully.* "Thank you for your help, Hudson. My brother is calling me back. I'll keep you posted."

I switch over. "Tell me something good."

"Saint is on his way with backup. You know he's always extra."

"I do." Saint thinks his life is a movie.

"He said he's about thirty minutes away. Did you want me to meet you there?"

"Nah. We'll be okay. I've calmed down little."

"Good. Saint will be there. All of this will be handled. Did you talk to Hudson?"

I tell him what Hudson said, peeking over my shoulder to see what Reign's doing before I say my next words. He's looking at his phone. I turn back around, taking a breath. "Do you think I'm crazy for wanting to be his guardian?"

"No. I don't. Is this what you want?"

"This isn't something I realized I wanted until today. Just now. I hope he doesn't think I'm trying to replace his dad."

"You could never do that. I doubt he'll see it that way."

"Reign deserves to feel loved and whole."

"He does," Snow agrees. "And it won't just be you. He's got all of us."

"Yeah... you're right."

"We'll support whatever you decide to do. Plus you know Mom will love that boy down."

"She'll take him herself." I chuckle. When she met Reign, she didn't waste any time talking about him visiting her in Sapphire Shores.

"Hell yeah she will. It'll be good for him."

"He was just coming out of his shell." I try to keep my voice even, but it cracks anyway. "And then this shit happens to him. Has been happening to him. I just—"

"Winter. Not everything is your fault. You respected his boundaries. Didn't force him to tell you anything. Why do you think you two get along so well? Because you're cool? That may be part of it, although I beg to differ, but you see and respect him without expecting him to be anything else but himself."

I'm silent for a few beats. "He deserves that."

"And you deserve to stop beating yourself up about shit. Sometimes things happen that were never in our control to begin with. That doesn't mean to let it go, it means you need to understand that you did your best. You are doing your best and it will never be perfect but it will always be enough for those who love you."

His words settle over me like a weighted blanket, quieting my guilt and fears. "Love you, Snow."

"Love you too. I'll get in touch with our legal team so you have one less thing to worry about."

"Thank you."

"Text me later if you feel up to it or need anything else."

"Will do."

We end the call. I let out a long, low sigh, moving my head side to side, making my neck crack. Turning around, Reign is still looking at his phone. When I slide into passenger seat, I see he's scrolling through photos of him and his dad. I sit with him in the silence for a minute.

"Reign..."

He presses the button on the side of his phone, making it go black, turning his attention to me.

"Unfortunately, I can't just take you away, and I can't go into that house–" I point at it "–like the terminator either."

He gives me a faint smile.

"We have to do this the right way if you really want me to take you away from this."

Reign scrubs his hands down his face. "I figured it wouldn't be easy..." He looks out the window. "Nothing has been."

"No, but I'll make it as easy as I possibly can."

"I'm tired. Not physically. Mentally. I've tried my best to not let the intrusive thoughts win, but sitting on that curb, I wondered what it'd be like to see my dad again. To just not be tired anymore. To be gone." His voice cracks and the cry returns.

I pull him toward me, wrapping him in a hug, hoping it'll hold him together a little longer until he feels okay again. Until he doesn't feel like slipping under.

"I got you," I repeat while he sobs.

After a few minutes, he pulls away, wiping his nose on his shirt. "What do we have to do?"

I tell him what Hudson said. "Our friend is a police officer. His name is Saint. He's on his way here to make the police report and to be with us when we go in there to get your stuff. Snow called our lawyers. They'll make sure we have everything we need for the hearing." I hesitate saying the last part, not sure how he'll react. "If you want me to be your legal guardian, I will be."

"Does that mean you'll be like my parent?"

"Yes... in a way. It's not like adoption where you'd take on my last name or anything. You'd be my responsibility. I'd take care of you and everything you need. I hope you understand I'd never try to replace your dad. I just thought—"

"Okay." He nods, considering my words.

"Okay?" I ask, hoping he'll elaborate.

"I think our dads put us in each other's lives." He looks up at the sky through the sunroof. "Maybe they bumped into each up there, or wherever they're at, and decided we had to meet because they knew we needed each other."

"You knew the mentorship was just as important to me as it was to you?"

"Yes." He nods. "I just knew that when you walked into the rec room everything was going to be okay. Even though right now it doesn't feel like it will be, but I trust you."

"Everything will be okay." A Hope Valley squad car passes by with two more trailing behind it. Saint parks in the driveway, blocking the grandma's car and the other two park at the end of the driveway. "I know this is scary, but I promise I'm here for you, okay?"

"I know." Reign gives me a smile that makes me hopeful.

Saint is making his way toward my car while the other two officers stand at the foot of the walkway.

"It's okay to get out if you want to." I open the door, getting out. "This will all be over soon."

Reign gets out, rounding the car, standing behind me. "Saint." He gives me a dap, pulling me into a brief hug. "Thank you for coming."

"Not a problem. Always happy to help you and your brothers out."

"This is Reign." I step aside.

"Hi Reign. I'm Officer Windlow." He holds out his hand and Reign shakes it. "Over there is Officer Palmer," Saint points to the guy on the left. "And the other, GI Joe looking motherfucker is Officer Wallace."

Reign chuckles.

"We're here to help and get some information. Once that's done, you'll be free to leave with Winter."

Saint turns his attention to me. "Snow said something about boxes so we brought a few."

"Thank you, Saint." I grab the boxes from the back. "Ready to get your stuff?"

Reign shakes his head. "I don't want to go in there with her."

I look at Saint and then at Reign. "Okay. I can get your stuff. Anything specific?"

"Everything. There's not much."

I feel the adrenaline kicking in. I'm not sure what we're going to walk into. He never invited me in, and I never asked. The first time I've seen his grandma was today through the window.

"We'll have Officer Wallace sit with you, is that okay?" Saint asks.

Reign nods. "Yes."

"Alright. Let's go."

I follow behind Saint, securing the boxes under my arm. He whistles at Officer Palmer and Wallace. They jog toward him. "Wallace, keep an eye on Reign."

He nods, standing beside my car like a personal bodyguard for Reign.

"Palmer, you're with me."

Reaching the door, Saint knocks on it. There's no response. Saint hooks his thumbs into his vest as if he has all the time in the world. He smiles at me, knocking again. A little harder than the last.

"Hope Valley PD." His voice is deep and commanding. Not one I'd want to hear on the other side of my door.

Eventually, we hear the sliding and clicking of locks. The door opens a crack and an eye appears in it. For a second, it reminds me of Reign's except hers are cold even if there are tears in them.

"Hello, Ma'am. I'm Officer Windlow, and this is Officer Palmer. We're here to collect the belongings of Reign DeLeon. And you are?"

"Amaya." Her voice sounds small.

"Are you his grandmother?"

"Yes. Where is he?" I have to keep from rolling my eyes when I know the woman has been watching us like a hawk through her window.

"He's in our custody now, Ma'am."

"I didn't do anything." She opens the door, revealing she's the same height as Reign and looks like a grandma who enjoys her weekends in Vegas.

"As of now, we are here to collect his belongings. The court—"

"The court?!" She shrieks loudly for sounding so small only seconds ago. "Ever since that boy's daddy died, he's been nothing but trouble. Always needing or wanting something. Not the least bit grateful for what he already has."

Saint nods. "I hear you ma'am; however, you are aware Reign is a child, correct?"

She raises her chin in the air.

"That means he *is* going to have needs and wants, which are your responsibility as his guardian."

She kicks the door the rest of the way open, making it hit the wall. "Come in, get his shit, and then get the hell out. I want nothing to do with you or that boy."

"Wise choice," Saint says with a smile.

She sneers at him, and it takes everything in me to not snuff the woman as I walk past her, following behind Saint with Palmer behind me.

"Down the hall. Second door on the right. Don't touch nothing else."

"So welcoming." Saint sighs like this is another casual day.

He opens the second door on the right. The room isn't very big, I can tell it's Reign's. There's art covering the walls. For a moment I stand in the center of the room because it's my first time ever seeing his work in person. He has a sketchbook with him all the time that he safeguards with his life, and the rest of his paintings he's never shown me. Reign's art is breathtaking. Bright colors and bold lines with a softness to it. It's him.

"Palmer, watch the crone."

He chuckles, leaving me and Saint alone.

"What are we packing?"

"All of it."

Between the two of us and how small the room is, it takes no time to grab all of Reign's things. I grab his paints, brushes, empty the dresser, closet, and look under his bed to find two boxes filled with what looks like his dad's belongings. Saint carefully takes the art of the walls, laying it in its own box. There's an easel in the corner that I didn't notice when we first entered. A medium sized canvas sits on it. Getting closer, I can tell it's a half finished portrait of his dad. I grab it and the easel.

"Palmer!" Saint shouts a little while later when he's packing even the curtains in a box. We left nothing behind. "Take these boxes out. Put them in Winter's car. We're ready to head out."

"Yes, sir." He nods, grabbing the first box off the mattress.

"Ready?" Saint asks me.

I look around the room one last time, seeing if I missed anything. "Yeah. I'm ready."

"Let's go."

Walking down the hall, I see pictures of Reign with his dad hanging. I look down the hallway, not seeing his grandma in sight, and grab every single one of them. His grandma is sitting in the kitchen, smoking a cigarette, looking annoyed.

"Tell that boy he's no longer welcome here. He's dead to me. Just like his daddy."

"You know..." I can't help myself, needing to say something. " I'm going to make sure that you regret the way you've treated Reign every moment, of every hour, of every single day for the rest of your miserable life."

She shrinks with every word.

"Just like how you tried to take his light, I'm going to take everything away from you until you're destitute. You won't have a pot to piss in by the time I'm done with you."

She tries to sound bigger than she is. "And who are you?"

"I'm Winter fucking King. Don't forget that name because I'm coming for your life."

Saint nods with a smile, continuing to the front door. Once we're out, it slams shut behind us.

"You just couldn't help but name drop, huh?" Saint asks.

I adjust the boxes in my hands. "You have to admit, I sound pretty fucking cool."

Reign doesn't speak during the ride home. We listen to music and sit in companionable silence. Pulling up to the gate of my house, the security guard waves me through. Reign has been to my house countless times, but he's never spent the night. I keep having to remind myself he's going to be staying with me... forever. Well, at least until he's ready to go off on his own. Even then, he'll always have a home with me.

Pulling into my garage, my heart drops when I see Eve's car. I was meant to be here hours ago. My only focus the past few hours has been Reign and making sure he's okay. After parking, I feel around in my pockets for my phone, remembering I never had a chance to take it off silent. Then when I went to pack Reign's stuff and sit with him while he gave his statement, I left it in the car. Where in the car though? Climbing out, I look on the seat and around it.

"What are you looking for?" Reign asks, standing beside me.

"My phone."

He points to the center console. "You left it in there."

"Thanks. C'mon. Eve is here." I'm wondering if I should tell him she's probably going to light my ass up right now. Looking at my phone with all the missed calls and texts from her, there ain't no probably. She *is* going to light my ass up.

"Oh... is she staying with you?"

"Yeah. Probably the weekend. Is that okay with you?"

"I'm sorry to ruin it."

I place my hand on his shoulder, making him look at me. "I'm not. I like having you around. I'm happy you're here."

"Me too." Reign gives me a genuine smile. "I can grab the boxes. I need a few minutes to just..." He lets out a breath.

"I get it. Take your time. I'll be right inside." Getting yelled at, I'm sure.

Hurrying inside, I find Eve sitting in the kitchen, drinking a glass of wine. She looks up when she hears my footsteps. Her brown eyes are swimming in tears. Fuck. It wasn't intentional, but I still feel guilty for leaving her wondering–*doubting*.

"I was so scared you left again." She visibly relaxes, letting out a deep sigh, swiping her hands over her eyes.

Her words settle on me like lead. "Sweetheart..."

She gets up from the bar stool, wrapping her arms around me, burying her face in my chest.

"I'm so sorry." I kiss the top of her head. "I didn't mean to worry you. I didn't think–there was– "

"Winter," Reign says from behind me. "What room did you want me to put the boxes in?"

Eve pulls away, looking up at me, and then peeks around my shoulder. "Reign?"

"Hi." His voice sounds uncertain. "Sorry to crash your weekend. I need to know where to put the boxes and then I'll be fine by myself."

Eve steps around me, taking cautious steps toward him. His curls are hanging in his face again. He's been getting regular haircuts with Cru, keeping it longer on the top. I'm pretty sure it's for Calliope's sake. Eve slowly raises her hand, gently sweeping the curls out of his eyes.

"Honey, are you okay?"

"Are you?" he asks, taking in her swollen, red eyes.

"I'm fine," she assures him.

Reign looks at me briefly before shifting his gaze to the floor. "No. But Winter says I will be, and I trust him."

"You will be," she says, briefly glancing at me. "Have you eaten? Do you want to eat with me? Winter can handle the boxes. I also know how to keep the bruising from a black eye minimal."

"You've," Reign points at her, "had a black eye before?" He cocks his head to the side, looking at her with disbelief.

"Yes," she says, bringing her hand back to her side.

It's my turn to look at her with curiosity.

"You did?" Reign's eyes widen. "How?"

"Let's just say some people will lie about being single, leaving you caught in the middle."

I want to call her a homewrecker, but hold my tongue. Instead, I try to hide my laughter and end up snorting instead. She cuts me a look that only makes me raise my brows with curiosity, wanting to hear how Eve found herself caught in the middle of a couple.

"Did they beat you up?" Reign asks.

"Me?" Eve scoffs. "Two things about me. I'm a sweetheart with a hell of a mean streak."

Mean streak is putting it lightly. I'm surprised she's only had one black eye. Eve is akin to a rabid dog when she's angry. I'd never tell her that to her face though.

"She got two good licks in before I taught her a lesson. But," she claps her hands together, "enough about that. Let's get your eye taken care of, then I'll make us some food while Winter grabs the boxes and helps you get settled into your room. I think the one just down the hall from Winter's will be perfect. You'll have your own balcony overlooking the garden. What do you think?"

Reign's face lights up for the first time all day. "I'd love that."

Eve wraps her arm around his shoulders, guiding him out of the kitchen. She looks over her shoulder at me.

I mouth, "Thank you."

Her reply is a dimpled smile as she mouths the words, "Love you."

30
WINTER

WATCHING EVE WITH REIGN were moments I didn't know I needed. They've been together countless times. Tonight is different though. I can see the same love I have for Reign in Eve's eyes as she cares for him, making him comfortable in an uncomfortable situation. It makes me fall deeper in love with her than I already am.

After Reign is settled, Eve and I head for bed. Now that things have slowed down, I feel the exhaustion settling in. I take a shower, turning off the lights, before climbing into bed beside her. She snuggles up to me, molding her body to mine, swinging her leg over my waist, and laying her arm across my chest.

"Eve, I'm sorry about—"

"I'm sorry for doubting you. Reign needed you to show up for him tonight and you did. That's what matters."

"You matter too." I rub my hand up and down her back.

"I know, but I can share."

I'm silent for a beat. "You know I'm not going anywhere, right? You tried to curb me for months and now look at us."

Eve stifles a laugh. "A lot of good that did me."

"You put up the good fight."

"I'm not sure you could call my efforts a fight, but thank you." She buries her face in the crook of my neck. "I'm not going to lie, I panicked.

Have you ever got this morbidly gratifying feeling when you think the other shoe drops? It hurts but you're also thinking 'I knew this shit was going to happen' and somehow you feel good about it happening?"

"A self-fulfilling prophecy…" I fill in.

"Yes."

"I think everyone does that," I say. "We expect the worse, get the worst, and then are gratified that we were right."

"Isn't that weird?"

I rub my thumb against her arm. "It's human. A very human experience. We're given the narrative to expect the worst with everything. It's like here's this really good thing, but don't get too comfortable because it'll go to shit soon."

"That's unfortunately true. Elle says I'll die holding my breath waiting for everything to be perfect."

A chuckle resonates in my chest. "From the moment I met you, I knew you were a perfectionist."

"How?"

"You're the only person I've met who has the posture and grace of a dancer without any formal training—"

"I—"

"Yeah, the six weeks you took ballet when you were four don't count. Besides, your mom told me the ballet school practically begged her to not bring you back after you bit that girl for stepping on your toes."

"I still say she did it on purpose. I was better than her, and she didn't like me." Her tone is haughty.

"It was a beginners ballet class…" I remind her, and she sucks her teeth. "Speaking of fighting, I had no idea you were a homewrecker!"

Eve covers her head with the blanket, cackling. "I'm not! That man wrecked his own home."

"How did you find yourself caught in the middle of a lover's quarrel?"

"I'm not going to tell you. You're going to talk so much shit." Her voice is muffled.

"Hold up." I pull the covers off her head. "Do I know him?"

Her silence is an answer and I can't help but laugh. If she doesn't want to tell me, it means it's someone we talked shit about together.

"Who was it? Tell me."

Rolling away from me, she lies on her back, covering her head with the blanket again. "Titus," she squeaks.

My eyes widen. "Williams?! The fucking douche bag whose daddy owns the car dealership?! Ohhh!" I let out a rumble of laughter. "I'm talking so much shit! Didn't you say his breath smells musty, and you fucked him?! I would've taken that shit to the grave, Sweetheart."

Titus Williams is an entitled prick for no reason. He's done nothing for himself except spend his dad's money. Titus was supposed to be the next big thing in the NFL. He had a full ride scholarship and was expected to be a first round draft pick. Until he got drunk the night of graduation, getting into a wreck that ended his career after suffering a neck injury. Surviving a wreck that nearly cost you your life would humble most. It gave Titus Williams a God complex.

"I was desperate!" she defends. "I'm not afraid to admit it, okay?"

"Wowww. I've been desperate before but not last person on earth desperate. I must know who molly whopped your ass too then!"

Eve cackles. "You have no concern for my safety."

"I know I don't have to worry about you. You've got hands. Who was the woman?"

"Connie..."

"Grey?! You are a homewrecker!"

"I am not! He said they had broken up and that she moved away. The latter was true, except they were in a long distance relationship. She came home, dragged me out of his bed while I was half awake, and punched me. I was livid because his dick was trash and I got hit for it. After I choked Connie within an inch of her life, I slapped the shit out of him too."

I laugh so hard, my stomach hurts. "Aye, let me tell you something."

"What?"

"I smashed Connie a few years ago knowing she was with Titus just to be an asshole."

Eve gasps, falling into a fit of laughter. "We ain't shit!"

"We definitely belong together."

"Real bad! You know they're having a baby, right? Her petty ass sent me an invite because she's friends with Ilaria."

"If it's coming up, we should go."

"I may entertain the idea just to see the look on their faces," she mutters.

I pull her toward me, wrapping my arm around her neck, and press a kiss to her temple. We lie in silence after our confessions. The reality of what happened with her panicking because she couldn't reach me and Reign's situation presses in on me now that the laughter has stopped. "Eve..."

"Yes?"

"Are you sure you're okay?"

"I'm okay, Winter." She kisses my neck, wrapping herself around me. "Even though I was panicking, I knew deep down that you weren't gone. Or maybe I just refused to believe you'd leave again. Either way, I'm okay. The question is are *you* okay?"

"I don't think I've had a chance to process it because I'm worried about Reign."

"Do you want to talk about it?"

I don't want to put Reign's business out there. At the same time, Eve is my person. She's going to be a part of my life and his now too. I tell her everything that happened today.

"Reign talked about committing suicide, Eve." My voice is strangled, trying to get around the lump in my throat. "That terrified me. I want him to feel whole, happy, and carefree. Not like he's in this world alone."

"And we'll give him exactly that."

"What if... the hearing doesn't go in our favor?"

"Winter, we have a lot of luxuries, but doubting who and what we love isn't one of them. Remember we were talking about the other shoe dropping earlier?"

"Yeah."

"What if everything works out? What if the hearing *does* go in our favor, we become his legal guardians, and everything falls into place? We need to think of the best possible outcome instead of assuming the worst. We have about another year and half with Reign. Instead of teaching him to expect the worst, like the world already has, we need to teach him to expect nothing but the best."

I needed to hear every word from her lips. Tipping her chin up, I kiss her as if I can drink them and they'll become a part of me. "All I heard was *we*, and that means everything."

"Us." She kisses me again. "Then, now, and always."

I pad down the hall to Reign's room, knocking lightly on the door.

"Come in." His voice is muffled.

Opening the door, you can't tell there's daylight outside with the light canceling curtains. I push the door open a little more to let the light filter in from the hallway. He's a heap on the bed, submerged in the sea of blankets. Paints are scattered all over the desk, and the easel is sitting beside it. He's made some progress on his dad's portrait.

"Eve and I are going to Flapjack's Brew... did you want to come with us?"

A beat of silence passes. "No, thank you."

"Do you want us to bring you back something?"

"I'm not hungry... thanks though." He pulls the blankets up higher.

I stare at the lump for a moment, torn between giving him space and not letting him slip further into the darkness he's currently lying in.

"Alright... well, if you change your mind, my phone's on. Call me if you need anything."

"Okay. Thanks, Winter."

Reign is always polite. I can't believe his grandma tried to claim he's difficult. I gently close the door. Heading downstairs, Eve looks at me hopefully with her bright brown eyes.

"What'd he say?"

"He's not hungry..."

"We can do breakfast here." She slips her bag off her shoulder, setting it on the coffee table.

"No. I think he needs some space."

She glances at the stairs, then at me. I can tell she's fighting the urge to try and fix this. I lick my lips to keep the smile off them.

"What?"

"Nothing." I hike my shoulder.

Eve bites her bottom lip, nibbling on it, looking at the stairs again. "*Maybeee* if we just—" She creeps toward the steps.

"Eve."

"Okay." She holds up her hands in surrender, stopping in her tracks. "Alright. We'll leave him be. For now." Grabbing her bag, she puts it on her shoulder. "But we need to try a little harder when we get back, okay? He needs food. Light. Air. Water."

My shoulders shake with laughter. "What is he? A plant?"

She rolls her eyes, turning away from me, heading toward the garage. "Get me out of this house before I march up those stairs and get him out of bed."

I follow behind her, with a smile on my face knowing full well she would.

Eve made me keep my phone on the table during breakfast with the ringer on high in case Reign called. He didn't. No matter how many times I assured Eve he's fine, she needed peace of mind that we'd be there if he needed us. Instead of heading straight home after breakfast, we go to the store. We don't really need anything. But if we go home, I'm not sure I can give Reign his space. And I know for damn sure Eve isn't capable. While his relationship with his grandma was tumultuous, she was all he had left. I can only imagine the blender of emotions he's sitting in right now. Especially knowing his mom is out there with a new family she adores.

Eve casually suggests we go to Target as if she's not about to go in on my wallet. A cart full of stuff she swears Reign needs, and six hundred dollars later we're back in the car. And somehow, we end up at the Cartier store. At this point I'm just along for the ride, funding whatever she puts in the bag.

"I just want to take a gander…" she says with a dimpled smile as I help her out of the car.

"A gander? So we won't need my wallet?"

"Oh, my love. Don't be reckless." Grabbing my hand, she pulls me along behind her. Eve doesn't *expect* me to buy anything for her because she *knows* I will.

A gander turns into earrings, necklace, and a ring. When we get in the car, I side eye the Cartier bag on her lap and the blinding smile on her face.

"What?" She gives me an innocent shrug of her shoulders. "You know I love a good stress shop. A little retail therapy." She gives me spirit fingers, wiggling them. Shaking my head with the corners of my mouth tipped up, I focus on the road. "Ooo, babe! Do you know where we should go?"

"Nah, but I imagine you're going to tell me."

"That I am!" She sweeps her braids over her shoulder, batting her lashes. "Urbane Bites. How could Reign resist a plate of chicken alfredo?"

Glancing at the clock, I see it's ten minutes to noon. "Finally, a good idea."

Sucking her teeth she glares at me, turning up the music.

Pulling into the garage, Eve grabs the food and her Cartier bag, leaving me to carry the boxes and bags from Target. I take it all to the front living room and then join her in the kitchen.

"I'll take his food up to him." I reach for the container.

She slaps my hand away. "Uh uh. Winter, I respect he needs space, but he also needs to leave that room. I'll get everything ready and meet you guys in the dining room."

Her tone leaves no room for protest. I know she's right. "Hey." I put my hand over hers, stopping her from pulling stuff out of the bags. Her eyes meet mine as I pull her into my arms. "Thank you for being here with me—*us*. I couldn't do this without you."

Eve's energy has help balanced out the heaviness of the circumstances. I could tell Reign enjoyed spending time with her last night. Not once did Eve ask him why he's here. She welcomed him and let him know he's home. She is home. My home.

"I love you." She wraps her arms around my neck, pulling me closer.

"Love you too." I close the distance between us, meeting her lips.

She deepens the kiss, slipping her tongue into my mouth, pressing her body closer to mine. I walk us backwards, until she bumps into the counter, and grabbing her thighs, I lift her onto it. She wraps her legs around my waist, and I groan when she scoots to the edge of the counter, pressing me flush against her. I slip my hand under her shirt, teasing her nipple through the thin, lacy fabric of her bra. Gripping her ass with my other hand, I pull her closer to me, applying pressure to her center, and she drops her head back letting out a pleased sigh. Sliding my hand up her back, I grip her hair, making her meet my lips again. I'm about to pull her shirt over her head when she leans away from me, leaving me kissing air, and then shoves at my chest, hopping off the counter.

Wiping her mouth, she says, "Reign," and peeks around me.

"The fuck?" Wrapping my hand around her throat, I pull her toward me, kissing her again, making her melt into me.

"Winter," she mutters against my lips. "Reign is—"

I draw back. "He has a girlfriend. I'm sure he knows what kissing is."

Looking at him over my shoulder, he takes a seat on a barstool.

"Afternoon." I nod. His eye looks considerably better than it did yesterday, although it's still noticeable.

He smiles, averting his gaze to the countertop where he's sitting on a barstool. "I do and good afternoon."

"See." I turn back to Eve, making my voice low so only she can hear. "Try to wipe my kiss off your mouth again. I'll make sure everyone in this neighborhood knows my name as it spills from those pretty lips."

Eve, being the other half of my soul, brings her hand up between us, swiping it across her mouth, challenging my words.

I chuckle low and smooth, whispering in her ear, "Bet, Sweetheart. Keep that same energy when I'm deep in you and you're struggling to keep quiet."

She shoves me away from her, wearing a pleased smile. "We brought home—"

I smack her ass so hard she whimpers trying not to yell... or moan knowing her.

"Food." I finish her sentence, nudging her out of the way while she rubs her ass.

Reign looks at me with a smile on his face. "You two are funny."

"May as well get used to us and our bullshit."

Eve smacks my arm. "Watch your mouth."

"Antics. Sorry." I roll my eyes, making Reign laugh. "Are you hungry?"

"Starving," he says, pulling his hair out of his face.

Eve takes over, gently nudging me out of the way to finish taking stuff out of the bags. "We got chicken alfredo from Urbane Bites. Did you sleep good?"

While they talk, I set the table. A feeling of comfort settles over me, knowing no matter what we're going to be okay.

♔

Sunday afternoon, Eve heads back to her place. She says it's to get some clean clothes, but I think it's to give me and Reign alone time. I haven't wanted to bring up yesterday because it's nice to see him enjoying himself in spite of it all. We're sitting in the living room, watching Baki.

Eve gives me a kiss before she leaves. "I'll be back in a little while." She ruffles Reign's hair, making him smile. "See you in a bit. Don't miss me too much."

"He won't." I side eye her. She sucks her teeth, flicking me off as she walks out the door. "And you talk about me and language?!"

When the door shuts, Reign says, "Eve is... really cool."

"She's aight," I tease. "Nah. Eve is my soul and then some."

"She's okay with me staying here?"

"Eve Valentine is not nice for the benefit of others. You don't know her that well yet, but if she doesn't like something or someone, *everyone* will know."

He's silent for a beat. "I don't mind if you two kiss. Wait–" he sits up "–that sounds creepy."

My shoulders shake, trying to hold in a laugh.

"What I meant to say is that affection doesn't bother me because it's nice seeing an example of a healthy relationship. I've... never witnessed that." There's a hint of sadness in his tone.

I've grown up with nothing but healthy relationships. Mine and Eve's parents have been prime examples for me. Even my grandparents were married for sixty years. The only time relationships, if they could even be called that, were toxic was when I was smashing my way through half of Hope Valley. That's neither here nor there right now though. I hope Reign never goes through that phase. A release is nice but that's all it is–*a release*–when there's no connection with the other person.

"Hopefully I can change that experience."

"You already are," Reign says with one corner of his mouth tipped up. He looks down at his hands as if he has more to say. His voice is soft when he does speak again. "I feel like I've been alone since the day Dad died. It felt like there wasn't anything that could fill the nothingness he left behind. My grandma was withdrawn for a while. Dad was her only child, and it was like a switch flipped in her when he died. Everything became my fault. It got to the point I was grateful when she was gone because we'd fight when she was home."

"About a month after Dad's funeral, Hudson called from True's House. I guess a counselor at school gave him my information." He shakes his head, pushing that detail aside. "I wasn't gonna go, but my grandma came home drunk one morning, blaming me for everything under the sun. Instead of arguing, I left. Walked to True's House."

"Walked?" That's at least a ten mile stretch.

He nods, bobbing his head up and down. "Yep. Walked. Used the GPS on my phone and arrived right when Hudson opened the doors. And in some weird way–I was happy she came home drunk that day because that's when the nothingness was filled with something. True's House became my haven. I could be a kid. There wasn't the stress of wondering what I did to piss someone off. The gaping hole that was in the middle of me felt a little less lonely. I met Calliope and other kids who knew what I was going through. Then I met you, your brothers, your Mom, Noelle, Aspen, and Eve and suddenly..." He pauses for a moment, as if the revelation hits him as the same time he speaks it. "The nothingness wasn't swallowing me whole anymore."

"All of you feel like family." His eyes meet mine. "You feel like home."

I bury his words deep in my soul, letting them take root. My eyes water, and I let him see me cry. I swipe at the tears I wouldn't want to control even if I could. Reign climbs off the couch, crosses the living room, and wraps me in a hug that matches the warmth of the sun.

"You've got me. Us. Always."

31

WINTER

REIGN AND I SPENT the rest of the day together, watching shows and talking. Eve arrived home with a pizza around ten after spending the evening with Elle and Aspen. Reign has eaten half of it on his own. My phone rings and I fish it out of my pocket to see it's the lawyer. I leave Reign and Eve at the table to answer it.

"Tell me something good, Easton." I head for my office.

"The hearing is Tuesday at nine a.m.. Reign will need to be there with you. His grandmother has already been notified. By chance, did Reign tell you of any other incidents?"

"He didn't tell me what they were. Only that it wasn't the first time it's happened."

"Okay, when I did a bit of digging, there were– " I hear the shuffling of paper " – about five other police reports. One being a wellness check for Reign requested by a concerned neighbor and the others were noise complaints due to yelling. This happened after his father's passing. While I regret he had to go through that, this will only help our case. Also, does Eve live with you? If she does, I'll need to run a state and CPS background check on her as well."

It feels like an ice cube is sliding down my throat, and my chest feels tight when he mentions a background check. I shut my office door. "Will my time in rehab be an issue?"

"No. You don't have a criminal record."

Relief washes over me. "Good." While I've been sober for years, the shadows of that time still haunt me. I clear my throat. "Uh... Let me talk to Eve and get her information. Is it okay if I text it to you?"

I know her social security number, birthdate, address, and blood type. But we haven't discussed her moving in, and I don't want to assume. I know she said her lease is up soon on her place. I'll talk to her once Reign goes to bed.

"That works. I'll call you if anything else comes up. I'm very confident in our case."

"Thank you, Easton. Have a good night."

Ending the call, I head back to the dining room. Reign gets up from his seat, stretching. "I think I'm gonna go to bed," he says, letting out a yawn.

"Okay, good night. Wait," I take my seat at the table. "Are you going to school tomorrow?" I'm not going to make him go. While his eye isn't as bad as I thought it was going to be, it's clear he got into something over the weekend.

"Yeah." He rubs his non-injured eye with the heel of his hand. "Eve told me she could make this," he points at the bruising, "less noticeable. Calliope and Ian already know what happened. They're the only two who pay close enough attention to me to notice anyway."

Reign is mistaken. He's the leader of his little pack of friends whether he realizes it or not.

"Okay, I'll give you a ride in the morning. I'm up at five during the week."

"Five?" Reign's eyes widen. "For what?"

"Swimming and to hit the gym. Want to join me?"

"Uh..." He runs a hand through his curls. "Nice of you to invite me, but no. I'd rather sleep." Cringing, he gives me a look that says "sorry".

Eve snorts into her cup of soda, setting it aside, wiping some off that got on her chin. "Reign, you're the sweetest."

"Never feel sorry for telling me no. Or anyone for that matter."

"I'll remember that." He rubs the back of his neck, looking at the floor. "Well... good night."

Eve gets up from her seat, wrapping Reign in a hug. "Night." She tousles his curls when she releases him. "See you in the morning."

Reign smiles bright. "Night."

Eve nudges my arm, sliding her eyes to Reign then back to me. Getting up, I give him a hug too. "Night. Let us know if you need anything." He gives me a half hug at first and then wraps both arms tightly around me.

Looking at the floor, he says, "Good night." Turning on his heel, he leaves us at the table alone.

Eve watches the doorway after he's gone. "Such a good kid. Ughhh! I just wanna squeeze him and make everything better."

"The hearing is on Tuesday at nine."

"That soon? When are you going to tell him?"

"Tomorrow." I grab my cup, pouring more soda into it. "I didn't want to fuck up his night, making him worry about it. Easton says we have a good case, though."

"If it comes down to it," Eve cracks her knuckles one by one, "I'll fight everyone in that courtroom."

I nearly spit my soda out onto the table. "That definitely won't help our case, Lara Croft."

Laughter tumbles from her lips. "Let's hope that doesn't need to happen."

Setting my soda aside, I lean back in my chair, fixing my gaze on her. "When is the lease up for your place?"

"Next month." She licks the tip of her pointer finger, chewing her bite of pizza slowly. "Why?"

"Would you want to live here with me? Us?"

Eve's smile glitters like stars. "You want me around?"

"Always."

"Even when I call you Win Win?"

Shaking my head, I let out a huff of laughter. "Unfortunately, yes. Even then."

Grabbing a paper towel, she cleans off her hands, setting it aside. "I'd love to be here with you both."

I wrap my hand around the leg of her chair, sliding her closer, placing her legs between my thighs. Picking up her hand, I interlace my fingers with hers. "One day, when you're ready, I'd love to walk down that aisle into forever with you."

It's Eve or no one. Us or nothing.

"You still want to marry me?" Her voice is hoarse, barely a whisper. Looking at her, there are tears sitting on the rim of her eyes.

"Yes. Why wouldn't I?" I swipe away a stray tear.

"Because of everything before."

I cup her face in my hands, bringing her eyes to mine. "I want everything with you, Eve. All of it. You're my past, present, and future."

Closing her eyes, she smiles as if basking in my words. Opening them again, they're alight with a depthless love.

"Is this a proposal?" She places her hands on my thighs, leaning closer. "Because if so, yes. I'll marry you."

I slide my hands down her arms, picking up her hands. "You don't want me to get on one knee? And—"

"No." She closes the distance between us, kissing me. "Just you. That's all I want."

I wrap my hand around the back of her neck, making her lips meet mine again. Pulling away, I ask, "Eve Valentine, will you marry me?"

"Yes." She crashes into me, straddling my lap, and wraps her arms around my neck.

Matching her intensity, I wrap one arm around her waist, gripping her thigh with my other hand, and pick her up. I carry her through the dining room, living room, and up the stairs to our room. Never breaking the connection our lips have. I kick the door shut behind us, gently placing her on the bed. I waste no time, grabbing her ankle, pulling her to the edge.

"If I remember correctly, I have a debt to collect." I unfasten my jeans, sliding them down, and kick them off to the side.

Eve simpers, looking up at me.

"Wiping your future husband's kiss from your lips is a criminal offense, Sweetheart."

"Technically," she holds up one perfectly manicured finger, "when I did that, you hadn't asked me to be your wife yet."

Tugging on the bottom of her sweats, I slip them off her legs. "Eve, you've been mine in every way since the day I met you."

She parts her legs with my words. "Prove it."

Wrapping my hands around her waist, I flip her onto her stomach. "Are you sure you want me to prove it, Sweetheart?"

Eve brings her knees under her, putting her ass in the air. She backs up so she's flush against me. "I said prove it."

Smacking her ass, I pull her panties down, giving me a perfect view. Instead of slamming into her, like my dick is straining to do, I drop to my knees, wanting a taste first.

Eve lets out a guttural moan when I glide my tongue along the length of her wetness. She tries to part her legs further, but her panties only give her so much allowance. I grab them, making them tighter around her thighs, keeping her in place.

"Stay where you are, keep quiet, and take what I give you. Got it?"

"Mhmm..."

"I need words, Eve." My hand connects with her ass cheek again.

"Shit. Yes. I got it."

"That's my girl."

I dive back in, licking and sucking, bringing her closer to the edge. Just like I knew she would, she struggles to keep quiet.

"Do you need me to stop?"

"What?" she pants, looking back at me. "No. Why are you stopping?"

"I told you to be quiet."

"Winter." She moans, burying her face in the comforter. "Please," she begs. "I can't, okay? You feel too good." Her voice is muffled. "Now, please." Biting her lip, she looks back at me again. "Be a good husband and eat your wife's pussy."

How can I tell her no when she begs so nicely? Wrapping my arms around her thighs, I lap at her center. She tries her best to keep quiet. I wouldn't say she's failing, but there's really no point. Eve is vocal about the pleasure she receives. I love it. If I allowed myself, I could get off on the sounds of her alone.

I bring her near her release just enough for her to feel it to only pull her back, edging her a few times before I let her fall. When she does, she calls out my name while I savor her sticky, sweet release. Standing, I pull down my boxers, freeing my hard length and wrap my hands around her waist as I sink into her from behind. Eve grips the sheets, dragging her nails across them. Reaching underneath her, I wrap my hand around her throat and bring my other hand to her clit.

"Are you mine?" I mutter in her ear.

"Yes." She cries as the pleasure consumes her. "I'm yours."

"Mmm... you don't sound needy and desperate enough, Sweetheart." I plunge into harder, making her breath hitch. "Say it like you mean it."

"Winter..." she breathes. "I'm yours."

Eve falls over the edge again, and I jump after her. I hold onto her hips, steadying myself as the shockwaves of my release wash over me. When I'm spent, she slowly slides up and down my length, prolonging the pleasure, before melting onto the bed. I roll onto my side, catching my breath, feeling like I'm on the verge of passing out. Eve stays in the same position lying on her stomach, sprawled out on the bed. I smack her ass for good measure.

Giggling, she groans. "I can't move."

Sitting up on my elbow, I sweep her braids aside and press kisses to her neck, shoulders, and back. Laying back down, I pull her into my arms. Lying in the aftermath of us, it sinks in that the woman who I thought I lost forever is going to be my forever.

"When should we get married?"

Sitting up, she rests her chin on my chest. Her face is lit by the moonlight shimmering through the window and an uncontainable smile is on her lips. "I think we should have a small one. Just us, family, and a few close friends."

"Love that idea."

Our first wedding was going to be featured in a bridal magazine. It was meant to be the event of the year. The guest list was exclusive, our budget was limitless, and at the time, that's what we wanted.

Then everything changed and we did too.

"I don't really care about details. I want you," she points at my heart, "a to-die-for gown, and a ring, of course. Nothing else matters."

"I have one picked out already... a ring I mean."

"What?" She sits up. "How? If we just—"

"I only brought it up now. I've been thinking about marrying you... well, since the day I met you. And after everything, I knew if I ever got a chance again, I needed to be ready."

"You've been carrying a ring around with you? All this time?"

"I don't carry it around. I bought it a few weeks after seeing you at Fireside. Snow took me with him to buy a ring for Elle at a custom jewelry shop in Seattle and there was—let me show you."

She gapes at me as I climb off the bed, pulling on my boxers. I head for my closet and open the safe at the back of it. A black velvet box rests on the bottom shelf. Grabbing it, I rejoin her on the bed. Eve stares at the box intently as if it holds the answers to the secrets of the universe. Opening the box, I reveal a three carat trillion cut natural green diamond with clusters of champagne colored diamonds on either side of it set in a rose gold band. Eve gasps, placing her hands over her mouth and nose as her eyes jump between the ring and me.

"Winter..." she whispers.

"I didn't realize how rare natural green diamonds are until the jeweler told me. When I first saw it, it was only the diamond. I customized the rest."

"Winter..." Eve says my name again like she's short circuited and is needing a moment to process.

"It reminds me of you and how rare you are." Pulling it out of the box, I grab her shaking hand. I press a kiss to the back of it before sliding it on her ring finger. "Perfect."

I give her time to process the gravity of this moment. Eventually, her eyes meet mine.

"Winter, I'd say yes to forever with you a million times across every lifetime."

Eve wraps her arms around my neck, straddling my lap, bringing her lips to mine.

She loves me slow, giving me all of her yeses.

32
WINTER

AFTER BREAKING THE NEWS to Reign that the hearing is tomorrow and seeing his carefree smile slip from his face, I head for Dr. Maddox's office instead of my own. I've gone through a lot of highs and lows in forty-eight hours, and I can feel myself beginning to spiral. I text Snow, letting him know I'll be an hour later than usual.

Snow: You don't have to come in today.

I'm tempted to take the day off. What am I going to do by myself though? Spiral?

Winter: I'll be there.

I climb out of the car, tugging at the neck of my button down that's feeling too tight, and cross the parking lot to Dr. Maddox's office. Trying the door, it's locked. I'm ready to shout expletives when he appears, looking confused, and meets me at the door.

Opening it, he asks, "Winter?"

"I'm sorry for showing up unannounced—"

"You're fine. Are you fine?"

"I am... but I'm not." I pace the length of the lobby. "Stuff is good–it's okay–I feel like I'm losing it though."

"Do you want to talk about it?"

I stop pacing, looking at him. "Yes. Please?"

He leads the way to his office, stepping aside for me to enter, and I unload before he even has a chance to close the door.

"Remember the kid I told you I was mentoring?"

"Yes." He nods taking a seat.

"Okay, well, he called me Friday evening..." I tell him everything that happened with Reign's grandma. "And now, I have emergency custody and am seeking legal guardianship, but– " I collapse onto the couch "–what if I fuck up? What if I fuck him up more than he already is? Not saying he's fucked up but trauma is trauma. What if they make him go back to his grandma? I'm spiraling." I press the heels of my hands into my eyes, letting out a heavy sigh.

There's a beat of silence before Dr. Maddox speaks. "Is that what you want? Guardianship?" He brings his leg up, resting his ankle across his knee.

"It is. But maybe it was an impulsive decision. Maybe there's a more suitable guardian out there for him."

Dr. Maddox tilts his head to the side. "Do you honestly believe that?"

"No." I stand, pacing again. "What if I fuck up though?"

"You will."

I stop in my tracks, turning to face him. "What?"

"You will fuck up, Winter." He enunciates each word. "It's an inevitability of life. Instead of stressing perfection, try your best. Your best is enough."

I lean back against the couch. "And if they make him go back?"

"You can still be there for him. I know that's not what you want to hear. You can be impactful, even from a distance. You haven't been his guardian this whole time, yet you've made a difference. Have you not?"

"I like to think I have."

"I *know* you have or you wouldn't be pursuing guardianship," he says with a smile.

"I want him to know he's loved and deserving of the absolute best."

"Whether or not you're his legal guardian, you can provide that."

I relax my shoulders, letting some of the tension leave my body. "You're right."

"Your best, Winter. That's all he needs."

Is that all Reign needs? My best? That's all I've been offering him since we met. If it wasn't enough, he wouldn't have called me Friday, trusting me to pick him up. I'm hopeful the hearing will go in our favor, but I can't be naïve and not ask what happens if he is placed back in his grandmother's custody again. Regardless of what happens tomorrow, Dr. Maddox is right, I can be there for him. Even from a distance.

"There's more..." I say, switching gears like I always do when I spiral, unable to stop the smile that I know lights up my face.

"Whatever the more is, I can tell it's good."

"You know Eve and I got back together." He nods. "Yesterday, I asked her to marry me... again."

Dr. Maddox smiles brightly. "I'm assuming she gave you a resounding yes?"

"She did. We haven't told anyone yet. All of this is overwhelming. It's a good overwhelm though. Is that possible?"

"It is. It's why people cry when they're happy. People forget happiness is just as powerful as sadness."

"I'm learning that. Everything finally feels right, you know? I guess the fear of wondering if it's *too* right lingers in the back of my mind."

Dr. Maddox nods his head, furrowing his brow with though. "May I offer a different frame of thought?"

"Please." I wave my hand as if giving him the floor.

"What if it's too good to be false?"

"Huh?" I know I look as confused as I sound.

Dr. Maddox sits up, leaning forward. "All the goodness and rightness you're feeling right now, what if it's too good to be false?"

"I..." Leaning back, I repeat the question to myself–too good to be false? "I've never thought of it that way."

"It's a narrative shift. Instead of thinking things are too good to be true. Maybe they're too good to be false instead."

Dr. Maddox gives me space to process his words, sitting in silence with me. "You really blew my mind right now with that question."

He chuckles. "I also felt like it was a mind fuck when my colleague posed the question to me."

"It's simple, yet powerful."

"If you tell other's they're deserving you must believe it for yourself too."

Dr. Maddox graciously gives me a full hour of his time, I leave his office feeling less chaotic and a lot more hopeful.

Tuesday morning, Reign, Eve, and I show up at the courthouse for the hearing. When I told Reign about the hearing, he didn't say much. In fact, he hasn't said much in the past twenty-four hours. After school yesterday, he came home and went straight to his room. He did join us for dinner only to push the food around his plate and then disappeared to his room. If I'm stressed, I can't imagine how he's feeling. I'm not sure what I'll do if the judge decides he has to return to his grandma's house. That'll be like ripping my heart out.

Sitting in the court room with Reign by my side and Easton on the other side of me, we wait for the judge to arrive. Eve is sitting on a bench behind us in spectator seating along with a few other witnesses that Easton asked to be here this morning. Reign's leg won't stop bouncing as he swivels the chair from side to side. I don't even have the heart to tell him it's going to be okay because what if it isn't? What am I going to do if—

The thought leaves my mind when the judge enters the room and we rise. I quickly glance at my watch, thinking she's early. She's not. It's nine a.m. on the dot. Which means Reign's grandma is late. I'm filled with hope that this will work in our favor. The judge looks at our table and then to the table that only the court appointed attorney is seated at.

"Mr. Decker, where's your defendant?" She looks down at him from the judge's stand over the rim of her glasses.

"Your honor," he clears his throat, pulling at the collar of his too large button down, "Ms. DeLeon is on her way."

"She should've been on her way," the judge glances at the time. "Five minutes ago. Was she not aware of the time?"

"Ms. DeLeon is aware of the time."

"That remains to be seen." The judge purses her lips, adjusting herself in her seat.

Another five minutes ticks by, and another, and another until we've been waiting for nearly twenty minutes. Judge Coldwell let's out an annoyed sigh, roughly shuffling the papers on her desk to let Mr. Decker know she isn't happy.

"Enough of my time has been wasted. Mr. Easton, thank you for being on time. Let's get to why we're here, guardianship of Reign DeLeon. Mr. King wants to become his legal guardian, correct?"

"Yes, Your Honor."

"Present your evidence," she says, sitting up in her seat.

Easton is very well prepared. He presents information we didn't discuss the other night but I already knew. Reign's grandma spent most of her time at the casino, spending his dad's life insurance money. Suspecting and hearing it are two different things. It makes my stomach roll. I couldn't imagine squandering my grandson's inheritance from such a tragic incident. Once he's done, the judge shuffles her papers again–a little more calmly.

"Unfortunate circumstances." Judge Coldwell shakes her head, glancing at Mr. Decker disapprovingly as if he is a co-conspirator of Reign's grandma. "Due to Ms. DeLeon not being here and the information presented, I must rule in favor of Mr. King and Mr. DeLeon. He is to remain with Mr. King at his home. In sixty days, we will return for another hearing in which legal custody may be granted. During that time, guardian training must be taken and the appropriate documents filed. Mr. Easton is well versed in this process and I'm sure will be more than happy to help you, Mr. King."

"We've begun the process already, Your Honor," Mr. Easton says.

"Good. Mr. DeLeon."

Reign nervously meets her gaze. Eve was able to tame his hair this morning so it isn't hanging in his face.

"Yes ma'am. I mean–Your Honor."

"Hang tight. This will all be over soon. You're in good hands. Court is adjourned." She slams her gavel, rising from her seat, and disappears through the same door she came from earlier.

Everything happens so quickly; I don't even have time to blink. One minute I'm a ball of stress, and the next we're being told what we had hoped to hear. It doesn't take long for it to sink in. Reign tightly wraps his arms around me, followed by Eve who wraps her arms around both of us. Sure, we have another sixty days to go, but now I feel like him living with us permanently isn't just a hope. It's going to be a reality.

Reign pulls away, giving me a watery smile. "Thank you for everything, Winter."

"I promise to always do my best, Reign. Even when I feel grossly underqualified and don't know what the hell I'm doing."

Reign wraps me in another hug before turning his attention to Eve.

"Calliope and Ian are waiting for you out there." She points to the doors. "If you want to see them, I'll go with you while Winter wraps up with Mr. Easton."

"They are?" Reign asks with wide eyes as Eve nods.

"Yeah."

His face lights up. "I want to see them."

She loops her arm through his, guiding him out of the courtroom. "We'll be right outside when you're ready," she says over her shoulder, giving me a dimpled smile.

I turn to Mr. Easton, going directly back into business mode once Reign is out of earshot. "I want all of it. The house and any assets, her bank accounts frozen, and the money put into an account for Reign. Everything. I want it transferred to Reign's name."

While his grandma was smart to not show up today, that doesn't mean I'm going to offer her grace. Sometimes, people don't fucking deserve it.

"I will get that process started right away, Mr. King. I'll be in touch about the hearing. As I've said before, I feel confident about this."

"And you weren't wrong." I clap him on the shoulder. "Thank you, Mr. Easton."

Despite the hearing going well, I still want to check in with Reign to make sure he's doing okay. His grandma not showing up worked for us, but I know that still had to affect him in some way. After the hearing, we went out for a celebratory lunch with Calliope and Ian. Snow, Noelle, North, and Aspen joined us. Snow hadn't told them about what happened on Friday. I was grateful he didn't. I know they care about Reign as much as I do, but I didn't want them overwhelming him. Once I told Snow how the hearing went, he shared with them what's been going on so they weren't asking questions over lunch. Not that I would have to worry about them treating him differently. They've considered him family since I first told them about him.

Climbing the stairs, I reach his door, and lightly knock on it.

"Come in," he hollers.

Opening the door, I'm happy to see he's wasted no time making the room his own. To distract him last night, Eve helped him decorate and hang the pictures I stole and his art on the walls. She was certain he'd be coming home with us today and wouldn't hear otherwise. I was barely able to stop her from going to the home improvement store for paint last night. Eve assured me it would happen next weekend when she moves in, regardless of what I say. I'm happy her stubbornness kicked in because Reign is clearly in his element. I recognize a song by 6lack spilling out of the speaker Eve bought him at Target. His room smells like paint and the garden outside with the French doors of the balcony open. An oddly comforting, refreshing scent.

Looking over his shoulder at me, I catch a glimpse of his father's portrait. It looks like he's done and is now adding finishing touches. His hands are speckled with paint, and there's a streak of it in his hair. No doubt from him trying to keep it out of his face so he can see.

"I just wanted to check in on you." I sit on the edge of his bed.

He returns to the painting, perfecting his already stunning art. "I'm okay." After a few beats, he stops, setting his brush down, and turns to look at me. "I thought she'd show up today. Is it bad that I wanted her to show up? To show that she cared?"

"No. I'd be worried if you didn't care about her not showing up. She's all you've known aside from your dad."

"Yeah..." He nods, falling silent. "She wasn't a bad grandma until she was. I think losing Dad crushed her... like it did me... except she crumbled under the pressure. And me..." His voice trails off as he glances at the portrait. "I crumbled too..."

Reign looks down at his hands, rubbing at a dried paint smudge, before meeting my gaze again. "Except, I'm picking up the pieces and making something new."

"You're amazing, Reign. I'm honored you're trusting me to be a part of your life. I hope you know I love you. And if not, I'm letting you know now that I love you."

Reign's lips part, staring at me with wide eyes. Maybe I shouldn't have said it? I'm not sure what the etiquette for love is when it comes to familial relationships.

"You do?" he asks after a few stunned moments of silence.

"I do."

He looks away from me, glancing at the painting, and then rubs his eyes. "For a while, I thought I was difficult to love."

"Never. It's like breathing. Automatic. No thought."

"I really needed to hear that," he says softly.

Getting up, I give him a hug. He holds onto me tightly before letting go. I look around his room, not wanting to make it awkward for him if he doesn't want to say it back.

"I'll let you get back to your painting." I point at the canvas. "It's amazing by the way. The people in Paris will be lucky to have you." Padding toward the door, I place my hand on the knob. "Let us know if you need anything. Night."

Before I can step through the open door, he calls out, "Winter."

"Yeah?" I turn to face him.

"I love you too... and Eve... all of you."

"We all love you more than you know, Reign."

33

EVE

TO SAY OUR LIFE has been a whirlwind over the past two weeks is an understatement. I've only had time for Winter, Reign, a dinner with our parents to announce our engagement – which was met with teary eyes and indescribable happiness – and work. I haven't had time to see Elle and Aspen to tell them about the engagement in person. Which is why they've threatened to share embarrassing photos and jump me if I don't go to dinner with them tonight. The embarrassing photos part worries me more because I know what they have. I'd consider it blackmail, honestly. To diffuse their proposal of war, I pull into Fireside's parking lot ten minutes early.

They're already at a table with my favorite drink waiting–a Moscow Mule.

"Well, well, well…" Noelle raises her chin in the air, looking down her nose at me. "Look who finally decided to not be too busy for us, Aspen."

Aspen leans closer to Elle, giving me side eye. "Do we even know her?"

"No. She doesn't even go here."

I snort with laughter at their Mean Girl reference. "I'm here to hang out, not be ridiculed."

"Now you want to hang out?" Elle pins her arms across her chest, dramatically tilting her head to the side.

Rolling my eyes, I pick up the cool copper cup, taking a sip of my drink. "Mmm..." I lick my lips. "This is tasty. Brielle is working tonight, isn't she?"

"What is that?" Aspen points a finger at me.

"What?" I look down at my chest.

"That!" She points again.

"What?!" I feel my lips and cheeks, attempting to wipe some imaginary thing off.

Elle scrunches up her face, looking at Aspen like she's crazy. "What are you talking about?"

"That big ass rock on her finger, dodo brain." Aspen smacks the back of Elle's head.

"Oh." A smile lights up my face, setting my cup aside, I hold up my hand. "This?" I thrust my hand in front of their faces, giving them spirit fingers.

They put their heads together, each holding onto my hand as they stare at the ring. "Winter proposed two weekends ago."

"Excuse me?" Elle has the nerve to look offended. "Two weekends? You saw us Monday for lunch after Reign's hearing. You couldn't have shared it with us then?"

"First of all," I snatch my hand away, "you didn't even tell me about your engagement to Snow. I had to find out over brunch when I saw the rocks blinding me on your hand. Second of all, like you, I wanted to tell you in person."

Aspen snorts into her drink. "Elle, you can't be butt hurt when you did the same exact thing. Besides, she's had a lot going on. How's Reign?"

"He's good. Settling in. I think he's happy."

Reign has relaxed into life with us. At first he walked around the house like he needed permission. Now, he takes up space.

"I'm happy Reign is happy, but please, tell us more about this engagement," Elle says. "Look at that smile on her face."

"I can't help it." I press my palms against my cheeks. "I'm unbelievably happy you guys. He asked if I wanted to move in with him, because you know my lease is up at the end of the month..." I tell them all the words Winter said to water my soul, the imperfectly, perfect proposal, the sex—minus the details—and the custom ring he's had made for months.

"He had the ring already?!" Elle's eyes well with tears. "That is romantic and beautiful. You're getting the happy ending you've always deserved."

"Happy beginning," Aspen corrects, raising her mojito in the air.

"To happy beginnings." I toast my glass against theirs and drink a few gulps.

Elle gets up, wrapping me in a hug, Aspen joins us, squeezing us tight. I can't contain the tears. My eyes water as they drown me in love.

"What'd I miss?" Brielle asks from behind us, carrying a basket of our usual wings.

Aspen grabs my hand, thrusting it in Brielle's face as if my hand is her own. Brielle gasps, dropping the wings on the table, causing a couple to topple out.

"Winter proposed?!" Brielle didn't strike me as someone who squeals, but she lets one out that could possibly break glass. She wraps me in a hug that makes me question the strength of my clavicle and grabs my hand to look at the ring. "I knew that man was gonna marry you. Wasn't a doubt in my mind."

"He said you always told him to come back to me."

"Damn right, I did. You two belong to each other."

They gush over the color of the ring, the design, and speculate our future wedding plans. I take in the moment, fading into the background, listening to them talk, and am overwhelmed with happiness. Marrying Winter is something I was too afraid to dream of. I never imagined we'd be back in one another's lives again.

I know I was stubborn in the beginning, terrified of getting hurt, even though I saw no semblance of the Winter I knew all those years ago. Reconciling that he had changed, that he was truly wiser, and definitely a hell of a lot sexier, was hard. Coming to grips with the fact that I was as culpable as him in the dissolution of us was hard.

But loving Winter has always been easy. *We've been easy.*

"Do you have a wedding date?" Elle asks.

Aspen gives her an incredulous look. "Let the engagement sink in a little bit, Elle."

"I know whatever you two decide, it will be beautiful." Brielle smiles. "I've gotta get back to work. I'll bring some extra wings to replace the ones that fell victim to my excitement."

I let out a huff of laughter. "Thanks, Brielle." I turn my attention back to Elle and Aspen. "No wedding date, yet. But it *will* be beautiful." I raise my glass in the air.

Arriving home much later than intended, I put my hand on the railing to climb the stairs, but pause, seeing the flicker of light from the TV on in the living room. Trudging down the hall, Winter is lying on the couch, watching some–boring, I'm sure–documentary. I kick off my heels, letting them clatter to the floor, and wiggle my toes.

"How was it?" Winter asks without looking away from the TV.

I pad toward him, taking off my earrings and bracelets along the way. "You know I always love seeing my girls." He scoots over when I near the couch, making room for me to lie beside him. Setting my jewelry on the coffee table, I happily do, burying my face in his neck, breathing deep. "But I love coming home to you more."

He kisses the top of my head. "They were sending me increasingly threatening text messages."

Laughter tumbles from my lips.

"I was worried they wouldn't let you come home."

"Eh." I say on a long stretch, letting out a yawn. "They're harmless. We spent most of the time discussing wedding stuff. Elle wants us to have joint wedding planning sessions."

"That sounds... fun," Winter says encouragingly, but I hear the amusement in his tone.

I suck my teeth. "No it doesn't."

Noelle and Aspen do everything together. They often forget I'm not the same.

A chuckle vibrates in his chest with my cheek pressed against it. "Okay, it sounds like torture."

"I want an intimate wedding. Family, close friends, and a photographer. Since the night you proposed, I've known what I've wanted."

Winter turns off the TV, leaving us in the soft light of the lamp, giving me his full attention. "And what's that, Sweetheart?"

34

EVE

TWO MONTHS LATER

Reign knocks on our bedroom door, looking more like a man than a boy in his bespoke suit and shorter than usual hair.

"I'm heading outside to welcome everyone."

Setting my makeup brush aside, I stand, giving Reign a hug. "I'm happy you get to be a part of this day. You make us a family."

The legal guardianship hearing was a week ago. Over the past two months, we've become a family. This isn't how I imagined our life being, but I can't imagine it any other way.

He hugs me back. "Me too."

"You look handsome by the way." I nudge his arm when I pull away. "Calliope is coming with her dad, right?"

We've become good friends with her dad, Vincent. Since his wife passed, he focused solely on Calliope and his work, avoiding a social life. When we'd invite him out, he'd decline our offers. So instead of asking, we picked him up one evening, introducing him to everyone. Since then he's become a part of our group as if he's always belonged. Winter has blocked every single one of my matchmaking efforts, reminding me how long it took Snow to be ready.

Snow wasn't ready. Noelle just happened.

"Yeah. I saw them arrive just now."

"Perfect. I won't keep you. Winter and I will join the party soon. Thank you for welcoming the guests."

He nods. "Of course."

I look in the mirror, catching a glimpse of Winter appearing behind me, fastening his cufflinks–with diamonds that match the rich green of my ring–to his button up. He stops in his tracks, his eyes rake over me from head to toe.

"Eve, you look... sublime."

Unable to contain my smile, I turn to face him, gently sweeping the voluminous curls Elle gave me out of my face.

"Beautiful." He takes another step toward me. Fastening the cufflink, he places his hand on my waist. I tip my head back slightly to meet his eyes.

"Exquisite." Bringing his other hand up, he cups my chin. "There isn't an adequate word to describe how stunning you look. Know that you've successfully taken my breath away."

"Let me give you some of mine." Holding his face in my hands, I press a soft, yet tempting kiss to his lips. Winter slips his hand around the nape of my neck, pulling me flush against him. Instead of giving him air, he steals my own.

He pulls away first, resting his forehead against mine. "Unless you want me to ruin you before the party, I suggest we stop."

I wrap my arms around his neck, looking up at him through my lashes. "Would that be such a bad thing?"

"Don't tempt me, Sweetheart."

"Me?" I take a step back from him, splaying a hand across my chest, attempting to look innocent.

"I'd never..."

Kicking the door shut, I lock it.

"Ever…"

Winter's gaze is trained on me, tracking every one of my movements.

"Think to…"

Doing a curtsey, I lift up the fabric of my skirt, exposing my thighs, and the garter belt wrapped snugly around them.

"Tempt you." Turning around, giving him a view of my ass, I place my hands on the back of the chaise, and look back at him.

Winter's eyes light my skin on fire, he saunters toward me as if our family and friends aren't waiting for us in the garden to show up to our own engagement party. Standing behind me, I hear him unfastening his belt and the pull of his zipper. He fists the fabric of my dress, pulling it up over my hips, and slips my panties down. My breath gets caught in my throat as my heart races with anticipation.

"You want me to ruin you?" He palms my ass, smacking it, making goosebumps pepper my skin.

"Yes."

"I'm always—" He slides the tip along my wetness, resting at my entrance.

I grip the back of the couch, resisting the urge to push back onto him.

"—going to give you what you desire."

Caging my waist with his hands, Winter slams into me. My knees buckle, and I bite down on my lip to keep from alarming our guests. He hits the spot that makes me feel transcendent. Wrapping his arm around my middle, he brings his fingertips to my clit, amplifying the already overwhelming pleasure. Grabbing the back of my neck, he bends me further over the couch, and nudges my legs apart with his knee. He maintains a rhythm that pushes me closer to the edge with each thrust. Bending at his waist, he wraps his hand around my throat, making his chest flush against my back.

"I get to have you forever," he whispers into my ear, "and still, that will *never* be enough."

Grabbing my chin, he brings my mouth to his, sealing his words with a kiss. It becomes too much–his touch, the feel of him in me, his body pressed into mine–and the release that's been building finally breaks free. I shatter for him, moaning into his mouth. Stars burst into color behind my eyes as I plummet into the place only Winter can send me. He breaks the kiss, keeping a firm hold on my throat, plunging into me. Reaching behind me, I wrap my hand around the back of Winter's neck, pressing into him, needing to feel *all* of him. The depth is the perfect crescendo of pleasure and craveable pain.

"I love the way you feel inside me."

Winter responds with guttural moan. His body momentarily tenses before relaxing as the wave of his release washes over him. His hips come to slow halt. He presses all of his weight onto me. Flush against my back, I feel Winter's heart beating as wildly as my own. My phone rings from somewhere in our room. I'm about to ignore it when I remember I have to let the photographer in. Trying to get up, Winter doesn't budge.

"Winter! Move!" I shove against him. He bites my neck, making me squeal with laughter. "I have to let the photographer in."

He groans, reluctantly pulling out of me. "The only reason I'm getting up is because you're about to become my wife."

Righting my dress, I turn to face him with a smile that hasn't left my face since the day we got back together. Instead of taking months to plan a wedding, we decided to plan an engagement party and have a surprise wedding. The only people who know what's happening are me, Winter, and Reign. I thought it'd be easy to keep our plan under wraps.

I've had to catch myself a few times before I spilled any of the details. Our moms have been unknowingly involved in some of the planning.

They went with me when I met with Delilah for her to design my dress. I went back and forth about a regal gown and something modern and chic. I chose modern and chic since our wedding is disguised as an engagement party and I loved the dress more anyway. Winter's reaction was all I needed to know I made the right choice.

Elle will be bummed that we aren't planning our weddings side by side. I love her, but I'm not the least bit sorry. Winter and I already went through the stress of planning one wedding and didn't want to experience it again. All the people who matter are here. It's perfect for us.

I look at myself one last time in the mirror, adjusting my dress and hair to hide the freshly fucked look. Winter wraps his arms around me from behind after slipping on his suit jacket.

"You're perfect, Mrs. King."

Bringing my hand up, I rest my palm against his cheek. "As are you, Mr. King."

Grabbing my hand, he twirls me around, making my dress spin out around me, and then pulls me back into him for a kiss. "Are you ready for this?"

"Since the day we met."

Heading downstairs, we meet the photographer out front. I thought it'd be impossible to book her for a surprise wedding, given how well known she is, but she was more than happy to take the two hour drive to Hope Valley from Seattle. I've been following her on Instagram for a while. I love the way she captures people and I knew if I ever had the opportunity to get married–I wanted her to be behind the lens.

There's a baby blue Ford Bronco with a woman stepping out of it who is even more stunning in person. She's tall with golden brown faux locs, glinting with hair jewelry, flowing down her back. Her eyes are a bright brown, and her smile is warm and inviting.

"Hi. I'm Harlow DeConto." She holds her hand out to me. It's adorned in gorgeous gold jewelry and a couple of intricate tattoos.

"I'm Eve Valentine."

"About to be King." She winks, tying half of her hair up on top of her head. "Your dress is to die for, by the way. Is it custom?"

I look down at my dress, beaming. While I loved it from the moment Delilah presented me with the design, I worried it was too simple. It's two pieces. The white top is a halter design, wrapping around me snugly like a bandeau, cupping my breasts, and dipping low with pleated details. It gives a tasteful peek of my midriff. The skirt is voluminous and floor length. It's made of tulle, cinching tightly at my waist with a belt of fabric, and has a peek-a-boo style cut out on my lower back.

"Yes." I nod. "Thank you."

"And I'm Winter." He shakes Harlow's hand.

"Pleasure to meet you. You designed a beautiful ring."

"It was easy with her as my muse." Winter kisses my temple.

Harlow's husband steps out of the car behind her–I know who he is from her IG posts. That sounds creepy, but true. He's the same height as Winter, covered in tattoos– none on his face–and looks at Harlow like she's the universe.

"This is my husband, Acyn."

"I know," slips from my lips before I can stop myself. "I mean–I know because I follow you online. Okay, I sound like a total fan girl right now."

"Stalker," Winter teasingly mutters in my ear.

"It's okay, I fan boy over Harlow, too." Acyn kisses her temple before extending his hand out to Winter and me. Internally, I'm screaming because they're just as amazing in person as they are online. Acyn turns his back to us after shaking our hands, and opens the back door of their car, pulling out their baby girl who is a spitting image of Harlow, but has Acyn's light brown eyes and jet black hair. "Say bye to Mommy, Evie."

I can't help saying, "Aww. She's adorable." Round, chubby cheeks and thick, dark lashes. "You guys are welcome to stay," I say, hoping I don't sound weird.

"She's cute." Harlow kisses her cheek. "But she needs a nap or you'll have a screaming baby interrupting your wedding."

"Yeah," Acyn agrees. "Thank you for the offer. If there's left over food, I wouldn't mind that though."

"Acyn!" Harlow nudges his side.

"Aye, I'm the same way." Winter says. "If there's no food, what's the point?"

"Exactly." Acyn bumps his fist against Winter's while Harlow and I roll our eyes. "See. He gets it, Sunshine."

"We'll be sure to give Harlow some food for you guys," I assure him.

"Enough about my husband's eating habits." She side eyes Acyn who smiles at her as she grabs her camera bag from the back. "I'm ready when you guys are."

She says her goodbyes to her family and gets to business as soon as they're on their way again.

After Harlow takes countless pictures of us, since we didn't have engagement photos, we let Reign know we're ready to start the wedding. Harlow heads out, leaving us and Winter alone again.

"Nervous?" Winter asks.

"No. Excited," I say as he interlaces his fingers with mine. "Everyone is going to lose their shit."

"Let them." He kisses the back of my hand. "It's about us."

"Always." I smile up at him.

Standing near the back doors, Reign's voice carries to us.

"Everyone, if you could please take your seats." He gives them a moment to do so.

"Look at our boy," I whisper to Winter. A lump lodges itself in my throat, and for a second I feel like I can't breathe. These past two months with them have been the best of my life. Glancing at him, I see he's teary eyed too. I squeeze his hand, and he squeezes mine back, keeping his eyes on Reign.

Clearing his throat, Reign continues. "We'd like to thank each of you for joining us today to celebrate the engagement of Winter and Eve. Since finding each other again, they've learned the importance of living in the moment and not getting caught up in plans. The only thing they want highlighted this evening is their love as they walk down the aisle."

It takes a moment before Reign's words sink in. There are a wide range of emotions on our family and friend's faces. Shock, tears, squealing (yes, Brielle was the loudest), and applause.

"This is it, Sweetheart." Winter turns to me, and I can't help the tears that spill from my eyes. Cradling my face in his hands, he swipes them away with his thumbs, and presses a kiss to each cheek. "I love you."

"I love you."

He kisses me. "See you at the end of the aisle."

Squeezing my hand, he walks out to the backyard, met by applause and asks my dad to come and walk me out. I lose it all over again when Dad walks toward me with tears in his eyes.

"Bug, I'm so happy for you, my beautiful girl." He wraps me in a warm embrace and kisses my temple.

"Thank you, Dad." I kiss his cheek.

Pulling away, he holds his arm out to me. "Ready?"

"Absolutely." I loop my arm through his.

When I step into the backyard, everyone rises, and "Melting" by Kali Uchis pours from the speakers. My eyes immediately find Winter's. He's swiping tears from his face, focused on me. I'm aware of our family and friends surrounding us, but all I see is him.

At the end of the aisle, Dad gives me to Winter, embracing us both. Winter reaches into his suit, pulling out a handkerchief, and dries my eyes.

"Let's get married, Sweetheart."

I intertwine my hand with his as the music fades away and the officiant begins the ceremony.

Our wedding day was teeming with love, joy, celebration, and laughter. Once the party's over, and our family and friends have gone home, I sit with my *husband* outside underneath the stars. Winter stands, holding his hand out to me.

"I want one more dance with my wife."

I slip my hand into his and he pulls me to my feet, wrapping his arms around my waist. "At Last" by Etta James plays softly in the background. I loop my arms around his neck, meeting his gaze, and move with him to the song.

"It's me and you, Sweetheart."

"Then," I softly brush my lips against his.

"Now," I mutter against his mouth.

"And *always*." Winter pulls me flush against him, deepening the kiss, and I taste forever on his lips.

EPILOGUE

WINTER

A WARM SUMMER BREEZE, lightly scented by the blooming garden outside, flows into Reign's room through the open balcony doors. Music streams from the speaker sitting on his nightstand while Eve and I double check with him that he has everything ready for his trip.

"T-shirts?" Eve asks Reign.

Sitting on the bed, Eve delegates, checking things off the "Packing for Paris" checklist she happily created for him, while I help Reign pack. It's been a little over a month since the wedding. We waited to go on our honeymoon so it aligned with his summer art program. He leaves tomorrow and then we leave the following day for a weeklong trip to Oman, a country in West Asia.

"Yeah," Reign answers, digging in his dresser drawer for socks.

"How many pairs of shoes are you taking?" I ask, pulling some new sneakers he got today out of the box to pack.

"I think three extra? A pair for walking, one for painting, and then one in case they take us somewhere nice. I'll wear the new ones tomorrow."

I set the shoes atop the dresser in his closet while Reign packs things into his suitcase. Well, more like tosses.

Eve plucks up the shirt he just threw in, shaking it out. "Reign, you've gotta fold it properly, babe, or you'll get to Paris and everything will be wrinkled. Let me show you how, okay?"

He stops, giving Eve all of his attention while she shows him how to fold a shirt to ensure it stays wrinkle free. She hands it to him when she's done.

"Put it in the packing cube. It'll keep your suitcase organized," she says. "You can toss everything in haphazardly for your trip home."

She nudges his arm, making him smile before picking up the iPad to check t-shirts off the list.

"Is Ian spending the night?" I ask him.

"Of course." Reign smiles. "He hasn't shut up about taking the private jet to Paris. I hope he doesn't geek out about it the entire flight. It's ten hours, right?"

"Yeah." I nod, chuckling. "If his enthusiasm becomes unbearable, there's a bedroom you could lock yourself in."

Reign shakes his head. "I still can't believe this is my life. From not having much of anything or anyone to having a life so full I'm not sure what to do with myself other than tell you thank you as often as I can."

Wrapping my arm around his shoulders, I give him a squeeze.

"You don't have to thank me. Letting us be a part of your life and living the life you deserve is more than enough."

He smiles at me, zipping up the packing cube with his t-shirts and sets it neatly in his suitcase.

"Reign, did you pack your toothpaste?" Eve asks.

He nods.

"Toothbrush?"

He nods again.

"Underwear and extra underwear?"

Reign palms his forehead, tipping his head back to look up at the ceiling, letting out an exasperated sigh. I can't help but laugh. Watching them together is one of my favorite things.

"What?" Eve looks between us. "You can never have enough underwear on a trip." She turns her attention back to the list, rattling things off at random.

"Jackets? Just in case it gets cold?"

I take the hoodie and jacket he always wears off the hooks in his closet, handing them to him. He folds them, putting them neatly in the suitcase.

"Swim trunks?"

"I already packed those." He points at the brightly colored fabric in his suitcase.

"Deodorant? Body wash? Floss? Face wash—"

"Yeah, Mom. I got it all." Reign slides his hand down his face.

I shoulder check the sliding closet door on my way out of it, almost dropping his extra pairs of underwear in my hand, hearing the word "mom" tumble from his lips. Eve is too busy listing off items to notice initially. I'm not sure if he meant to say it or if it was jokingly. Judging by the way he's carrying on as if nothing happened, he meant the word even if he didn't consciously say it.

"Oh," Eve continues. "Don't forget to pack the extra charger. That way we can video chat. I really—"

Eve stops abruptly when the word finally registers, staring at Reign. Lips slightly parted, her eyes slide from him to me and then back Reign again. We both watch him until he looks at me and then at Eve.

"What?" he asks. "The extra charger is—"

"No..." Eve says cautiously.

"You just asked me about the extra charger. It's already in my bag. Should I pack another one? I think three is a bit excess—"

"No." Eve repeats. "It's just... you called me Mom."

"Did I?" Reign blinks, seemingly surprised by his own words.

Eve shakes her head "yes". Reign looks at me with a questioning look.

"You did," I confirm, setting his extra underwear in the suitcase.

"Oh." He sits beside Eve on the bed, looking at the floor. "That's how I see you in my head and how I refer to you when I talk to friends. I don't know what a mom is or how it feels to have one. I imagine... you're the best mom for me. If you don't want me to call you that then—"

"No, no." Eve scoots closer to him wrapping him in a hug. "You can call me that if you want. You can call me mom. Or Eve. Or whatever you want."

My hearts swells in my chest, feeling a lump of emotions lodge itself in my throat as tears sting my eyes.

"I didn't realize it slipped out," he says, looking at her.

Eve unravels her arms from around him.

"I won't make it weird. I promise." She sniffs, placing her hand over her heart. "I'm honored that you even see me that way."

Eve picks up the iPad, seemingly giving herself something to do when Reign wraps her in a tight hug. She can't help it and starts crying, wrapping her arms around him again.

"I know I'm making it weird." Her voice is wobbly. "It's just I love you so much Reign." She kisses his temple. "You're my boy–*our boy*–no matter what. Now and always."

The emotions I tried to swallow break free, witnessing the love between them.

Reign pulls away first, giving Eve a watery smile. He gets up, looking around the room and continues packing. I pat his shoulder, giving it a squeeze and then plant a kiss on the top of Eve's head. She wipes tears from her cheeks before picking up the iPad with a dimpled smile on her face.

Later that evening, I'm sitting in the kitchen, scrolling through my phone, eating some food Eve's mom dropped off. Reign rounds the corner, grabbing a plate, and helps himself to the chili lime chicken and sides. While it warms up, he leans against the counter.

"Winter... are you mad at me?"

I set my fork and phone down. "No. Why do you think that?"

"Because..." His voice trails off. "Because I called Eve mom and... I don't want you feel left out. It's just that I have a—"

"Dad," I finish for him. "I understand, Reign. I don't want you to ever feel any pressure to call me that."

"I do see you that way, though."

"Oh..."

"At first you were like a big brother, but you love me like my dad did. And sometimes... I feel guilty because he's not here and I'm enjoying myself. Loving my life without him. I didn't think that would ever be possible."

"I get that."

The gaping hole of grief that losing a parent leaves in its wake makes it feel like it's impossible to ever feel anything other than sadness again. Slowly life continues, and eventually you do too. Until one day, you stop in the midst of your beautiful life and realize you somehow wriggled out of the clutches of grief long enough to live on. It's a bittersweet feeling because you're happy in spite of them not being a part of the happiness.

"You know what I think, Reign?"

He gives me an inquiring look.

"That our dads are celebrating that we have each other and are happy."

Reign considers my words for a moment. "Yeah." He smiles.

Getting up from the stool, I round the kitchen island and pull him into a hug, kissing his unruly curls.

"Call me what you want. No matter what, I love you."

He wraps me in a hug so tight I can feel the love radiating from him without him needing to say it back.

The following morning, we see Reign off at the airport.

"Has anyone told you this morning that you're beautiful, Mrs. King?" Ian asks as we walk across the tarmac toward the jet.

Snow and North snort with laughter while I give Ian side eye. He's been enamored with Eve since he met her.

"Just call me, Eve, Ian." She smiles, interlacing her fingers with mine.

Reign shoves him. "Bro, chill. That's my mom."

Again, Reign calls her mom as if he was always meant to. Elle, being the most emotional out of all of us, gasps with tears in her eyes.

Aspen nudges her, whispering, "Keep it together, crybaby."

Originally, it was supposed to be only me and Eve dropping him off, but somehow it always becomes a family affair with Reign.

"You're annoying, Ian," Calliope says, scrunching up her face.

"Reign," Eve says. "You have your passport, wallet, and ID, right?"

"Yeah. I do. Cal made me triple check this morning."

Eve gives Calliope a smile. "A girl after my own heart."

We make it to the jet. It's all black with "King" emblazoned on the side. Rowan, the pilot, is waiting at the top of the stairs.

"Good morning, King family and friends." He descends the stairs, holding his hand out to me.

"Rowan." I smile, shaking it. "How have you and the family been?"

He's been our pilot since we were teenagers.

"Good. Thank you for letting Charlotte and the girls fly to Paris with Reign and Ian."

"Girls?" Ian perks up.

"Two daughters." Rowan smiles proudly. "Aurora and Astrid."

I give Ian a warning look and he holds up his hands in retreat, returning to his conversation with Calliope and Reign.

"Enjoy your time in Paris."

When Rowan asked if his family could travel with him, I was more than happy to tell him yes. They've traveled with us in the past. Plus, I'll rest a little easier knowing Charlotte will keep an eye on them until they get there. I trust Reign. Ian can be questionable at times even though he always means well.

"Of course, Mr. King." Rowan checks the time on his watch. "We'll take off in five minutes." He turns, heading back up the steps.

"Alright, Reign." I smile. "Call us if you need anything at all."

"Yeah," Eve says. "We're only a flight away."

"I'll be fine." Reign smiles.

Eve wraps him in a hug so tight his eyes bulge. "I love you, and we'll see you in two weeks."

Giving him a little slack, Reign hugs her back. "Love you too."

"I'm serious, call us if you need anything at all. Even just to say hi."

"Eve..." I say.

"Okay, okay." She lets him go. "Have fun."

"I promise I'll call," he assures Eve.

I give him a hug. "Love you. Eve is right though, call us for anything."

"Love you, Winter." He wraps his arms around my middle.

Snow, North, Elle, and Aspen say their goodbyes. Each of them shove money into his hand as if I didn't just transfer more money than he could ever possibly need for a two-week stay in Paris into his bank account this morning. The money he gets from his dad has been transferred into a trust, at his request, that he'll have access to when he's twenty-one.

Calliope is the last to say bye to Reign. We all pretend to be in a riveting conversation while they talk. Eve asked Vincent if he'd let Calliope spend the last weekend of Reign's summer program in Paris with him. He agreed as long as he could go with her. I'm pretty sure he trusts Reign with Calliope's life, but he's a dad after all.

Once they're done, Reign turns to me. "Ready."

"Alright," I say. "We love you and see you in two weeks. Enjoy yourself. You deserve it."

"Love you guys, too." He waves to everyone.

"Bye, Ian. Make sure you check in with your parents."

"I will, Winter. Thanks for letting me fly with Reign."

"Any time."

His face lights up at the promise of enjoying more trips with Reign.

With those last words, Reign and Ian climb the steps to the plane. Standing behind Eve, I wrap my arms around her shoulders, pulling her against my chest as we watch them board the plane.

"You two look like proud parents," North says.

"We are," Eve and I answer together.

Our honeymoon in Oman has been something out of a movie. I already feel like I'm dreaming with her choosing to spend the rest of her life with me. Another layer of surrealism is added when we're in a place that looks otherworldly with picturesque views. Eve being the most stunning of course.

During our stay, we visited the Sultan Qaboos Mosque, then we stepped into a fairytale at a four-hundred-year-old castle in Nizwa, swam in the Bimmah Sinkhole with the clearest blue water I've ever seen in my life, and after a little convincing, I got Eve to swim with me and the whale sharks. We stayed in a local mud village, Misfat Al Abriyeen, that overlooked a lush garden with fresh fruit, mainly bananas and dates. Now, we're ending our trip at a resort in Jabal Akhdar, the Green Mountains, before we head back home on Monday.

I watch Eve dive into the infinity pool, resurfacing looking like every single one of my dreams. Her eyes catch mine.

"Are you going to dive in or just stare at me?"

I smile, peeling off my shirt and dive in after her. The cool water envelopes my skin, bringing relief from the days sweltering heat. I immediately heat up again when Eve wraps herself around me, bringing her lips to mine.

"This week with you has been unforgettable."

I rest my hands on her ass, walking toward the edge of the pool holding her.

"I have to agree, Mrs. King."

She gives me a blindingly dimpled smile. "Want to watch the sunset?"

"I'll do anything with you."

Unraveling her legs from around me, I let her feet touch the bottom of the pool. She rests her forearms on the ledge, and I stand behind her, pressing my chest to her back. I wrap my arms around her, looking out over the cliff at the setting sun, feeling a deep sense of gratitude. After everything – the grief, pain, and uncertainty – here I am, standing on the edge of the earth with the woman who commands my heart and is the other half of my soul.

Leaning forward, I press a kiss to her neck. She tilts her head to the side as I give her another one just below her ear right over her dove tattoo.

"Winter, we're going to miss the sunset."

The way she presses her body into mine lets me know the only thing on her mind is me.

"We have forever, Sweetheart. We'll watch the sunset tomorrow."

Caging her waist with my hands, I turn her to face me. She wraps her arms around my neck.

"Right now, and always, I just want you," I say.

Pulling me toward her, she presses a kiss to my lips.

Thank You

I haven't written acknowledgements in my past few books because I didn't want to leave anyone out. However, there are people who poured goodness into me while writing this book when I was going through one of the hardest times of my life and for them I am grateful.

Latosha, my author manager, my ace. Thank you for sharing your light with me. I appreciate you and all that you are. Love you deep!

Mihaela, thank you for checking in on me and letting me know you care. That meant the world to me and so do you.

Beth, thank you for encouraging me. You're not just my editor. You're my friend too and for you I am grateful.

Maria, my (second) mom, the woman who I believe was handpicked by my mom to walk with me in this life because she could not, I love you.

Bienvenida, gracias por venir dos mil millas para cuidarme eso me curo mental y fisica mente se lo agradesco con todo mi alma.

My other half, I'll always walk with you.

My boys, you've taught me that my presence is enough. You're pieces of my soul walking outside of my body.

My beautiful, amazing readers, without you I wouldn't be here. Thank you for loving me and my work. Be gentle with yourselves and love deep!

KEEP IN TOUCH

Thank you for reading. If you enjoyed this novel, please consider leaving a review on Amazon, Goodreads, and wherever else you can so other readers can enjoy it, too!

Visit my website or take a picture of the QR code below to subscribe to my newsletter, get exclusive updates, explore my other books, follow me on social media, and to stay up to date!

www.aevaldez.com

ALSO BY A.E. VALDEZ

All I've Wanted, All I've Needed

Colliding With Fate

The Beginning of Forever

A Worthy Love

Three Kings Billionaire Series:

Snow King Catches His Snowflake